HOW TO BE A SCOTTISH MISTRESS

"Ye're trembling. Tell me true, are ye afraid of me, Fiona?"

"I don't fear you, my lord. I'm nervous. And worried that I will not please you."

"Where's the bold lass who offered herself to me so brazenly this afternoon?"

She lifted her chin, a blushing spot of color burning on each cheek. "I am here, my lord. As we agreed."

"Gavin. Call me Gavin." He sighed, then touched a finger to her mouth. "We'll go slowly. Though I cannae promise fer how long."

Wrapping one arm around her back, he tipped her off balance. Her eyes widened as she gazed up into his face. Gavin leaned down and kissed her. He tasted her shock and wondered if she had underestimated her own sexual allure. He molded his mouth to her soft, yielding lips and pressed harder.

She let out a quiet moan, then opened her lips to let him inside.

He kissed her again, unprepared for the torment that spread rapidly through him.

More. I want more . . .

Books by Adrienne Basso

Published by Kensington Publishing Corporation

How To Be
A SCOTTISH
MISTRESS

ADRIENNE BASSO

ZEBRA BOOKS
KENSINGTON PUBLISHING CORP.
http://www.kensingtonbooks.com

ZEBRA BOOKS are published by

Kensington Publishing Corp.
119 West 40th Street
New York, NY 10018

All Kensington titles, imprints and distributed lines are available at special quantity discounts for bulk purchases for sales
promotion, premiums, fund-raising, educational or institu-
tional use.

Special book excerpts or customized printings can also be created to fit specific needs. For details, write or phone the office
of the Kensington Special Sales Manager. Attn.: Special Sales
Department. Kensington Publishing Corp., 119 West 40th
Street, New York, NY 10018. Phone: 1-800-221-2647.

Zebra and the Z logo Reg. U.S. Pat. & TM Off.

ISBN-13: 978-1-4201-2902-1
ISBN-10: 1-4201-2902-3

First Printing: July 2013

eISBN-13: 978-1-4201-2903-8
eISBN-10: 1-4201-2903-1

First Electronic Edition: July 2013

10 9 8 7 6 5 4 3 2 1

Printed in the United States of America

To my agent, Pam Hopkins.

*Many thanks for your encouragement,
insight, and support.*

*It's truly a privilege to be working with
the best in the business—for more years than
either of us will ever admit.*

Chapter 1

"We'll have rain by nightfall, I fear," Lord Henry Libourg, Baron of Arundel, declared solemnly as he slowed his horse's canter, drawing closer to his wife so as to be heard above the pounding hooves. "'Tis bound to make a mud pit in the middle of the bailey, but the newly sowed crops will benefit."

"Rain? Are you daft, my lord?" Lady Fiona matched her mare's pace to that of her husband's war steed, then eyed him with healthy skepticism. "There is nary a cloud in the sky to mar the perfection of sunshine."

"Rain it will be, my lady," Henry insisted with authority. "I feel it in my bones."

He slapped his gloved hand deliberately against his thigh, then grimaced. Fiona turned her face upward toward the bright sunshine, shaking her head. It was moments such as this when the nearly twenty-five-year age difference between her and her spouse became glaringly apparent. Only an old man spoke of his joints aching when rain or snow approached.

The unkind thought had no sooner entered her head when Fiona silenced it. Henry was a good husband— dear to her in many ways. She had been sent to his manor as a young girl of twelve, to serve his wife and learn the duties of a proper lady. When that good woman had died in childbirth five years later, Henry had surprised Fiona by asking her to be his wife and mother to his infant son.

Born to a family of minor nobility that took little stock in the welfare of its female members, Fiona had been relieved when her father agreed to the match. Relieved and grateful, for it allowed her to stay at the first place she had truly considered home.

She knew others could not understand why she would eagerly wed a man of modest means and position so much older than herself, but as the Baroness of Arundel, Fiona had found a purpose that filled her with confidence and self-worth. She had come to accept that her marriage, though affectionate, was not, nor would it ever be, a marriage of passion. Yet Fiona loved Henry truly, in a way that stretched far beyond a sense of duty.

All in all, it was a good life.

Fiona turned her eyes away from the sunlight twinkling through the leaves and gazed out at the trees surrounding them. Summer had finally arrived, but a thick layer of dead brown leaves carpeted much of the forest floor, mingling with the green of the smaller bushes and ferns.

"Oh, look, Henry, 'tis a cluster of blooming feverfew," Fiona exclaimed. "Please, may we stop so I can gather some? Two of the kitchen lads have broken out in a fierce rash. They are suffering mightily, and treating them with my usual ointments has proven useless.

I am certain the addition of feverfew will make all the difference."

Filled with excitement, Fiona tugged on her reins with a short, sharp motion. Her horse protested, rearing in response.

"Careful now, you don't want to take a tumble on this hard ground," Henry admonished. With impressive skill, the baron reached out a strong arm to ensure his wife kept her seat.

Fiona cast him a grateful smile, tightening her thighs around her mount instinctively. She was a competent, though not especially skilled, horsewoman. Fortunately, Henry was near to keep her safe.

Once her horse was calm, the baron peered over at the soft white flowers she pointed toward, his expression perplexed. "Feverfew? Are you certain? They look like ordinary daisies to me."

Fiona smiled. Henry was a man of solid intelligence as well as experience, but medicinal herbs and flowers were completely foreign to him. "With their yellow centers and white petals, I'll allow there is a strong resemblance, but you must trust me, sir, when I tell you those are not daisies."

"I trust you, Fiona. I'm just not certain 'tis wise to delay our return home. We have been gone for most of the afternoon and there are duties that await us both. If I can spare the men, you may return tomorrow to collect your flowers."

"They are not merely flowers, Henry, they are medicine. And truly, the need is so great that I fear tomorrow might be too long to wait. The sooner I try a new treatment, the sooner the lads will be healed."

Henry made a soft sound of resignation beneath his breath. "God's bones, Fiona, I think you are the only woman in all of England who would make such a fuss over kitchen lads."

Graceful in victory, Fiona smiled sweetly. "You are the one who taught me to care so diligently for our people, good sir. Now come, there looks to be enough to fill my saddle pouch as well as yours."

The baron slid off his horse, then caught his wife around the waist when she began to dismount from hers. Their eyes met briefly as he set her gently on the ground. Impulsively, Fiona leaned forward and playfully kissed the tip of Henry's nose.

"Impudent baggage," Henry bristled in mock annoyance.

A deep chuckle bubbled through Fiona and she laughed merrily. The sound echoed through the forest, startling a flock of blackbirds from the branches of a nearby tree.

"Wait here," Henry commanded, handing her the leads of both horses.

Fiona nodded in understanding, waiting patiently. Even though they rode on their own land, it was wise to be cautious, especially in these uncertain times.

She watched the baron make slow progress toward the clusters of feverfew, his shrewd gaze darting back and forth. Bored at being stopped on the journey, the horses ambled a few steps and lowered their heads to drink from a large puddle at the edge of the forest. Fiona allowed it, securing their leather leads to a tree trunk. She then turned back to Henry, anxious to begin her harvest.

At last, he gave the signal and she scampered forward, glad she was dressed in her new pair of leather boots. The ground was moist and springy, her feet sinking nearly to the ankles in some spots.

"I don't suppose I can ask you to hurry," Henry muttered, as she strode past him to reach the first large bunch.

"I shall try my best," Fiona replied. "But doing a proper job of harvesting takes time."

Though his expression was wry, Fiona heard the twinge of pride in her husband's voice. She had never shied away from hard work and took a marked interest in all who lived at the manor, be they peasant, servant, or knight. And it was no secret she was well loved for her dedication.

Determined not to take a minute longer than necessary, Fiona sank to her knees, surveying the bounty growing before her. Gathering a large handful of blossoms growing at the base of an oak tree, she skillfully twisted her wrist, breaking the stems near the base of the roots. She made certain not to take every flower, ensuring the plants would survive and produce more feverfew in the coming weeks and months.

With such a great number of soldiers, servants, and others depending on her for care, Fiona knew well the importance of keeping the castle stillroom stocked with precious medical supplies, ever at the ready to treat the ills of those who needed help.

Moving forward on her knees, Fiona reached around the trunk to harvest another bunch of the precious flowers. As she broke off the stems, an odd sense that something was amiss surrounded her. It was quiet, almost too quiet. She turned her head to check on Henry, who stood several yards behind her.

His sword was drawn, his stance vigilant, yet relaxed. Telling herself she was being fanciful, Fiona returned her attention to the feverfew. Stretching forward, she tugged on a few remaining flowers, then suddenly, a masculine hand shot out from behind the tree and seized her wrist in a cruel grip.

A scream lodged in Fiona's throat, her body too stunned to react. The grip tightened and pain radiated through her arm, but fear and shock kept it at bay. Lifting her head, Fiona looked up into the eyes of the fierce warrior who held her captive. A knight, she surmised, from the style of his garments, and one not needing to resort to thievery, judging by the fine quality of cloth he wore.

He was broad of shoulder, with deep-set blue eyes, framed by dark lashes. Though crouched before her, she could see he was tall and well muscled. His hawklike nose was straight and masculine, his mouth sensual. He wore his thick, dark, wavy hair longer than the current fashion, reaching just below his chin. There was a thin scar slashed across his left temple, ending at the corner of his eye. A memento of a long-ago battle, no doubt.

The sharp angle of his square jaw was covered with the dark stubble of several days' growth of beard, adding to his menacing appearance, which bespoke of power and authority. Strangely, he was a man Fiona realized she would have considered handsome, had the situation not been so terrifying.

Who was he and why was he hiding on their land? Fiona knew this was hardly the time for questions. She needed to escape. Now! Still on her knees, she tried to scramble away, but he was too fast. And much too strong. Pulling her by the wrist, he lifted her to her feet in one smooth motion, hiding her from view behind the large tree trunk.

Tears welled in Fiona's eyes at being manhandled so roughly, but it was his softly whispered words that drained the blood from her face.

"Be silent, lass, or we'll gut yer man where he stands."

Her captor's steely blue eyes spoke his emotions as clearly as any words. Cold, remote, intense. A jolting fear slithered through Fiona's slight frame, as she realized he would kill without hesitation.

In the line of trees ahead of her, a branch snapped. Panic coursed through her veins when she spied five more men hidden among the tall oaks. Dear God!

She fought to break free of the man's grasp, but he anticipated her move, yanking her tightly with a bruising, iron grip. Fiona let out a strangled gasp as her body collided with his solid chest. Swift as lightning, his right arm snaked around her waist, gripping her like a vise, effectively pinning both her arms against her body. The moment she was secured, his other hand clamped tightly over her mouth.

"Fiona?" Henry called. "Where are you?"

She felt the fear rising, her heart thudding within her chest as she heard her husband moving toward them. *God have mercy, he will be killed! I must warn him!* With a renewed burst of energy, Fiona struggled to free herself: kicking, twisting, throwing her head frantically backward, banging it repeatedly against the chest of her captor. It made no difference. As if made of stone, the man never moved, his heavily muscled arms holding her as though she were nothing more than a pesky insect.

Still, Fiona fought to break free, refusing to give up so easily. Working her jaw up and down, she was able to catch the edge of her captor's hand between her teeth. Heart racing, she summoned all her strength and bit down. Hard. Once, twice, three times.

She tasted the wet, dirty leather of his glove on her tongue, but ignored the discomfort and continued her assault, biting, then tugging, like a hunting hound with a captured rabbit. There was a split second of triumph when she heard a dull grunt from her captor—he had felt it. But despite any pain she caused, any wound she might have inflicted, he did not loosen his grip. If anything, it became tighter.

Helpless, Fiona watched Henry stride directly into the ambush. A muted cry of pain bellowed up from her chest as one of the brigands stepped out from his hiding place, lifted his sword and swung at her husband's head. Henry reacted quickly, arching his own blade in a wide circle, effectively deflecting the lethal blow. Repositioning himself, Henry stepped to the side to avoid a second thrust before striking back with several short, heavy blows.

Advancing, he managed to drive his opponent against a tree trunk. Praying for a miracle, Fiona's heart remained frozen as she watched him battle a much younger, larger man.

The flurrying crash of steel on steel intensified, the piercing sound reverberating through the forest. She could see Henry's muscles flexing as he swung his sword, proof of the many hours he spent with his men on the training field. But Fiona could also see that her husband was tiring, his endurance no match for a man nearly half his age and a full head taller in size.

Yet Henry would not easily succumb. He landed a blow to his opponent's upper arm, drawing blood. Startled, the brigand stumbled and fell to the ground. Fiona's moment of joy at her husband's triumph was short-lived, however, as two other men immediately joined the fray.

Within minutes one of them struck a stinging blow that clearly drove the air from Henry's lungs. She cried out as Henry fell, barely noticing that her captor had taken his hand from her mouth.

"No, please." Fiona's voice was loud and sharp, dripping with emotion. Her heart lurched at the sight of a sword pressed so menacingly against her husband's throat. Instinctively protective, she tried to move forward, but she was pinned in place with a paralyzing force.

"Wait! 'Tis Arundel. Dinnae harm him!" Her captor's voice rang out and the other men instantly obeyed, pulling away. They exchanged glances and Fiona watched in astonishment as Henry was helped to his feet by his first opponent, the man he had wounded.

"Release my wife." Though hoarse, the level of command in Henry's voice was evident.

Stunned, Fiona felt her captor's arms slip away. Fighting to control her shaking, she stumbled forward to stand at her husband's side.

Astonishingly, the brigand who had held her captive bowed gracefully in a gesture of supplication. "I beg yer forgiveness, baron, fer our inhospitable greeting. But I dinnae realize who ye were until my men attacked."

"Kirkland?" Henry huffed with indignation, his arms moving briskly as he brushed the dirt and leaves off his chest. "God's bones, I should knock you on your arse for this," he shouted.

"An understandable though unwise reaction, my friend." Fiona's captor took a step forward and his men moved in closer, forming a protective ring behind him.

Light-headed, Fiona struggled to release the breath she was holding. Who was this fierce stranger? Someone Henry knew, yet hardly the friend he claimed. Though their weapons were lowered, there was no doubt this man would fight if challenged. Or insulted?

Fiona pushed away the newest fear that had taken root in her brain, knowing it would be foolhardy to add more drama to an already puzzling situation.

"You're on my land," Henry declared flatly. "I would have thought that would be a clue to my identity, forgoing the need to attack."

"We dinnae attack, we surprised ye." Kirkland's lips rose into a slight grin, but the hardened glimmer in his eyes revealed he felt little mirth.

Henry let out a snort. "You frightened my wife," he persisted, and Fiona nearly groaned. Why would he not leave the matter alone? They were outnumbered and vulnerable. Did he not realize the danger? "Are you hurt, Fiona?"

All eyes turned toward her. It would be madness to admit the truth, so instead Fiona lifted her chin and smiled. "I'm fine," she lied, ignoring the throbbing of her wrist.

"I fear I was too harsh in my treatment of ye, Lady Fiona. 'Tis not my usual way to accost a gentlewoman."

The words were spoken with a gentle flourish, and accompanied by a courtly bow, but the Scot's face remained stoic and impossible to read. Fiona felt her cheeks turn hot and she silently cursed her keen eyesight. If she had not caught a glimpse of the feverfew from the road, they never would have stopped and gotten into this mess.

"Why are you here, lurking in my woods?" Henry asked. "'Tis hardly our usual method of contact."

"We had to come farther south than we intended in order to avoid some nasty business at Methven. I can assure ye, we willnae be here much longer. Just until we know it's safe to return home."

Henry's eyes filled with surprise. "You fought at Methven?"

"Aye." Kirkland's upper lip twitched. "My men did me proud."

"We were defeated," one of the brigands declared bitterly.

"We were deceived," another protested hotly, before spitting on the ground. "The English refused an honorable challenge to meet us on the field of battle, preferring instead to act like cowards, invade our camp, attack at dawn, and slaughter us while we slept."

Henry's eyebrows rose. "No quarter was given?"

"None," the earl replied, his tone flat. "Most of those who escaped have fled to the Highlands. But I must return home, to defend my lands and protect my people."

Henry stroked his chin thoughtfully. "So, you've finally decided to pledge your sword to the Bruce? 'Tis a gamble."

The earl shrugged. "An abundance of caution has kept us under England's thumb fer too long. I might not always agree with his methods, but I believe the Bruce is Scotland's best chance fer freedom. At the very least, we deserve to have our own king."

Fiona was surprised to see the hint of sympathy in her husband's eyes. It was a well-known fact that King Edward was determined to exert his authority over Scotland and expected the Scots to pay homage to him. As a loyal subject of the king, Fiona had always believed that Henry supported that position.

"Not all your countrymen are in agreement that Bruce is the man who should wear the Scottish crown," Henry said. "I heard the MacNabs and the MacDougalls fought alongside the English at Methven, against King Robert."

"'Tis true." The earl shrugged again, his brows

pulling together in a frown. "Led by John MacDougall of Lorne himself. He's driven by blood vengeance and means to have it. Ye'll not find a more formidable foe in all the land."

Henry snorted. "Sacrilegious murder of one's nephew in a churchyard will do that to a man."

Fiona crossed herself. She remembered well hearing of this abomination against man and God. Robert the Bruce was one of several claimants to the Scottish crown. He had disposed of his main rival, John "the Red" Comyn, by calling him to a meeting at a church and then killing him.

This barbaric act served to solidify in Fiona's mind what the English believed for decades about their northern neighbors—for all their profession of faith, the Scots were a heathen people. Yet somehow Henry had befriended one?

"The Bruce's cause was just," the earl admonished. "He and Comyn had signed an agreement to unite the clans and gain independence. To secure the crown fer himself, Comyn saw fit to share a copy of that agreement with the English king. A clear act of treason."

"Perhaps," Henry conceded, though his expression remained skeptical. "Though it is now Bruce, and his followers, who are labeled traitors after being defeated in battle. Still, I believe that all men must choose their own path in this life, though it behooves them to remember they will answer to God in the next."

"My conscience is clear," Kirkland said coolly, an unmistakable edge in his tone.

Henry was silent as he studied the other man. Finally he spoke. "What do you want from me?"

"Safe haven in yer forest fer a few days—a week at most."

Henry nodded and a chill swept through Fiona. Knowingly harbor wanted men on their land? Was he mad? If it were ever discovered, such an act would surely bring the full wrath of the king down upon them all.

"Henry, we cannot—"

"Quiet, Fiona."

The sharpness of his tone stung, but she obeyed without further comment, knowing in her heart she needed to trust in Henry's judgment. He was wise and worldly and caring and would do what was best.

Fiona reached down and grasped her husband's hand, squeezing tightly. Her faith in him was unconditional. Yet as she gazed at the broad, powerful shoulders, hard eyes, and stonelike expression of the Scotsman who had brought this turmoil into their lives, she realized why she was so frightened.

'Twas indeed true that her loyalty and trust in her husband was steadfast. Her opinion of this heathen Scot, however, was another matter entirely.

Gavin McLendon, Earl of Kirkland, tried to ignore the play of emotions that flitted over Lady Fiona's face when she realized her husband was going to aid them. He swore he could almost hear the spirited objection that sprang to her lips, but somehow she kept it at bay and held her tongue. Gavin could not help but be impressed at her self-control.

He vaguely recalled hearing that the baron's second wife was considerably younger than her husband, but somehow he had not expected her to be so pretty. Beautiful, really.

She had a buxom figure with lush breasts, perfectly curved hips, and an angelic face that looked as if it had been carved from marble. Her head was uncovered and a long, thick braid of honey-blond hair trailed down the middle of her back, ending at the base of her spine. It made her appear maidenly, innocent; an odd occurrence for a married woman.

Her eyes were an unusual shade of green, vibrant and sparkling with intelligence—a trait he did not often ascribe to the female sex. His own wife, though not a simpleton, would never have grasped the enormity of this current situation on her own.

And if by some miracle she did, she would never have been so calm. Or cooperative.

"How many men are with you?" Henry asked.

"Twenty-five. But most are wounded," Gavin answered readily, then cursed his loose tongue. After being on the run for nearly two weeks, exhaustion was finally starting to overtake him. Though his relationship with the baron was of long standing, it was never wise to be so trusting.

The tension in the small clearing subtly began to rise. Gavin saw his men look warily from one to the other, their hands drifting down to the weapons at their sides. From the corner of his eye, Gavin noticed Lady Fiona give her husband an anxious glance.

"I will do what you ask of me," the baron declared. "And provide whatever medical assistance I can for your men. But in turn, I expect a boon from you."

Gavin stifled a curse. He had never assumed the aid would come without a price, but at this moment in time he had little to give. "Aye. Name yer price."

"Before the end of summer, I expect you to lead a raid on my village and steal my cattle."

For the first time in many days, Gavin felt his lips move into a smile. "I'll take the entire herd, if ye want."

"Most obliging of you, my lord. And don't forget to steal some grain," Henry added, his broad face breaking into an answering grin. "Though I expect it to be promptly returned and my fields left as they stand."

"'Tis the usual agreement. The plundered grain returned and the fields left trampled, but not burned."

"The usual agreement?" Lady Fiona's voice climbed to a high, wavering pitch and her chest rose and fell with quickening breaths. "So, you have done this before? And yet, you both act as though it means nothing. I can't imagine that our people share your opinion, Henry. How terrified and helpless they must feel when they are attacked."

"We attack no one, shed no blood," Gavin insisted. Her obvious dismay rankled, though he wasn't sure why. He and the baron had done nothing wrong. On the contrary, they had found a way to live in peace and harmony and avoid any suspicion over their secret alliance by outwardly appearing as enemies.

"We devised this agreement years ago. The McLendon clan come under the cover of night," Henry explained. "They are rarely seen by the villagers."

She shot her husband a startled look. "And that makes it acceptable?"

"That makes it safe," Henry countered, his voice rising with impatience. "For all concerned. Our people suffer no injury and nearly all of what is taken is eventually returned. It would look suspicious if we were the only castle along the border to suffer no raids from our thieving northern neighbors. King Edward does not look kindly upon the Scots, but I do not share his belief that they must be conquered."

"As if ye could," Duncan said tersely, stepping forward, his hand moving down to the hilt of his sword. "Damn English. Yer a bunch of dishonorable cowards."

"Duncan!" Gavin pinned his cousin with a cold, hard stare. Duncan was a fine soldier and a loyal retainer, a man not inclined to run from a battle. It had been harder on him than most to accept this defeat, but Gavin could not allow him to jeopardize the one alliance that could save them now.

Duncan did not wilt under his glare. For an instant he looked confused and then he mumbled something beneath his breath. His manner still proud, the chastened man released his grip from his sword handle and took several steps backward.

Fortunately, the baron took no offense at Duncan's remarks. Gavin slowly exhaled, blessing whatever reasoning had pushed the Englishman to propose a truce between them, along with a radical plan to ensure its survival. It was a rash act on Gavin's part to agree, but one he had never regretted. Especially now.

"At nightfall for the next five days, I will bring food and drink for you and your men and leave it at the base of this tree." Henry pointed at the massive oak. "You can hunt for game in my northernmost woods to supplement the fare. I shall keep my men away from the area for the remainder of the week, so you won't be discovered."

"We will keep to the north." Gavin attempted a smile of thanks, yet failed, for there was one more thing he needed. It galled him to ask, but it was necessary to improve the chances of survival for several of his more severely wounded men. "Clean linen bandages would be useful, along with some medicine."

Lady Fiona bit her lower lip. "I have just begun to replenish our supplies," she said quietly, her voice anxious. "I can give you some linen, but our stores of medicines are low. 'Twould be a waste—"

The baron held up his hand and Lady Fiona quickly fell silent. "My wife will send what we can spare."

"The medicine will be of little use if none of you have the skills to properly use it," Lady Fiona snapped.

A glance from the baron had her looking contrite at her sudden outburst, but Gavin wasn't fooled. The firm set of her jaw bespoke of her true feelings on the matter.

"We know enough to drink the potions and put the salves on our wounds," Gavin offered, attempting to break the tension.

The baron chuckled, along with a few of Gavin's men. Lady Fiona bestowed an obliging smile in his direction, but the look in her eyes was hardly hospitable.

A prickling sensation of guilt washed over Gavin. She had a right to be upset, afraid. They were taking precious supplies, putting yet another burden upon the baron and his household. Gavin wanted to tell the lady that she would not regret her part in this, that in these uncertain times, when loyalties were tested, there was comfort to be found in acting bravely and honorably.

But the sad truth was, he could not.

Chapter 2

Summer, one year later

"Are you certain you wish to leave tomorrow, Lady Fiona? I've heard rumors that the king's army will soon be marching north again. 'Tis hardly the safest time to venture across the border into Scotland."

Fiona wiped her damp palms against her skirt and forced herself to stay calm as she gazed into the weathered face of the knight standing before her. It had taken her months to formulate this plan and even longer to put the pieces into place. Now that the moment was at hand, she must not allow anything to sway her commitment.

"I believe that King Edward is determined to lead a victorious campaign against the Scots, Sir George. Yet I fear if we wait for a safe time to make this journey, we shall never leave." She tried smiling, but her lips refused to cooperate, doubt and fear keeping them frozen.

Sir George's dark eyes softened. Though only of average height, he appeared larger, due to his thick, muscular build. The scars on his face and arms were a testament to his years on the battlefield, and Fiona knew she was lucky to have a loyal, honorable knight with his skills on her side. It brought a small measure of comfort to her heavily burdened heart, though in truth there was little that could be done to appease the bitterness she felt.

That some called the death of her husband and the loss of their lands a cruelty of fate was viewed by Fiona as an insult. How could an event of such anguishing loss be given such a trite explanation? No, it was not fate that brought such devastation into their lives—it was betrayal.

Fiona was convinced that somehow the alliance Henry had forged with the Scottish Earl of Kirkland had reached the ears of King Edward. Lacking any substantial proof, the king had decided not to outright accuse Henry of any wrongdoing. Instead, he had allowed Sir Roland DuPree, one of his brutish minions, to petition a blatantly false claim to their lands. And when Henry refused to yield the property, Sir Roland and his army, with the king's silent sanction, had stormed the castle and taken it by force.

It had hardly been a fair fight. Fiona closed her eyes and once again relived the nightmare of the fateful event that had destroyed the only happiness she had ever known, forever changing her life.

It had been quiet that night—too quiet. The soldiers who stood guard in the watchtowers had died swiftly, their throats slashed to prevent a warning of the impending invasion, to delay a call to arms. Roused from their beds, Henry and his knights had fought bravely to defend the keep and protect the inhabitants, but they were no match for the men who had devised the ruthless attack.

Outnumbered and unprepared, Henry and his soldiers

fell one by one. With the tide turned against them, many of the surviving guardsmen laid down their arms and pledged their allegiance to the conquering Sir Roland.

But not Sir George. He had been the first to pledge his sword to Henry's son and heir, ten-year-old Spencer. And it was Sir George who had managed to safely spirit her and Spencer away after Henry had been fatally struck.

Sobbing and in shock, Fiona, her maid, and Father Niall had followed Sir George through the dank, musty, secret escape tunnels that ended outside the bailey walls. Together, Fiona and Father Niall carried a badly injured Spencer on a makeshift stretcher, each moan uttered from the child's pale lips a fresh pain in Fiona's bruised heart.

The fear had been almost paralyzing. Even now Fiona could still smell the dampness, hear the skittering sounds of the rats in the tunnel and the clash of swords from above as a few brave men fought on.

The tunnel ended in a cave, and they hid there for what felt like hours, while Sir George scouted ahead. Finally, he returned, stolen horses in hand. Just as dawn was starting to break, the weary group rode away, ears attuned to the sounds of pursuit.

Thankfully, no one followed. In her greatest time of need, Fiona had no choice but to turn to her eldest brother, Harold. They arrived at his keep six days later, exhausted and in shock. He had hardly been gracious in receiving them, but at least he had not denied them sanctuary.

"Sir George! You're here!"

The boyish voice rang out with pure delight. Fiona turned and watched Spencer make his way across the crowded bailey. Her heart jumped with worry as it became necessary for the boy to move with speed and agility to avoid the carts, animals, and people hustling through the courtyard.

Even from this distance she could see how badly Spencer limped. The broken bones of his right leg, an injury suffered during the attack, had fused together at an odd angle, leaving it shorter than the left leg. It was a constant reminder of what they had endured, of what had been broken that could never be fully restored.

As Spencer drew closer, one of the castle hounds suddenly darted in front of him. His balance compromised, the boy's face contorted into a grimace as he stumbled and fell. Fiona gasped, biting her lip until she tasted blood. No, she refused to cry out, to show any outward sign of distress. The last thing Spencer wanted or needed was her pity—he got that in buckets from others.

More than anything else, her child needed her to believe in him, needed to know that she had faith he would overcome this physical infirmary, that he would one day be whole again. And by God, no matter how difficult it was for her, she would give that to him.

Arms flailing, Spencer shoved the hound, who was now trying to lick his face, pushing the animal away. Though it was only a few seconds, to Fiona it felt like hours, as she watched the boy lie flat on his back, panting with the effort it took to right himself. Finally, with slow deliberate movements, Spencer rose to his feet. His misshapen grin of triumph when he regained his balance wrenched at Fiona's heart. Swiftly, she brushed away her tears, replacing them with a confident, supportive nod.

A nod her son answered with one of his own.

"After these many months, I had hoped the boy would

be stronger," Sir George mused, his eyes narrowing with worry.

"He improves each week," Fiona replied sharply.

"Can he wield a sword?"

"Yes."

"With authority?"

Fiona skewered the knight with a piercing look. "He's barely eleven years old."

"He began learning how to fight at his father's knee when he was but a lad of five," Sir George responded. "I supervised the making of his first wooden sword myself."

"My brother has refused to allow Spencer any time on the practice field," Fiona replied, embarrassed to admit her own flesh and blood had so little confidence in Spencer's abilities. "Father Niall works with him, but the priest's skill is limited. With the proper training, I know Spencer will be able to compensate for the weakness in his leg. All he needs is the opportunity."

Sir George took a breath. "If the lad cannot be trained here, then perhaps he can be fostered at another castle?"

"Believe me, Sir George, as much as it would pain me to be separated from him, I have tried to find him a place. Father Niall helped me compose the letters I sent to all the holdings in the area, both large and small." Fiona felt her face flush with heat. "No one will take him."

Sir George's eyebrows rose. "No one?"

Fiona frowned. She had begged her brother to intervene and when he refused, she had taken matters into her own hands. Though possessing only a rudimentary knowledge of reading and writing, Fiona had put all her efforts into the task of securing a future for Spencer. Yet even with Father Niall's aid, it had taken her hours to write those letters.

Waiting had been the hardest part. For as each reply—and rejection—was received, hope for Spencer's future had slipped further and further away. Now all that was left was the reality of her situation. No one was going to come to their rescue and willingly take up Spencer's cause.

They would languish in her brother's castle for the rest of their lives—an unwanted burden with no true place or purpose. For Fiona, the idea was equally repellant and terrifying and completely unacceptable.

What had started as a mother's duty to protect her child was now a compulsion for Fiona, burning like a fire within her chest. She would give her own life if it prevented any further harm from coming to the boy. But she was greedy in her wishes and dreams, wanting more than mere survival for Spencer. She wanted him to thrive, to flourish, and when the time was right, to regain his birthright.

"Henry was never openly accused of treason, but 'tis common knowledge that the king did nothing to prevent the attack on our lands," Fiona said. "That, coupled with Spencer's injury, has made it impossible to find a nobleman willing to foster him, to give him the proper training needed to attain knighthood."

Sir George stared at her somberly. "Have you considered the boy's future might lie with the church?"

"Oh, Sir George, not you, too," Fiona said, bristling at the remark. "'Tis bad enough that I must listen to my brother harp upon how Spencer's infirmary makes him fit only for a priestly life. I expected more from you."

Sir George bowed his head. "I only want what is best for the boy."

"As do I," Fiona huffed, though there were moments she had questioned her own motivation. Was her need for revenge putting Spencer in a dangerous position? Should she listen to men like Sir George and her brother, who were so certain the only course for Spencer was a life of spiritual devotion?

Feeling a twinge of uncertainty, Fiona watched Spencer finally make his way to their side. His smile was wide and genuine as he embraced Sir George. It renewed her spirits to see the boy so happy. And renewed her determination. She refused to languish here at her brother's keep, wasting precious time. She would not quietly accept the future that others wanted to foist upon her son. She would fight for the future he deserved.

Had not Father Niall himself reluctantly agreed the boy had no true calling to be God's servant? And when further pressed, the priest had added that he highly doubted Spencer would be happy living a quiet life of faithful devotion.

Seeing the hunger and longing in Spencer's eyes when the men were training was proof enough of the boy's true desires. He deserved to inherit his father's lands, to lead and protect their people. Somehow, someway, Fiona was going to make certain he had the chance.

"Will we be ready to leave soon, Sir George?" Fiona asked.

The answering silence from the knight was disturbing. Fiona suppressed a shiver of alarm. If Sir George abandoned them now, they would be stuck here for months. Maybe even years. So great was her distress, Fiona failed to notice her brother, Harold, sauntering smoothly across the bailey toward them.

"Ah, I see your chivalrous knight has finally arrived."

Harold halted beside her, his arms crossed, booted foot restlessly tapping. His narrowed gaze slowly swept from her to Spencer, and then rested speculatively on Sir George. "Good day to you."

"My lord." Sir George favored Harold with a curt nod before turning toward Fiona. "The preparations for our journey are nearly complete. If it pleases you, Lady Fiona, we will depart tomorrow at first light."

Spencer tilted his head in interest. "Am I going, too?"

"Yes, of course." Fiona smiled. He looked so young, so eager. With great effort she resisted the urge to run her hands affectionately over the lad's dark curls, knowing the gesture would embarrass him in front of the other men. "Sir George and his men will escort us north, to the Abbey of St. Gifford, so we may visit the holy shrine."

Harold scoffed. "I don't know why you insist on traveling such a great distance to pray. The brothers are not known to perform miracles or cure the infirmed."

"Harold!" Fiona felt her ire ignite, not only at her brother's words, but at the smirking expression on his face. "We have no need of cures or miracles."

Her brother's perceptive eyes narrowed further. "Then why go at all? Why travel these dangerous roads?"

Fiona swallowed. Lying had never come easily, and with so much depending upon keeping her true plans secret, it was hard to find a response. But find one she must. "I need to show proper respect for the anniversary of Henry's death. A retreat of prayer and reflection seems fitting."

"My chapel is at your disposal, as is my priest. Hell, your priest still resides within my keep. Are these two holy men not enough?"

"I need to show proper respect," Fiona repeated,

forcing humility into her tone. Why was her brother taking such an interest in her now? He had hardly been welcoming when she arrived a year ago, dazed and shocked and desperate. His lack of attention and concern had been hurtful, and even more upsetting was the eventual realization that her brother's feelings would not change.

'Twas obvious he had little use for Spencer, with his infirmary, and even less for her, a widow with no dowry. Harold's neglect and disinterest was one of the reasons she was making this journey. No longer could she tolerate the bleak, barren future her brother saw for her son.

"A holy pilgrimage is a fitting tribute for the baron," Sir George interjected. "I am proud and honored to be of service to Lady Fiona."

Harold sniffed and Fiona could see the resistance in his eyes. And while she certainly appreciated Sir George's support, she feared the knight's agreement with her had further angered her brother.

"Sir George informed me earlier this year he intended to make this pilgrimage when the weather turned warmer. It made sense that Spencer and I join his party," Fiona said, trying to shift the focus of the conversation. "You and your knights have far more important matters to occupy your time, or else I would have asked for your assistance."

Harold's mouth twitched at the blatant, and clearly false, flattery. They both knew her brother would never have granted her request nor spared any of his men to protect her on the journey.

"Since you have found the means, 'tis clear you will do as you wish, no matter what I say." Harold's words were tight and controlled, but his disapproval was obvious.

"I find such independence a very unattractive quality in a female."

Fiona closed her eyes, feeling her stomach churn. As bad as things were, she knew they could get much worse. If she were wrong, if her plan failed, she would be forced to grovel, to beg for her brother's forgiveness, leaving herself, and Spencer, totally at his mercy. "I'm sorry to disappoint you, brother. But I must follow my conscience, and my faith."

"So be it." Harold relented, his manner deliberately ungracious. "Let it not be said that I didn't warn you of the folly of your actions."

Fiona refused to reply, instead lowering her eyes and bending her knee in a graceful curtsy. Clearly unimpressed, her brother snorted and turned away.

Fiona sighed, feeling the tension ease out of her shoulders with each step Harold took. Her brother believed she was going to the Abbey of St. Gifford, but that was a ruse. Oh, they would indeed stop at that holy place. Very briefly.

After respects had been paid to the brothers and prayers offered for Henry's soul, Fiona was going to continue moving north, to their true destination. Once there, she would appeal to the one man she believed could grant her the justice she so desperately sought, could help her secure the future that Spencer deserved.

She was going to cross the border into Scotland and plead her case to the enemy—Henry's secret ally, the Earl of Kirkland.

"I want him found and brought to me." Gavin McLendon, Earl of Kirkland, declared. "Alive."

A hush fell over the hall at the pronouncement, the

silence most eerie. The soldiers gambling in the corner held their dice, the servants cleaning the remains of the noonday meal stood still, the castle women seated in the bright sunlight at the far end of the vast chamber halted their sewing. Even the castle hounds ceased foraging for food scraps among the rush-strewn floor, heads raised, ears pointed.

Alone on the dais, Gavin leaned back in his seat, his sharp gaze pinned to the three men standing before him. Yet their expressions, each more stoic than the next, never changed.

Gavin fingered the ornately carved armrest of his chair and waited. There would be no excuses—his men knew him well enough to avoid that mistake. But there might be some sort of protest, since what he was asking them to do was akin to impossible.

And they all knew that, including Gavin.

"We've tracked the bastard fer over a week, but the trail has gone cold," Duncan admitted, his stare unapologetic.

Connor, standing beside his older brother, crossed his arms over his chest. "Gilroy has fled to the hills. He willnae be back fer a while, especially since he knew we were chasing him."

There was a ripple of agreement from the two other men. Looking past them, Gavin noticed several of the soldiers nodding their heads, while the women clucked a few loud sounds of disagreement.

Frustrated, Gavin cast a hard look at his three best trackers, letting out a soft curse beneath his breath. "Why would Gilroy need to hide from ye in the hills? 'Tis clear from his bold actions he believes he has nothing to fear from me or my men. Two years. Fer two full years that bastard has walked freely among us, doing whatever he pleases, taking whatever he fancies. Why? Because he believes my men lack the wits to stop him. And dammit, he's right!"

Duncan stiffened, his expression tightening. "'Tis not our lack of brains or skills, as ye well know. Gilroy's a wily one. And he's got plenty of help from our own."

"Aye," Connor added. "Half the lasses in our clan fancy themselves in love with him. They offer him shelter, then when we follow his trail to their village, they claim not to have seen him."

Gavin slapped the chair arm beneath his hand, putting every ounce of frustration he was feeling into the blow. His bastard half brother was running amok, stealing cattle and grain and making a general nuisance of himself. Such behavior threatened Gavin's authority, calling into question his ability to lead and rule his clan.

Something he could ill afford at any time, but never more so now, when Scotland was still a divided land. Even members of his own clan had questioned the wisdom of Gavin's decision to support King Robert, for the would-be king was little more than a fugitive in his own kingdom. Yet Gavin had no intention of forsaking his pledge, nor did he intend to suffer the same gruesome death as others who had defiantly sided with Robert against England's King Edward.

Not content with the mere execution of his enemies, King Edward had captured and then brought to London good men like William Wallace and Simon Fraser. Once there, he had ordered them hung, drawn and quartered and, as a final humiliation, had their heads impaled on spikes on London Bridge.

These barbaric acts had scared some sympathetic to King Robert's cause, but not Gavin. Instead, it had strengthened his resolve to do all that was necessary to help King Robert break from England's rule and achieve independence.

Yet how could he expect his people to trust his judgment and follow his lead when he couldn't control the raids of his bastard half brother? If word of this weakness spread, Lord only knew what other dangers they would be inviting. For in Scotland, if you didn't hold fast to what was yours, another clan was more than happy to claim it for themselves.

Allowing the determination that burned in his chest to be freely reflected in his face, Gavin stared down at his men.

Duncan, Connor, and Aidan were his cousins, sons of his father's brother and three of his most experienced, skilled fighters. He was confident of their loyalty, their devotion to him personally, and their regard for the welfare of the clan. A part of him regretted having to speak so harshly, but results were imperative.

Gilroy *must* be captured. Soon.

"Intruders have been seen in the south woods, milord!"

Gavin bit back his additional words of reprimand as the young soldier bringing the news hurried into the great hall. Was the opportunity he had been waiting for finally here? Gavin felt his pulse race at the thought of ending this irritating problem once and for all.

"Is it Gilroy?" Gavin asked, his expression eager.

"I dinnae think so." The young man hung his head, his disappointment obvious. "James saw them and sent me here with the message. There are two women in the party, a lad, a man wearing a priest's tunic, and six mounted knights. James dinnae get too close, but he said I must tell ye he believes they are English."

English? On my land? Gavin could feel the muscles

in his body tighten, but outwardly he remained calm. Not his half brother, but who could be certain? This could easily be another trick, a diversion created in one place while mischief was accomplished on another front.

"Take some men and ride out to meet these intruders," Gavin commanded. "That is, if ye think ye are capable of bringing them to me without any difficulties."

Duncan flushed, Connor fumed, and Aidan grimaced.

"We willnae have any trouble," Connor shot back.

With a stoic grimace, Gavin lifted a hand and waved off the comment. Clearly annoyed, the three men stomped away. Good. Perhaps the possibility of further humiliation would ensure their success. Reaching for his half-empty tankard of ale, Gavin took a long swallow, then leaned back in his chair.

He eyed a few of the soldiers gambling in the corner, but none would meet his gaze. Not surprising given his current mood. Unperturbed, he lifted his goblet, took another deep swallow, then leaned back in his chair and waited.

Concealed behind the large trunk of a fallen tree, Ewan Gilroy watched through the dense foliage as the McLendon men approached the encampment. When they crested the hill a cry arose from the camp sentry. One of the women moved forward as if to greet the McLendons, a short, broad-shouldered knight at her side. The rest of the men circled the edge of the camp, yet their weapons remained sheathed and they made no outward moves to defend themselves. Ewan wiggled forward on his belly to get a better look, but this closer view confirmed what he had seen.

Curious.

Though in truth, Ewan knew he shouldn't be surprised. He had been tracking this odd group for four days and nothing they had done made much sense. In the beginning, they had traveled on the public highway, but once they gained a foothold on McLendon land, they had taken to the forest, blatantly trespassing. 'Twas almost as if they were challenging the earl's authority, as if they wanted to be discovered.

"If we're fixing to raid the traveler's camp and take their bounty fer ourselves, we best make a move now or else the McLendons will reach them first."

Ewan froze, recognizing the voice of Magnus Fraser. Magnus was not part of his regular band of men and more often than not, Ewan had regretted his decision to bring him on these last few raids. Aye, he fought well and hard, but there was an arrogance to the man that was distasteful, an attitude bordering on threatening. With other skilled fighting men available to ride with him, Ewan had come to the conclusion that Magnus was far more trouble than he was worth.

"There's no need to bother with this lot," Ewan responded. "The McLendons believe us to be far away. 'Tis foolish to show ourselves fer whatever meager trinkets those travelers carry."

"I like trinkets." Magnus cleared his throat and spat on the ground. "We should have gone in at first light, like I said. When there were no McLendons around to see us."

Ewan avoided Magnus's stare, knowing he was right. They should have attacked sooner, but something had made him hesitate, hold back. Something he didn't want to acknowledge nor admit.

He was weary. Of the constant raids, the running and hiding, of not having a true home to call his own.

Lately, they had been even more successful in disrupting the business of the clan, an occurrence that should have given Ewan a sense of triumph. Instead, it left a hollow, almost empty feeling way down in the pit of his gut.

Given a choice, this was not the life he would have chosen for himself. Fugitive, outlaw, thief. It had been hard growing up as Moira Gilroy's bastard son, especially since his noble father had not laid claim to him until he was on his deathbed, mere minutes before meeting his maker.

By then, it was too late. Though born a daughter of a laird, Moira Gilroy had been cast out by her family when she shamefully revealed her pregnant state. Her lover, the grand and mighty Earl of Kirkland, also turned his back to her plight, refusing to acknowledge the child as his own.

Terrified and alone, Moira had repeatedly pressed for aid and finally the earl relented. His concession provided his former mistress with a crude hut on the outskirts of one of the villages, along with a meager stipend that shrank each year. If not for Ewan's quickly learned hunting skills as a lad, the two would have perished from starvation years ago.

Weaned on his mother's hatred for the earl, her constant wailing over the injustices done to her, and her almost daily recounts of her pain and suffering, Ewan grew to manhood with a bitterness eating at his heart. Two years ago, at the age of twenty, he had started the raids on the clan as a means to exact revenge, and in a short time they had increased in frequency, size, and intensity.

But so, too, had McLendon's pursuit. Though Ewan swaggered with rash boldness in front of his men, the truth was they had nearly been caught on this last raid. The incident had given Ewan pause and for the first time he began to think about how—and when—it would all end. The earl was long dead and in his place Ewan's half brother ruled. 'Twas said that Gavin McLendon was a fair and honorable man, yet he treated Ewan with the same contempt as their father.

"If we cannae pluck any treasure from these travelers, then I say we go to Kilmore," Magnus grunted. "Their grain house is near to bursting. What we cannae use fer ourselves, we can sell."

"Kilmore village is one of the earl's strongholds," Ewan said. "We have few allies within it."

"They'll not be so loyal with an empty belly and their bairns crying out from hunger when they try to go to sleep," Magnus snarled.

Ewan closed his eyes and felt a ripple of emotion flood his heart. "I willnae starve innocent folk to make a point."

Magnus's eyes gleamed. "'Tis the smart move."

There was a low grumble of agreement among several of the men who had drawn near when the discussion began. Ewan cocked an eyebrow. "And when exactly did ye get a brain in yer thick skull? Tell us true, Magnus, was it left to ye by the wee fairies while ye were sleeping?"

The men laughed and Ewan could feel the building tension leach away. Well, most of it.

Magnus was smiling as broadly as the rest of them, but his knuckles were white where his fingers wrapped around a tree branch. Ewan noted the telltale evidence of anger and defiance and casually reached for the dagger hidden in his boot. 'Twould be a pity to kill such a skilled fighter, but if challenged, he would not hesitate. Ewan had no illusions about the character of many of the men who followed him.

Heartless bastards, the lot of them. And Ewan knew he was the worst of the bunch.

The color in Magnus's cheeks heightened and a tiny muscle beneath his left eye twitched. Ever on the alert, Ewan waited, but the attack never came. Magnus glanced at a few of the men, then looked away uneasily.

Ewan slowly lifted his hand, keeping his dagger hidden. There would be no fight—this time. Yet Ewan was wise enough to realize that one day soon the time would come when Magnus *would* challenge him.

By all that was holy, he'd best be ready for it.

Chapter 3

Fiona stirred the meager pot of rabbit stew and wondered if it could be deemed a surprise attack when you knew it was going to happen. Not precisely the time, or even the place, but a confrontation was an eventuality. They were deliberately on the earl's land—trespassing. And they were being watched. It was now only a matter of time before they were confronted.

Her stomach turned with restless agitation. If she was wrong about the earl, all their lives were in grave peril. The only thing that kept her calm was Spencer. Basking in the innocence of youth, he had seen this trip as a grand adventure. His boyish delight in the simplest of things had kept them all in good spirits.

But even Spencer's sweet charm could no longer dispel the tension inside the camp. Fiona's frayed emotions were stretched to the breaking point.

"Why have the McLendon men not approached us?" Fiona asked as she tossed a bunch of wild onions in the cauldron.

"They'll be waiting for orders from the earl," Sir

George responded. He leaned forward and sniffed appreciatively. "Is it ready?"

Fiona sighed. *Saints alive, how could he possibly be hungry?* Since crossing the border into Scotland four days ago, she had barely been able to choke down a few bites of hard bread and cheese. Fiona supposed she should be grateful that Sir George was not so easily rattled, yet it was still unsettling.

After a final stir, she ladled a hearty portion of the stew into a wooden bowl and passed it to the knight. "I hope you do not regret your decision to aid me, Sir George."

Sir George took a big bite of the concoction, noisily sucking in his breath when the hot food hit his mouth. "Riding into Scotland is the last thing I wanted for you and the boy, my lady, but I understand why you had to leave your brother's keep."

Catching a whiff of the food, a few of the other men drifted toward the cooking fire. Fiona handed the ladle to her maid, Alice, and the older woman diligently assumed the task of distributing the meal.

Not wanting to be overheard, Fiona stepped away from the others. Sir George took a second helping of stew before following her.

"The men all understand what they are to do when the earl's retainers show themselves?" Fiona asked.

"I have ordered them to stand firm and wait for my signal before drawing their weapons." Sir George frowned. "But I'm still not certain that will work. The Scots are warriors, men known to strike first and ask questions later."

"I know. That is why 'tis so important that we not challenge them."

Fiona carefully avoided looking at Sir George when

she spoke, knowing her words had the potential to insult the knight. He was not the sort of man who ran from a fight and that was exactly what she was asking him to do.

"I will do as you wish," Sir George said begrudgingly. "But I give you fair warning. At the first thrust of a Scotsman's sword, my men and I will retaliate in kind."

"I understand. Though I shall pray it won't be necessary."

Sir George ate the last bite of food in his bowl, then wiped his mouth on his sleeve. "Tell me again, Lady Fiona. Why are you turning to this Scottish earl for aid?"

"Believe me, he is hardly my first choice. But I am long past the point where I must face the facts. There is no one in England who will support Spencer's claim to his birthright, including my own kin."

"And you think a Scottish earl will?" Sir George asked, disbelief evident in his tone.

"He is my last hope," she whispered, hating how weak and pitiful she sounded.

"And if he turns you away?"

Though his tone was gentle, the cruelty of the question struck at Fiona's core. What would she do if the earl turned her away? It was almost too frightening to consider.

"The good Lord will provide," she replied, secretly wishing her faith was that invincible, that strong. Disregarding the pain squeezing her heart, Fiona smiled up at the knight. "Now, come and have another bowl of my stew before it is all eaten."

Momentarily distracted by his stomach, Sir George complied. They sat companionably among the others, engaging in low conversation. Spencer, unaffected by the rising tension, kept them distracted with his endless questions.

Suddenly, the thunder of horse hooves cut through the tranquility of the afternoon, the sound far louder than Fiona expected. Brushing the wrinkles from her skirt, she rose slowly to her feet, eyes widening when she caught sight of the men galloping toward them.

There were three in the lead and another dozen retainers behind them. Even at this distance, they were an intimidating force. Bare-chested, wearing a variety of fierce-looking weapons strapped to their upper bodies, they looked like a band of frenzied beasts on the scent of fresh prey.

The closer they came, the faster they rode, bearing down on the small camp with a single-minded determination. Fiona threw a hand over her mouth to still a cry of fear. What if they attacked before she had a chance to speak?

Suddenly, the plan she had so carefully conceived seemed fraught with incredible risk and danger.

Heart pounding, she turned to the knight at her side. Sir George looked uncertainly back at her, his eyes narrowing to small slits. "Hold steady, men," he ordered. "Await my signal."

The restless sound of shifting feet and metal armor failed to offer her comfort. Silently, Fiona held out her hand, gesturing for Spencer to stand between her and Sir George. Trying to instill a confidence she didn't feel, Fiona rested a reassuring hand on the boy's shoulder, not surprised to feel him trembling.

The sound of the riders grew louder. Her fingers tightened on Spencer's shoulder as her gaze scanned the surrounding woods, searching for an escape route in case things went terribly wrong.

One of the riders pulled slightly ahead of the others, then raised his arm. The men behind him pulled up and quickly dismounted. Fiona was dismayed to discover the Scots were no less intimidating on foot.

"Yer on McLendon land," the leader said. "Why?"

"Our lady has business with the earl," Sir George announced, stepping forward.

The leader scoffed. "What sort of business?"

"Private business."

"With an English lady? Not likely."

There was a chorus of hearty chuckles and Fiona felt every set of Scots eyes shift toward her. Her cheeks heated, but she blithely ignored the sudden sense of helplessness that surrounded her, keeping her attention on the leader.

She knew this man. He was among the soldiers that had sought sanctuary on their land after the battle. But for the life of her, she could not recall his name.

"Ask her again what kind of business she has with the earl, Duncan," one of the men jeered.

Sir George growled low in his throat and reached for the hilt of his sword. Fiona thrust her arm across his waist to keep him back, ignoring the burst of angry rumbling from the men standing behind her. If Sir George broke rank, a fight was certain to ensue.

Fiona cleared her throat delicately. "Duncan? Do you not recognize me? I am Lady Fiona, wife of Baron Arundel."

The corners of Duncan's lips twitched. "Wife? Widow is more like it."

"Yes, widow." Fiona swallowed the lump in her throat. "You must forgive our intrusion upon McLendon land, but Sir George speaks the truth. I have come to see the earl."

"Yer not expected."

"Yes, I know. I am sorry. There was no means of sending a message asking his permission." She tried smiling, achieving only a wane grin.

Duncan looked mildly annoyed at the gesture. They all stood silent and uneasy for a few moments. "Now then, on a usual day we'd be chasing the lot of ye off our land—and not real politely, either. But today is a lucky day fer ye, Lady Fiona. The earl told us to bring ye to him. So, ye'd best be getting on yer horse."

Lord be praised. Releasing the breath she had been holding, Fiona scrambled to obey. One of Sir George's men boosted her onto her mount and she quickly gathered the reins. The others started toward their horses, but Duncan's voice halted their movements.

"Only the lady comes with us. The rest of ye will wait here."

Sir George and his knights exchanged glances. "My men will stay behind, but I will accompany Lady Fiona," Sir George insisted.

"Nay." Duncan's voice boomed.

Fiona flinched. Several of her knights became more vocal in their protests, shifting restlessly on their feet. Out of the corner of her eye, Fiona saw one of the Scotsmen reach for his sword.

No! They had come too far to risk failure now.

"Silence!" Fiona held up her hand. "We are guests of the earl and as such must act accordingly."

"I'll not allow—"

"Since he is the earl's man, I trust Duncan's honor implicitly," Fiona shouted, interrupting Sir George's protest. "I'm sure he will gladly guarantee my safety."

Everyone's attention shifted to Duncan. There was no mistaking the annoyance in his eyes, but there was something else there, too. Integrity. His word, once given, would not be broken.

"She'll not be harmed on my watch," he said grudgingly.

"Thank you." Fiona felt her belly tighten. The last thing she wanted was to ride into the earl's castle without her knights at her side, but there appeared to be no other way. "I entrust you with Spencer's safety, Sir George."

Somewhat mollified, the knight nodded his head.

"I'll be leaving some of my men to keep ye company, Sir George," Duncan announced as he swung himself effortlessly onto his saddle. "Just to make sure ye dinnae get lonely."

There was barely any time for Sir George to argue. Within seconds Fiona could feel the press of horses and men as the Scots formed two columns around her. The moment they began to move, her startled horse meekly followed the surge.

The brisk pace left Fiona breathless. She resisted the urge to turn and look back upon the camp. Instead, she concentrated on keeping her seat, determined to show the Scotsmen that she was able to keep to their grueling pace.

They rode through a large meadow, covered with sweet-smelling green grass and tiny lavender flowers, then entered a dense forest. Here they were forced to ride single file, with Fiona placed firmly in the center of the pack. They eventually emerged from the dense woods into a valley with a picturesque stream meandering through the center of it.

Pressing the back of her hand to her forehead to shield the newly emerged sun, Fiona gasped as she caught her first glimpse of the earl's castle. Dominated by four massive gray stone towers, it was perched at the top of a large hill, looming over the landscape below and allowing for sweeping views of the countryside from all directions.

Stone walkways on the ramparts connected each of the towers, and Fiona could see the heads of the men who patrolled them. As she and the riders drew closer, she realized that there was a second curtain wall of stone surrounding the entire complex. Here, the battlements were numerous, allowing for even greater protection against attack. Her mind whirled as she tried to calculate the time and expense required to design and construct such an elaborate stone structure.

Though clearly built for warfare and defense, there was an unmistakable beauty surrounding the fortress. The stone shimmered when hit by sunlight and the water in the wide moat sparkled like gemstones.

Surrounding the great castle was a sizable village of thatched-roofed homes, cooking smoke rising from many of them. As they rode down the main path through the village, the sounds of laboring hands and bustling activity filled the air. Hammering, sawing, nailing. Children's laughter and mothers' scolding, braying livestock and clucking hens.

Word quickly spread of their presence. People abandoned their work, emerging from their dwellings to stare openly as they passed. Several of the children waved, and a few of the young women simpered and cast appreciative, flirting eyes toward the men.

Fiona could not help but notice how healthy they all looked, with round cheeks and sparkling eyes. There were barely any holes in their clothing and most had shoes upon their feet. It was a sharp contrast to the thin, dirty rags and gaunt faces of the peasants on her brother's land. It buoyed Fiona's sprits to see the common folk so well cared for by their lord and bespoke of the earl's compassion and generosity.

Pray God, that giving spirit would extend to her and Spencer.

"She's English."

The accusation was hurled from a faceless voice. A chill crept inside her, reminding Fiona that here she was considered the enemy, an unwelcome and unwanted intruder. Word quickly spread among the villagers and the friendly smiles turned to harsh glares. She braced herself for any verbal taunts, but a glowering stare from Duncan silenced the growing crowds. Still, Fiona could clearly see that the villagers' simple curiosity had given way to mistrust.

Quiet surrounded them. Fiona nudged her mount closer to Duncan. Another dark scowl twisted the young man's face and a feeling of gratitude swept through her. He had given his word to keep her safe and was now intent on keeping his promise.

Still, a pang of loneliness dug into her heart. If only she had Sir George or Spencer by her side to give her courage.

Finally, they left the village behind and resumed a fast pace. Soon they arrived at the castle entrance and Duncan gave the signal to slow their mounts. When they rode beneath the raised metal portcullis Fiona's back was as rigid as the stone curtain that surrounded the great castle, giving no hint of the fear tearing her apart inside.

I know I am doing what is right, she repeated to herself. *The earl is a man who values honor. He will not forsake us in our time of great need.*

As Fiona expected, the inner bailey was bustling

with activity. Here, the retainers were barely given a second glance. Boys came forward to take their horses and several of the men joked with them. Duncan jumped off his horse, then assisted Fiona from her mount, his hands barely touching her waist. She cast him a shy smile, grateful for his respectful treatment.

All but two other men and Duncan drifted away. Nervously, Fiona followed the trio up the stone stairs into a large receiving hall. The room was massive in size, nearly as wide as it was long, with a high, soaring ceiling lined with thick, dark wooden beams.

A clan banner with the McLendon plaid woven around the edges hung from the center beam and finely embroidered tapestries depicting various battle scenes decorated the walls. Four large hearths were set in the stone walls, two on each side. On this summer day only one was lit, the fire barely blazing.

Slits in the stone at the very top of the walls let in light and fresh air, yet there was a heavy darkness that permeated the vast chamber.

At the far end was a raised dais where one man sat and several others stood.

"Wait until ye're called," Duncan commanded before he marched over to the dais, leaving her behind with the two other men.

Hunching over, Fiona craned her neck forward and squinted into the gloom, trying to distinguish the features of the men on the other side of the chamber. Was the earl among them? Or would she first have to speak to another of his retainers? That thought was most discouraging, so she pushed it aside.

"Come forward, Lady Fiona."

A hush fell over the chamber at the sharply spoken command. Gingerly placing one foot in front of the other, Fiona began the long walk, biting her bottom lip to keep it from trembling. It felt as if every eye in the chamber was trained upon her. No matter. To save Spencer she'd walk through fire, if that's what it took.

After what felt like an eternity of steps, Fiona finally reached the dais. Her relief at discovering that the man seated in the chair was indeed the earl was short-lived. He met her tentative smile with a fierce gaze that pierced her to the core.

Showing respect and deference, Fiona lowered her head and sank into a graceful curtsy. "I thank you most humbly, my lord, for receiving me."

The earl snorted, then gave her a humorless smile. "Ye've given me little choice in the matter, Lady Fiona. Let me assure ye, the McLendons are not often this lenient with those who trespass upon our land."

Disappointment rushed through her. She might be an uninvited guest, but there was no need to treat her like a common criminal. Why, he hadn't even offered her a seat, or a glass of ale or wine to quench her thirst.

"Duncan warned me of the reception I was likely to receive. I see now that I should have trusted his word, but I believed a noble Scottish earl would show a chivalrous hand to a lady in distress. Especially since he had been treated as a friend when he dared to trespass upon *my* land."

The earl raised an eyebrow in surprise. "Are ye scolding me, Lady Fiona?"

"I am relating the facts, my lord."

His mouth tightened. "With a boldness that many would find insolent."

His words gave Fiona a chill. For one horrible moment, she worried she had gone too far and he meant to dismiss her. But then the pride that had given her the courage to take this risk flared to life. Her chin lifted, her spine straightened.

"It would be tragic, indeed, for you to perceive an insult when none was given."

"Aye, it would," he mused.

Subtly wiping her damp palm on her skirt, Fiona forced herself to smile. "Friends are not easily acquired in these uncertain times. 'Twould be tragic to turn one unjustly into an enemy."

"Aye." His gaze slid from the rounded neckline of her gown to her leather-shod booted feet. "Is that what we are, Lady Fiona? Friends?"

Fiona's breath shortened. She knew the scrutiny was meant to intimidate, but there was something intimate, almost sensual in the earl's hooded gaze that caught her completely off guard. "My husband counted you a friend."

Lord Kirkland's gaze slipped downward. "I was saddened to hear of Henry's death. He was a good man."

"The finest." Fiona blinked, refusing to get teary-eyed.

"Ye were attacked?"

"Ambushed in the middle of the night. My son and I barely escaped with our lives." Fiona's voice softened. "That is why I have come. I seek justice."

"From me?"

Fiona's cheeks reddened. "You are my last hope."

The earl's surprised expression did not alter. "These are dangerous times to be forging alliances, milady. Especially with a Scottish earl."

"Spencer and I have been squarely placed in danger's path ever since Henry's death. Though he believes otherwise, King Edward cannot live forever. His son and heir is a very different sort of man. It will be difficult for him to rule England's nobility with the same iron fist as his father. I need to be ready to reclaim my son's birthright the moment an opportunity arises."

"What do ye want from me?"

"Spencer is intelligent, passionate, and eager to learn. All he lacks is the proper training."

The earl furrowed his brow. "Is there no one in England to foster the lad?"

"None will have him."

"Why?"

Emotion rose inside Fiona, clutching at her throat. "He was wounded during the attack. His injuries have been slow to heal."

"He's a cripple?"

"No!" The tension in her stomach twisted. She couldn't lie; the moment the earl saw Spencer he would know the truth. "His right leg is not as strong as the left. But it will improve."

"There's those that can be taught when they are lacking," Duncan remarked. "Old Douglas wields a sword as good as any man, and he has but one hand."

"Hmmm." The earl settled back in his chair. He didn't seem entirely convinced, but at least he was still listening. "What do ye offer in return for my aid?"

Fiona's heart leapt. "A half yield of our grain crops for three years."

"What else?"

"Hunting rights in our northernmost woods."

"And?"

Fiona nervously licked her lips. "Twenty bolts of our finest wool. The weavers of Arundel are known throughout the kingdom for their skill. You'll find no finer material in all the land."

The earl studied her for a moment. "As far as I can see, ye have neither crops, nor land, nor cloth. I'll grant ye 'tis rather clever offering things ye dinnae possess in exchange fer what you want, but only a fool would agree to such a bargain."

Fiona could feel her heart beating harder than it ever had. "With your help, someday I will have it all again. And I shall keep my word and give you what we agreed upon."

His expression grew quiet, contemplative. Fiona allowed herself to hope, making the earl's next words all the more crushing.

"Someday is far away. Yet even if I were willing to wait, I must maintain that ye are offering nothing to make it worth my time and effort."

Fiona stood stunned for a moment, struggling for words, her nails flexing deep into the cloth of her overskirt. "I appeal to your honor, my lord, to your sense of decency."

"Sadly, ye are gravely misinformed as to my character."

He is turning me away. Disappointment slammed into Fiona's chest like a fist. She had expected the negotiations would be challenging, but had been confident a satisfactory solution would be found. But what use was compromise when the earl showed no interest at all in anything she offered?

There had to be something he wanted, something he would prize enough to strike a bargain with her. More often than not she had heard Henry say that every man had his price. What was the earl's?

"There must be something, my lord," Fiona's voice trailed off, her pride keeping her shoulders straight, her head high.

And that's when she saw it. A flash of passion glowing

from the depths of his eyes. A gleam of male interest, a spark of masculine admiration. Sexual desire.

It startled her. Henry liked to tell her she was pretty and would often compliment her golden hair or fair complexion or green eyes. And she enjoyed hearing it. But those words were never spoken with overt desire. At first, she had been too young to realize there was a lack of physical intimacy in her marriage. By the time she learned that her marriage was different from most, it was no longer important.

Henry treated her with respect, showered her with kindness, favored her with devotion. One night, after drinking too much ale, he had confessed that his lack of physical attention toward her stemmed from always thinking of her as he first knew her. She had come to his castle as a child, and though she had grown to womanhood beneath his roof, he forever saw her as a young girl.

Gradually, Henry's lack of passion had woven itself into Fiona's mind, but the spark of interest in the earl's eyes reminded her that she still had one weapon at her disposal, one move left to make.

The earl was twice a widower. Did he feel the loss of a wife as keenly as she felt the loss of a husband?

Holding steady, Fiona forced herself to look at the earl's handsome face. "You are very much mistaken when you say I have nothing to offer. There is one thing that is mine, wholly and completely—my person. And thus, in exchange for training my son, I offer myself to you."

A deep, soulful hush fell over the hall, letting Fiona know that others had heard her remarks. But it was their lord's reaction that mattered.

Slowly, the earl lifted his gaze to hers, his deep blue eyes burning into her own. Fiona swallowed hard. Embarrassment washed over her, along with a single ray of hope.

Clearly, he was not repulsed by the idea.

"'Tis a tempting offer, but I cannae marry ye, lass. I feel no great urgency to wed again, but when the time comes and I do take my next wife, she'll be a Scottish lady, through and through."

"I'd expect nothing less." Fiona hardly knew how she was able to speak so calmly. She had known that a marriage between them was highly unlikely, yet her desperation had been so strong, she was willing to humble herself with the outrageous suggestion.

The earl stood, his posture dismissive. *Oh, no.* Crestfallen, Fiona's heart sank and her breath quickened as her mind worked frantically, desperately searching for the words that would miraculously change his mind.

He would not marry her. It had been a rash, desperate suggestion. But there was no time to feel the sting of rejection. She must act.

Ignoring the voice that told her she was about to make an even bigger fool of herself, Fiona took a bold step forward. If the price she needed to pay to secure Spencer's future was her own humiliation, then so be it.

"Clearly, you misheard, my lord. When I offered myself, I said naught about marriage, did I?"

Chapter 4

Every person in the great hall seemed to be holding their breath, Gavin among them. Surely he had misheard Lady Fiona's remark? Misheard or misunderstood.

But Lady Fiona had lost her shy smile, had abandoned her quiet demeanor. Her expression now was quite bold, though beneath the bravado Gavin could swear her hands were trembling.

As well they should be. Why, the daft woman had just proposed becoming his mistress!

"Do ye know what ye are saying?"

"I know precisely what I propose, my lord. And I'd thank you to have the good manners to acknowledge it."

Good manners? Aye, the woman had lost her wits, there was no doubt. He uncoiled his long limbs, stood, then took a step closer, looming over her. "I heard ye well enough, Lady Fiona. I can assure ye, 'tis not every day an English lady enters my hall and asks to be my leman."

"These are desperate times. I must take desperate measures," she replied steadily.

"Och, so now it's my fault yer turning yerself into a whore?"

She cringed at the remark, yet recovered quickly, an expression of calm on her face. Still, he was close enough to see her reaction, to feel the bolt of pain his words had inflicted.

Aye, now that will be the end of it. She'd just acknowledged that the offer was made in desperation and she now needed a graceful way to withdraw it and still keep some pride. Gavin stole a quick glance at her winsome mouth and for a single moment regretted his decision to give her one.

Lady Fiona was a rare beauty, with a face and figure that could easily haunt a man's dreams. Looking at her, he felt a familiar eagerness in his breath. Mud was splashed on the hem of her cloak and gown, wisps of blond hair had escaped from her silken veil, and a weariness hung about her person. Yet none of that dimmed her appeal or lessened the fierce, fiery attraction he felt for her.

He would have enjoyed having her in his bed, would have relished the chance to explore the sensual curves of her body, to taste the delights of her flesh. He had been too long without a woman and there was something unique, different about this one that captured his attention like none other.

She tilted her chin and cast him an unrepentant glare. "I am a free woman. I shall willingly barter whatever I can, including my person, for I answer to no one but myself and the good Lord."

"I doubt the Lord would approve of yer choice," he muttered.

"Neither of us can know that," she answered. "God is merciful and forgiving. He understands human weakness and frailty. Besides, what harm do we do? Neither of us is married. We are breaking no vows, forsaking no others."

Oh, she was too clever by half. Gavin could see that her pride had taken a beating, but she was not about to give up. So why was he resisting her? Well, for one thing, her proposition was ridiculous.

Or was it? His cock certainly didn't think it was a bad idea at all. Quite the contrary—that part of his anatomy had stood at attention the moment she had risen from her graceful curtsy, her sweet beauty nearly bewitching him.

Even now, his pulse was pounding hard and fast and a rising heat had captured his loins. Thankfully, the hem of his embroidered tunic concealed most of his ardor and his stoic expression hid the restlessness teaming inside him.

Disconcerted that his rampant desire would cloud his common sense, Gavin searched for a different topic of conversation. But there were none to be found. Not while Lady Fiona watched him with such a pensive look on her face and the rest of the hall's occupants openly stared.

Accept. The word echoed in his brain, and Gavin was surprised by how strongly he was tempted. Yet still he held back. Always aware of his position, Gavin was cautious and very particular when choosing his bed partners. It was something his men liked to joke about, though seldom directly to his face.

Twice married, Gavin had been a faithful husband— out of respect and empathy. Respect for the woman who bore his name and presided over his castle, and empathy for the suffering endured by an innocent bairn born out of wedlock. It was a fate no child deserved.

Thanks to his philandering father, he was forced to contend with the antics of a bastard brother whose actions were rooted in resentment and misery. Many would find it difficult to believe, but every now and again Gavin felt a pang of sympathy for Ewan Gilroy and the place he occupied in the world.

Gavin refused to place a child of his own in such a tenuous position, refused to have his heir contend with the same difficulties; praise God he would one day be so blessed as to have a son. This attitude made for many a cold night swim in the loch to relieve his ongoing sexual frustration, but for him, it was the right choice.

Gavin kept away from female servants and peasant girls, seeing how it could lead to talk of favoritism and breed jealousy among his people. Straying wives and curious virgins were also avoided at all costs. That left clean, experienced whores to dally with and the most desirable bedmate of all—a barren widow.

Pity, really, that Lady Fiona could only fulfill half that requirement.

"Do ye have other children in addition to Spencer?"

"No." She hung her head.

"Have ye buried many bairns over the years?" he asked gently, recalling with pain the three small grave markers in the valley.

Gavin's son had lived the longest—five days, dying hours after his mother. The two infant daughters his second wife had borne him had each lived only a few hours.

"Alas, I've not ever experienced the joy of carrying a babe." Lady Fiona's mouth turned white with regret. "Sadly, Henry and I were never blessed with children of our own."

"Spencer?"

"Is the prodigy of my husband's first marriage to Lady Catherine."

"The boy is yer stepson?"

It didn't seem possible. Why would she fight so hard and sacrifice so much for a lad who wasn't even her own blood?

Lady Fiona gave him a stifling glare. "Spencer is my son in every way that matters," she declared hotly. "He is the child of my heart and will forever remain there."

Her loyalty surprised him. 'Twas a quality Gavin greatly admired and Lady Fiona obviously possessed it in abundance. Yet another mark in her favor.

"How many years were ye Henry's wife?"

"Ten."

And no pregnancies? Clearly she was barren. His interest piqued, as this fulfilled his first requirement in a lover. And she was a widow, accomplishing the second. *An English widow.*

That was a complication that might cause some difficulties in time. But standing at this juncture, the promise of a sweet, lovely, willing bedmate pushed those repercussions to the very back of Gavin's mind.

"Leave us!"

Gavin's booming order rang out through the hall. Soldiers, guardsmen, and servants alike scrambled to obey, the more bold among them risking a curious glance in his direction before departing.

Duncan was the last to leave and he dared to push himself forward to mutter in Gavin's ear. "I'll grant ye she's a bonnie piece, and there might be a good reason or two to offer her aid, but dinnae be letting yer cock make that decision."

"When I'm in need of yer counsel, I shall ask fer it,"

Gavin declared hotly. *Bloody hell.* Allow a man the chance to freely speak his mind and he'll seize every opportunity to tell you precisely what you don't want to hear.

At last alone, Gavin advanced upon her. Her eyes widened with something he could not define. Fear? Nay. 'Twas more like resolve. His admiration grew yet again.

"Ye ask much of me, Lady Fiona."

"But I am prepared to give much in exchange." She lowered her lashes coyly. "Whatever you require, whatever you want."

Gavin nearly stopped breathing. Anticipation surged hard inside him. The idea of her giving herself to him so openly ignited his baser desires, sending sensual images through his mind. Hell, he could almost feel the fiery stroke of her tongue against his own, see her lying naked on his bed, her golden, unbound hair flowing around her, framing her creamy flesh.

But there was another feeling gnawing at him, this one not nearly as pleasant. 'Twas guilt. How could he allow the widow of a man he once called a friend to debase herself in such a manner? Even worse, how could he convince several key Scottish nobles to shift their loyalty and support the Bruce's cause if he had Lady Fiona and Spencer, the rightful heir to an English barony, living within his castle walls?

Why, the Bruce himself might question Gavin's loyalties!

For appearance sake, he had to ensure there was a plausible reason, with no political implications, for the lovely widow to be under his protection. Surely, there was no true-blooded Scotsman alive who didn't understand the allure of the fairer sex.

Some of the more conservative lairds might question his self-control, but not his politics. Then again, once they met the fair Lady Fiona, there was no one who would gainsay his choice.

"Have you made a decision, my lord?"

He groped for a final grain of sense, an answer that was not purely rooted in blind lust, and was pleased he could justify this decision with at least some rational thoughts.

"Aye. I shall do as ye ask." Gavin circled slowly around her, stopping at her back. He could see the nape of her neck through the silky gauze of her veil—'twas slender, delicate, and alluring. He leaned close, his lips almost touching the creamy flesh, and whispered, "In exchange fer my help, I'll take a half yield of yer grain crops fer three years."

She shivered. "Agreed."

He blew softly beneath the fabric, causing the wisps of golden hair to flutter. Her entire body appeared to jump. "The hunting rights in yer northernmost woods."

"Fine."

Smiling at her reaction, he repositioned himself so they were toe to toe. "Twenty bolts of yer finest wool."

She averted her gaze. "Yes."

He curved his hand beneath her chin and ran his thumb slowly across her lips. She sighed and looked up into his face. Her gaze fixed on his mouth, lingering until Gavin's loins tightened. She looked like a girl, innocent, vulnerable, but there was a poise and grace about her that was all woman. "And finally, my good lady, I'll take ye."

Her cheeks flamed with embarrassment, but she held his gaze and nodded.

"So, we have struck our bargain, Lady Fiona?"

"We have, my lord."

Her voice was a startled whisper and for a moment she looked flummoxed. The expression bothered him, niggling at his conscience, forcing him to ask a question he did not want to broach.

"Are ye certain? Ye agree to *all* the terms?"

"Yes." The word was barely audible, but she squared her shoulders and repeated it, this time forcefully. "Yes."

A feeling of bliss raced through Gavin's veins. Not knowing what else to do, he bowed to her. She dipped her knee and curtsied with queenly dignity. When she rose, she met his gaze full on, her eyes wide with a myriad of unsettled thoughts.

His heart lurched. She had agreed to the terms with conviction, but her lingering doubts were impossible to ignore. It left him with the strangest yearning to pull her into the circle of his arms and soothe away all her misgivings.

And that's when Gavin knew he was in trouble.

For several long seconds Fiona was unable to breathe. Had she really just agreed to become the earl's mistress? By all that was holy, the world had gone mad.

A soft sigh passed her lips. She has just willingly abandoned every lesson on propriety and morality that had ever been preached to her. She blinked and stared at the earl, wondering if he was also feeling a sense of shock.

"Ye'll move into the chamber next to mine," he said.

Fiona nodded, though in truth she barely comprehended his words, listening with a curious detachment, as if she were watching everything from a great distance. Her mind and emotions were reeling with the enormity of what had just transpired and it was difficult to find a place in reality.

She had gotten what she had come for, had achieved her goal, had secured the one thing most important to her—a future for Spencer. Yet at what cost?

Unexpectedly, a strong instinct to turn and walk away rose up within her. To flee to a place of refuge and safety and never look back. But where would she go?

Nowhere. There was nowhere to go. She had chosen this path and sealed her fate when she proposed the arrangement to the earl. It was now her duty to accept this role, to embrace her future.

Their eyes met and the fog around Fiona abruptly vanished. Something in his expression made the hair on the nape of her neck stand up. He was gazing at her as though she were a tray of sweetmeats and he a hungry, greedy boy just waiting to reach in and stuff his mouth full.

He drew closer, his gaze intent on her lips. *Oh, no.* She cast a helpless look about, seeking a way to distract him. A swatch of color fluttering above caught her eye.

"Are those your clan colors?" Fiona inquired loudly, pointing to the banner that hung above their heads.

"What?"

"The tartan. Many clans have a distinctive tartan, do they not? And a motto. Tell me, my lord, what is your clan motto?"

"My motto?"

"Ah, I see it now, stitched in the banner. *Invictus Maneo. I remain unvanquished.* Is that correct? My Latin is far from perfect as I have only recently begun to learn to read and cypher."

The earl regarded her with a look of perplexed annoyance, stretching thin the faint scar that slashed across his left temple. Oddly, it gave his handsome face a more approachable appearance. Fiona's nerves began to settle. Her chattering had succeeded in breaking the intimate mood, had lessened the hungry look in his eye. For now.

"Ye've a solid knowledge of the language if ye can read it," he said. "A most unusual skill fer a female."

"A woman alone has need of all sorts of skills, my lord."

"Yer no longer alone." His gaze grew possessive as it meandered over the length of her body. "*I remain unvanquished* is not just our motto, but the creed the McLendons live by. Ye'll do well to remember that, milady." He turned away. "Hamish!"

A stocky man with thinning gray hair arrived so quickly Fiona wondered where the servant had been waiting. Close enough to hear the entire exchange? Most likely.

Fiona closed her eyes in mortification, but then chastised herself for being so foolish. There were few secrets kept in a castle, especially concerning the lord of the manor. By the time the evening meal was served, news of the earl's new English mistress would have spread far and wide.

"Hamish is steward here," the earl explained. "He'll see that ye are settled."

"Hamish." Fiona attempted a friendly smile. The steward cocked his head and stared at her curiously.

"Lady Fiona is to be our guest," the earl announced. "Have the chamber next to mine prepared at once."

The corners of the servant's mouth turned down. "Will the lady be with us long?"

Fiona's pride bristled as her cheeks heated. She had

hardly been a welcomed guest at her brother's keep, but at least she had been spared any open scorn by his servants. It hurt to be so quickly judged, yet if she was going to live here, she'd have to find a way to endure.

The earl's expression hardened. "I expect ye to see to her every comfort, Hamish. Is that understood?"

"Aye."

The servant drew himself up. Understood perhaps, but obviously not agreed upon. While Fiona was glad the earl attempted to save her dignity by giving her a chamber of her own, he would not be able to force his people to show her respect.

"What will become of the men who accompanied me here?" she asked when Hamish departed.

"They will be told that ye and yer son are remaining here, as my honored guests."

"Sir George will want to hear the news directly from my lips."

To her surprise, the earl nodded approvingly. "Any soldier worth his salt would do the same." The earl cast her a mischievous grin she found so out of character, she nearly missed hearing his next question. "Do ye wish to write Sir George a note? I can send fer parchment and a quill?"

Fiona smiled. "I would gladly compose a missive, but alas Sir George cannot read. In any event, I owe him the courtesy of releasing him from my service." Fiona paused as a new thought struck. "Unless you would consider allowing him to stay? He is a landless knight with great skill and experience and a credit to any lord he serves."

The earl grimaced. "My allies will tolerate a great deal, but I doubt they will understand the presence of an English knight in my garrison."

"Better in your garrison than fighting outside your walls."

"It will take more than a few of King Edward's puny knights to breach my walls. He learned that well enough last year."

Fiona's blood chilled. "Edward laid siege to your castle?"

"He tried. But surrender took far longer than he anticipated. Thankfully, an early frost and a biting winter wind sent him back across the border." The earl met her gaze unflinchingly. "He might try it again in a few weeks, as he marches north, though the Bruce is his true quest. Word has it that he plans to capture and punish him once and for all."

Fiona blanched and alarm flared through her. This was one complication she had not considered. Having experienced the brutality of battle firsthand, she was not eager to once again be a part of the fray.

Almost as if reading her mind, the earl asked, "Are ye sure ye want to stay?"

A flash of indecision seized her. She had made her decision. And yet . . . "The castle appears to be well fortified, with strong outer walls that can withstand a significant attack."

"They've never been breached," the earl replied.

His words were not spoken boastfully, but rather with a reassuring confidence that offered Fiona some comfort. Still. "There are other ways to gain entry inside a castle," she pointed out.

The earl's eyes flashed with resentment at the implication. "My people are loyal. There'll be no one opening the gates in the middle of the night."

She forced her rapid heartbeat to slow. "I pray you

are right, my lord. For I am entrusting you with the safety of myself and my son."

Out of the corner of her eye Fiona caught a movement. A pair of serving women passed near them, their expressions openly curious. Fiona then noticed that quite a few others had drifted back to the hall and decided some silent signal must have been given. There were a few soldiers, though none she recognized. And a contingent of women that grew steadily in size. The whispering among them increased and they didn't bother to hide their efforts to overhear her conversation with the earl.

"No harm will come to ye while ye're under my roof," the earl insisted.

The whispers from their growing audience grew louder, along with the resentful looks. In a way, Fiona could not fault the feelings—the McLendons were a proud people and she had cast aspersions on their leader.

"I understand that my escort must depart, but I was hoping you would allow my maid, Alice, to stay," Fiona said. "We have been through much together these past years. It would be a comfort to have her by my side."

And a relief to the female servants of the castle, Fiona silently added, knowing none of them would willingly serve in that capacity.

The earl shrugged his broad shoulders. "I see no harm in it."

"Thank you." Fiona cleared her throat delicately, hating to ask for more, but there was one other member of her household she wanted near. "Father Niall has also asked that he be allowed to remain with me. His mother was a Highlander who married an Englishman.

Father Niall would relish the chance to live for a time in the land of his mother's birth."

The earl's jaw locked in a formidable line. "A priest willnae approve of our arrangement and I'm in no mood to have a man of the cloth lecturing me on the evils of the flesh day and night."

Fiona struggled to keep the color from rising to her cheeks—without success. "He will not interfere," she replied.

"Priests cannae help themselves. 'Tis part of their training."

Fiona blinked back the sudden rush of emotion. Her sense of loss at having to give up Father Niall cut deep. Her shoulders slumped and she hugged her arms to her chest, but she could not hold back one final plea. "I shall make certain that Father Niall keeps his opinions to himself."

A short silence fell between them.

"See that he does," the earl finally said.

Grateful for the unexpected boon, Fiona broke into a smile. Without thinking, she reached out and squeezed the earl's hand. His warm fingers covered hers, his hand tightening fractionally in response.

A shiver tingled over Fiona's skin. Strangely disoriented, she withdrew her hand and looked away. "Where will Spencer be housed?"

"He'll spend his days training with the other squires and sleep in the hall with the rest of my retainers. 'Tis important that he not be given any special treatment, or else the others will come to resent him."

She sent him a troubled look. "You won't allow him to be teased or bullied by the other boys, will you?"

The earl barked out a short laugh. "Ye want me to

make a man out of him, to train him to fight and lead. I willnae succeed if ye try to mollycoddle the lad."

Fiona twisted her hands against her overskirt and leaned closer to avoid being overheard. "You must understand a mother's fears."

"Aye. That's why training is done by men. They'll be hard on him, make no mistake about it. But fair. I dinnae tolerate brutality of any kind among my retainers. We save that passion fer our enemies."

"But we are your enemy," Fiona whispered.

The earl squinted and tiny lines fanned out along the corners of his eyes. "If the lad can survive the Scots, he can manage anything. Isn't that what ye wanted?"

"Yes. Yes, of course." Fiona's throat closed as she tried to look confident. This was why she had come, to ensure that Spencer was trained. She had known the Scots were a people engrossed in warfare, but she had not realized how threatening and predatory they could appear.

Even the earl, who was dressed as finely as any English lord she had ever seen, was formidable and unyielding. How would a physically deficient Spencer fare against these warriors? Was she unwittingly placing her child in mortal danger?

Fiona closed her eyes, awash in confusion. There were too many conflicting emotions coursing through her veins, making her feel off balance.

"Are ye feeling unwell?"

Fiona's eyelids fluttered open. The earl had taken a few steps closer to her. At this distance he towered over her, his muscular physique clearly outlined beneath his clothes. But it was the strong angles of his face, the sharp line of his cheek and jaw that held her attention.

He was, without question, the most physically striking man she had ever met. And she had just agreed to become his mistress. Her face flooded with a mortified blush. "Forgive me. I'm a bit tired. It's been a most eventful afternoon."

He nodded. "I'll have a servant see ye to yer chamber."

The earl's words drew the attention of the women gathered at the foot of the dais. Most looked away, a clear indication of their unwillingness to serve her. Undaunted, the earl chose one. "Margaret. Escort Lady Fiona to her chamber."

A petite young woman with lovely reddish-blond hair and a smattering of freckles across her nose stepped forward. She nodded, apparently struck mute by the earl's orders. And who could blame her? Fiona was also having difficulty believing this had come to pass.

"I'll see ye at the evening meal, Lady Fiona." A faint smile crossed his mouth, the gleam in his blue eyes setting her pulse to an unsteady beat.

Casting a final glance at the earl, Fiona turned to follow the servant, praying the fear in her breast didn't show. She could feel him watching her, but she kept her eyes on Margaret's back.

They climbed a winding flight of steep, stone stairs that led to a narrow hall. As they walked down it, Fiona counted six heavy oak doors, impressed that the castle boasted so many private chambers. She was even more impressed when Margaret revealed they were all for sleeping. Apparently, on the top level there was a large solar, a weaving room, and a chamber where the steward worked on the castle accounts.

Margaret opened a heavy oak door. Curious, Fiona stepped over the threshold. It was a small and simple chamber, with a narrow bed, a single chair, and a table. But a fine pelt of fur covered the bed, a plump cushion rested on the chair seat, and several beeswax candles were on the table.

There was a small window covered with a stiff leather shutter to keep out the chill, though on this summer afternoon it was fastened open to allow in the fresh air. Fiona was pleased to note there was room for a pallet for Alice to sleep on and a small wooden trunk in which to store her clothes.

"This will do very well, Margaret. Thank you."

The servant flushed, clearly surprised by Fiona's gracious reaction. "I'll come and fetch ye when it's time for the evening meal," she said. Then, after a hasty curtsy, she departed.

Alone in the chamber, Fiona allowed herself to feel a measure of relief. Blowing out her breath, she walked across the room and gazed out the window. The sweeping vista was breathtaking, with a clear view from all sides, making it impossible for even a small contingent of men to approach the castle without being seen.

We will be safe. And one day, Spencer shall reclaim what was unjustly taken from him.

Fiona smiled. She had done it! Gained access to the earl's castle without bloodshed, established a place for Spencer, secured the possibility of one day regaining their lands. Despite any lingering misgivings she had over her host, it was still a heady feeling.

She turned away from the window and her gaze landed on the bed. Her triumph quickly faded, and reality sliced through her like a blade.

How would the earl react when he discovered his new mistress had almost no experience as a lover?

Chapter 5

"'Tis true, then? Yer going to keep her here as yer mistress?"

Duncan spoke quietly, yet Gavin could not miss the note of doubt in his voice. It was a feeling he shared, though he was not about to reveal that to anyone. He stepped down from the dais and strode across the great hall, Duncan following closely on his heels.

"Lady Fiona's needs are few. I can easily accommodate them," Gavin replied.

"I'm not sure the other lairds will see it quite the same way," Duncan insisted, displaying a frown of disapproval.

"Well, since I willnae be asking their opinions, it willnae matter."

Duncan shifted uncomfortably. "We need to rally as many good men as we can to fight fer our king. Ye know better than most that it hasn't been easy convincing our kinsmen to support Robert. Having an English lady and her brat under yer protection willnae help the cause."

Gavin halted. "Our kinsmen hesitate because they

fear if we lose, King Edward will seize their lands, strip them of their titles, and then chop off their heads."

Duncan rubbed the back of his neck vigorously. "Ye cannae blame a man fer being attached to his head."

Gavin grinned. "Nay, ye cannae."

"But will the others doubt yer loyalty to the cause with an English widow and her son under yer protection?" Duncan asked.

Gavin's jaw hardened. He never expected his cousins, nor his most trusted and experienced men, to follow him blindly and thus encouraged them to speak their minds. At times it could be an annoyance, but more often than not Gavin felt it kept him honest.

"I owe Lady Fiona a debt of honor," Gavin said. "When we sought sanctuary on her land, it was given."

"The debt was owed to her husband," Duncan countered.

Gavin tilted his head. "Have ye never wondered if Baron Arundel's death was due in part to the aid he offered us?"

Duncan frowned as he weighed the notion in his mind. "'Tis possible."

"'Tis more than possible." Gavin looked Duncan straight in the eye. "We will aid her and her son. The McLendons pay their debts. Always."

Duncan nodded, though he didn't look completely convinced. Still, Gavin knew that would be the end of the discussion about Lady Fiona. He allowed those close to him whom he trusted to freely express their concerns, but he made the final decisions. And to a man, they abided by them. While they might disagree, they knew Gavin always put the welfare of the clan before his own.

Gavin exited the hall, Duncan at his side. They

crossed the bailey and headed toward the practice field, but detoured first at the smithy.

The heat struck full force the moment they entered the stone building. The forge glowed a fiery red as two heavily muscled smithies pounded metal into weapons, the tandem clanking and clattering noise nearly deafening.

Upon spying Gavin, one of the smiths paused, wiping the sweat from his brow. "We're working as fast as we can, milord."

"Aye. I can see that ye've made progress." Gavin ambled closer and lifted a chain mail coif off the workbench, pleased with how tightly the links were forged. Few of his men wore them into battle, but he knew if he could convince them to use it, the mail could offer some much-needed protection.

"I copied it as closely as I could," the smith said.

"'Tis fine work," Gavin assured him.

"I dinnae know why ye are wasting the time and metal to fashion these," Duncan said, bending close to get a better look at the piece.

"It could protect yer thick skull," Gavin said bluntly.

"A well-placed arrowhead can pierce any mail, no matter how fine the links." Duncan picked up a two-handed long sword and swung it in a wide arc. "This is all that I need to fend off the enemy."

The smith grinned, then shifted back on his heels and ducked to avoid the menacing path of Duncan's sword.

"Nevertheless, I want the coifs made," Gavin instructed. "Helmets, too."

Duncan shrugged. "We need more battle-axes and arming swords. A sharp, double-edged blade is best fer cutting and thrusting."

"I've a pile of those over here," the smith said.

Gavin moved to inspect the swords, pleased with the result. There was a good number of them and they were each finely crafted and well balanced.

"Have one of the men take these into the armory, and then count all our weaponry," Gavin ordered.

"Everything?" Duncan asked.

"Aye. Swords, pikes, war hammers, spiked targes, daggers, bows, arrows, all of it."

"Expecting trouble, milord?" the smith asked.

"Always," Gavin replied.

Duncan grinned, but the smith nodded solemnly. Gavin appreciated the man's understanding of how serious a position they were in—being prepared for war was most assuredly the only way to win it.

"I'll also need a smaller-sized sword made," Gavin said. "Duncan will give you the details once we measure the lad."

The smith leaned in, dropping his voice to a respectful whisper. "Fer the English lad?"

Gavin nearly smiled. 'Twas a good thing their survival didn't depend on secrecy, for it seemed that no one within his castle walls could keep their mouth shut.

"Aye, the sword is fer the lad. He'll start his training with a wooden one, but I expect him to progress quickly."

The smith's brow quirked with interest at the remark, as Gavin had hoped. He wanted his faith in the boy's abilities to be part of the gossip about the lad. He just prayed that it wasn't misplaced.

With his errand completed, Gavin progressed to the practice field. The shattering clash of metal reverberating through the air could be heard well before he arrived. Pairs of guardsmen and soldiers engaged in sword training were scattered through the castle yard, trampling down the few hearty blades of grass that refused to die under their stomping assault.

A sweaty Aidan trotted over. "Will ye be joining us?"

The question was meant for Duncan, but Gavin seized the opportunity. A spirited training session was as good a way as any to clear his mind. "Hand me a newly forged arming sword."

"I'll be yer sparring partner," Duncan said, pulling his own sword free.

"'Tis my turn," Aidan insisted.

"What about me? I outrank ye both." Connor stepped forward to stand beside his brothers.

Gavin nearly grimaced. He didn't want to dwell on the reason the trio was so eager to draw steel on him, remembering well how he had called these men to task earlier in the day.

"I'll start with Connor," Gavin said. "Duncan's next and I'll finish with Aidan."

A ripple of murmurs went through those men close enough to witness the exchange. By the time Gavin had stripped off his tunic and stood bare-chested in the sunlight, a sizable crowd had formed.

Duncan tossed Gavin a sword. He tested the balance of the weapon, liking the feel of it in his hand. Lately, he had cut back on his training, concerning himself with political matters. Yet it was unwise to stay too long without practice and conditioning, especially with war looming.

Without warning, Connor suddenly charged.

The clash of swords could be heard throughout the courtyard. A shout went up and the men pressed forward to see the exchange. Wagers were placed, but Gavin ignored the chatter, knowing he would be vulnerable if he allowed himself to be distracted.

It took every ounce of Gavin's concentration to fend off Connor's blows. It hurt, the pain radiating up his arm, through his shoulder each time Connor's sword struck his own. *Damn, just a few weeks of inactivity and I'm as weak as a lass.* Gritting his teeth, Gavin dug deep to find his strength. Pushing forward, he managed to pivot away from the next blow, but lost his balance and nearly fell on his arse.

Connor charged. Gavin thrust out his leg, curling his foot around the younger man's ankle. He regained his footing just as Connor lost his. Seizing the advantage, Gavin flew toward him, the tip of his sword notched against the visibly beating pulse at Connor's throat.

Connor slowly released the grip on his sword, then raised his empty hands in surrender.

"Yer turn, Duncan," Gavin shouted harshly, pulling away.

The warm-up gave Gavin a clear advantage in the next match. Before Duncan had a chance to get his bearings, Gavin attacked. Wielding his sword with agility and power, he alternated his striking blows from left to right, forcing his opponent to move swiftly in every direction to fend off the attack.

As Gavin intended, there was no opportunity for the younger man to take the offensive. Knowing he was outmatched in brute strength, the only possible way to win against Duncan was to stay in control of the match. With cold purpose and precision, Gavin continued to advance. Tension and excitement surged among the men, followed by shouts of encouragement.

"Stay strong, Duncan," Aidan cried. "He'll tire soon."

"Not soon enough," another man shouted.

"I'll grant he's swift fer an old man," Duncan taunted. "But I'll have my fun before I lay him low."

"Aye, I'm fast," Gavin replied with a sneering grin. "And cunning."

Ducking low, he launched himself forward, driving his shoulder into Duncan's stomach. Unprepared for the attack, Duncan let out a loud grunt, then landed on his back in the dirt. Gavin immediately stepped on Duncan's wrist and his sword fell from his hand, resting harmlessly beside him.

"Next!" Gavin cried out.

Aidan began to circle just as Gavin raised his sword. Needing a moment to catch his breath, Gavin stayed beyond striking distance. Of the three, Aidan was the most methodical fighter, his movements sharp and crisp. And predictable.

So Gavin waited. For the war cry and charge he knew would be coming. It didn't take long. Aidan let out a chilling cry and swung his sword, nearly taking off Gavin's head. Gavin turned at the final moment and thrust his blade to block the blow, pressing back with all his strength. Aidan groaned as the force knocked him down to one knee.

Sweat poured from Gavin's brow as he pressed down with all his might, then with a sudden flick of the wrist he sent Aidan's sword flying across the courtyard.

Releasing a war whoop of his own, Gavin plunged his sword deep in the ground near Aidan's leg. "Anyone else?"

The men shuffled their feet and gazed at the dirt. None met his gaze or his challenge. Connor spat blood on the dirt, Duncan rubbed his midsection, Aidan struggled to his feet. Coins were exchanged as the wagers were settled, accompanied by wild gestures as the matches were reviewed and discussed.

It took two squires to pull Gavin's sword from the dirt. The admiration in their eyes as they reverently handed it to him was impossible to miss. It made Gavin feel old. Was he ever that young and impressionable?

Seeing the lads brought to mind the young man he had just agreed to take into his household—the rightful heir to an English barony. *Dammit, what madness have I taken upon myself?*

"Did ye see Lady Fiona's lad when ye were at their camp?" Gavin asked Duncan.

"I caught a glimpse. There was nothing remarkable about him." Duncan paused, then answered Gavin's unasked question. "I dinnae see the weakness Lady Fiona alluded to when she spoke of the lad in the great hall."

"If we're lucky, it willnae be so bad."

Duncan nodded. "Even if 'tis, we can prepare him mentally, teach him fighting skills and strategy, build his endurance, make him tough in mind, body, and spirit."

For a moment Gavin kept silent, the doubts and discomfort crowding his thoughts. "Will it be enough?"

"Only God can provide miracles."

"Aye," Gavin agreed, yet a part of him longed for that miracle. Not for himself, or even the boy, but for his mother. Remembering the hope in her lovely green eyes as she pleaded for his help had touched a chord inside Gavin. He wanted to succeed beyond Lady Fiona's expectations or at the very least, not disappoint her.

Duncan's stance relaxed. "I've been thinking. If the infirmary is in the lad's leg, it willnae hurt to train him to throw a dirk. A man who can throw a blade with skill and accuracy can be a real danger."

"A dirk? 'Tis not a very knightly weapon."

Duncan snickered. "I'd smack a man on the head with an iron cooking pot if that's all I could get my hands on to fight fer my life."

Gavin shook his head. "I always said ye lacked the proper respect to become a true knight, Duncan."

"Thank God. We've enough nobility in the clan having an earl as our leader."

"Well, now, this noble earl stinks. I'm off to the loch to wash away the grime before the evening meal. Are ye coming?"

"I'll be along after I collect my winnings."

Gavin halted, frowning in puzzlement. "Ye lost our fight, Duncan. Ye'll need to be paying off yer debts, not putting coin in yer pocket."

Duncan lowered his chin and for a moment Gavin thought the man was blushing. But that was impossible. Duncan was notoriously thick-skinned. Even the bawdiest tales brought little reaction from him.

"Ye heard me right," Duncan replied, a twinkle in his eyes. "I am indeed *collecting* my winnings today. I wisely followed the creed of every loyal Scot, even when I gamble."

"What creed?"

"Never bet against yer laird."

It was much harder saying good-bye to Sir George than Fiona had expected. The knight had been allowed into the inner bailey, and the earl, dressed in fresh garments and sporting damp hair, escorted her through the defensive wooden palisade that surrounded it.

Encircled by a contingent of Scots, many looking ready to strike at the mere hint of trouble, Sir George stood with quiet dignity and authority.

"Five minutes, Lady Fiona," the earl said softly. "Sir George and his men need to ride fer the border while there is still some daylight."

The words sounded far too much like a threat for Fiona's liking, but she was not foolish enough to challenge the earl's authority.

Sir George stepped forward and Fiona did the same. The circle of Scots around them kept their distance and she felt grateful for the privacy.

"I thank you, most sincerely, for all that you have done, Sir George, but the time has come for us to part. I release you from my service. May God protect you and keep you safe."

"Are you certain you wish to stay?" Sir George asked, his brows drawn together with concern.

Fiona bit her lip to stop its trembling. The afternoon had gone by very slowly. Sitting in solitary silence in her chamber had given her far too much time to think. But she could not allow any of her doubts to show, for then Sir George might not leave, which would place his life in peril.

"This is the only way to get what Spencer deserves," she said.

Sir George's shoulders lowered and Fiona knew she had successfully made her point. With a dramatic flourish he dropped to one knee. "We shall meet again, my lady. Under far better circumstances, I assure you."

Fiona swallowed back her tears, refusing to mar the dignity of the moment by crying. The determination she witnessed in the knight's eyes gave her courage. He would never forsake Spencer's cause.

"I pray that you are right, my friend."

Fiona extended her hand and Sir George rose to his feet. Looking over his shoulder, the knight locked his gaze on the earl. "If any harm comes to her or the boy while she is in your care, you'll answer to me."

The words were boldly spoken, with a wealth of meaning infused in every one. Fiona flushed and turned to look at the earl. His eyes narrowed as he went very still. Fearful, she held her breath, but the men exchanged some kind of unspoken understanding and Sir George backed away without further incident.

The tightness pressing against her chest increased as she watched the proud knight mount his horse and ride away. He had been a strong, constant support through all the pain and grief of the past year and she truly had no idea when she would once again set eyes upon him.

She clenched her mouth and turned away, concentrating on keeping her emotions steady and even. She would not break down in front of this curious crowd of strangers, would not give them the pleasure of seeing her cry.

Her jaw still tight, she walked to the earl's side. He gave her a slight nod. Her heart skipped. Strange how this small gesture gave her a measure of comfort, made her feel less alone.

For one impulsive moment she wanted to reach out, grab his hand and squeeze tightly. *Saints alive, wouldn't that get their tongues wagging?*

"The evening meal will be served soon," the earl said. "Let us retire to the great hall."

"Fine."

His brow cocked at her cool tone. He watched her closely for a very long minute, then gestured for her to walk ahead of him. But she was not to be left alone.

After only a few steps the earl clutched her arm, rather possessively.

Fiona drew in a stiff breath, feeling a jolt of awareness as her flesh leapt at his touch. She looked over at his handsome face, locking her gaze on his. His expression was completely unreadable. How unfair! Her body was responding to him in ways she had never before experienced and he felt nothing.

Unsettled, Fiona extracted herself from the earl's touch the moment they reached the high table. Attempting to hide her thoughts, she looked at her hands, which were shaking in her lap. Gracious, it felt as though every feeling coursing through her body was on display for one and all to see. She felt as exposed as if she were sitting there with nary a stitch of clothing on her body. Even the arrival of the servants carrying heaping trays of hot food didn't spare her the scrutiny of those seated in the hall.

Mother Mary, it is going to be a long meal.

Oddly enough, the one person who was not paying attention to her was the man seated by her side. Goblet in hand, the earl was engaged in a rather heated conversation with a group of men seated to his left. They were debating the merits of different weapons and battle strategy, and relating the gory outcome of a recent fight.

It was astonishing to hear how spiritedly the men offered their opinions and argued their points. None had any difficulty disagreeing with the earl. Nor did he deny his men the right to express their thoughts.

How unusual. Henry had, on a few occasions, sought the opinion of his captains, but they rarely disagreed with his views. At least not within her hearing. It was a confident leader, indeed, who allowed such liberties among his retainers.

Lost in thought, Fiona did not at first notice when a servant plunked a large tray of meat between her and the earl. 'Twas the smell that finally caught her attention. She wrinkled her nose at the strong odor, realizing few herbs or little if any seasoning had been used when roasting the meat. And from the char on the outside, it was obvious the flesh had been thoroughly cooked.

Perhaps too thoroughly.

Fiona's stomach flipped. She glanced beneath her lashes at those seated around her and saw everyone was eating with gusto. Resolved, she sliced a piece of venison off the bone and popped it into her mouth. It tasted like sand, but she chewed it purposely, though she needed a large sip of wine to wash it down.

She picked at the food on her trencher, grateful the earl was occupied in conversation with the men seated around them.

"Do ye not like our food?"

Fiona glanced up and met Duncan's challenging stare. "It's delicious," she countered, forcing a large piece of meat into her mouth.

"Shall I offer ye a bit of friendly advice?" The warrior sat back in his chair, lazily surveying her. "Work a tad harder at hiding yer true feelings."

"Or else?"

"Ye'll never survive."

Merciful heavens. She didn't doubt he was offering her friendly advice. Which naturally begged the question—what would those who wished her ill say?

Fiona let out a long breath and looked across the hall. Father Niall was seated one table below, his head bent close in conversation to a man dressed in priest's robes. Her maid, Alice, was nowhere to be seen. *I must remember to make sure food was provided to her.*

Fiona glanced down at her nearly full trencher of bread, wishing there was an easy way to spirit it out of the hall. 'Twould rather neatly solve two problems—bringing food to her maid and freeing Fiona from trying to choke down another morsel of the heavy, rich fare.

Distracted, she picked at her food while taking in all the activity of the great hall. There were plenty of servants moving about, bringing food and drink to the men and women seated at the lower trestle tables. 'Twas a large crowd and most were in good spirits, talking and laughing amongst themselves, though one table of guardsmen was shouting and rudely banging their empty tankards on the table, demanding more ale and wine.

It was then that Fiona spied Spencer among the ranks of the squires, his features twisted with anxiety as he scurried to do the soldiers' bidding. Her stomach heaved with fear at the sight of his clumsy movements. He shouldn't be there, serving these heathens. 'Twas bound to end in disaster.

No sooner had the thought formed in her mind, Spencer lost his footing and pitched forward. Instinctively his arms thrust out and he was able to save himself from hitting his face on the stone floor. But the metal pitcher of ale he carried did not fare as well. It bounced as it crashed to the ground, the contents splashing high in the air.

Laughter rang out as most of it landed on a brutish-looking warrior with a nasty scar on his thick forearm.

"The ale goes in the tankard, lad, not on the face," one of the men shouted.

"About time Donald had a proper bath," another teased, and a second round of laughter erupted among the men.

"Dammit, lad, watch what yer doing!" Donald's beefy hand swung out, cuffing Spencer on the back of the head. "Spill another drop of that good ale on me and I'll be spilling yer blood on the rushes!"

The hall went silent at the outburst. Fiona rose purposefully from her seat, but the earl placed a restraining hand upon her arm. "Leave it."

"But, my lord—"

"I told ye, Spencer willnae be given any special treatment. He must learn his duties just like the other squires. And he must also learn the consequences of failure."

"Beg pardon, sir," Spencer said to the angry soldier.

Fiona heard the trembling in Spencer's voice as he offered an apology. Which was soundly ignored. His eyes grew enormous in his pale face as he stepped aside to elude another blow from the unforgiving Donald. Spencer wobbled, yet through sheer force of will managed to stay on his feet.

Fiona's heart sank like a rock. She felt powerless, sitting there like a witless fool, watching the drama unfold without being able to do anything to prevent it.

"If that oaf harms my son . . ." she began, clamping her hands together until her knuckles turned white.

"He willnae," the earl insisted. "Trust me."

Sod off. Dear Lord, that's what she wanted to say—nay, to shout. But instead she held herself very still, allowing the words she dared not speak to reverberate in her head.

Donald bit out a crude oath and lunged for Spencer, but this time he never got close. One of the men seated at his table blocked the blow, then two others held him back.

Donald couldn't mask his fury or frustration. He struggled to free himself, his expression nearly murderous. Fiona's heart stopped. If either man lost his grip, Spencer would be grievously injured.

Do something! She wanted to reach over, grab the earl by his broad shoulders, shake him until his teeth rattled, and then scream the words at him in her loudest voice.

The earl visibly tensed, and she realized the hysteria in her eyes had alerted him to her anguish. He turned to Duncan. The two men exchanged a look, then Duncan nodded.

"A swim in the loch will cool Donald's temper," Duncan shouted, rising to his feet. "Shall we help him, men?"

"Into the loch!" One of the retainers took up the challenge and the hall soon reverberated with the chant.

"Into the loch! Into the loch!"

Fists pounded on the trestle tables as the cries grew louder. The mood turned celebratory. A protesting Donald was lifted on the shoulders of several men and carried from the hall. A few giggling serving wenches followed, along with some of the squires, a smiling Spencer among them.

The noise level returned to a hum of conversation as the attention shifted back to the meal. Fiona lifted her goblet and took a long sip of wine, hardly believing that disaster had been averted.

"I told ye there was no need fer worry. My men are tough, but they know I willnae tolerate thoughtless cruelty," the earl said, placing his hand over hers.

Fiona's pulse spiked. The feel of his flesh against hers made her tremble. The residual effects of her anxiety over Spencer? Or was it something else?

He moved his fingers lightly, a gentle caress over the top of her hand. Fiona started trembling more, embarrassed that he could feel her reaction. She could sense the passion surging inside him, could see how he wanted to hold her closer, press his hard strength against her softer curves.

She wanted it, too. Her hands exploring the contours of his broad chest, her lips touching his softly, teasingly before thrusting her tongue into his mouth and stroking it against his.

The boldness of her longings shocked her. Fiona searched his face, seeking to understand how he could have caused such a reaction. But she found no answers in the depths of the earl's blue eyes. In fact, he looked every bit as puzzled as she felt.

Enough! Fiona rose. "With your permission, my lord, I will retire."

Though she had asked, as any meek, well-trained subservient female should, Fiona did not wait for his approval. Instead, she tried to sweep past him, but he caught her hand, pulling her to a halt.

Fiona shivered. Lord, what was wrong with her? Was it the venison? The ale? The—

"Gavin."

"What?"

"My Christian name is Gavin." His gaze intensified. "Fiona."

She looked hastily away from the growing passion in his eyes. "Gavin." His name rolled off her tongue awkwardly. "I bid you good evening."

'Twas only years of practicing restraint that kept

Fiona's back straight and her steps steady as she exited the great hall. Her maid, Alice, was waiting to greet her when she arrived at her chamber.

"Shall I help you prepare for bed, my lady?"

Alice's simple, familiar words shocked Fiona out of her trance. Ignoring the hint of trepidation in the older woman's eyes, Fiona nodded, and then sat silently as the maid performed her usual nighttime duties.

Fiona's gown and underskirt were removed, replaced by a linen chemise that had seen so many washings it was nearly transparent. Her tightly woven hair was unpinned and unbraided, then brushed until it shined like a glossy veil of gold. Lastly, she washed her face, neck, and arms in a basin of lavender-scented water, then rinsed her mouth from the pitcher of water.

"Shall I stay with you, Lady Fiona, un . . . until he arrives?"

Fiona blanched. She knew her maid was only trying to be helpful, but her fussing made Fiona even more nervous. "I think it best if you leave now. Oh, I forgot to ask. I didn't see you in the great hall. Did you eat any dinner?"

The maid shook her head. "I couldn't swallow a bite."

"I imagine it will take us some time to get used to our new surroundings."

The maid's wry expression conveyed how likely she believed that would occur. Fiona couldn't blame her—everything seemed so very foreign.

A moment later Fiona was alone with her thoughts, sitting rigidly in the chair, her eyes staring at the closed door. Her heart was racing and her hands felt like ice as she gripped the edge of her seat.

She was not feeling scared precisely, but anxious.

Very anxious. Not anxious because she was ignorant and unaware of what was going to happen the moment the earl—Gavin—stepped over that threshold.

Quite the opposite. She was anxious because she did know.

Chapter 6

With heavy-lidded eyes, Gavin watched Fiona leave the great hall when the meal ended. 'Twas a struggle to hold the yearning he felt for her tightly in check, but he did. Even as his mind was imagining her clothes being slowly stripped away while his lips kissed the sweet, tender skin as it was revealed.

For the last hour he'd been shifting restlessly in his seat, trying to control his raging desire. His stones were hard and aching, his hands nearly itching to explore and caress Fiona's luscious flesh. Even with his eyes wide open, visions of their bodies joined so tight that naught could separate them haunted him.

It felt as though his loins tightened every time she cast an eye in his direction. Hell, even watching her chew her meal sent a surprising surge of lust through him. Chewing her food!

Christ's bones, he'd lost his mind.

He had known beautiful women in his lifetime—had even bedded a few. But this attraction he felt for Fiona was different somehow—it held a power over him that chased his good sense to the bottom of the loch.

He remembered her beauty and feisty spirit the first time he had seen her—and a feeling of surprise at having such a strong reaction to an unknown woman. He also remembered feeling a twinge of disloyalty for having lustful thoughts for the wife of his friend and ally.

"She's a proud one, our English lady," Duncan commented, as he refilled Gavin's tankard.

"Aye, and a true beauty," Aidan agreed. "Yer the envy of every man in the hall tonight."

Gavin grimaced. He didn't feel confident. He felt unsure. He'd visited alehouses and whorehouses, where the female companionship was experienced, lustful, and plentiful. He had been married twice and each time submitted to a rowdy bedding ceremony, with the male guests and his retainers accompanying him to the bridal chamber amid bawdy comments.

But he had never bedded a mistress within the walls of his own castle, while his household was gathered below, their ears most likely attuned to every sound. It somehow felt base, sordid.

Yet this twinge of conscience in no way diminished the desire he felt, nor lessened his determination to take Fiona to his bed. Damn if he wasn't becoming addled over the lass.

Gavin glanced toward the stairs for the tenth time in as many minutes, then quickly looked away, worried one of his men might have noticed. The last thing he needed was Duncan's jesting or Aidan's sarcastic quips. He was nervous enough.

Ignoring the pointed stares he was receiving from Duncan, Connor, Aidan, and God only knew who else, Gavin casually lifted his tankard.

"Will we not have some singing tonight?" he asked.

"How can it be that ye've got songs on yer mind

tonight?" Duncan inquired with a wry expression. "That's the telltale mark of an old codger, wanting to stay with his men drinking and singing instead of joining the bonnie lass who's waiting fer him above stairs, warming his bed."

"An old codger! I'll have ye know I'm a man in my prime," Gavin declared, trying not to smile.

"Yer actions tell a different story," Aidan insisted with a teasing grin.

Gavin gulped down another mouthful of ale and then banged the tankard on the table. "I bested ye on the practice field today," he said smugly. "All three of ye."

Duncan grumbled, while Aidan mumbled something under his breath about getting lucky at catching him off guard.

"Well, that only proves yer not too old for *some* things," Connor said, smiling like a buffoon. He drained his tankard, then started singing. Before long, the rest of the men joined in.

Hark, hear it now—
those ale brewers are turning Arras into Scotland!
By St. Andrew, hear it!
Good men and good times,
cry charity to Holy Mary!

The songs became progressively lecherous as the drink continued to flow, but it provided the distraction that Gavin craved.

It was late when he finally mounted the stairs to his chamber, taking them two at a time. Drawing himself up to his full height, Gavin reached for the door latch, then hesitated. Would Fiona be sitting in his bed, naked and alluring? Or would she be in the small chamber he had assigned her, waiting to be summoned?

He glanced back and forth between the two doors, trying to decide. Going with his gut instinct, he yanked open the heavy wooden door of the smaller chamber.

There was a gasp, followed by an odd little squeak. Fiona stood. Gavin stepped forward. The door closed behind him, leaving him in uncomfortable seclusion with his brand-new mistress.

No candle was lit, only moonlight brightened the room. Still, he could make out the glow of her unbound golden hair, the fine curves of her lush body. He was a man who appreciated beauty in its many forms and Fiona's was special, rare.

She seemed to expect him to say something. Perhaps give her a command? *Strip off yer nightclothes, lay on yer back, and open yer legs.*

If he said it, she would obey. Like a supplicant before her master, she would do his bidding. Hell, he could rip off her thin nightgown, toss her on the bed and have his way with her and she'd never utter a word of protest. But the idea did neither heat his blood or raise his passion, nor did it give him a heady feeling of power and command. Instead it made him feel like a brutal tyrant.

He was a leader of men, having taken the mantle of leadership of his people as a young man of twenty-three. Dominating, commanding, being in control was as much a part of his nature as it was a fulfillment of his duty.

Yet Gavin had learned as a youth that bed sport was far more enjoyable if both partners participated. With patience and skill he had coaxed a passionate response from his virgin brides. Did his mistress not deserve the same consideration?

"Why are ye standing here in the darkness?" he asked. "I expected to find ye in my chamber."

Her color flared, yet when she spoke, her voice was even. "You gave me no specific instructions. I thought it best to wait here instead of invading your bedchamber."

She was watching him, but nothing in the depths of her emerald-green eyes gave any hint to what she was truly thinking, what she was feeling. She presented a placid facade, but Gavin would wager every gold coin he possessed that her heart was fluttering like a trapped bird.

"We can stay here, if ye like," he offered.

She nodded. Gavin moved closer, deeply conscious of the small space. He inhaled her spicy lavender scent, and a heady warmth encircled him, far more powerful than all the ale he had drunk earlier tonight. The tangle in his gut drew into tight knots. He felt hot. Needy. Primed.

How was he possibly going to keep his lust at bay and not frighten her witless?

He tried a smile. She squinted up at him.

Ah, hell.

He had fantasied about what was hidden beneath the confines of Fiona's simple gown from the moment she had knelt before him in the great hall. Now, at last, was the time to indulge that curiosity.

Gavin stepped between her legs, bringing the full length of Fiona's body flush against his, with only a thin layer of their garments separating them. Groaning, he cupped her lush buttocks, pressing her softness against his stiffening manhood.

She seemed confused, opening her mouth to speak, then closing it. He pulled her closer and she stiffened in his embrace, letting him know she had no true desire for him. The gesture disturbed him. He didn't know why. Or maybe he just didn't want to believe that the object of his intense passion was indifferent to him.

Well, there really was only one way to uncover the truth.

"Ye're trembling. Tell me true, are ye afraid of me, Fiona?"

She turned her head away and his heart sank.

"I don't fear you, my lord. I'm nervous. And worried that I will not please you."

She was lying. Her gaze wouldn't meet his and she worried her bottom lip back and forth between her teeth so rapidly it turned bright red. Dammit! The last thing he wanted was for her to be afraid of him.

"Where's the bold lass who offered herself to me so brazenly this afternoon?"

She lifted her chin, a blushing spot of color burning on each cheek. "I am here, my lord. As we agreed."

"Gavin. Call me Gavin." He sighed, then touched a finger to her mouth. "We'll go slowly. Though I cannae promise fer how long."

Wrapping one arm around her back, he tipped her off balance. Her eyes widened as she gazed up into his face. Gavin leaned down and kissed her. He tasted her shock and wondered if she had underestimated her own sexual allure. He molded his mouth to her soft, yielding lips and pressed harder.

She let out a quiet moan, then opened her lips to let him inside, the erotic sensation of her tongue dueling with his igniting a flame deep within him. She tasted faintly of wine—and mint—a lustful, heady combination.

He kissed her again, unprepared for the torment that spread rapidly through him. *More. I want more.*

He nibbled at the tender spot behind her ear, savoring the sweetness. Everything about her tasted delicious.

Returning to her plump, ruby lips, Gavin ravished her mouth as his hunger grew. For an instant the world seemed to spin away. The taste of her mouth was more intoxicating than the finest French wine. Moving down, he lowered her nightclothes and pressed his mouth to the valley between her breasts, nuzzling that tender spot.

It was torture, but Gavin waited until he felt her body relax and slacken before taking one of the nipples fully into his mouth and twirling it around his tongue.

Fiona moaned, louder this time, and plunged her fingers into his hair. Encouraged, Gavin peeled away the rest of her nightclothes and eased her back on the small, narrow bed. 'Twas impossible to believe the fire coursing through his veins could have flared any hotter, yet when Gavin positioned himself over her and looked down, his control nearly snapped.

She gazed back up at him with hooded eyes, darkened with passion and curiosity. His eyes had adjusted well to the moonlit chamber and he could see the outline of her ample breasts, small waist, and slim hips. He took a moment to study her exquisite form, the sight hardening his already pulsing erection.

"Shall we go a wee bit faster now?" he whispered.

Her hands fisted in his hair, giving him the answer he desired. Gavin dragged in a shaky breath and slipped his hand between her long, shapely legs, gliding down her inner thighs and back up. Her eyes blazed like glowing emeralds, her face flushed a delicate shade of pink, deepening her beauty. Gavin's erotic imagination took flight, making him wonder what she'd look like after spending a carnal night in his bed.

"Ye're so beautiful," he murmured.

Fiona snorted. "There's no need for false flattery. We made a bargain, you and I. I shall freely give you what you seek."

He pulled back. "Ye doubt my words, lass?"

"I . . ." She lowered her chin, averting her eyes. "I am unused to hearing such tender expressions. Henry was the only man who ever called me beautiful."

"Does it pain ye, remembering him?"

"At times. But my memories are mainly joyful and for that I am grateful. And lucky." She tilted her head. "Do you think often of your wife?"

"Wives," he corrected, shrugging sheepishly at her widened eyes. Christ, he sounded like an old lecher, having survived two young wives. "They were both fine lasses. Alas, my marriages were too brief to have many memories at all, joyful or otherwise."

She wrinkled her brow, her expression wry. "How calmly we speak of our past lovers. Is that not cold?"

"Life goes on," he said simply, brushing a long strand of her golden hair away from her eyes.

"As best it can," she said in a sad voice.

Deciding that melancholy had no place in their bed, Gavin brushed his thumb beneath Fiona's chin, tilting her head so he could reach her mouth and kiss her. She murmured something as their lips met and he pressed deeper.

Tentatively she reached out, extending her fingers to touch his chest. Slowly she worked her way across the wide expanse, rubbing in a circular motion with her palm. Gavin felt each tender stroke as it left a burning trail across his covered flesh.

Greedily, he moved his head lower, tonguing her navel, licking the curve of her hip. He playfully rubbed the stubble on his chin against her tender skin. Fiona jumped. Her fingers curled and she restlessly shifted her legs. Gavin smiled in satisfaction. There was fire inside his little English rose—all he need do was set the flint to the dry timber and let the flames engulf them both.

Removing his tunic, he let it fall to the floor, then hastily pulled his shirt over his head and tossed it aside.

"Touch me again," he whispered.

Fiona's hands rose up until they rested on Gavin's bare shoulders. Lifting one arm higher, her fingertips lightly raced across his nose and mouth, down his chin and along his throat.

The tender gesture of intimacy made Gavin forget she was doing her job as his mistress. He groaned encouragingly, pressing her legs open with his knee, the blood pounding so loudly in his ears, he swore he could hear it.

The sounds in my head. In my head? Nay!

The loud, almost frantic knock on the chamber door had them both stiffening.

"Milord!"

"Go away," Gavin snarled.

There was only a brief pause before the pounding started again. This time louder and longer.

"Are ye deaf, man?" Gavin shouted. "Leave me be!"

"I cannae," came the quivering voice from the other side of the door. "Duncan says 'tis urgent."

"If this is a prank, then ye best be preparing to meet yer maker," Gavin shouted. He stomped to the door and yanked it open. "What?"

The squire leapt back, almost as if fearing he'd be struck. "They sent me to fetch ye. 'Tis Gilroy. He's raided the grain at Kilmore."

Gavin stiffened, cursing his bastard brother beneath

his breath. The knave had the most incredible sense of timing in all of Christendom. Was he never to find a minute's peace from his antics? "Have they caught his trail?"

"Aye. Duncan believes he's heading fer Dunfield's Cross. He knew ye'd want to be told of it straightaway."

"Fine. Ye've done yer duty and told me." The temptation to slam the door and return to Fiona's warm body tore at his gut, but Gavin couldn't resist adding, "If the men take the Sterling pass, they should be able to intercept the raiders."

The young squire nodded eagerly. "That's just what Duncan said they're going to do."

Gavin grimaced. "Have they left?"

"They're gathering in the bailey right now."

Gavin hesitated for a moment and that troubled him. No woman should ever come between him and his duty. Especially an English mistress.

"Call fer my squire and have my horse readied. I'm going with them."

The lad smiled and hurried off. Gavin turned to a silent and still Fiona. She had retrieved her nightgown from the floor and gathered it close to her chest.

"Is there danger?"

"Of a sort. An outlaw who thinks he can raid my villages and frighten my people is once again on the loose. He needs to be taught differently."

"Must you go? Can you not send your men?"

"'Twould be better if I lead them."

He was pleased to see she understood his answer, perhaps even approved of it. It took maturity and a serious regard for a man's leadership position for a female to fully comprehend the notion of duty.

*Or else she's simply happy that I'm leaving her
alone.*

One look at Fiona's rumpled, doe-eyed countenance
was all Gavin needed to dispel that disconcerting
thought. He took a long, deep breath, struggling to beat
back the lusty demands of his body. Once in command
of himself, he placed a knee on the bed and leaned forward, looming over her.

"I'll not be gone long. Keep the bed warm. Better
yet, move yerself into my chamber and keep that bed
warm. 'Tis larger."

Then, giving her hip a hard squeeze, he left.

With a flushed face and a quivering body, Fiona
stared at the closed door. Gavin being called away was
a stroke of good luck for her, was it not? A close escape
from having to pleasure him, to allow him intimate liberties, to experience feelings and emotions that she
could not identify.

No man had ever touched her the way Gavin had.
Even more shocking was her answering response and
the deep feeling of longing for more of the same. When
he encircled her within his arms and kissed her, it felt
as though her insides were floating.

She was completely unprepared for the strong rush
of emotions that invaded her the moment his lips
touched hers. There was promise in his caresses. Promise of fulfillment, yes, but promise of compassion and
caring. Dangerous emotions for any woman to expose
her heart to, but a vulnerability that no mistress could
afford.

It should have felt tawdry, allowing a man who was
not her husband to take such liberties. Maybe that was

what was bothering Fiona most—it hadn't felt wrong. It had been comfortable and natural. It had been glorious and she craved more.

How could that be? She had lived her life striving to do what was good and proper and moral. Her reward from the Almighty for following this path had been the tragic death of her husband, abandonment by her blood relations, and days lived in fear.

The earl had changed it all. Fiona knew it was only temporary, knew she would leave his castle one day, would leave him. But while she stayed, was it so terrible to search for and nurture any bits of pleasure she could find?

Was that really so wrong, so wicked?

She needed to find the courage to ask Father Niall. Her priest and confessor had said nothing about this bargain she had struck with the earl, but she knew he must have an opinion.

Was she ready to hear it?

Fiona sat on the edge of the bed, shook out her crumpled nightgown, and then slipped the garment over her head. The earl had asked her if she was afraid. She had lied and said no. But deep inside Fiona acknowledged the truth. She did fear him. But not in the way he thought. Not physically. She feared the emotions he stirred within her breast, the feelings of promise and hope. She feared she would grow to care for him, and no good would ever come from that situation.

Fiona's mind turned to Henry. Guilt rose up within her like a murky tide. She had never felt this passionate intensity with her husband, had never craved him so completely, longed for him so defiantly.

Henry is dead. For once the thought did not bring the usual well of intense sadness. Instead, Fiona felt a calming acceptance of the reality. There was no need for her to lock away the memory of her love for her dead husband. 'Twas better to recall the joy of life and living, to remember what it felt like to love and trust a man.

Henry's death had taken so much away from her, but it had also given her the strength to move forward, to admit that a part of her hoped to one day find the love of a good man. It felt honest acknowledging these feelings, for they would help protect her. From Gavin. She had agreed to be his mistress and she would uphold her part of the agreement. She would be sweet and accommodating and giving. She would do all that he asked of her—and gladly.

But, she would exercise prudence and self-preservation. She would not fall prey to the earl's charms. For that road most assuredly led to heartbreak and despair.

Gavin was awake. He shifted restlessly to his side and pulled the edge of his cloak to his chin. The hard dirt dug into his hip and shoulder, but he knew it was useless to try and find a comfortable position sleeping on the forest ground.

Grunting beneath his breath, Gavin stared out into the thickening woods ahead. The canopy of tree leaves hid the moon and most of the stars, yet he could still make out the silhouette of the man posted on watch.

Closing his eyes, Gavin adjusted his head on the log he was using as a pillow and once again tried to sleep, hoping the rustle of leaves and the creak of the wind-blown trees might lull him into an hour or two of slumber. But the rumbling sound of the men snoring around him and the hoots and growls of the woodland creatures inhabiting these woods made sleep impossible.

That, and the thoughts running through his mind. When dawn broke, it would be up to him to decide if they would continue the pursuit or make their way back to the castle. Without capturing Gilroy.

They had tracked the outlaws to Dunfield's Cross, only to discover Gilroy and his men had already come and gone. Discouraged by the now-cold trail, they had ridden another ten miles before making camp. Gavin knew patience was required to vanquish an enemy. Following that creed had proven successful in the past with many of his foes. But in the case of his bastard half brother, Gavin's patience was gone. He was tired of playing games.

Abandoning the pretense of sleep, Gavin stood. *I might as well relieve the soldier keeping watch. Mayhap that poor sod can get a few hours of rest.* Gavin took a step, then froze at the faint sound of thunder rumbling in the distance. Shifting his feet to see through the thick tree leaves, he squinted up at the night sky, surprised to see twinkling stars dotting the blackness.

No storm would be coming on a clear night. Then why the thunder? Gavin turned at the exact moment a spine-chilling war cry shattered the stillness of the night. A line of men on horseback burst out of the underbrush. Swords drawn, they charged the camp.

"To arms!" Gavin roared. "'Tis Gilroy!"

The camp erupted in confusion. Men shouted and cursed and scrambled to find their weapons in the darkness. The ringing of steel on steel soon filled the night.

A rider charged Gavin just as he reached for his

sword. He leapt to his right and the warrior swung ineffectively into thin air. Heavy sword clasped between both hands, Gavin pivoted around and slashed his foe in the leg, striking nearly to the bone. The man screamed and fell to the ground while his riderless horse disappeared into the woods.

The night air thickened with the energy of battle. Swords clashed and arrows flew, as each side fought for dominance. Gavin fought his way into the center of the fray, his mobility hampered by the darkness, his determination increasing with each swing of his sword.

It ends here and now!

A body hit the ground next to him, coming so close it brushed against Gavin's boot as it fell. Gavin glanced down briefly, noting the arrow protruding from the man's chest, then felt a stab of relief when he saw it was not one of his soldiers.

Realizing they were outnumbered, and the tide of the skirmish was turning against them, Gilroy and his men fled into the dense forest.

Gavin watched them retreat, his breath coming in harsh gasps. Ignoring the bodies strewn on the hard ground, he faced Aidan. "Did we lose any men?"

"Nay. We sustained some gashes and bruises, but these bodies are Gilroy's minions."

Using his foot, Connor rolled one of the prone men onto his back. A single shard of moonlight bathed the corpse in a ghastly glow. Blood seeped from the gash across the man's chest and pooled onto the soil, making it slippery.

"I dinnae recognize him," Duncan said, bending low to peer closely at the man's features.

"I'm not surprised," Aidan said. "Outlaws and

brigands are the only kind of men who would follow Gilroy and ye don't know many of them."

"They can fight," Connor said. "I'll give them that."

"Not as well as they die." Gavin felt the intensity of his emotions blazing in his chest and knew he needed to ignore them. Calm, steady, controlled. 'Twas the only way he would win this contest.

"There were at least two dozen of them that attacked us," Aidan said, as he wiped the bloodied end of his sword on a nearby bush and carefully sheathed the weapon back in its scabbard.

"Did anyone see which way they went?" Connor asked.

"They scattered like leaves in the wind," Aidan replied.

"North," Duncan said with confidence.

"Leave one man to care fer our wounded and bury these bodies," Gavin commanded. "The rest of ye mount up. We ride north."

The constant sound of a ringing church bell startled Fiona awake. Rubbing her eyes, she tried taking in her surroundings, but it was too dark to see much. *'Tis not yet dawn. Why do they rise so early?*

Shaking her sleep-clouded head, Fiona reached out and fingered the unfamiliar heavy bed curtains, realizing they were the reason for the dimness surrounding her.

Cautiously she pulled them back and a shaft of daylight caressed the length of her bare leg. Opening the fabric a fraction wider, she peeked out and peered about the room.

It was empty. Gavin was nowhere to be seen. Actually, judging by the neatness of the chamber, it appeared that he had not returned last night. She probably should not have heeded his command and slept in his chamber, but her mind had been occupied and in the end it seemed easier to obey.

Footsteps sounded in the hall. Fiona froze, hoping it meant the household was answering the toll of the bells and going to Mass. But one pair of feet did stop, opening the chamber door and entering without a knock.

Fiona wasn't certain who was more surprised—her or the female servant who entered.

"Glory be, what are ye doing in here?" the woman asked as her disapproving gaze swept Fiona from mussed hair to bare toes.

Fiona smiled mysteriously. She was not about to explain herself to this sour-faced servant. "Has the earl returned?"

The servant propped her hands on her hips and assumed an indignant air. "And why would ye be needing to know that?"

Deciding it was too early in the morning to be answering questions, Fiona sprung from the bed. She stalked out of the chamber and returned to her own and found Alice waiting for her.

"A group of wounded men arrived in the bailey not a half hour past," Alice reported in a rushed whisper. "I heard two squires speaking of it when I went to the kitchen to fetch some food for you to break your fast."

"What of the earl? Was he injured?"

"I don't believe he was hurt. Apparently, they were set upon by a man the squires called Gilroy and his band of brigands, but the earl and his men fought off the attack."

"Where is he now?"

"Giving chase. The squires were arguing over whether he would take Gilroy prisoner or kill him the moment he was captured."

Fiona shuddered. As much as she understood the need to vanquish one's enemies, killing always left a bitter taste. "From what I understand, this Gilroy is a fierce fighter, an enemy of long standing."

"Oh, my lady, there is more to this sordid tale." Alice took a deep breath, then blurted out, "Gilroy is the earl's brother."

"What?"

"'Tis true." Alice's head bobbed enthusiastically. "He's his half brother. His bastard brother."

"Truly?"

"Yes. They share the same sire, and according to the squires, much of the same tenacity. They spoke almost with admiration as they declared he might call himself Gilroy, but he was a McLendon through and through."

"That is indeed a peculiar way of referring to one's enemies," Fiona agreed. She selected a simple, formfitting green kirtle with tapered sleeves, a full skirt, and a short train, and Alice assisted her into the garments.

"'Tis only one of the many things I don't understand about these people," Alice commented, as she tied the silk ribbons across the bodice of Fiona's gown.

The maid efficiently brushed, then plaited and pinned Fiona's hair on the top of her head. She added a delicate pure white veil and over that placed a gold circlet mitre to keep it in place.

Feeling better prepared to face the others, Fiona turned to Alice. "We might not understand these people, but that is no excuse for neglecting our devotions. I shall attend Mass this morning and pray for the safety of the earl and his men."

Alice's mouth pressed into a thin, disapproving line. "Prayers for the earl are all well and good, but I think it would be wise if you asked the good Lord for some help for yourself, Lady Fiona. I fear you're the one who'll be needing it more."

Chapter 7

The church was filled when Fiona entered, nearly every bench packed tight. Spying a space near the front, she tried sliding into place as unobtrusively as possible. But it was near impossible to remain unseen, as the whispers of her presence spread through the chapel like wildfire.

Pay them no mind, she told herself. She carefully adjusted the skirt of her gown, then glanced beneath her lashes to see who sat beside her. 'Twas Hamish, the castle steward. She offered him a shy smile. Hamish grunted, his expression leaving little doubt that he was displeased with her seat choice, but at least he had the good manners to stay in the pew. Fiona was sure any of the women seated so piously around her would have made a scene and stomped away.

It was difficult to concentrate on the service with so many resentful glares trained upon her back. Fiona could almost hear the snickers when nerves made her stumble over the words of a familiar prayer, but she refused to bow her head. Her pride demanded she stay, but more importantly, she needed the familiar comfort of the Mass to calm her nerves.

Plus, she assumed the castle squires would be required to attend the Mass, which meant she would have a chance to see Spencer and hopefully speak with him. Though it had been only a day, she missed him terribly and wanted to see for herself how he was fairing in this strange new environment.

It was a pleasant surprise to look up and find Father Niall upon the altar, assisting the castle priest. The two men worked together in harmony, their common faith overcoming any political differences. Of course, the fact that Father Niall was half Scots didn't hurt either, Fiona thought, as she knelt on the hard wooden floor.

Fiona had a much better view of the inside of the chapel from her kneeling position. She felt a shiver of joy when she spied a pew filled with young squires, Spencer among them. Contented, Fiona folded her hands together, not taking her eyes off Spencer for a moment. His face was paler, but his back straight. The lad beside him leaned close and whispered something in Spencer's ear, causing him to break into a wide grin. Fiona's spirits lifted. Spencer seemed to be adjusting to his new position.

Far better than I.

When the Mass ended, Fiona waited outside the church, ignoring the stares of the people who walked past by refusing to meet their suspicious gazes. But then Spencer appeared and Fiona's heart lightened.

"Spencer! Good morning."

At the sound of her voice he turned, then gave her a bow. "Good morning, my lady."

Fiona bit her lip. She had taught him proper manners

from the time he was a small boy, but never expected to be on the receiving end of such formality.

She wanted to push the other lads aside and wrap him in a tight embrace. Unsure, she controlled the impulse, knowing how mortified he would be at so public a display of affection, especially in front of the other squires.

"May I have a word?" she asked.

Spencer shifted his gaze, not meeting her eyes. "I have duties," he replied.

Her heart tugged with longing for the young boy who had always been eager to be in her company. She knew things would change once they arrived at the castle, but she hadn't expected it to happen so quickly. Nor for it to hurt so much.

"I shall only keep you a few moments," Fiona said.

Spencer shrugged his shoulder. Hardly the response Fiona desired, but she seized her chance and gently guided him away from the other boys so they could have a moment of privacy.

"How are you faring? Do you have enough to eat? Is it warm enough where you sleep?"

The questions rolled off Fiona's tongue faster than Spencer could nod his rather sullen answers. She could not help but notice how often, and anxiously, he turned toward the other boys. Not having his full attention for these few precious minutes was maddening. Spencer turned his head yet again and that's when Fiona noticed the yellow and blue bruise on his cheek.

"You've been injured!"

Fiona reached up to touch the wound, but Spencer swatted her hand away. "Mother, please."

Fiona's hand fell to her side. Unused to such an awkward exchange, she tried a different approach. "Tell me about the other squires. Who is the young man in the red tunic?" Fiona asked, picking the boy she had seen earlier in church standing beside Spencer.

Spencer immediately perked up. "That's Travis. He's teaching me how to fight."

"Is he?" Fiona struggled to keep her tone casual. "Is that how you got that fine bruise on your cheek?"

Spencer gave her a lopsided grin. "I was slow to duck. Angus says it's good practice to have my wits scrambled every now and again. It will make me a more agile fighter when I've got a sword in my hand."

"Oh?"

Spencer nodded. "And Travis showed me that sometimes it's better to strike with the heel of your hand instead of a closed fist. Especially if you can swing upward and catch your opponent square in the nose."

"I was unaware of that tactic," Fiona said faintly.

As she listened to Spencer, the impact of what she had done fully hit her. She was training him for battle, for war, perhaps even his death. The realization shook her. Doubts crept into her head. Would it have been better to listen to the advice of her brother and send him to the priesthood, where he would be safe?

"Violence for violence sake alone is not a wise attitude," Fiona lectured. "Just because you have the means to kill a man, doesn't mean that you should."

Spencer paused. "Even if he is your enemy?"

"It all depends. If he threatens your life, or the lives of those you are sworn to protect, then you must act. Swiftly. Decidedly. But there are other ways to resolve your differences. A good knight knows how to skillfully wield a sword. But a great knight knows how to use his brains as well as his weapons."

It was a good speech and Fiona was proud of it.

Unfortunately, Spencer paid her little notice. He was shifting his weight from one foot to the other and staring at the group of squires.

Fiona gazed at them, too. The infamous Travis was motioning for Spencer to join them, yet when he realized he had been caught by Fiona, Travis's eyes widened in feigned innocence.

A shiver of alarm ran through Fiona. Was he Spencer's friend or foe?

"I have to hurry or else I'll be late," Spencer announced suddenly. "Angus gets mad when we are late."

"Best run along," Fiona replied. Then not caring one wit who was watching, she leaned down and kissed Spencer on the forehead. "Stay safe, my dearest."

Gulping back his groan, Spencer scurried off, his limp seeming even more pronounced. Heart heavy, she stood alone in the bailey, watching Spencer until he disappeared from view.

Unaware of how long she remained in that spot, Fiona suddenly sensed the presence of someone near her. Startled, she glanced down and found one of the castle hounds sitting at her feet. It was a large, unattractive-looking beast with an enormous head and fawn-colored fur that was long and mangy and none too clean.

His chest was wide, the muscles strong and defined. He would have been a terrifying beast, if not for his wide, brown, trusting eyes.

"I've no scraps or treats to give you," Fiona said, expecting him to hurry away.

The animal seemed to consider her words for a moment, then nudged Fiona's hand in an insistent manner, demanding to be petted. With a rueful smile, she stroked the beast's ears, surprised at their softness.

The hound's tail thumped happily on the dirt, pleased at the attention.

After one final rub, Fiona turned to leave, and the dog trotted along beside her. He stayed by her side when she entered the great hall. Tensing at the sight of several unfriendly faces, Fiona halted.

The beast stopped, too. He nudged her side. She didn't budge. Then, almost as if sensing her distress, he comfortingly licked her palm with his large tongue.

Fiona could not hold back her smile. The uncertainty of the morning fell away, the anxiety of her decision to come here faded.

It appeared that she had at long last found a friend.

Fiona stood at one end of the great hall and stared at the circle of women gathered near the fireplace. It had been five days since Gavin had so abruptly departed and there was still no word on when he and his men might return.

Well, no word that had been shared with her. Though she had asked. Every morning. And at each of the noon meals. Then again at the evening meal and once more before she retired for the night.

She bade Alice to inquire also. And Father Niall. But the answer was always the same—no one knew.

Fiona didn't believe it. Just last night, from the small window of her bedchamber, she had seen a young soldier return to the bailey, obviously bringing news. She had hastily thrown her cloak over her nightgown and rushed to the great hall. But the messenger was nowhere to be seen, and when she had asked, several of the servants had denied he even existed.

Perhaps today the earl will appear. There are several hours of daylight remaining.

Fiona's spirits were momentarily buoyed at the thought. Time had hung heavy these last few days, mainly because she had little to keep her occupied. The earl's castle was a stark, unfriendly place. Her brief encounters with Spencer had been unsettling, for it was obvious he preferred to converse with the other squires. She was glad that he had so quickly adjusted, but seeing Spencer's easy acceptance of this new life made her even more lonely.

If not for the large hound who had befriended her at Mass, there would be none but Alice and Father Niall to greet her with a smile. For whenever she came across the hound, Fiona could swear he was grinning, with his tongue hanging out of his mouth and his tail wagging so fast and furiously his entire back end shook.

It was a momentary bit of joy in an otherwise dull day. Fiona had not been foolish enough to expect any overtures of friendship she extended would be welcomed by the castle folk, but she had thought she could at least work alongside them.

The women studied her with the sharpness of a hawk, yet whenever she met their gaze with a hesitant smile, their hard stares passed coldly over her. Gossip was rampant throughout the castle, spreading out to the village. Fiona tried hard not to imagine what horrid tales were being told about the earl's English mistress, but so much idle time led to far too much thinking.

It was starting to become depressing. Knowing her position in the household was rather . . . uhm . . . unique, Fiona had kept to her chamber after Mass that first day. Making her bed, sweeping the floor, tidying the small chamber, then darning every article of clothing she possessed had taken half the morning. But when she was finished, she quickly became bored.

Knowing her idle hands would make the hours hang heavy, Fiona had boldly entered the earl's chamber. It was large and well appointed, and above all masculine. Feeling like an intruder, she worried at the reaction if she was discovered. *Probably be thrown into the damp dungeons and left there until the earl returned.*

But the monotony and boredom of being idle soon overtook her fears. Cautiously she lifted the top of a wooden chest, slightly disappointed to find it was filled with the earl's clothing. Curious, she unfolded the top piece, a deep blue tunic, edged with gold thread. The center medallion was a gold falcon, with bright red eyes that had clearly taken someone many hours to create.

Running her hand slowly over the intricate embroidery, Fiona discovered several loose stitches, along with a tear of the fabric on the shoulder. Resolved, she placed the garment on the floor and reached for the next piece. It was a fine linen shirt, dyed an unusual shade of light green. That too sported a large tear, acquired perhaps when yanked off the body carelessly and too quickly.

By the time she had gone through every garment, Fiona had a substantial pile that needed repair. Enthused at having something to occupy her time, she gathered the pile in her arms and returned to her small chamber.

Alice nearly accosted her when she entered. "Is that the laundry, Lady Fiona? How dare those Scottish crows make you carry it!"

"Be calm, Alice. It's not the laundry. These are the earl's garments, sorely in need of repair."

"Why do you have them?"

"I intend to make the repairs. Fetch my sewing kit, please."

The maid's eyes flashed. "What about the earl's squire? He should be attending to this mess. 'Tis his job to keep his master's clothes in good order."

"I suspect the poor lad has been hiding these things. They require a delicate hand to be properly mended. A talent I'm sure the squire lacks."

"Well, there are plenty of others to do that sort of work. No need to soil your delicate hands." Alice tilted her head and sniffed. "You are a lady."

"I am. And as such will showcase my skills with a needle. Now fetch my kit."

"But—"

"Alice, fetch my kit and that's the end of it."

The maid did not bother to disguise her groan of disapproval, but she obeyed. "The light in here is dismal," Alice complained. "You'll go blind doing all this sewing."

"Yes, it is rather dim," Fiona agreed, but she would not be deterred. "Please pull back the window covering to allow in the light."

With another heavy sigh, Alice followed the order. A sharp ray of sunshine filled the room, followed by a burst of fresh air. Experiencing both uplifted Fiona's spirits. Keeping busy was also a boon, making the afternoon pass quickly. But by midmorning of the next day, she had finished all the work and been unable to uncover anything else to do.

In the days that followed, Fiona's numerous attempts to be helpful at other castle tasks had been met with a resounding no, followed by a stony wall of silence.

Fiona knew they saw her as an enemy, yet that logic did not prevent the hurt from squeezing her chest.

The truth was, their outright rejection made her feel inadequate. She meant them no harm. She had not come here to disrupt their lives or cause them any difficulties. How could they not understand it? She was merely trying to survive, a powerless woman in a world run by men. One would think she would receive support and empathy from the sisterhood, instead of censure.

Well, today she was not going to turn away and allow herself to be treated like an unwanted stray dog. By all that was holy, she was going to work no matter what anyone said. Just let them try and stop her.

"I shall help to spin the wool," Fiona announced as she joined the circle of women gathered together in the great hall.

Swinging around, Judith stared at her with an open mouth. "There is no need fer it," the older woman proclaimed.

Judith was the unofficial leader and the most outspoken of the women. Handsome, middle-aged, with streaks of gray in her dark hair, she ruled the gaggle of female servants with an iron fist.

"Aye, we need no help," Maggie chimed in, and the others nodded in agreement.

"Oh, but you shall have it nonetheless," Fiona announced, refusing to be turned away.

The women did not look happy with the dictate. But Fiona wasn't doing this to gain their acceptance or approval. She needed something to occupy her time, else her wayward thoughts would drive her to despair.

She took a seat and gathered her materials. Poking the dense ball of wool with her forefinger, Fiona searched until she found a strand. She felt every female eye in the great hall trained diligently on her as the spindle began to slowly spin and the weight on the end began to pull the wool thin. Fiona's fingers stiffened as she manipulated and twisted the fiber into a thread, straining to create an even string.

"Dinnae be making it too thin," Judith warned in an agitated tone. "Or else it will snap the minute we put it on the loom."

"I know," Fiona answered tersely, wanting very much to add that she hardly needed any instructions, since she, like nearly every woman in the world, had been making thread since she was a young girl.

Trying to prove her worth to these thorny Scotswomen was a losing venture, Fiona decided. She assumed they objected to her English heritage, but lately she wondered if they also resented her rank.

From what she could tell, the Scots were not all that impressed by titles—though treated with respect, the earl was hardly fawned over by his retainers, or his servants.

Suddenly, the earl's booming voice cut through the cackling female conversation. *He's returned!* Fiona's hands faltered and she nearly dropped the spindle. Now, wouldn't that reaction give these crows a fine morsel to gossip over?

By the time the earl reached the end of the hall, she had mercifully regained her composure. Her greeting was no more enthusiastic than that of the other women. Still, Fiona felt horribly exposed, certain he was aware of how excited she was to see him again, how relieved she felt that he was safe.

"Have there been any difficulties while I've been gone?" he asked.

"No," Fiona lied, admitting she would have bitten

her tongue till it bled before complaining to him about the petty insults of these women.

"Good. Very good."

He looked right, then left, then gazed up at the rafters. If Fiona didn't know better, she would have sworn he was looking for a way to escape. The earl moved to the fireplace and motioned for Fiona to follow.

He removed his leather gloves and she found herself staring at his hands, remembering the feel of his fingers against her heated flesh. The faint smell of leather and horses clung to his skin. Fiona inhaled. It was odd— Henry, too, had smelled of horses and dirt and leather, but it was very different.

Why?

"Since I heard no cheering from the bailey, I assume that Gilroy managed to elude capture?" she asked, trying to turn the conversation away from these heightened emotions.

"Aye."

The terse answer reminded Fiona that it was probably unwise to highlight the earl's failure. Men could be ridiculously prideful over these matters, but honestly who did they think they were fooling? Clearly, Gilroy had not been found. Were they all supposed to pretend that he had, in order to spare the earl's feelings?

"Will you try again?"

"When we have a solid lead. There's no use putting good men's lives at risk without just cause."

The earl's comment erased Fiona's earlier impression— he had been concerned about the fate of his men, an opinion that had him rise considerably in her estimation.

Embarrassed by her waspish tongue, Fiona sought to make amends. "Are you hungry?"

"Aye, thirsty, too."

"We've got everything ready, milord," Judith called out. "Come, eat and restore yer strength."

Ignoring his usual place on the dais, Gavin took a seat on one of the trestle tables, beside his soldiers. Judith and the other women sprang into action, bringing out platters of food for the returning men, filling their goblets with hard cider and ale and pressing them each for details of their quest.

Feeling out of place, Fiona melted into the background. She picked up the ball of wool, but it was impossible to concentrate on spinning thread with the earl so near.

The men were speaking in low tones, making it difficult to follow the conversation. At best, she caught only small bits here and there that made little sense. Distracted, she glanced about the great hall and noticed one of the squires with a wooden yoke on his shoulders. Dangling on a rope from each end were two heavy-looking wooden buckets.

"What are you doing?" Fiona asked, when the boy passed near.

"Bringing hot water to the earl's chamber for his bath," the squire replied, his face straining with exertion.

A bath. Of course. After he's eaten, the earl will want to remove the grime from his skin. Well, here was some way she could make herself useful. She had helped to bathe many a visiting knight and lord when running her own household and knew precisely what needed to be done.

Preparations were well in hand when she arrived at the earl's bedchamber. A high-sided wooden tub had been set near the fireplace, where a small fire was burning to keep away the chill. The leather shutters had been

pulled tightly closed, to ward off a draft and prevent
the earl from falling ill, though Fiona had long doubted
the validity of that precaution.

Fiona carefully draped the padded linen cloth inside
the tub, then brought it up over one edge. At her nod,
the squire dumped the steaming hot water inside. It
barely covered the bottom. It took five additional trips
for the water to reach a substantial level. By then, the
squire was red-faced and breathing hard.

Fiona organized the rising buckets, then took the
soap pot and towels from the beleaguered squire. He
gave her a grateful smile and hurried away. Fiona rolled
up her sleeves, wishing she had an apron to cover the
front of her gown. She only owned a few garments and
this was by far the best of her clothing.

"I wasn't sure where ye had gone."

Fiona's heart gave a silly jump at the sound of the
earl's deep voice. "I'm here to assist you with your
bath," she explained.

Fiona heard the audible breath he drew. Anxious, she
waited to see if the earl would voice any objections.
When none were forthcoming, Fiona stepped forward.
She reached for the edge of his tunic, intending to lift it
over his head. He stiffened, his muscles going rigid, his
chest barely moving as he breathed.

"Would you prefer to have your squire attend you,
my lord?" Fiona asked.

"Gavin," he grunted.

"Pardon?"

"Ye're to address me by my name. We agreed."

"Of course. I'm sorry. Gavin." She added the last deliberately, trying to show her obedience. His winsome
grin told her he wasn't believing it for a minute.

Unperturbed, Fiona continued with her duties. He

went very still as she began to unlace the leather ties of his chausses. Fiona pulled them apart and Gavin flinched.

Confused, Fiona raised her head. "Are you certain you do not wish me to call for your squire?"

"Nay. I want ye."

A warm hand cupped her chin. There was raw strength in that grip, but it was tempered by hard control. Fiona wondered what would happen if that control ever snapped; then decided she'd rather not find out.

The tread of footsteps sounded in the hall. Fiona looked over Gavin's shoulder toward the open doorway. The earl's squire stood there hesitantly, peering at them with wide, curious eyes.

"I brought ye more hot water," he said uncertainly.

"Pour it in the tub," Gavin instructed, his eyes still locked on Fiona's. "Then leave."

Unused to such intimacies, especially in front of strangers, Fiona shook her head and broke his grasp. The chamber grew heavy with the sound of pouring water. Fiona busied herself near the fire, turning abruptly when she heard the unmistakable splash of water.

He's climbed into the tub, she thought, unable to decide if she felt relieved or disappointed. *More disappointed, I fear, having missed the opportunity to see him in all his naked glory.*

Fiona took a deep, steadying breath that nearly lodged in her throat when she turned to face him.

Gavin was indeed in the tub, resting his head and shoulders against the cloth she had laid there for that very purpose. His left arm dangled over the side, the right rested on the wooden edge. Mesmerized, Fiona stared at his bare, tanned forearms and large, strong hands.

For the past few days she had secretly listened to the men and women of the castle spin yarns about his prowess. How he could ride faster and longer than any of his men. How he could pierce the smallest target on the first attempt. How he could wield a sword with the power of ten men.

Seeing his physical strength with her own eyes, she no longer doubted the truth of those claims.

Flustered, Fiona turned to reach for the pot of soap. Oil of eucalyptus melded with the spicy scent of lavender as she lathered the washing cloth. Intending to start with his back, she began moving behind him. Quick as lightning, his hand shot out, grasping her wrist.

"Nay, Fiona, dinnae hide yerself," Gavin drawled. "Stay where I can see ye. If yer going to wash me like a wee lad, then I'm going to enjoy the view."

She forced herself to obey without protest. She was his mistress and needed to do what he commanded. Though in this instance, 'twas hardly a battle of conscience to do as he asked.

As she came closer, Fiona saw the whirl of hair on his chest and the dark line that trailed from his navel downward, disappearing into the water. A twist of excitement ran through her loins. A normal reaction, she decided. He was magnificent. She'd have to be made of stone not to feel something when she gazed upon his masculine beauty.

He leaned forward so she could reach his shoulders, then lifted his head to stare into her eyes. She could clearly see the hungry desire shimmering in the blue depths. Unexpected pleasure flashed through her. Fiona swallowed, feeling the heat rising over her body.

She pressed the cloth to his shoulders and rubbed vigorously, trying to regain her equilibrium as she hurried to finish washing him. She had already decided she was not going to scrub any parts of him that lay beneath the water. He was perfectly capable of doing that on his own.

The room grew quiet, save for the sound of the cloth rubbing his flesh and the occasional splash of water. Gavin reached out and trailed the tip of his finger lightly across her throat and up to her chin. Fiona froze. The cloth slipped from her fingers, fell into the water and floated aimlessly in the tub.

"Are ye finished with me, darlin'?"

She blinked, the sound of his silky voice breaking her trance. Fiona pulled away, swirled two fingers in the soap pot and began washing his hair. Lifting the pail, she poured the warm water over the earl's head, rinsing away the suds, admiring the clean gleam of the dark tresses. His hair was wet and curling, resting on his shoulders.

"Shall I get my scissors so I can trim your hair?"

He opened one eye and stared lazily up at her. "I learned long ago, 'tis never a wise idea to expose yer throat to a female with sharp instruments."

Fiona placed the empty bucket on the floor. "Don't you trust me?"

He shrugged his shoulders, causing a wave of the water to lap over the side and spill onto the floor. Reacting quickly, Fiona kicked his tunic out of the way, so it wouldn't get wet. Presenting her back to him, she knelt on all fours and mopped the spill with one of the towels.

"Are you staring at me?" she asked, feeling the prickly sensation of being watched.

"I cannae help myself. 'Tis a bonnie view yer treating me to, lass."

Fiona's smile bubbled into a giggle. A bath was not sexual in nature. At least none that she'd ever taken. Yet somehow Gavin was able to make mopping a wet floor an erotic experience.

She turned her head and raised an eyebrow at him. He looked at her from beneath heavy-lidded eyes, examining her figure in a slow, measured way, causing her to look away in embarrassment.

"Join me, lass," he said in a silky voice.

"There's no room," Fiona whispered, scandalized.

"Of course there's room," he admonished.

"Where would I sit?"

"On my lap, where else?"

Merciful heavens! A flush of heat shuddered through Fiona's body at the very idea. Gavin continued staring at her with a mesmerizing gleam in the depths of his blue eyes, causing an odd weakness in her knees.

Then he flashed a grin that was pure boyish mischief. *He's flirting with me.*

The realization momentarily robbed her of speech. No one had ever done that before. It was not part of Henry's nature to be playful with her. He'd been kind, sweet, and even indulgent at times, but never once lighthearted. 'Twas somewhat astonishing to discover that she rather liked it.

Avoiding his gaze, Fiona pushed back the lock of hair that had fallen over her face. "The bath is meant for you, my lord, not me."

"Well, if it's my bath, then 'tis mine to share, is it not? And I've decided to share. With ye."

Chapter 8

Gavin liked how expansive Fiona's eyes grew when he asked her to join him in the tub. She wasn't shocked—well perhaps a wee bit. But she was also curious, intrigued by his suggestion, and that did all sorts of things to his already fired blood.

It was fun toying with her. He liked watching her face as she ministered to him, noting the wrinkle of concentration on her brow, the small lines tightening around her mouth as she tried to maintain a proper, dignified approach to her duty.

Tried, yet failed. Thank God.

He had enough duty and obligation surrounding him. He wanted, needed, something different from Fiona.

"Why willnae ye join me in the tub? Dinnae ye enjoy yer bed sport with a bit of boldness and adventure?" he asked.

She tossed him a doleful look. "I'm starting to think you are a very wicked man."

"Aye, lass, ye dinnae know the half of it."

Gavin stood. The water cascaded off his body in

sheets, forming a large puddle around the tub. But this time Fiona did not scramble to mop it. In fact, this time Fiona did not move at all.

Her eyes widened, her lips parted, her cheeks turned a delicate shade of pink. The tips of her breasts were straining against the fabric of her gown, the nipples clearly outlined. His cock, already hard and straining, jumped. She must have seen, because something went still in her eyes and she became totally focused on him. The air grew hot, steamy, thick.

Temptation pulled at him. His body fairly twitched with need. She was his for the taking and he'd waited far too long already. Gavin caught her in his embrace and kissed her mouth, opening her lips to delve inside to taste. She moaned and tightened herself against him.

He began to slowly kiss his way down her golden flesh, paying close attention to her responses. He didn't always have such patience at the start, especially when he was so aroused. But Fiona shivered and groaned each time he landed on a particularly sensitive spot, the sound encouraging him to continue.

He took his time kissing and caressing her, savoring and relishing each moment. It was as though he were driven by some unexplained need to know her intimately, not just her luscious body, but her soul.

With impatient hands, Gavin stripped off Fiona's clothing until she was as naked as he. Her fathomless green eyes seared into his and an unaccustomed wave of tenderness washed over him. If he didn't know better, he would swear she was a virgin on the eve of discovering the mystery of becoming a woman.

He smiled at her affectionately. She returned it with one of her own, though her lower lip trembled. Gavin reached for her breasts, marveling at how perfectly the plump softness fit his palms. He thumbed the dusky rose nipples, playing lazily with his fascinating prize. Fiona's breath hitched and he could feel her body quiver.

As her gasps escalated, he nuzzled her throat and whispered, "Shall I have a wee taste?"

Gavin didn't wait for her response. Bending his head, he caught the burgeoning nipple between his teeth, then rolled his tongue in a slow circle around the entire areola. Fiona's breathing grew harder, more ragged, as Gavin continued his sensual assault, licking her breasts, tasting their sweetness, relishing their softness.

Her knees started to buckle. *Aye, she was a passionate lass.* Gavin chuckled softly, mightily pleased with himself, and her. He swept Fiona into his arms and carried her to the bed, pressing her back onto the clean linens. Almost as if dazed, she sprawled languidly on the large mattress, her beautiful body on wanton display.

For him. Only for him.

Gavin closed his eyes and inhaled. The scent of her arousal nearly drove him crazy. With gentle fingers he reached between her thighs and parted her folds, opening her feminine secrets to his heated gaze. She was soft and pink, like a lovely, delicate flower.

Unable to resist, he lowered his head and tasted her with his tongue, caressing her sweet essence. She reacted with a cry of sheer torturous delight. He laid his hands on her thighs to hold her still, then blew on the wet curls. She shivered and arched off the bed, her moan louder this time.

Triumphant, Gavin swirled the tip of his tongue

through her folds, slow and thorough, paying special attention to the sweet pearl in the center. Fiona bucked and writhed, thrashing her head from side to side.

He continued pleasuring her with his lips and tongue, angling her body so he could see the rapture and wonder brighten her face. Fiona opened her mouth, then closed her eyes. She let out a surprised shriek and her body jerked and shuddered. Her climax nearly brought on his and he almost pulled away to prevent himself from spilling his seed too soon.

But he would not be so cruel as to deny either of them this bliss. Seeking time to regain control of himself, Gavin, pressed light, soothing kisses along her inner thigh, prolonging her pleasure. Finally mastering his raging passion, he sat back on his knees and took a deep, shuddering breath.

It gave Gavin no small measure of pride to see Fiona so sated and content, basking in the glow of sexual release. His eyes remained on her face as he grabbed her waist and pulled her toward him, drawing her legs up on either side of his hips, spreading them wide.

"And now, I claim ye," he said hoarsely.

She whimpered in anticipation as he pushed the tip of his penis against her wetness, demanding entrance. Probing and insistent, he guided himself a little bit inside her moist heat, immediately feeling her tense.

"Open fer me, lass," he coaxed, stroking her golden hair. "Let me inside and I promise I'll bring ye to the heavens again." He thrust his hips, but she tensed again.

"I'm sorry," she whispered in misery. "I'm trying. 'Tis just that you are so very large and—"

He leaned over and plunged his tongue into her mouth. The moment it met hers, Fiona bumped her hips against his. Gavin could feel Fiona's inner muscles flexing around his engorged shaft. It was blissful torture. And he wanted more.

He moved his hips again and she gradually unfolded, allowing him a bit deeper inside. His body wanted him to go faster, deeper, harder, but Gavin resisted the urge. Instead he rocked his hips back and forth slowly, moving with sure strokes inch by inch until she fully accepted him. Fully submitted to him.

It felt . . . indescribable. The warmth and wetness was familiar, but the closeness, the connection, aye, that was different. Gritting his teeth, Gavin held himself in check. It had been too long since he had enjoyed a woman's softness and he wanted the moment to last.

"I dreamt of ye while I was gone," he admitted.

Her brow furrowed. She reached up and tenderly glided her fingertips along his temple, tracing the scar he bore with a gentle stroke. "I've been counting the days that you've been gone, always hoping that today was when you would return. And finally you have come back."

She had missed him? The revelation snapped the thin thread of Gavin's control. Unceremoniously, he grabbed the soft globes of Fiona's buttocks and lifted her closer to him. She trembled and shook, but he would not be denied.

His questing fingers found her nipple and he rubbed the tip of his finger over the peak until it hardened. With a strangled cry, her hips rose to meet his. She gripped his shoulder and thrust herself upward. He slid one hand between them and brushed the pad of his thumb over her pulsing flesh.

The moment she started to climax, Gavin knew he

could hold back no longer. Mindlessly, he thrust and drove himself deeper, pumping furiously. His climax caught him hard and fast, racking his body with deep spasms, nearly blurring his vision when it came upon him.

Gavin could feel Fiona's body tighten around him as he pumped his seed inside her womb. Shuddering, he collapsed on top of her, fearing he was crushing her but feeling too damn satisfied to move a muscle.

The scent of their passion mingled with the damp air. He inhaled the fragrance, pleased to feel a slight stirring of his cock. With just a wee bit of rest, he'd be primed for a second round. And maybe a third.

Feeling more than a tad smug at his virility, Gavin rolled to his side, taking Fiona with him. Playfully, he pressed his face into her golden hair and lazily stroked her back. She sighed and snuggled closer.

And in that moment, Gavin's burdens eased; the worries about his bastard half brother, Gilroy, the uncertainty of Robert's kingship over Scotland, and the fate that awaited them, all slipped away.

With a contented, satisfied sigh, Gavin allowed sleep to claim him.

Gavin's lax body and gentle snores let Fiona know he was asleep. This meant it was the best time for her to quietly return to her chamber. She squinted in the darkness, trying to locate the door, deciding how she would navigate around the furniture without disturbing Gavin. Avoid the chair, watch out for the table, step around the tub. Yes, that should work well.

'Twas a solid, practical plan. Having a plan was always a comfort for her. A necessity, really. Yet Fiona never moved. *I'll leave in a minute. Or maybe two.*

She snuggled closer to his broad strength, burrowing her head into his shoulder, not daring to think too hard on why she wanted to stay. Gavin's warm breath whispered against the top of her head, the steady, even rhythm a strange comfort.

So this is what it means to make love. Saints preserve her, he had acted as tender and considerate as a besotted bridegroom. Was that how all men treated their mistresses? If so, that would certainly explain why women took lovers.

Fiona shook her head, marveling at the experience. She had shared more with Gavin in a few hours than ten years of marriage with Henry. And it wasn't only physical. They had laughed, he'd teased and flirted with her. He had made her feel like a woman. A *desirable* woman.

If only they could have a future together.

Fiona sat up immediately, as if struck by a bolt of lightning. No! She must never allow those thoughts to creep inside her head, to burrow in her heart. It would be her undoing, a heartache that would forever haunt her. Mind racing, she turned to leave the bed, but Gavin caught her at the waist, holding her tight.

"Where are ye going?"

"To my chamber."

He made a noise deep in his throat that sounded like a growl. She started to protest, then realized she had no right to refuse him. Her emotions in turmoil, Fiona allowed herself to be pulled into his embrace. She could feel the rough hair on his legs brush against her thigh beneath the covers. It was a ridiculously erotic sensation and her body responded with trembling need.

Gavin's kiss was hard and seeking, his hand traveling immediately between her thighs. Fiona gasped, intoxicated by the feeling, admitting the very last thing she wanted was to leave his bed.

It went much faster this time, but felt even better. Within moments she was on her back and spread out beneath him, like some pagan goddess, a virgin sacrifice to appease the gods. His hands and mouth were everywhere, stroking and suckling her bare flesh, exciting and torturing her at the same time.

"Now," she panted. "I need you now."

Gavin grinned wolfishly. "As milady commands."

Her blood flowed hot and raw when he thrust inside, claiming her as his own. Sobbing with restless passion, she held him close, moving her hands over his shoulders and the corded muscles of his biceps, bucking beneath him with blind compulsion. Arching and shuddering, she moaned loudly, feeling the whole length of him buried deeply inside her.

Close, she was so close.

Sensing her need, Gavin slipped his hand to where they were joined, his clever fingers knowing precisely where to stroke. Instantly, the sensations within her spiraled out of control. Higher and higher they climbed and Fiona stretched and strained to reach the pinnacle, to achieve the passionate bliss she now knew awaited her.

A keening wail burst from Fiona's throat as the raw hunger inside her finally crested, shattering into a million pieces. She locked her legs around Gavin's waist and let the pleasure engulf her, surround her, possess her. When it subsided, she lay gasping beneath him, still feeling the ripples of sensation deep within her.

"Open yer eyes, Fiona."

The commanding voice reached through her hazy bliss and Fiona obeyed. His fiery gaze was straining with need and unfulfilled passion.

Just a few hours ago, the sight of his intense desire would have frightened her, for she had no experience with it and knew not how to appease him. Yet now she understood exactly what he needed, how to bring him the satisfaction he craved.

Wantonly, Fiona bent her knees, then glided her fingertips over his shoulders and down his spine, resting at the base. Digging her heels into the firm mattress, she surged upward, at the same time pressing against his lower back.

Gavin's deep-throated groan of ecstasy let her know he appreciated the resulting deep, heavy penetration. He needed no encouragement to continue the swift, sure strokes. Fiona quickly adapted the same rhythm, sending him into an even more fevered pitch.

His body surged forcefully into hers, each thrust deeper, harder, longer, setting her very flesh on fire. She could feel the ripple and tightening of his muscles as the spasms of release overcame him, and then the warm rush of liquid as his pulsing seed filled her.

They lay locked together for a long while. Fiona barely noticed when he rose from the bed. With great effort, she turned her head and watched him dip a rag into the now-cold bathwater. He wiped himself, swirled the rag through the water a second time, wrung out the rag, then approached the bed.

She lay in stunned silence as he casually cleaned her upper thighs and between her legs, feeling totally embarrassed by such an intimate gesture. The carnal haze so deliciously surrounding her vanished, replaced once more by uncertainty. Was this typical? Is this how most men treated their bed partners?

Anxious, Fiona sat up, pulling the bed linens high on her chest, waiting to see what he would do next. 'Twas almost a disappointment when he simply climbed back into the bed, until he reached over and flipped her on her side, facing away from him.

"I keep my back to the wall and my head at the door when I sleep," he declared, pulling her into the curve of his body.

"Even in your own castle?" she asked, feeling an odd sense of pity for him for needing to take such precautions. Was his life truly in such jeopardy?

"I know I'm safe among my clansmen, but 'tis best to keep to the habit at all times."

He wrapped his arm around her, pulling her back tighter against his chest. She wriggled to get into a more comfortable position, tucking her limbs between his, then realized exactly what the long, hard object was that was pressing so insistently against her buttocks.

"I . . . uhm . . ." She tried to pull away, but his arms were clamped so tightly she could barely move.

"Pay it no mind. Ye've worn me out fer now, lass," he murmured in her ear. "Go to sleep."

The suggestive stiffness hardly felt *worn out*, but Fiona was not about to argue. She, too, needed sleep, but it was not easily found. Closing her eyes, she started counting the stars, a trick Henry had often employed. It didn't help. She next tried matching her own breathing with Gavin's deep and even breaths, but all that did was make her light-headed.

Her thoughts began to wander, with fears and uncertainty over the future surfacing first. *Did I do the right thing coming here? Will the earl keep his word and protect me and my son? I believe so—but what if he does not? What happens then? Where will I go? What will I do?*

Stop! Restlessly struggling to shut down these

dangerous thoughts, Fiona shifted her legs. Then her hips. And then her legs again.

Gavin's steady breathing abruptly ceased and she felt his body tense. "Well, lass, now that ye've woken me, ye'll be needing to do something about this." Reaching for her hand, he pulled it behind her, placing it on his erect penis.

Ah, more bed sport will surely exhaust me. Fiona smiled in the darkness, wrapping her palm around him. He shuddered. She smiled again, running her hand languidly up and down the length of him, caressing the round head, marveling at the satin smooth feel of the turgid flesh.

He groaned and arched under her hand. Still holding him in her grasp, Fiona turned, nuzzling her chin in the mat of springy hair on his chest. There was comfort to be found in his strength, pleasure in his arms.

"I shall gladly handle this, my lord," she whispered, surprised to realize she meant every word.

Ewan Gilroy stood at the top of the craggy hill and watched the sun slowly set in the valley below. The golden hue had turned to a brilliant red, bathing the scene in a crimson glow. From this distance the small cluster of thatched roof cottages were barely visible, blending cleverly into the wooded landscape. Precisely as he intended when he had selected this spot—a hideout built to keep them safe.

Now, wasn't that a fine laugh.

Despair was an emotion Ewan rarely felt, even managing to conquer it that terrible, harsh winter when he and his mother were on the brink of starvation. But despair had crept into his voice earlier today when he

136 *Adrienne Basso*

informed the families of the men who had died in the raid that their loved ones had been killed. And failure had touched his soul when the newly widowed Jenny, her belly large with child, had swooned with grief at his feet.

"So, this is where ye've been hiding."

Ewan didn't need to turn his head to know who had spoken—the voice was nearly as familiar as his own. "I'm not hiding, Mother. I'm thinking."

"Too much of that will put ye off yer food," she replied, patting his hand awkwardly. "Best not to dwell on it."

Ewan resisted the urge to glower at his mother, knowing she would never understand. Compassion was not a word she had ever embraced and she often mocked those who did. Life had been unkind to Lady Moira Gilroy, youngest daughter of the Laird of Gilroy, and she took her resentment out on those around her, including, at times, her only son.

"We lost four men," Ewan said steadily. "Two of which had families."

Lady Moira scoffed. "What about the earl? I'm sure ye gave as good as ye got."

A creeping feeling of unease shivered through him. He had no idea if any of the earl's men had been killed, making this loss all the more senseless. "A few were wounded, the rest . . ." Ewan's voice trailed off and he shrugged. "I dinnae know fer sure."

"Ye're not gonnae allow him to get away with this, now, are ye?" Lady Moira asked, her brown eyes accusing.

"I attacked him."

"'Tis what he deserves."

Was it? Ewan massaged the bridge of his nose with his fingers. He had been weaned on animosity and resentment, taught to blame the earl and his kin for all the ills that befell him and his mother, raised to fight against the injustice of his fate. Yet even he conceded that the crimes against his mother were not the fault of the current earl.

"I just wish I had more to show fer the loss of my men," he said. "'Tis a high cost, with little reward."

Lady Moira huffed, dismissing the sentiment. "They made the choice to follow ye, knowing the risks," she insisted, unsympathetically.

Her words were not unexpected. As a lad there were times he thought her heart was made of stone. Idly he wondered if she had passed this trait on to him, but the knot twisting his gut told him otherwise. Was her way better?

"We'll need to lay low fer a while and stay out of sight," he said. "'Tis the only way to keep safe."

"Nay! Now is the best time to strike! They willnae expect it." She tugged sharply at his arm and Ewan turned to face her. "Ye must never forsake yer vengeance. They mock ye, belittle ye. Call ye the McLendon bastard."

Ewan's smile was filled with irony. "That's who I am."

"Nay! Ye're more, so much more. Ye've got Gilroy blood in ye, too, proud and noble. Dinnae ever forget it." She took a step closer, her features turning anxious. "I raised ye to have a purpose, Ewan."

"To hate."

"Aye, to hate—those who treated us unfairly, as though we had no worth, no value." Her eyes got a faraway look. Lady Moira was nearing fifty, but looked

older. The lean years and hard living had taken the
sparkle from her eyes, the glow from her complexion.
"Yer father could have married me and had a legitimate
son. He was a cruel, hard man, taking advantage of a
girl's tender heart. But even more of a fool to toss aside
such a fine lad as yerself."

With an inward oath, Ewan held his tongue. His
mother could drive a saint to sin, make no mistake.
Especially when she was in the mood to harp on her
favorite tirade—the Earl of Kirkland.

"Ye're my mother. Ye're supposed to sing my praises."

"Not all women would have done the same in my position. I stood by ye." Her eyes narrowed with emotion.
"And now I expect ye to stand on yer own and avenge
the wrongs done to us both."

Ewan gave her a pained expression. Aye, she had
stood by him. When the earl had denied the babe she
carried was his, when her family tossed her out, pregnant and unwed. She hadn't abandoned her bastard
infant son at the gates of the castle, or placed him on
the steps of the chapel, or set him in the woods to be
carried off by wild animals. But she had raised him to
seek the vengeance she was unable to achieve on her
own, and he feared the cost of that was too high.

"Is my death truly what ye seek?" he asked.

Lady Moira paled. "Never," she replied in a low,
trembling voice. "'Tis McLendon blood I want spilled
on the ground."

"In all likelihood, if I meet the earl in open combat,
'tis my blood that will be shed. He has more men, all
better trained than mine, finer weapons, faster horses.
He'd cut me to ribbons in a fair fight."

Lady Moira's brow wrinkled. Was it imagination or did his mother's vehemence fade a wee bit?

"Then dinnae fight fair. Cease yer raiding and direct yer actions at him. Track him, follow him, catch him off guard. Or better still, alone. Slit his throat, then hide the body. The loch is wide and deep. Ye can easily slip his corpse into the dark waters where it will sink to the murky bottom, never to be seen again."

Ewan barely contained his shudder. Even after all these years, the depth of his mother's hate still had the power to startle him.

"As much as it would bring ye joy, I willnae kill my brother in such a cowardly manner."

Clearly displeased, Lady Moira crossed her arms and pursed her lips into a hard, thin line. Ewan let her stew in her anger for a few moments, the sight easing some of his own distress.

"Smile, Mother. I willnae be able to easily kill the earl, but I vow to do everything I can to make his life a living hell."

A sudden movement at the door woke Gavin from a sound sleep. Stark naked, he leapt from the comfort of the bed, reaching for his dirk.

"No, don't hurt him!" Fiona squealed, grabbing Gavin's arm. "He's harmless."

He was a large, mangy, rather dirty-looking dog, with scruffy fur and an enormous head. At the sound of Fiona's voice, the beast raised his head and moved clumsily into the chamber. Gavin backed up, but refused to relax his stance or put down his weapon. He didn't recognize this particular hound and he certainly didn't like the look of him. Especially since the animal was heading straight toward them.

But before he reached them, the dog suddenly stopped, sniffed, then bent his head in the tub and began lapping at the water energetically.

"Christ! Willnae that soapy water make him sick?" Gavin asked.

"It might," Fiona conceded, sounding concerned. "Naughty boy! Shoo, shoo. Now get away from there!"

Naughty boy? Gavin raised his brow. "Aye, now that will get his attention, make no mistake."

Fiona bounced to her feet, making no comment as she pulled on her linen chemise. Disappointed to see her clothed, Gavin watched curiously as she stomped across the chamber and hauled the dog away from the tub by the scruff of the neck.

She dragged the reluctant beast to the door, wrinkling her nose with each step. "It might be a good idea to dunk him in the tub," she remarked. "He smells rank."

"There's no need for him to be clean. He should only be coming indoors when the weather is vile."

Fiona glanced down at the dog, looking somewhat guilty. The beast began wagging his tail enthusiastically, bestowing a look upon her that could only be described as adoring. "I'm afraid I've broken that rule. This mangy fellow has been my most faithful companion while you were away."

Gavin didn't bother to hide his surprise. "I would have thought ye'd be spending yer time with Spencer."

Fiona's hand moved down and she absently began stroking the dog's head, causing his tail to move faster. "I've seen Spencer a few times, but he's busy learning his duties. He appears to have taken well to his new surroundings."

"And that displeases ye?"

Her hand stopped. "Why would you say that?"

"Yer brow is wrinkled and yer mouth is turned down on the corners," Gavin answered, pleased that he was able to so easily read her emotions. "'Tis obvious ye aren't happy."

She gave a dainty, resigned shrug. "I suppose no mother likes to realize that she is no longer an essential part of her child's life."

"A lad needs to think fer himself, especially if he hopes to one day lead other men. A lass, now, that's an entirely different kettle of fish. She does well learning to take orders."

As Gavin hoped, that remark brought a flash of fighting spirit to Fiona's eyes. Pleased, he reached out and rubbed the dog behind the ears. The animal sighed with gratitude, leaning close. So much for loyalty. The beast could easily be bribed with a bit of affection and most likely a large soup bone.

"You are wrong about women," Fiona said. "Being able to think for themselves might one day save a female's life."

He opened his mouth to reply, but was quickly distracted. Gavin tensed and the hair on the back of his neck stood on end. The heavy sound of running footsteps outside the chamber was unmistakable. Beside him, the dog stood at attention, then let out a low, throaty growl.

"Get behind me, Fiona," Gavin ordered, a surge of danger heating his blood.

Silently, she obeyed. Shifting the dirk to his left

hand, Gavin reached for his sword with his right. Naked and battle ready, he faced the door, his sword ready to strike.

Gavin whirled as the chamber door burst open.

"We have news! Glorious news. King Edward is dead!"

Chapter 9

"Dammit! Are ye daft, Duncan, bursting in here with no other warning? I nearly sliced yer fool head off!"

Seeming unconcerned, Duncan cast him a lopsided grin. "Aye, I can see ye have both yer swords out, ever at the ready to protect and defend."

Both? Gavin scowled, then glanced down, remembering his naked state. He lowered his sword and sauntered to the chair to retrieve his braies.

"Better?" he asked, pulling on the garment.

"Much. Ye were putting the fear of God in me, wagging that mighty snake in my direction."

"Yer just jealous of its great size," Gavin countered. "Now tell me yer news."

"Longshanks is dead!" The width of Duncan's smile matched the excitement in his voice. "He was leading his army north, preparing fer another campaign. But when they reached Burgh-on-Sands he fell ill, and thanks be to God's wisdom and mercy, he died."

"At Burgh-on-Sands? That means he never even made it over the border into Scotland," Gavin replied, raising his arm in triumph. "'Tis the most rewarding news I've heard in years."

Gavin's heart lightened, while his mind raced. With Edward gone and his young, weaker son on the throne, Robert Bruce would now finally have the chance he had been waiting for to unite the clans and free them all from England's iron fist.

"I can scarce believe it myself," Duncan declared. "The Hammer of the Scots is dead. I've prayed fer this day fer as . . ." His voice dropped off and his nose wrinkled. "Lord save us, what is that smell?"

"Lady Fiona's pet."

Almost as if knowing he was being discussed, the dog let out a low growl. Duncan jumped back, reaching for his sword. Fiona gasped. Gavin smiled. "Calm down, Duncan. It's a dog, not a wolf. He willnae eat ye. At least I dinnae think he will."

"Of course he won't," Fiona said, crossing the chamber to stand protectively beside the dog.

As she walked past, the faint scent of lavender assaulted Gavin's nose. It was intoxicating. He was suddenly glad he had put on his braies, since the swelling evidence of his reaction to her was starting to stiffen.

Unfortunately, he also realized Duncan was having his own reaction to the lovely Fiona. Unable to fully dress without the assistance of her maid, she had donned her linen chemise. The modest garment hung to her ankles, but the fabric was so worn it was nearly transparent in places.

Gavin's ire rose. He didn't like the idea of Duncan seeing so much of her. The delicate slope of her shoulders, the sensuous curve of her buttocks, the alluring shape of her long legs. He had fallen asleep with her soft, round bottom nestled against his groin, his arm wrapped possessively around her waist.

And woken up several times throughout the night to lay claim to that luscious body, delighted in the enthusiastic welcome he had received. The thought of another man sampling the sweetness of her charms was unimaginable, but so too was the idea of another man catching a glimpse of her body.

"The dog belongs outside, with the other hounds," Duncan said.

"And thus I have explained that to Lady Fiona," Gavin interjected. "Remove the animal at once."

Duncan and Fiona turned to him in puzzlement. "Duncan," he added with emphasis. Damn, did they honestly think he meant for Fiona to traipse outside with only that flimsy piece of cloth covering her?

Duncan reluctantly obeyed the order, getting behind the beast and literally pushing him toward the door. The dog looked none too pleased with the circumstances, but with another insistent shove from Duncan's booted foot, he allowed himself to be taken away. Duncan's grumbling blasphemies were easily heard all the way down the corridor.

Fiona sank down in the chair, then tilted her head up to gaze at him. He could see the speculation in her eyes. "So, the king is dead."

"Aye." Gavin grinned. "Long live the king."

"Edward is rumored to be a different sort of man than his father. Less inclined to war, more inclined to indulge his many pleasures."

"An attitude that bodes well fer Scotland." Gavin's eyes roamed over her face. "And ye, Fiona."

She nodded. "Do you think I should petition him to

recognize Spencer as the rightful heir to the barony and plead for the return of our lands?"

Gavin thought a moment. He was flattered that she sought his advice, but her question left him in a quandary. If the English king granted her request, there would be no reason for her to stay in Scotland with him. And while he had never expected their arrangement to be long-standing, the thought of her leaving rankled. Nay, 'twas much too soon for him to release her from her role as his mistress.

"There are certainly cases when 'tis better to settle matters of property and title by law and decree, rather than battle," Gavin began. "But the key to asking favors from a king is all in the timing. Edward will have many important affairs to attend to, the least of which will be securing the crown upon his head."

"I know you are right. Now is not the time for me to be asking for favors." She folded her arms across her chest and released a heavy sigh. "Even though my cause is true and just."

Gavin smiled. Seeking justice for her child never failed to ignite a spark within Fiona. He admired her tenacity, her determination to protect her cub with all the ferocity she could muster. 'Twas even more miraculous when one considered the lad wasn't even her blood kin—a fact that lifted her even higher in Gavin's estimation.

"Yer time will come, Fiona. 'Tis best to wait until the lad is older, tougher, experienced with leadership. The king might be able to grant him his legacy, but Spencer will have to hold it on his own."

"True."

She seemed disappointed, yet resigned. Gavin felt

a twinge of guilt, knowing his reply had been colored by his desire to keep her near. Trying to be objective, he examined the dilemma again, satisfied when he reached the same conclusion. Conscience clear, he approached her.

She might appear soft and vulnerable on the outside, but her heart had courage and spirit. Still, for all her proud boldness, she had a woman's frailty. She could throw herself upon the mercy of a king, or any man of power, hoping and praying for fair treatment. Yet there was no recourse if she were denied. She could not pick up a weapon and solve her problems as a man would, on the field of battle. She needed others to do that for her.

She needed him.

The soft cascade of blond tresses falling down her shoulders glowed with a golden hue in the morning light. He knew that it felt as silky and fine as it looked and for a moment Gavin imagined digging his fingers through it. Rubbing it over his face and chest, pressing the strands against his nose and inhaling the fragrant scent.

She truly was lovely. And irresistible.

"Now that we're finally alone, I can do what I've been waiting fer all morning." Without another word, Gavin swept Fiona into his arms and kissed her senseless.

Fiona grasped a weed between her thumb and forefinger and pulled. It came out cleanly at the root, bits of rich soil clinging to the spidery veins. With a smile of satisfaction she shook off the excess dirt, then tossed it onto a third pile of weeds. Remaining on her knees, she shuffled down the neatly planted rows and attacked a new section.

The castle herb garden was located near the kitchen, in an area protected by high, stone walls. Fiona had only recently discovered it, and the privacy it afforded. She had been dismayed upon seeing the condition of this important household asset. Underwatered and choked with weeds, the precious herbs were scrawny and wilting—a possible explanation for the often bland fare served in the great hall.

Bending to her task with vigor, Fiona dug with the tip of her finger at the base of a very large weed, realizing she'd have to soak her hands in warm water in order to get rid of the dirt beneath her fingernails. No matter. The mindless work was a godsend. It kept her hands busy, served a useful purpose, and took her out from under the watchful, critical eyes of the other women.

Since hearing the news of King Edward's death earlier this morning, Gavin had been cloistered with his men. She doubted she would see him until it was time for the evening meal. 'Twas just as well. All it took was a few minutes in his company and passionate thoughts she could not control were conjured in her mind. It took but a scant minute more for her to act on those thoughts—a teasing smile, a seductive glance, a sensual kiss and she was lost.

It was an unsettling reaction, something she needed time and distance to explore and examine. For that was the only way she would ever come to understand it.

The gate swung open, and to her amazement, Gavin walked through, a purposeful stride to his step. "I've been searching everywhere fer ye," he said.

"Well, I'm not hiding," she replied defensively, not

wanting him to realize that was precisely what she'd been doing.

"I never said ye were."

Fiona flushed and turned her head away. "'Tis a crime to let such precious bounty whither from neglect. I've been working for two days and should be done with the job in another two. Provided there aren't too many interruptions."

Hoping he would take the hint and leave her to finish her task, Fiona gathered the pulled weeds, condensing them into one pile. But instead of moving away, the earl came closer, casting a shadow over her.

"Ye'll have to finish this another day. Though why ye would want to is a puzzlement. As I recall, there are pages aplenty in this household. Isn't weeding the kitchen gardens one of their jobs?"

Straightening, Fiona rose self-consciously from her kneeling position and vigorously rubbed the knotted ache at the base of her spine. "Tending herbs requires knowledge that most young boys do not possess. They're likely to pull out as many herbs as weeds."

"Oh, so it's skilled labor, is it, playing in the dirt? Something fit only fer a lady?"

Fiona tried to assume a formal, dignified air, but the boyish glint in Gavin's eyes made it difficult. "'Tis honest labor," she said lamely.

"I never said it wasn't. I merely questioned why ye had chosen to do it."

"I enjoy the solitude and being out-of-doors. I also like being able to easily see the fruits of my labor." She waved her hand elegantly over the large plot where it was instantly apparent which sections she had tended and which had yet to be weeded.

"Ye've done enough fer one day," Gavin said as he held the gate open for her.

His meaning was clear, yet Fiona balked at obeying. There were still hours and hours of daylight left. If she kept working at her current pace, she could clear an entire section before the evening meal.

"Yer frowning," Gavin observed. "Is something amiss?"

The question thrust Fiona into a quandary. This wasn't merely about the weeding. It was about her freedom, her ability to make her own decisions about how she spent her time. Should she press the point now? Or wait for a better opportunity?

Then again, did she even have a point to make? She had agreed to be his mistress, devote herself to his pleasures. Being surly and arguing would hardly bring the earl any pleasure. She might not be his slave, but she was subject to his whims.

"I'll start working again early tomorrow," Fiona said, deciding not to avoid a direct confrontation.

"And I'll tell Hamish to send a few of the pages to help," Gavin added.

Fiona's back stiffened, but she managed a slight smile. Gavin must have noticed, since he quickly added, "The lads will work under yer supervision."

"Thank you." Her reply was not as gracious as it could have been, but Gavin gave no indication that it angered him. Or perhaps this time he took no note of it?

Fiona's mood improved as they walked through the bailey. Having Gavin at her side afforded her the immediate respect of anyone they passed, though Fiona felt compelled to make eye contact with each and every person, to show that she was not timid. Or worse, ashamed of her position in the household.

If I act like a lady, they will treat me as such.

"I had planned to leave immediately, but I see ye'll need a few moments to refresh yerself," Gavin remarked, gazing down at her hands.

Fiona curled her dirt-encrusted fingers into a fist, hiding them from view. "I'm to accompany you? Where?"

"Ye'll see."

His cryptic smile gave her no further clue. But any resentment she felt at being ordered about quickly faded. They were leaving the castle—together. An afternoon of freedom!

There was no time for Fiona to change, nor much choice of another gown to wear, so she spent the time cleaning the dirt from her body and having Alice braid her hair. Excitement starting to build, Fiona returned to the bailey, heading directly for the stables, where Gavin stood impatiently tapping his foot. His squire waited beside him, but as Fiona drew closer she realized . . .

"Spencer!"

The boy turned at the sound of her voice, a trace of a smile hovering on his lips. But it faded as she drew closer and he took a step back. Fiona surmised he was concerned she would bestow some unmanly affection upon him in front of the earl. At least that's what she hoped was causing this reaction.

Fiona hardly cared. She had only caught an occasional glimpse of him these past few days, relying on Father Niall to give her the specific details of the boy's activities. A few private moments with Spencer was a gift and she was not about to squander it.

"Tell the stable master to saddle my horse and two others, Spencer," Gavin instructed.

"Two?"

"Aye. One fer Lady Fiona and one fer ye."

"Me? Why do I have to go?"

The pinched disinterest in Spencer's face struck at Fiona's heart like a well-aimed sword thrust. Was it really such a torturous proposition spending the afternoon with her? Or perhaps it was the earl's company the boy objected to so strongly?

Cringing inwardly, Fiona neither spoke nor looked at the earl while they waited, though she knew she had Gavin to thank for this opportunity to be with her son. They were a silent, rather solemn group as they mounted their horses and rode from the bailey. Once they passed through the open portcullis and cleared the castle gates, Gavin's powerful stallion twisted his head in annoyance, eager to be let loose for a spirited gallop. But he held the horse in check, making him ride beside Fiona's palfrey.

Spencer rode behind them. *Most likely slumped in his saddle.* But Fiona resisted the urge to turn around and check, worried if she saw his face filled with sullen misery she might just start crying.

With her mood so unsettled, she barely noted the direction they traveled, nor appreciated the beauty of the countryside. Since there were no retainers accompanying them, Fiona assumed they would not ride too far, and her assumption proved correct when Gavin reined in his horse after only thirty minutes of riding.

Gavin vaulted from the saddle. After helping her dismount, he returned to his horse, emerging with several long poles, one sporting a net hanging limply at the end of it.

"Are those fishing poles?" Fiona asked, displeased that in her distress over Spencer she hadn't even noticed when the gear was strapped to Gavin's horse.

"They are indeed." With casual ease Gavin tossed the poles at Spencer, one at a time. Fiona felt a smug sense of pride when the boy caught them with ease.

"Follow me," Gavin commanded. "I know where to catch the really big fish."

"I've never been fishing," Fiona admitted, her curiosity piqued at the notion. She turned to see Spencer's reaction, regretting it almost immediately. The boy's mood had not improved—if anything, he seemed even more annoyed.

Determined not to let Spencer spoil the outing, Fiona trained her eyes upon Gavin's broad shoulders and followed him around the shore of the lake. He leapt onto a flat rock, then turned to assist her. Skirts flying, Fiona managed to scale the hard slope with only a small bit of her dignity still intact, then realized it didn't matter. She was enjoying herself.

"Not much farther." Gavin paused in front of a fallen tree trunk that stretched across the water from one group of rocks to another. He stepped carefully onto the natural bridge, testing its strength, then made his way across.

Not to be outdone, Fiona gathered her skirt in one hand and slowly picked her way over to the other side. A smiling Gavin was there to greet her. They turned together to wait for Spencer, but the boy stood frozen on the rock.

"Concentrate on keeping your footing and walk slowly," Fiona advised.

"I—" Spencer hesitated, the doubt in his eyes growing.

"Can you help him?" Fiona whispered under her breath.

"Aye, I'll help the lad. But not the way ye think."

Gavin made his way to the center of the log, then stretched out his arm. "Hand me the equipment."

Spencer inched his way forward a few feet before passing over the rods and net. Once they were in his grasp, Gavin walked back to join Fiona. Spencer's eyes darted nervously from the rocks to the log to the water, then back to the rocks. "If I lose my balance I'll fall in the water."

"Then ye'd best stay on yer feet." Gavin cocked his head. "Can ye swim?"

Spencer swallowed hard. "No."

"Well, that's more of a reason not to fall in the loch. I've heard tell that the water's so cold at times it will steal the breath from yer lungs the moment you sink beneath it."

"Gavin," Fiona hissed. "The boy is scared enough without you adding fuel to the fire."

"Overcoming his fear will make the victory all the sweeter," Gavin insisted. Turning back to Spencer, he said, "Yer legs might not always work the way ye want, but there's ways to compensate fer it. Can ye think of any?"

Spencer pulled his bottom lip between his teeth as he looked both ways, taking stock of the situation. Fiona's heart sank as Spencer backed away. The boy had been resentful at coming in the first place. Now he was going to stomp away like a spoiled brat, insulting Gavin and shaming her.

It was therefore a relief when he soon returned with a very long, sturdy-looking branch in his hand. Grasping it between both hands, Spencer tentatively lowered it into the water. As he put his weight on it, the branch slipped on the murky bottom and slid out from under him.

Fiona gasped, not knowing how Spencer was able to keep his balance. Once righted, he lifted the branch from the water and flung it into the lake.

"A good idea, but unsuccessful." Gavin crouched down on his haunches and spoke in a low, encouraging tone. "Think, Spencer. And dinnae be afraid to fail. The only way to learn anything in life is to try and fail, then continue trying until ye succeed."

Sweat gathered at Spencer's brow. He stood a few minutes longer, thinking, then sat on the ground, removed his boots, then strung them across his neck. Fiona soon realized this would give his feet and toes a firmer grasp on the log. Arms akimbo, he started across, his shorter leg challenging his balance with each step.

As he drew near, Fiona could see how firmly his jaw was locked, how tightly his teeth were clenched. 'Twas a miracle she didn't hear them cracking. 'Twas a miracle also that he didn't land in the lake. She held her breath with each step, fearful any sound would break his concentration. As he got close, Gavin extended his arm. Spencer hesitated for an instant, then grabbed it.

"Clever lad!" Gavin exclaimed. "There's no shame in taking help when ye need it. Ye cannae hide the infirmary in yer leg. If ye do, then others will view it as a weakness. So let it stand in the open and let everyone see ye can overcome it.

"Ye'll have to prove yerself more than others, but I believe ye've the courage, strength, and intelligence to conquer this affliction. If ye work hard and learn to properly wield a sword, there's none that will be able to best ye."

Spencer's chest fairly puffed out with pride. He pulled on his boots, then without being asked, bent and lifted the poles. "Will you teach me how to swim?"

"I will. When the weather gets a wee warmer and we have some privacy. 'Tis a lesson best taught only among men. We swim as we were born, in nothing but nature's clothing."

Spencer blushed. Fiona did, too. Breaking the awkward mood, Gavin urged them to the other side of the rock. From here the sparkling water stretched nearly as far as the eye could see. Gavin told them to spread out on the flat rock, instructing Fiona to sit in the middle. When they were finally settled, Gavin explained the finer points of fishing, set the bait on their lines and cast the lines in the water.

It was impossible to miss the worshipful glow in Spencer's gaze when he looked at Gavin. Fiona felt the moisture gathering in her eyes. Mortified, she turned away, not wanting either of them to see. After the turmoil of the last few days—well, in truth the last year—this carefree outing was a tonic.

They sat in companionable silence for nearly an hour. A gentle breeze kept the sun from becoming uncomfortably warm. Fiona removed her veil and gold circlet, reveling in the freedom. She turned her face to the sun, feeling an odd sort of renewal seeping into her bones.

A sudden rustling sound in the trees on the shoreline behind them spun Gavin around. Fiona marveled at the quickness of his body, the fluid motion he used to draw his sword. It was as though the weapon were a part of him, a mere extension of his flesh.

Alas, the precaution proved unnecessary. A most familiar hound came bounding through the underbrush, tongue lagging, tail wagging.

"I cannae believe he followed us all the way here," Gavin marveled.

"He's a very clever boy," Fiona said proudly, rubbing the special spot behind the pup's ears that never failed to delight him.

The beast sighed in ecstasy, and pushed closer, nearly knocking Fiona over. She laughed, tossing her head to one side to swing her braid over her shoulder, so the dog would not be tempted to gnaw on it, then allowed herself to be licked on the face. It truly was impossible to resist such faithful, loving devotion.

"Mother!"

Fiona, Gavin, and the dog all turned at the sound of Spencer's frightened cry. But it was Gavin who quickly ascertained what was upsetting the boy.

"No cause fer alarm," he called out. "This great beast is yer mother's new friend."

"I thought it might be a wolf," Spencer admitted sheepishly, and they all laughed.

"He's an odd-looking fellow, isn't he?" Fiona said, rubbing the dog's muzzle. "I think I shall call him Laddie, in recognition of his Scottish heritage."

Curious, Laddie abandoned Fiona and trotted over to greet Spencer. After receiving an acceptable response, the dog lumbered to the edge of the rock, dipped his head and began lapping noisily.

"He's scaring the fish away," Spencer complained.

"Don't whine," Fiona admonished. "'Tis unbecoming and unmanly. He'll stop once he's drunk his fill."

Her words proved true, however a moment later the beast sighted something that prompted a round of excited barks. Spencer said nothing further—his look of annoyance was enough to convey his feelings.

"Fine, I'll take him for a walk on the other side of the lake so you can fish in peace and quiet," Fiona said.

"I'll come with ye," Gavin volunteered, springing to his feet.

"But Spencer—"

"Will be fine."

Spencer nodded. Still, Fiona hesitated.

"We'll stay close to the shoreline, so ye can keep the lad within yer sights at all times," Gavin offered.

Fiona nodded, satisfied with the compromise. Yet she took her time making certain that Spencer had everything he required within easy reach before moving.

They made a slow circuit on the shoreline of the lake, the dog running happily ahead. Every now and again Gavin would pick up a stick and toss it into the underbrush for the beast to eagerly chase.

"Well, he seems to understand one part of the game," Fiona remarked, when the dog returned with the stick, yet refused to yield it.

"Are ye enjoying yerself?" Gavin asked, as he picked up another stick and hurled it over the treetops.

"Yes. Thank you." The thought flew in her head and the words swiftly followed, before she had time to think. "Why did you arrange this outing today? Why are you being so kind?"

"Ye don't know?"

She shook her head.

"Isn't it obvious? I want to please ye, to make ye happy." He reached up and drew his palm gently across her cheek. "I'm trying to woo ye, lass."

He's jesting. Yet the deep timbre of his voice called to her. To the lonely, forgotten place in her heart. But it wasn't only her heart. Her body had a weakness for Gavin, and a part of her worried what would happen if she didn't try harder to quell it—or at least control it.

Despite her best efforts, Fiona felt herself being

pulled in by the curious emotions she saw reflected in his eyes. Desire, excitement, but most astonishing of all—possibility.

The possibility of finding someone to care for her. To protect her. To love her. Such foolish, dangerous thoughts.

Gavin reached down and grasped her hand, entwining his fingers with hers. His touch sent tiny sparks through her. The sensible part of Fiona's brain urged her to lower her gaze and conceal her true feelings, but there was simply too much delight coursing through her to comply. What did it matter if he knew the truth? She found him attractive, exciting, desirable. Was it so wrong to let him know?

His wicked grin let her know he was aware of the effect he was having on her. Well, two could play at that game. With an innocent smile, Fiona ran her palms down the hard contours of his arms. The tight muscles flexed beneath her sensual touch.

She leaned closer, until their chests were touching, then raised her chin and slowly outlined his lips with the tip of her tongue. He trembled against her. The power of their passion awed her, almost frightening in its intensity.

"Spencer?" she asked breathlessly.

"Is safe. He's in my direct sights. Damn, he's just caught a fish!"

Fiona sighed heavily. "Well, if you can see him, then he can see us."

Gavin groaned. Fiona stepped back. It seemed as though every muscle in his body flexed with restraint, yet he impressively remained in control.

"Until tonight," he said gruffly.

Fiona nodded, the sensual promise in his eyes making her shiver.

Perched behind a boulder on the ridge above, Ewan watched the scene below with restless interest. There were easily a dozen things he could name that were far more enjoyable than sitting on a rock for hours with a line thrown into the loch, waiting for some hapless fish to bite. Merely observing the earl and his companions had at times bored Ewan senseless.

Thankfully, there were a few distractions. The lad successfully conquering the fallen log had brought a shout of joy and a smile so wide from the woman he could see it from this great distance. She was a bonnie thing and Ewan had recognized her and the lad without difficulty. It was not a common sight to have an English lady on McLendon land, and he wondered if any of the soldiers that had accompanied her were still at the castle.

The sudden appearance of a mangy dog had also caused a commotion. Ewan had taken note of how quickly the earl reached for his sword when the beast charged from the brush, how swiftly he was ready to attack and defend. Even without a contingent of guards around him, the earl would not be easily caught unawares.

He had spoken the truth to his mother when he said he would not kill the earl. But he also meant it when he declared he would cause him a considerable amount of trouble.

All men were mortal. All men had weaknesses. What was the earl's? Could this English woman be the key?

Ewan had heard tell of besotted men. Perfectly

normal lads who lost control of their thoughts—and sometimes their tongues—at the sight of a bonnie woman. He would never have believed the earl to be one of those men, but observing the scene below had raised the possibility.

Then again, he knew very little about his half brother. They had never spoken, had never met face-to-face. All he really knew about the earl were the tales he had heard: of command and harshness, of strength and dominance, of courage and character.

Ewan was astute enough to realize the details and emphasis of the stories were often dependent on the attitudes of those relating the tale. Even with a dirk held against her throat, his mother would be hard-pressed to find one good or kind or fair thing to say about the earl.

There was good mixed with bad in all people. Though in Ewan's experience, one side almost always dominated the other.

Yet as he melded back into the dense woods, two questions remained foremost in Ewan's mind.

Who was the blond beauty? And why was she so important to the earl?

Chapter 10

It was a cheerful trio that returned to the castle, Gavin leading the way. Fiona sat relaxed and content on her palfrey. An impressive string of fish hung from the end of Spencer's fishing pole. Gavin, too, felt an uncharacteristic sense of well-being. It had been a rare treat to escape his ever-present responsibilities for an afternoon.

"We've received an important message fer ye," Aidan said, as he grasped the lead on Gavin's horse and pulled him toward the stable.

"More messages?" Gavin grinned as he dismounted, his mood too uplifted to manage a serious response. "Is the new King Edward dead also?"

Aidan smiled faintly. "Not yet. But there is a king wanting yer attention."

Gavin's heart quickened. There could only be one king to which Aidan referred. The Scottish King Robert.

"With the news of Edward's death, I expected he would move south," Gavin said in a hushed voice.

"Ye've got that right." Aidan glanced around the

crowded area, then leaned in close. "He's waiting fer ye upstairs in yer private solar."

"Why not the great hall?"

"That's where he wanted to go. I thought it wise not to question his request, but 'tis clear he dinnae want to attract much attention. He arrived with a small contingent of heavily armed soldiers, none bearing the royal standard. As it was, only Connor, Duncan, and I recognized him."

"Has he been here long?"

Aidan shook his head. "Less than an hour. Connor rode out to fetch ye, but ye've returned before him."

"We didn't see Connor. He must have taken a different route to the loch." Gavin laid a hand on Aidan's shoulder. "Take charge of Lady Fiona. And make certain I'm not disturbed."

Gavin took the stairs to the private solar two at a time, arriving at the top slightly out of breath. Without knocking, he swung open the heavy wooden door and found the king lounging comfortably in a padded chair, a meager offering of refreshments set before him.

"Sire, welcome. I humbly beg yer pardon fer not being here to greet ye," Gavin said, bowing low.

"As I gave ye no warning of my arrival, 'tis understandable," Robert replied, coming to his feet. "'Tis good to see ye, my old friend."

The king extended his hand and Gavin shook it. Robert looked well. He was lean and fit with a natural air of authority and regal command surrounding him. 'Twas hard to believe that a scant year ago his kingship had been in grave peril, his cause all but lost. With his army defeated and his support scattered, Robert had been lucky to make it out of Scotland with his life.

But he had done what he promised: gathered more

troops, secured greater support, and returned to fight for his crown. "I had not expected to see ye so soon after Loudon Hill," Gavin said.

Robert grinned cheekily. "'Twas pure delight watching Mowbray and his cavalry force flee, was it not? And besting the Earl of Gloucester a few days later added a certain element of justice to our fight."

"A victory fer all of us to savor," Gavin agreed.

"Aye. And now we've had the best possible news of all." Robert shot Gavin a look of pure glee. "Longshanks is dead."

Gavin returned the grin. "Praise God. My people are planning a grand celebration as we speak. Will ye join us?"

"Regretfully, I cannae stay long."

"Then at least allow me to offer more fitting hospitality to my king," Gavin said, gesturing toward the goblet of ale and simple platter of cold meat, cheese, and brown bread on the table in front of Robert.

"Nay, this has more than appeased my hunger and assures me that few in yer household are aware of my true identity. I find it easier to evade my enemies when I dinnae travel with all the royal trappings. There will be plenty of opportunities to make a royal progress when the crown sits more securely upon my head."

"Do ye anticipate much resistance from young Edward?" Gavin asked, taking the seat opposite the king.

"No. The whelp lacks his father's shrewdness and taste fer blood." Robert remained silent for a moment, then cleared his throat. "The next threat of war will come from within our borders. That's why I'm here. I need to know that I can continue to count on yer full support."

"I've pledged my sword and my men to yer cause, fully committing all to defeating the English." Gavin tightened his jaw. "I've never made any secret of the fact that I'm not nearly as eager to spill Scottish blood."

"That's hardly my choice either," Robert exclaimed. "I will accept the fidelity of any man who swears allegiance to me and forgive any past transgressions. But we both know there are some clans who will never accept me as their rightful king."

"I know. As we speak, they are taking sides against ye with the MacDougalls and the MacNaghtens leading the way."

"Dinnae forget the MacNabs and the McCullochs." Robert smiled grimly. "They, too, crave a piece of my hide."

"Fer some it's less about yer sovereignty and more about their history. They'll line up against ye solely because their blood feud rivals are siding with ye."

"Aye, 'tis how the English were able to gain a foothold inside our beloved country in the first place. But the clans must see reason, must look beyond their petty differences to the future." The king slid a folded piece of parchment across the table. "You see before ye a list of those men who have not yet chosen sides."

There were no surprises as Gavin read through the list of names. "Some will still try to avoid the conflict, delaying as long as possible before choosing sides."

"Time for delay is fast running out. I need to work quickly to secure as many clans as possible to my banner."

"I know most of the men on yer list. I can speak with them, plead fer yer cause, but I'm no silver-tongued diplomat."

"I dinnae think many of those men would understand the art of diplomacy if it struck them over the head." The king sat back, folding his arms across his chest.

"I need these alliances to strengthen my claim to the crown and fight those who would oppose me, Gavin. Seven of the men on the list have marriageable daughters. McKenna's sister is also of an age to be married.

"If ye take one of these women as yer wife, the allegiance of her clan will shift to our side. And they, in turn, can aid ye in convincing some of the others."

Marry? Gavin felt an unexpected trickle of sweat start on his neck. Kings had long dictated the arranged marriages of the nobility, requiring that they give their approval for many of the matches. He really shouldn't be surprised. Yet he was. Gavin glanced again at the list. The letters grew fuzzy before his eyes.

"Is there anyone in particular ye prefer?" Gavin asked, stalling for time.

"All on the list are suitable and will be beneficial to the cause." Robert took another swig from his tankard. "Too bad ye can only marry one of them."

Gavin tightly gripped the arms of the chair and tried smiling. He knew this day would come eventually. He owed his clan a rightful heir and his king a sovereign duty. That much was clear. Yet a part of him resisted. Why?

"When do you require the deed to be done?" Gavin asked.

"The sooner ye make a choice and achieve a formal betrothal, the better. The actual wedding can wait a few months, since the promise of a betrothal is binding."

Gavin's chest tightened. "I'll send word to ye once the agreement is signed," he replied, deliberately ignoring the trace of misgivings tugging at his heart.

The king's gaze was not without sympathy. "I know I ask much of ye, Gavin."

"I willingly serve my king," Gavin replied forcefully.

"I know. Yer loyalty is noted and appreciated and will be rewarded."

Gavin grit his teeth. He did not support the king in hopes of winning favors or rewards. He did it because he loved his country and believed in the cause. "Yer success as our king is reward enough," he insisted.

"Well said, yet I'm grateful nonetheless. Truly." Pleased with getting his own way, Robert flashed a generous smile. "I've heard tales of a recent addition to yer household," he continued casually. Too casually. "An English widow and her son?"

Gavin stiffened. "Since when is it a king's business to be concerned about another man's mistress?"

"If that female becomes an impediment to my goals, she therefore becomes my problem." Robert lifted his tankard and studied Gavin over the pewter rim. "Will the lady be a problem?"

Gavin bristled. "Nay. She understands her place in my life. Hell, 'twas the lady herself who suggested our current arrangement."

"Curious." Robert drained the tankard and set it on the table. "I suppose she found yer manly charms irresistible."

"Not at all." Gavin grinned and shook his head, then leaned close so his gaze was level with the king's. "The lady needed my help."

"Ah, 'tis the duty of every chivalrous knight to protect a lady in distress."

The mockery of the king's words bathed Gavin in guilt. His actions toward Fiona had been anything but chivalrous. "My relationship with Lady Fiona will in no way impede my obligation to ye or my commitment to the cause. I will do as ye ask and take one of these women as my wife."

Robert stood and extended his hand a second time. Gavin accepted it with considerably less enthusiasm than before, knowing it was the final seal of his pledge to obey.

Robert pulled on his leather gloves, then glanced around the chamber. "Perchance, is there a back staircase?"

"I'm afraid not. I shall escort—"

"No fanfare, Gavin. 'Tis safer. Trust me."

Still, Gavin insisted on checking the hallway first, to ensure that no one was in sight. Satisfied, he signaled for the king. Robert slapped him on the shoulder as he left, and Gavin watched the king's back as he descended the staircase. The moment he stepped foot in the great hall, a small contingent of soldiers emerged from the shadows, quickly surrounding the king. They drew almost no attention as they walked through the nearly deserted hall and out the front door.

The minute they disappeared from his sight, Gavin hurried back to the solar. Leaning out the window, he saw the group head for the stables. One of the soldiers spoke briefly with Aidan. Horses appeared and the men swung onto their mounts, riding out without a second glance.

Gavin was still preoccupied with the scene outside the window when the door burst open. Aidan, Duncan, and Connor stood in the doorway, their expressions openly curious.

"Is Robert safely away?" Gavin asked.

"Aye, and looking mightily pleased with himself," Aidan replied. "Are we off to fight again?"

"Not yet," Gavin answered, almost wishing that were the case. Though the idea of killing his fellow Scots was distasteful, the idea of another marriage to a woman he had never met and didn't know was not much better.

"If we aren't going into battle, then what did the king want?" Duncan asked.

"We know that whatever it was, ye agreed," Aidan added.

Gavin raised his brow. "Now, why would ye say that?"

"'Cause Robert was grinning like a half-wit when he called fer his horse," Aidan explained. "'Twas obvious he was pleased with the outcome of yer meeting."

"I need a drink," Gavin declared.

"I'll fetch some ale," Connor volunteered.

"Nay. Tell Hamish to bring a jug of whiskey."

Gavin's command was met with surprise by all three men. Distilled locally, the potent liquor was used mainly for medicinal needs and by the earl's decree, drunk only on special occasions.

They remained quiet until the whiskey arrived. Gavin solemnly filled each cup and passed them around. "Robert wants me to take a wife," he announced, hoisting his vessel and gulping the contents. It burned like fire as it ran down his throat and spread through his gut—a welcome distraction from his current woes.

"Damn! 'Tis no wonder ye're needing a dram of whiskey," Connor exclaimed, refilling Gavin's cup.

"Has he chosen yer bride fer ye?" Duncan asked.

"Nay. He's given me a list." Gavin brandished the parchment in front of the trio, waiting for a reaction. It took a few moments before he realized they were unable to read it.

Taking another fortifying sip of his drink, Gavin then slowly recited the names, combing his memory for any glimmer of recognition. There was one woman on the list he had actually met—Shana Agnew. She was attractive, with dark hair and striking blue eyes. She also possessed a shrill voice that grated on the nerves and a propensity for talking about everything and nothing. In his head, Gavin immediately shifted her name to the very bottom.

Connor idly picked at the cheese on the king's platter, then tossed a piece into his mouth. "I saw Margaret Colville at a tournament in the Highlands two years ago."

"And?" Duncan prompted.

"There's more to a woman than good looks," Connor said philosophically. "Perhaps she has a sweet countenance or a kind heart."

Gavin restlessly tapped the tips of his fingers together. "I dinnae require a beautiful lady, though given the choice, I would prefer a woman who is passably attractive."

"Then ye'll need to consider someone else besides Margaret Colville," Connor said with a good-natured laugh.

"That's unkind," Aidan admonished.

Connor shrugged. "'Tis harsh to judge a lass purely on her looks, I know, but Gavin's the one who'll be sleeping beside her. And we have to think about the clan. We dinnae want his bairns to look like a herd of horses. Or worse, a litter of piglets."

The men all nodded solemnly as Gavin refilled their cups.

"What about the McKenna lass?" he asked. "I heard tell that she's a bonnie one. Though if she shares her brother's fiery temperament, there willnae be a piece of crockery left unbroken in the entire castle."

"She's got the McKenna bright red hair," Connor confided.

"Any priest will tell ye that's the mark of the devil," Duncan warned.

"Though if she's as beautiful as they say, ye might enjoy being in hell," Aidan snickered.

The men broke into laughter, and Gavin couldn't help but join them. He took another long sip of the whiskey, conceding it was aiding him in this discussion.

"All right, then. I need to stay away from Colville, McKenna, and Shana Agnew," he said, wishing he had a quill to cross the names off the list entirely. No matter, he'd remember. And if he didn't, Aidan, Connor, and Duncan would remind him.

Duncan frowned. "What's wrong with Shana Agnew?"

"She's a whiny, frightened rabbit of a female who likes to wail with every passing emotion," Gavin muttered.

"Sweet Jesus!" Aidan swore. "Ye don't need to stay away from that lass, ye need to run as far as ye can!"

"Now, repeat the names of the lasses ye will consider," Aidan suggested. "'Tis easier to make a choice with fewer women."

"Nay," Duncan interrupted. "I say ignore the women and concentrate on the clan and the alliance. Which match is better fer all of us?"

"Excellent point." Gavin lifted his cup in a toast, then drained it and promptly filled it again. Squinting down at the parchment, he slowly read the names, leaving out the ones they had already rejected.

The three brothers listened attentively, yet remained quiet. Gavin mulled over the choices. "Sinclair?"

Duncan tilted his head. "Aye."

"Agreed." Connor let out a long breath.

Aidan nodded. "Sinclair is the best choice. He's a fierce warrior and his men are well trained. His lands are close, his coffers full, his judgment fair, though harsh at times."

"His daughter?" Gavin said quietly.

The men exchanged looks. "I've not heard anything about the lass," Aidan admitted, and his brothers nodded in agreement.

"No matter." Gavin sighed. "This is a political match."

"Still, it makes sense to set eyes on the lass before ye start negotiations," Connor insisted.

"Or at least make inquiries," Duncan added.

Gavin leaned back and gave the trio an amused look. "Bloody hell, just listen to us! Gossiping like a gaggle of old crones. The Sinclair lass will come with an impressive dowry of land, a noble pedigree, and the political alliance the king seeks. The rest is unimportant."

Yet even as Gavin spoke them, the words left a sour taste in his mouth. Despite the various benefits, he still hadn't fully accepted the notion of wedding a stranger. A picture formed in his mind of his unknown bride standing stiff and silent beside him outside the chapel doors while the priest prompted them to recite their vows. 'Twas not an overly appealing sight.

"Will ye present a formal offer in writing to Laird Sinclair, or discuss the terms in person?" Aidan inquired.

Gavin heaved a sigh of resignation. "I'll think on it a few more days and then decide."

Fiona felt the weight of Alice's censuring stare as the maid watched her add another pinch of herbs to the small pot simmering over the blazing fire.

"I need more wood, Alice. Kindly place another log on the fire."

Warily Alice obeyed the command, placing the wood on the edge of the fireplace, then pushing it into the flames with her foot. The small chamber was already beastly hot, noxious vapors permeating the entire space. But this was the only place in the entire castle where Fiona could be assured of privacy, leaving her no choice but to brew her draught in her tiny bedchamber.

Fiona knew there were many who would condemn her for what she was doing, including Father Niall. Preventing conception was a moral sin, but Fiona had always contended it was a woman's burden either way, and not something a man could decide.

Through the years she had shared her herbal knowledge with many a desperate woman, trying to offer counsel and solace to ensure that a lethal dose was not taken. Yet she never would have believed that someday she would be the one in need of assistance.

Several of the required herbs were growing in the kitchen garden she weeded. They had been the simplest to obtain. The rest could be found in the castle stillroom, which was kept unlocked so the cook could season their meals and Hamish could dispense medicines to those who fell ill.

Still, Fiona had been fearful of anyone seeing her taking what she needed, so after giving her very detailed instructions on what to look for, Fiona had sent Alice to the stillroom to fetch the other herbs.

"'Tis poison, my lady," Alice said in a nervous whisper.

Fiona gazed about the room. They were obviously alone, yet Alice felt the need to whisper. A clear indication of her fear. But it could not sway Fiona's resolve.

"This medicine will help to bring on my courses a bit sooner than usual," Fiona said calmly. "Nothing more."

"It could also bring on your death," Alice hissed, her eyes wide with worry. "I've heard tell of a woman who had the life bleed out of her after drinking a similar brew."

Fiona blanched. She was well aware of the dangers, to both her body and her mortal soul. But she had no other choice. "I cannot risk the earl's seed taking root inside my womb. 'Twould be a disaster."

"Father Niall says a child is a blessing."

"A babe is truly a miracle," Fiona agreed. "Lest you forget, I already have a son and he deserves my protection. What would happen to Spencer if I became pregnant?"

"Do you think the earl would abandon you?"

"I'm uncertain." Fiona rubbed her brow, confusion tearing at her gut. "His assumption that I was barren brought an odd sense of relief to his expression when he spoke of it."

"But you are not barren," Alice exclaimed. "Why would the earl think such a thing?"

"More than ten years wed and no children of my own. 'Tis a logical conclusion to reach."

Alice blushed and lowered her eyes. Having served Fiona all of her married life, the maid was well aware of how infrequently the baron shared her mistress's bed. "Can you not trust in the good Lord to guide your future?"

Regretfully, Fiona shook her head. "I cannot leave Spencer to an uncertain fate. The risk is too great. For all of us, but most especially for some poor innocent babe. Ewan Gilroy is proof enough that being born a bastard is a harsh life around here."

After wrapping her hand with thick cloth, Fiona carefully removed the bubbling cauldron from the fire and set it on the floor beneath the window. Alice peered inside and Fiona could see the maid's surprise at the meager amount. But Fiona knew she had made enough for an effective dose.

Fiona extracted a few spoonfuls and dribbled them into a cup. Well aware of Alice's disapproving frown, Fiona stared at the contents for several minutes, waiting for it to cool.

Then with a sudden stab of regret, she lifted the goblet to her lips, and drank.

Gavin sat brooding in the great hall after the evening meal, his eyes resting on the group of women clustered in front of the fireplace. Fiona was among them, spinning a ball of wool into thread. Well, not precisely among them. Though engaged in the same work, she sat slightly apart, an obvious outcast. Her dour maid was beside her and if not for the servant, she would be completely isolated.

Lifting his arms above his head, Gavin stretched out the stiffness in his back. The motion brought him higher in his chair and that's when he noticed Fiona did have one other companion. That mangy dog.

The beast was curled at her feet, no doubt snoring loudly. It gave him a queer sense of comfort knowing that she had a valiant protector, even if he was of the four-legged variety.

"I need to speak with ye on a delicate matter concerning Lady Fiona," Hamish said.

Gavin eyed his steward. After the day he'd had, he

was not in the mood to listen to any more problems. Yet duty always came first. "Aye."

Hamish cleared his throat. "The other women dinnae like the lady," the steward muttered.

Gavin twisted his head to see if anyone else had overheard the remark. Then feeling foolish for acting so concerned, he shrugged. "'Tis of no importance. What matters is that I like Lady Fiona."

"Forgive me, milord. Naturally yer desires are all that matter."

Gavin grunted with satisfaction and waved the steward away. Hamish turned, then paused. He took a breath and glanced again at the earl hesitatingly.

"Speak," Gavin commanded. "'Tis obvious there is more to say, which in all likelihood I willnae want to hear, but ye believe it needs to be told."

"The castle women resent Lady Fiona's interference in the daily routine. Her insistence on helping with various chores has caused resentment and discord among the women. They complain of it to me daily."

"Since when is working a crime? I should think they would be pleased at having her assistance or at least admire her efforts."

Hamish released a beleaguered sigh. "They are females, milord."

"I suppose ye want me to speak of this to Lady Fiona?"

"If ye think it best," Hamish said humbly.

Gavin drummed his fingers restlessly on the wooden table. Leave it to a bunch of women to make a problem where one shouldn't exist.

"Tell them that if they prefer, I shall instruct Lady Fiona to cease her efforts to work alongside them. She will instead conduct herself like a pampered, noble lady and demand to be waited upon. By them."

Hamish's face brightened with interest. "Very good, milord. I will take great pleasure in relating yer wishes."

Fiona was expecting the cramps and the headache, for they usually accompanied her menses, but she was unprepared for the exhaustion. She hoped concentrating on a task would help keep her awake, but her eyelids felt so heavy she couldn't control their drifting down over her eyes. At times she could barely catch a glimpse of the thread she was trying to spin—at others she saw two fuzzy strings through blurry, unfocused eyes.

More than anything she wanted to drag herself up the stairs and crawl into her own bed. Alone. So she could suffer in silent privacy. But no one left the hall without seeking the earl's permission and she was in no mood to ask him.

"Shall we retire, milady?"

Fiona's head snapped up and she stared at Gavin. Her mind had been drifting in a state of exhaustion and she hadn't even heard him approach. Relieved she could finally leave, she rose and Gavin caught her hand.

By the time they reached the top of the staircase, Fiona felt as though her legs would collapse if she took another step. She muttered a hasty good night to Gavin, then gratefully reached for the latch on her bedchamber door, but his booming voice stopped her.

"Where do ye think yer going?"

"To bed, to sleep," Fiona muttered, too tired to turn around. Besides, there was no need to see the scowl on his face when she could hear it so clearly in his voice. "I suddenly feel exhausted."

"Why are ye going into that chamber?"

Fiona closed her eyes and leaned her head against the door. "I cannot . . . that is to say, I need to be alone tonight. And the next few nights," she added hastily.

"Fiona, is something wrong?"

Yes! You are a half-wit! He'd been married before, surely he knew about this sort of thing. Her head still pressed against the door, she turned it and stared at him pointedly, hoping the truth would dawn upon him. Or at least he'd take the hint and leave her alone. Unfortunately, his gaze remained puzzled.

"'Tis my womanly time, Gavin," Fiona groaned, in too much discomfort to be delicate.

"I dinnae care. Come to my bed."

Fiona whirled around. Her head was starting to feel as though it were splitting in half. "I need to be alone," she repeated.

"I never put much stock in the teachings that a woman is unclean during her time of the month. 'Tis a part of nature; how can that be something so fearful?"

"'Tis a woman's burden, to be endured alone," Fiona grimaced.

"Are ye in pain?"

Her face whitened. "I . . . well . . . I cannot discuss this with you," she muttered.

"I'll send for yer maid. Now come into my chamber."

Alice arrived a short while later with Fiona's night-clothes, a basin of warm water, and other essentials. Gavin stayed on the opposite side of the chamber, allowing Fiona some privacy. But the minute Alice departed, he came to the bed.

"Turn on yer side, Fiona."

She lifted a corner of the cloth Alice had kindly

placed on her forehead and glared at him. "Have you lost your mind?"

Gavin looked insulted. "Och, I'm not an animal. Now do as I say."

Realizing that arguing would only deplete her strength and increase her headache, Fiona did as he asked, deliberately facing away from him. She could hear his deep chuckle and then his hands were on her back, first rubbing the tension in her shoulders, then moving to the center.

She let out a shuddering sigh of relief. It felt marvelous. The tight knots in her lower back began to ease. Fiona felt her entire body start to relax. Just as she was drifting off to sleep, she felt him kiss her neck, then lightly nibble a path to her ear.

"Gavin," she muttered in a warning tone.

"Shh," he murmured gently. "I'm merely saying good night. Though I dinnae want ye thinking I was too chivalrous that I'd deny myself the chance fer a wee taste of yer sweetness."

Fiona grinned, the trace of a smile still on her lips when the blissful oblivion of sleep claimed her a few minutes later.

Chapter 11

The shouting from the sentries was heard clearly in the bailey below. Gavin, who had been observing the squires' morning training on the practice field, immediately rose to his feet. Duncan and Connor joined him, and the three men climbed up the stone stairs to the battlements. They met Aidan coming down.

"The guards have spied a large party on horseback headed this way," Aidan informed them.

"Soldiers?" Gavin questioned.

Aidan nodded. "Archers, too."

"Are they flying a battle flag?"

"They're too far away to be certain."

"Sound the alarm fer the villagers to remain in their homes," Gavin commanded. "And put our archers and men on the wall."

Orders given, Gavin glanced at the keep, his eyes searching for the narrow slit of his bedchamber window. Fiona had stayed abed late every morning this past week, emerging after the noon meal. The first few days she looked pale and wan, but yesterday a spot of color had returned to her cheeks, along with the sparkle in her eyes.

'Twas a good sign that she was feeling better, yet Gavin hoped she would keep to her current pattern and remain in his chamber. It was one of the safest spots in the castle.

"Connor thinks they might be flying the McKenna banner, but they're still too far away to see it clearly." Aidan leaned close and whispered, "If I hadn't seen the king with my own eyes last week, I would say it was him. By all accounts, it looks like a very grand caravan. The soldiers are riding three abreast and their numbers are so large we cannae see the end of the column."

"We've no quarrel with the McKennas," Duncan exclaimed. "Why would they be marching on us?"

Gavin inwardly groaned. "I see Robert's hand at work. Apparently, he is more anxious fer me to select a bride than he claimed."

"We've already ruled out the McKenna lass," Aidan said. "Her fiery temper and matching red hair were more than ye were willing to take on."

"I remember," Gavin replied. He shielded his eyes against the sun, straining to get a better look at the approaching riders, searching for the one thing he hoped not to find. "God's wounds!"

"What? What is it?" Duncan asked anxiously.

"Women," Gavin grunted. "There are women riding in the middle of the line."

"Dammit." Aidan shook his head in sympathy. "Looks like McKenna has decided not to wait fer an offer and instead is bringing a bride to ye."

"Should we deny them entrance?" Connor suggested.

Gavin scowled at him. "And start a feud?"

"We could say there is sickness within our walls." Deep in thought, Duncan scrunched his face tightly, then suddenly brightened. "Or the plague. No one will pass through our gates if there is even a hint of plague."

Gavin groaned and lifted his head toward the sky. The only thing dafter than Duncan's suggestion was the strong temptation Gavin felt at agreeing with the crazy idea.

"The McLendons are not cowards. We willnae hide behind a lie like a gaggle of weak women," Gavin admonished. "Go find Hamish and tell him to prepare a fitting meal fer our unexpected guests. I want barrels of our best ale brought up from the cellars for all the McKenna soldiers, too."

Connor frowned. "Why are we wasting our best ale on that lot?"

"'Cause if things turn nasty, I want McKenna's men to be plied with drink," Gavin explained. "I'm sure the captain of their guard will make certain they dinnae lose their senses entirely, but their reactions with sword and bow will be slower."

"Christ Almighty, maybe it would be better to say we have the plague," Aidan grumbled.

Gavin almost nodded in agreement. He pictured the long line of soldiers being turned away at the gates, the McKenna lass with them. Now that would be a sight to bring a smile to his lips.

"Keep our men on the wall," Gavin ordered. "Best to be prepared without need than to be caught unawares."

He left the trio on the ramparts and walked to the bailey, deciding he would stand at the entrance to the great hall to greet his uninvited guests. However, his attention was diverted when Fiona came through the door and stood at his side.

"I heard the alarm and saw the approaching men. Will there be trouble?"

"Not if I can prevent it."

She nodded, her face visibly relaxing. The sight of her trusting eyes hit him like a punch in the gullet. Her faith in him was humbling and uncomfortable, for it was something he didn't fully deserve.

Guilt, swift and sure, stabbed Gavin's conscience. That trust would undoubtedly be crushed from Fiona's eyes when she discovered he was taking a new bride. The one small comfort was knowing that wasn't going to happen today.

"'Tis the McKennas, just as we thought," Duncan shouted from the wall, his deep voice booming through the bailey.

"Are they your enemies?" Fiona raised her hand to her mouth and began to nibble on a fingernail, a sure sign of nerves.

"Nay." *And I hope to keep it that way.* Gavin rested his hands on his hips and bowed his head. At all costs, he needed to remember his first priority was to secure support for Robert's cause. And that meant that Fiona must not be standing here when their unexpected guests arrived. As much for her protection as Gavin's convenience.

Laird McKenna was already going to be disappointed when he learned that Gavin had no intention of making an offer of marriage to the man's sister. 'Twould be a double insult to do it with his English mistress by his side.

"The McKennas are Highlanders, a breed with an unmatched Scottish pride," Gavin said.

Fiona recovered her poise, hastily lowering her

hand from her mouth. "I take it they do not care for the English?"

"More than most."

"Shall I retire to my chamber?"

"Nay, lass, go wait in my chamber. In my bed." He winked and she blushed. He wondered if she could feel him undressing her with his eyes. It had been six days since he had made love to her and the simmering passion inside him was starting to boil. "These uninvited guests shouldn't stay more than a few hours."

Fiona's back straightened. Then to his utter surprise, she took hold of his face between her palms and kissed him. "I shall await your pleasure," she whispered breathlessly.

Now standing alone on the steps of the entrance to the great hall, Gavin composed his features into impassivity. He could hear the shouts from the wall as the McKennas asked for admittance, the creak of the metal chains as the drawbridge was lowered.

The ground reverberated, the dust flew and swirled in the still air as the McKenna party filled the bailey. Gavin forced a tight smile on his lips and waited for the laird to dismount.

Brian McKenna was a bear of a man, very tall and broad-shouldered, with brawny arms and an expansive chest. His face was young, yet lined with the worry and strain of a man responsible for the fate and well-being of many.

Perhaps because of that responsibility, he was armed to the eyeteeth, carrying two swords, a battle-ax, and a long, thin-bladed dirk that sported a single red jewel in the handle. The sight of all those weapons gave Gavin pause, and he wondered if McKenna was indeed the ruthless brute many claimed him to be.

"I bid ye welcome and offer ye the hospitality of our clan," Gavin said formally.

"I thank ye fer receiving us," Laird Brian McKenna replied, his voice thundering through the bailey.

Several of the servants working in the area halted their chores to glance at them. Mayhap it was the wild winds and rolling hills of the Highlands that called for such a loud, booming voice. Or perhaps the laird just liked to bellow. Gavin widened his grin to assure his servants there was no cause for alarm, then motioned for them to resume their work.

"I've instructed my servants to prepare a respite for all of ye," Gavin said.

"'Tis a most gracious welcome," the laird replied. "We've been traveling since dawn and the dust of the road has left us parched. 'Twould be a great relief if my sister could rest fer a few hours before we continue our journey home to the Highlands. She's a delicate lass, unused to the discomforts of travel."

Gavin's eyes narrowed. There was an almost playful arrogance about the man that might cause one to under-estimate his intelligence. But Gavin was not so easily misled. McKenna had made a point of mentioning his sister within moments of their arrival. Clearly a calcu-lated move, since it forced Gavin to now follow polite custom and escort the lady inside himself.

He had no wish to insult McKenna, especially since the man would be leaving without securing a betrothal arrangement.

Gavin waited for the young woman to dismount from her palfrey and then extended his hand to her.

He heard her sharp intake of breath before she very gingerly placed her small hand into his. He felt her entire body tremble with each step she took, yet she kept moving forward.

She was delicate and fragile, a tiny bit of a thing. The top of her veiled head barely reached Gavin's shoulder. As they walked the length of the great hall to the raised dais, he shifted his gaze to glance at her face, surprised at what he beheld.

She had the same startling gray eyes as her brother, a bow-shaped mouth, and a healthy dose of blushing pink color on her cheeks. Her hair was hidden beneath a linen veil, but he swore the few wisps that had escaped were a deep auburn color.

Yet it was her age that puzzled him most. Why, she was no more than fifteen or sixteen. Was this the hot-tempered McKenna lass whose fiery tongue had skewered many a man with the sharpness of a blade? It hardly seemed possible.

Aside from her youth, the lass had the distinct sheltered expression of a female raised within convent walls. Clearly, Connor's information about the McKenna lass was wrong. Gavin's jaw hardened, wondering what other unpleasant surprises awaited him.

"Please, milord, I would prefer to sit here among my attendants," the lass said softly, stopping at the table closest to the dais.

Gavin paused. His conversation with her brother would be far more private if she were seated away from them and would spare her the humiliation of being spoken about as though she were an item to be bartered instead of a person of worth.

He almost said as much to her before catching himself. *God's wounds, when did I become so aware and concerned about a woman's feelings?* Shaking off the notion, Gavin agreed to her request. But only because it gave him an advantage.

With a fluttering breath, the McKenna lass perched herself on the very edge of her seat. Shrugging at the uncomfortable position, Gavin moved to the dais and sat in his chair, then motioned for the laird to take the seat on his left.

McKenna took to heart Gavin's offer of making himself welcome. The young man lounged comfortably in his chair, tankard of ale in one hand, elbow of the other arm resting on the wooden arm of the chair, his legs stretched out in front of him.

But Gavin was not fooled by this casual attitude. There was focus in McKenna's expression and a keen observation in his eyes as they scanned the great hall. Missing nothing, Gavin decided.

There was no need to struggle with polite conversation; McKenna drained his tankard, refilled it, then spoke. "Tell me, do ye still have a great affection for Robert the Bruce?" he asked.

"I do. And what of ye, McKenna? Will ye support yer king?"

McKenna cocked his head to one side. "I might, with the proper enticement."

Gavin raised a brow. "Is freedom from the English not enough fer ye?"

McKenna shrugged. "We are a long way from being separated from the harsh rule of England. Those who are on the wrong side when this war ends will suffer harsh reprisals, most likely losing everything they own, and very possibly their lives."

"Aye, the stakes are high. That's why we must win."

McKenna leaned back, folding his arms across his wide chest. "The Bruce is a man greedy fer power. Why should I trust that he will treat us any better than the English if he succeeds in keeping his crown?"

"He shares our blood," Gavin replied smoothly. "Many talk of the differences among Highlanders and Lowlanders, but there is no denying that we have more in common with each other than the damn English."

"Ye believe he will do what is best fer Scotland, yet I have my doubts," McKenna said bluntly. He speared a piece of cheese with the tip of his knife, pulled it through his teeth and began chewing. "However, a union between our clans would go a long way toward easing those doubts."

Gavin went completely still, determined to appear as though he were considering the notion. "I confess, I have heard some rather . . . uhm . . . outrageous tales about the redheaded McKenna lass."

"Yet ye still opened yer gates and bid me welcome?" McKenna hooted so loudly with laughter he began to cough. "Ye're either a very brave or very desperate man," he finished hoarsely.

"Neither," Gavin said dryly as he refilled the laird's tankard. He glanced over at the women. McKenna's sister had finished her food and drink and now sat with her fingers tightly intertwined, precisely as one did when praying. A quick glance at the scheming expression on her brother's face made that seem a wise precaution, though it was impossible to tell what the lass was asking for with her prayers. "Tell me about her."

"The rumors about my sister are all true," McKenna said in an almost cheerful voice. "She's a shrew of a female; disobedient, willful, and defiant to the end. A man could lose his mind trying to reason with her, and that's a fact. Truth be told, I wouldn't wish her upon my most despised enemy."

"Yet ye are offering her hand to me in marriage?" Gavin asked, astonished at McKenna's bluntness. He didn't seem to be a fool, yet it was a ridiculous approach for a man trying to negotiate a match.

McKenna smiled, revealing a row of large, even teeth. "My sister, Caitlyn, the hellcat, has run off with a landless knight; a French mercenary she professes to love with all her heart." McKenna scoffed in disgust, a hard edge entering his voice. "'Twill be a rude awakening when her new husband discovers she's forfeited her dowry by defying me and marrying without my permission. I'd like to see how much he loves her then."

Gavin took a healthy sip of his ale and waited for McKenna to continue.

"The lovely lass that is seated in yer hall is my younger sister, Grace, who is the very picture of womanly virtue and obedience. She was promised to the church, but since Caitlyn has disgraced our clan by refusing to do her duty and make a strong marriage alliance, Grace must now take her place. I fetched her from the Convent of the Sacred Heart three days ago. Thankfully, she hadn't yet taken her final vows, which leaves her free to become a bride of a Scottish lord, instead of a bride of Christ."

Gavin couldn't believe what he was hearing. McKenna sounded desperate. It was no small act of defiance going against the church. Men had been excommunicated for such treachery, their souls damned for eternity.

Then again, the young laird did not seem the type to be overly concerned about his soul.

Gavin glanced at the young woman in question. His assumption about her cloistered upbringing was correct. She was not the hellcat, but rather the saint. Yet still not for him.

McKenna was studying him, obviously watching for a reaction. Gavin deliberately gave him none, though tossed the man a bone. "Grace is lovely."

McKenna turned to him sharply. "But?"

"Pardon?"

McKenna made a low growl of displeasure. "There's clearly more ye want to say. So say it. I'm a man who appreciates a direct and honest approach. I haven't got the time or patience fer diplomacy."

"Neither do I." Gavin drew in a stiff breath, his face giving nothing away of his inner turmoil. McKenna was a man filled with Highland pride that could turn into rage at even the hint of an insult. "Grace is very young."

"She'll turn fifteen this winter."

Gavin barely held back an exclamation of surprise. "She's young enough to be my daughter." He tried, yet failed to completely contain a shudder. "While I'll make no judgments upon a man who chooses a child bride, I personally have no stomach for such a union."

"Aye, I see yer point." McKenna leaned close, his expression hardening, his eyes narrowing. "However, let me remind ye, they are far more pliable at this age. It takes less effort to mold them into what ye want, to teach them to serve and please ye exactly as ye desire."

This time Gavin did shudder. If McKenna thought to entice him with this revelation, he was sorely mistaken. Nay, a child bride was the very last thing Gavin wanted. Give him a woman with intelligence and opinions and the courage to express them. Anything else was unacceptable.

"By chance, have ye any unwed sisters older than the fair Grace?" Gavin asked.

'Twas a calculated risk, for if there was another sister

of marriageable age, Gavin knew he'd have to quickly find a reason that woman was unacceptable as a bride.

McKenna gave him a tight grin. "There's one more McKenna female, but she is my youngest sister. I've promised Beatrice to the church, since Grace has left the nunnery. The abbey was counting on a dowry as well as the protection of the McKennas, should the need arise. They were so reasonable in releasing Grace, I cannae go back on my word to them."

Gavin forced his expression into something he hoped was disappointment. Silently he wondered precisely how reasonable the young laird had been, but it didn't matter. Both Grace and her young sister, Beatrice, were too young to become his bride. And the fiery Caitlyn, bless her heart, was off on an adventure with her French knight.

Relieved the visit was going to end without insult, Gavin sat back in his chair. He was trying to think of an easy way to reopen the discussion about supporting the king, when McKenna pushed back his chair and abruptly stood.

"We thank ye for yer hospitality, but 'tis best that we depart while there's still daylight."

McKenna glanced at the laird's men. They hastily shoved the rest of their food into their mouths, and then quickly drained their tankards. Grace stared at her brother with watery eyes, but she rose to her feet, the determination in her spine strong. Gavin watched her closely, wondering if he had mistaken her character. She appeared to have more of the McKenna spirit inside her than first impressions revealed.

It was chaotic in the bailey as the large group made ready to leave. Grace gave Gavin a regal nod before mounting her horse, then waited as a group of soldiers protectively surrounded her.

Feeling the need to establish some camaraderie, Gavin clapped McKenna on the shoulder as he bid the man farewell. "The time for choosing a side in this conflict is fast approaching. I implore ye to search yer heart and support Robert's just and righteous cause."

"I promise ye that I shall think more seriously upon it."

"Good." Not precisely the answer Gavin hoped to receive, but it was better than an outright rejection.

"I confess it bodes well for the Bruce if he has men of yer ilk supporting him." McKenna swung up on his horse. "Be sure to tell him I said that the next time ye see him."

Gavin planned to return to his chamber the moment the McKenna clan departed, but castle business kept him busy until late in the evening. Taking the task of calling Fiona to the evening meal upon himself, Gavin took the stairs two at a time, only slowing his pace when he reached the chamber door.

He entered, surprised to discover the room was cloaked in darkness. He almost turned to leave, but the sound of a soft sigh from his bed let him know exactly where to find Fiona. Gavin went to her, feeling a quiver of anticipation roll through his entire body. After a tense afternoon with Laird McKenna and several hours of coping with various clan matters, time alone with her was all that he craved.

He sat gingerly on the side of the mattress and Fiona immediately stirred. She turned her head and opened her eyes, blinking several times before a smile lit her face.

"Have your unexpected guests gone?" Fiona asked, her voice groggy with sleep.

"Aye. They left a few hours ago." Gavin leaned over and wrapped his arms around her waist, marveling at how natural and right it always felt to hold her in his arms.

"I heard no sounds of swords clashing below stairs. Does that mean all went well between you and the Highland laird?"

"Mostly."

She reached up, gliding her fingers through his hair, a gesture he found equally comforting and arousing. What was it about her that drew him so strongly? That made him want to forsake his duty and instead fulfill his passion.

"You seem troubled, Gavin. Was there a problem?"

Gavin pulled in a stiff breath. "Laird McKenna wants me to marry his sister."

Fiona went rigid. Her hand stilled, her breath ceased. "Will you?"

"Nay."

An ache tore at him as she released her breath. *Tell her the rest.* Gavin knew this was the perfect opportunity. He was going to have to choose a bride, and soon, most likely taking Aileen Sinclair because an alliance with the Sinclairs was best for his people.

It was what the king wanted and Gavin knew it was his duty to obey. A part of him also knew that Fiona would understand that, yet try as he might, the words did not come.

Coward! His frustration nearly got the better of his temper. Fiona laid her head against his chest. Right or wrong, suddenly none of it seemed to matter. Gavin sighed and rested his chin on the top of her head.

The comforting position had an unexpectedly calming effect, spreading warmth through him like a long sip of the finest whiskey.

"Is there some way I can help?" she asked.

Oh, Fiona! Yer breaking my heart. "Ye just did, lass," he whispered, before turning her in his arms and pressing her back gently against the mattress.

She welcomed him as she always did, freely, openly, the sensual look in her vivid green eyes letting him know how much she wanted him. She invited closeness naturally, weaving a web around him that enthralled and delighted.

For a long moment he held her, the feelings twisting and seething inside him. Then, unable to resist, Gavin slowly, thoroughly made love to Fiona with an honesty and reverence that pierced his heart.

Chapter 12

The familiar sounds of clashing swords mixed with men's laughter drew Fiona's attention as she walked from the chapel across the bailey. Her heart quickened. Was Gavin on the practice field with his men? She craned her head and tried to get a good look, but her view was blocked by a wall of soldiers awaiting their turn to train.

She'd hoped to have at least a few private minutes with him this morning, but Gavin had risen from their bed while she slept. Nothing but cold linens and a faint, intoxicating male scent had greeted her. Though she tried to tell herself she was overreacting, Fiona was worried.

The concern in his eyes when he came to her last night was troubling. She believed it had something to do with the visit from Laird McKenna, even though Gavin claimed all was well in that quarter. But she wanted to know more.

It had been a shock to hear the laird was trying to broker a marriage between his sister and Gavin, but even more distressing was the feeling of dread that had gripped Fiona's heart. *I haven't the right to care!* In desperation, Fiona had repeated those words to herself last night, and again this morning, yet the disappointment curdling in her chest remained.

A cheer went up from the practice field, followed by a smattering of applause. Unbidden, the image of Gavin wielding his sword surfaced in Fiona's mind. Perhaps he was working right now, and the strain of his movements, coupled with the midday warmth, made it necessary for him to remove his shirt. Bare-chested, muscles rippling, torso glistening with sweat each time he lifted his sword and swung it down. *Oh, my.* Fiona's face flushed with heat at the very idea.

Merciful heavens, if Alice had not been walking beside her, Fiona might have given in to the temptation and turned to see what was happening. Her thoughts scattered, devoid of concentration, Fiona stepped squarely in the middle of a rather large puddle, soaking the hem of her gown with muddy water.

"Oh, now that will take more than a bit of scrubbing to get out," Alice complained when she saw the mess on Fiona's gown. "Though I know it's impossible to avoid so much mud in this gloomy place. Why, if it's not raining, then there's fog or mist, and when the sun does shine, 'tis only for a few hours. 'Tis no wonder the Scots are a wild, barbarous people."

"There was no rain yesterday," Fiona remarked, remembering the previous afternoon.

"I know. Yet the puddles from the previous five days remain large enough to sink up to your ankles if you fall into one," Alice grumbled.

Fiona smiled for a brief moment. Was the weather truly that gloomy or was Alice being overly dramatic? Honestly, Fiona had not noticed so much gray around the castle. "I understand that you might be feeling homesick, Alice. Do you wish to return to England?"

"And abandon you, my lady!" Alice clucked her tongue and shook her head. "Never."

Fiona's lips twitched. Alice's loyalty was appreciated, but she could not let the woman suffer. "It would not be a permanent separation if you went back to England. Some day we shall all return, when Spencer claims his rightful inheritance."

"An event I pray for nightly, my lady. But until that joyful day arrives, my place is here with you." Alice drew herself up. "You need me."

"I do," Fiona agreed.

"I cannot bear to think how ill served you would be by one of these Scottish wenches." Alice puffed out her chest. "I shall stay, of course, though I will confess that I shall be very happy the day we depart."

Depart? Fiona had difficulty imagining it. Though they had been here a few short weeks, she was most reluctant to leave. Despite being an oddity, and an outsider, she had a sense of security within these stone walls that gave her a feeling of peace and contentment.

Yet Alice had raised a legitimate point. How long could she stay here? Years? It might take that long for Spencer to be ready to assume control of his legacy.

Fiona sighed. The simple truth was that she would stay until Gavin tired of her. That brought on an even deeper sigh. And what if she tired of him first? Fiona grimaced. What a completely foolish notion. Tire of Gavin? As if that would ever happen!

Another loud cheer from the training area distracted Fiona. Unable to stop herself, she turned and peeked through the crowds. In addition to the soldiers, squires, and pages, several of the household servants and stable boys, as well as a number of villagers, were gathered in a wide circle, intently watching the events.

Moving closer, Fiona followed their gazes and saw that Gavin stood at one end inside the ring, his sword still sheathed in its scabbard, his arms casually crossed. Slightly disappointed, she noted he still wore his shirt, then silently laughed at her foolishness.

Turning her attention to the opposite side of the ring, she beheld his opponent. A much shorter, slighter man, shifting nervously on his feet—Spencer!

Fiona gasped her son's name in horror, but only Alice was near enough to hear. And her maid was every bit as shocked. As for the rest of the crowd, well, they appeared transfixed by what they were about to see. Spencer squared his shoulders, pulled on his helmet and drew his sword. The other squires hooted and clapped.

"Are ye sure about this, lad?" Gavin pulled his sword, easily tossing it from hand to hand.

"I wish to learn from the best," Spencer replied. "I am honored you accepted my plea to spar with you."

Gavin grinned. "Flattery willnae make this any easier fer ye, lad."

Spencer advanced, then assumed a fighting stance. "I never expected that it would."

Clutching the hilt with both hands, Spencer swung his sword in a high arc over his head and brought it down with far more strength than Fiona thought possible. Gavin blocked the blow easily and Fiona felt a moment of pride at her son's prowess, until the piercing clatter reminded her that these were deadly weapons. It would only take a small slip for Spencer to be seriously injured.

With poetic rhythm, the two took turns striking and

avoiding blows. Gavin shouted instructions that Spencer struggled to obey, yet Gavin steadily and easily continued to move Spencer back. It took but a few minutes for Spencer's chest to start rising and falling rapidly, his puffing breath heard clearly throughout the practice field. After one more exchange, Spencer wisely retreated to the other side. He bent at the waist and started wheezing. Fiona's concern mounted.

"Finish him off, milord, so we can eat our midday meal," one of the men shouted.

"Aye, we're hungry and need some humbled squires to serve us," another yelled.

The comment brought a round of boos from the squires, who then started cheering even louder for Spencer. Their support seemed to give the boy a renewed sense of vigor and strengthen his determination. No longer looking defeated, he straightened and stood proudly.

"Do ye yield?" Gavin asked.

Spencer shook his head and charged. Gavin stood at the ready, but instead of swinging his sword, he stepped aside at the last moment, causing the boy to stumble and fall. He advanced and the moment Spencer rolled onto his back, Gavin placed the tip of his sword on Spencer's chest.

Fiona smothered a terrified cry in her fist. At the sound, Gavin looked over at her. Fearing her horrified expression was showing, Fiona hastily backed away from view. It was then she heard a sharp cry of pain, followed by a hissing curse.

Fearing the worst, Fiona craned her head between the two burly men who stood in front of her. She saw Spencer cast his sword to the ground, toss off his helmet and rush toward Gavin. But a ring of soldiers had surrounded the earl, preventing the boy from getting close.

"Forgive me, my lord," Spencer cried. "'Twas a careless mistake."

Fiona could not hear Gavin's reply. He shouted something to the rest of the men. The circle around him melted away. Pointedly ignoring everyone, Gavin stomped away from the practice field, his right hand clasped over his upper left arm.

No one else moved. Most of the men were staring at Gavin with a surprised look of disbelief. The crowd parted silently to allow their lord through, then hurried away.

Fiona hurried, too—to check on Spencer. Alice tried to keep pace with her, but in her haste stepped in a long, shallow puddle. Fiona pressed forward, leaving her blasphemous maid behind.

As she approached, Fiona heard the astonished whispers and expressions of disbelief from Gavin's retainers. Had a squire truly landed a blow against the earl?

"I don't know how it happened," Spencer said, his face lined with worry. "I thought he would easily block the blow, just as he did with all the others. I never meant to strike so hard."

"Ye drew blood," one of the squires said, awe in his tone.

Spencer flinched, then took a few quick breaths. His face sparked with guilt when he caught Fiona's gaze. "Is the earl very angry?" he whispered.

"I suspect his pride is hurt far more than his arm," she replied, keeping the volume of her voice low. "What about you? Are you injured anywhere?"

Fiona sighed with relief when Spencer shook his head. Then the squires closed in, effectively pushing her away. They were giddy with excitement, patting Spencer on the back and congratulating him loudly enough for those still in the area to hear. For his part, Spencer refused to meet their gazes, hanging his head and looking utterly miserable.

After assuring herself that Spencer was physically unharmed, Fiona left. When she entered the great hall she met a scowling Gavin standing in front of one of the enormous fireplaces, a fretting Hamish at his side.

"Shall I summon the healer from the village, milord?" Hamish asked, his brow knit with worry.

"Nay. 'Tis only a scratch."

Fiona's eyes flew to Gavin's blood-coated fingers. "It appears to be far more than a scratch," she refuted, reaching up to touch Gavin's arm.

He hissed in pain and jerked away. "I said it was merely a flesh wound."

"Best allow me to take a look," Fiona advised. "I've seen many a good knight suffer mightily from a small, festering wound."

Reminding her far too much of Spencer when he was in a snit, Gavin reluctantly allowed Fiona to pry his fingers away from his arm. The moment they were removed, a well of fresh blood surfaced.

Fiona sucked in her breath when she saw Gavin's arm. The wound was deep and jagged, tearing away a good portion of the flesh.

"It will need stitches," she declared.

Gavin gave her a wary look. "Are ye certain? Or are ye just looking fer an excuse to stab me with a needle?"

Fiona leaned closer and whispered in his ear. "Well, my lord, you do take every opportunity you can to give me a poke. I think 'tis past time that I return the favor."

He smiled wolfishly, as she had hoped, the wound

momentarily forgotten. Taking advantage of the distraction, Fiona sat Gavin in a chair, then quickly dispatched Alice to fetch a needle and thread and Hamish to bring hot water, clean bandages, and medicinal herbs.

Gavin shut his eyes as she playfully removed his shirt, the tight, white line around his lips conveying the depth of his pain. When Alice and Hamish returned, the pair hovered over her curiously until a glare from Gavin had the steward bowing politely and both of the servants quickly leaving.

Fiona presented Gavin with a healthy portion of whiskey, which he downed in two gulps. Waiting a few moments for the strong spirits to take the edge off, Fiona began gently cleansing the wound. She sopped up the warm water as it trickled down Gavin's arm, wrung the cloth out, then started again. The water in the bowl soon turned red, but she was pleased to see the bleeding had slowed.

Fiona's brow furrowed as she threaded the needle. Pinching the jagged edges of Gavin's flesh together between her thumb and forefinger, she made small, neat stitches. Gavin clenched his mouth and turned his head, but he never once flinched.

Fiona was grateful. Though she had learned, and was often called upon, to practice the healing arts, it was never easy piercing a man's flesh, especially one who was squirming and screaming. Thankfully, Gavin had spared her that added difficulty.

When she finished, Fiona mixed a salve with the herbs and honey Hamish had brought. She spread it liberally over the wound, then wrapped it with a clean cloth. She placed her palm across his forehead, soothing him while at the same time checking for any sign of fever.

"I still cannot credit that Spencer was the one who did that to you," she murmured.

"A streak of sunlight flashed off his blade and temporarily blinded me," Gavin grumbled.

"Really? It must have been a very fleeting burst of sunshine," Fiona commented in a lighthearted tone. "The skies have been gray and cloudy all day."

"Cease gloating, please." Gavin flexed his arm and rotated his shoulder, grimacing slightly at the movement. "I plead an English conspiracy. Ye deliberately distracted me as ye were standing in the crowd while yer son attacked me."

"Oh, is that how it happened?" Fiona stepped back, resting her hands on her hips. "Lest I remind you, 'twas you who taught Spencer that fighting fair doesn't always win."

"Aye, but Spencer has no need of cheap tricks. The lad has real skill."

Fiona's heart gladdened at hearing the compliment. She had convinced herself that with the proper training Spencer would be able to overcome his physical limitations. 'Twas a tremendous relief to discover she was right.

"He's had a good teacher," she said.

Gavin shrugged. "I take little credit. Duncan trains the squires. He works them hard, but the results are promising."

Fiona smiled. "I know you've been giving Spencer extra attention. Thank you."

"No thanks are necessary. 'Tis part of our agreement, after all."

Her heart squeezed. "Yes, of course." She turned away and busied herself with clearing the medical supplies, trying not to react to his words. Words that struck at her heart, cutting her to the quick as they delivered a cold shock of reality.

This was a business arrangement between them. An exchange of bartered services. Gavin agreed to foster her son and train him to be a knight and in exchange she slept in his bed.

'Twas nothing more and nothing less.

Though painful, Gavin's remarks were a stark reminder that she was a fool to ever forget it.

Gavin saw Fiona's expression tighten with hurt and he wanted to bite his tongue until it bled. First, he'd humiliated himself on the practice field by allowing himself to become careless, and now he had opened his mouth and stuck his booted foot inside it.

He reached for her and she tried to push him away, but he persisted, catching her wrist and pulling her toward him.

"Curse my thoughtless tongue," Gavin said as he stroked Fiona's cheek. "'Tis far more than merely an arrangement between us, lass. We both know it."

"You owe me nothing, my lord."

She spoke the words with such pain in her voice it nearly tore his own heart in two. Logically, Gavin knew he had nothing to feel guilty about. He had not forced her into this position—hell, becoming his mistress had been her suggestion.

Yet there was no denying that their relationship had long progressed beyond a mutually beneficial arrangement. They shared something deeper, something whole and true. 'Twas something that Gavin freely admitted he couldn't define, yet couldn't ignore. To do so would be an insult to both of them.

"I fear we've gotten ourselves in far deeper than either of us anticipated," he said softly.

Her eyes fluttered open and met his. She exhaled a weighty sigh, a deep furrow wrinkling her brow. "What do you propose we do?" she asked.

He raised her hand to his lips and kissed it, a courtly, respectful gesture. "Enjoy every minute of it," he replied.

The following days took on a routine that Gavin found both exhilarating and oddly comforting. Each night, he would tumble Fiona into his bed and make love to her. Nay, with her. Sometimes it was quick and intense, when his ravenous hunger needed instantly to be fed. Other times it was slow and tender and surprisingly even more explosive.

They explored each other's body with reverence, delighting in discovering what brought the other pleasure. He was insatiable, unable to keep himself from touching Fiona, even as they slept. The heat and urgency he felt whenever he was near her was impossible to control, the feelings that surrounded him as she lay naked next to him indescribable.

Once sated, he would gather Fiona in his arms, basking in a feeling of completion. There in the darkness the conversations would begin—tales of their youth, who had been important and influential as they grew to adulthood, what dreams and hopes had they secretly kept. Who and what had brought them happiness—and sadness.

Gavin told her outrageous stories of his boyhood adventures, exaggerating his antics until her smiles turned to giggles. She spoke of her life as a young girl and the close bond she'd had with her mother along with the inconsolable sorrow she suffered when that good woman died from childbed fever when Fiona was eight years old.

Revealing who they were as children, and later young adults, established a deeper understanding between them. But it wasn't only the past they discussed. They talked—and argued—about nearly everything—politics, the tyranny of kings, the merits of French wine, and the best way to roast a flavorful haunch of venison.

The one subject they never broached was the future. Gavin wanted to believe it was because they had agreed to live in the moment, but that was only partially true. Looking too far ahead would jeopardize what they shared and he was not prepared to sacrifice this unexpected gift of happiness.

However, as this sharing brought them closer and closer, Gavin grew concerned. He had never opened himself to a woman as he had to her.

His dependency on Fiona had the potential to become a dilemma. He craved, nay hungered, for her day and night. No matter how often he had her, he still wanted more. It was dangerous, precarious, for he worried if his need would ever be truly filled.

Yet when these dark thoughts reared their ugly head, Gavin thrust them from his mind. He was happy now, in a way that had never before been a part of his life. He was no longer alone and isolated, and neither was Fiona. He would relish these rare glimpses of contentment while he was able to hold them in his grasp.

Still, he was not so naive to believe that the future would somehow take care of itself.

* * *

Aidan let out a battle cry and swung his heavy sword wide. Reacting at the last moment, Gavin barely had time to avoid a slice to his gut.

"Yer distracted," Duncan called out from the sidelines, scrutinizing him with narrow, speculative eyes. "First a squire lands a blow that has ye bleeding like a wild boar, and now Aidan nearly opens yer belly with one stroke of his blade. Maybe 'tis best if ye cut yer training short today."

Ignoring the remark, Gavin lifted his shield. Aidan struck again and their sparring quickly intensified. But when Gavin thrust his sword forward and hit nothing but air, he knew it was time to quit.

Duncan was right; he was distracted. Breathing hard, Gavin stepped back and held up his palm to stave off Aidan's next attack. Aidan instantly lowered his sword.

"Are ye hungry?" Duncan asked. "Ye dinnae break yer fast with us in the hall this morning. A man can't put up a strong fight with a growling stomach."

"I'd wager 'tis lack of a proper night's sleep that has his lordship so sluggish today," Aidan snickered.

"I believe ye are right, brother. Yet I must agree that winning the favor of the fair Lady Fiona is worth a few cuts and bruises," Duncan chided.

"Bugger off," Gavin grumbled, shooting them both a nasty glare.

The truth was Gavin was neither hungry nor tired, but rather clouded with indecision and inertia. With each passing day, the promise he'd made to the king weighed heavier on his mind. Just last night, after Fiona had drifted off to sleep, he'd reluctantly pulled himself away from the cozy warmth of the bed to once again study the matter. Lighting a candle, he sat at the table in his chamber and peered at the list of potential brides that the king had given him, his mind and gut churning.

That damn list, with names that were no longer letters on parchment. They were flesh and blood women and he needed to make a final decision as to which one of them he would take as his next wife. Aileen Sinclair was the logical choice. They had all agreed. Yet still he hesitated, refusing to make the final commitment.

Time was moving too swiftly. He wanted to halt it, freeze it, keep things exactly as they were right now. Peace and prosperity for his clan, good cheer and laughter in his hall, and Fiona at his side and in his bed. Was that such an unreasonable wish?

Gavin sighed. A reckoning was coming; he knew he could no longer put off making a decision. Robert requested a marital alliance and one did not deny a king. Especially since Gavin knew how important this alliance was for Robert's cause.

Yet every time he thought of taking another wife, the face that instantly sprung to mind was one of golden, refined beauty. With green sparkling eyes, a broad smile, and a fierce, loyal soul.

Fiona.

It was impossible, of course, a circumstance Gavin knew could never warrant any serious thought. Marry an English widow—never! Yet as he sat, brooding at that table in the predawn hours, he was almost astounded to realize that Fiona was, without question, the choice of his heart.

Why? Well, that brought forth another nearly incomprehensible truth. He admitted his feelings for Fiona were complex. He also admitted that he had great difficulty acknowledging the depth and strength of these emotions. How had this happened? How had she so seamlessly wound her way inside his head, inside his heart?

How had she changed his world so completely that he now experienced this sentiment so profoundly, so intensely? A sentiment that until this moment he was sure was mythical, something that very rarely existed between a man and a woman.

Love.

Gavin's mind fairly spun at the concept. Unselfish, all consuming, astonishingly intense.

Aye, love.

He had fallen in love with his mistress.

Chapter 13

The morning mist burned off slowly, and a golden hue spread throughout the countryside. The bright, sunny weather served to heighten the excitement that was already buzzing throughout the castle, for today was the start of the yearly fair. Fiona had been informed of this event by no less than three different people as she made her way to the great hall to break her fast, and their enthusiasm was impossible to resist.

She was disappointed to discover that Gavin had already eaten and was gone from the hall, but he left a message with Hamish requesting that she be ready to attend the festivities in the village with him as the noon hour approached.

Pleased that they would be able to enjoy the fair together, Fiona ate her meal in contemplative silence. This past week had been the happiest of all since her arrival in Scotland. Gavin had been very busy, as always; in fact, she had seen less of him than usual.

But the time they had spent together had been special, infused with intimacy and affection. Having these moments together had made it possible for Fiona to put aside her fears for their future and let the warmth of these emotions embrace her.

As promised, Fiona and Gavin set out for the fair at the appointed hour. As they walked past the village toward the open field where the merchants had set up their carts and tents, Gavin curved his arm across Fiona's shoulders, holding her close. The scent of him filled her, and her heart thudded in response.

Fiona couldn't resist the urge to smile. The enjoyment showing in Gavin's face reminded her of Spencer. Who would have believed such a fierce warrior could have such a boyish streak?

As they came closer, the strains of music could be heard; the trill of pipes and the rhythmic beat of the drums. There were couples dancing while others clapped and stomped their feet. Kegs of ale were set on a wooden table and both the dancers and musicians were imbibing freely.

Fiona observed one of the pretty maids, a tray filled with tankards, give Duncan a saucy wink. His brothers started hooting, their teasing yells carrying in the breeze. Fiona saw Duncan swagger up to the maid and whisper something in her ear that soon had her blushing.

"What do ye want to do first?" Gavin asked.

Fiona took a deep breath and immersed herself in the sights and sounds around her. There were acrobats, jugglers, and ropewalkers, along with merchants in rows on either side of a makeshift path, their carts and brightly decorated stalls showcasing their wares. Bolts of cloth, yards of ribbon, small jars of exotic spices. There were bags made of the softest leather and casks filled with imported wine. Soaps and candles and pottery of various shapes and sizes.

The smell of roasting meat mingled with the sounds of excited conversation. The lighthearted, festive mood was contagious. This was a day to leave behind the drudgery and monotony of daily life, to indulge and enjoy. It seemed something that Gavin's people understood very well and were undertaking with ease.

"I've never been to a market fair this large," Fiona confided. "I scarcely know where to look."

"First we shop," Gavin decided. "Then we feast."

He took her hand. She turned and he gave her a grin that melted her bones. Still reeling from his gaze, Fiona allowed herself to be led to the first cart. The pleasant, floral scent engulfed her as she gazed at the flakes and bars of soap and the long, tapered candles.

"Which items catch yer fancy?" Gavin asked.

Fiona's eyes widened. The ordinary, dark yellow candles were made from tallow, but the pale candles were fashioned from beeswax, which Fiona knew gave off a much brighter light.

"'Tis frivolous to buy something we already make ourselves," she whispered to Gavin.

"This is not at all like the ash or tallow soap we use," he countered. "Or the fish oil soap that's only fit fer the laundry."

"Or bathing my dog," Fiona said with a grin.

"I've heard the most luxurious soaps are made in Spain," Gavin said.

"Just so, milord," the merchant replied eagerly. "They use olive oil and add aromatic herbs. Try this one."

The merchant handed Gavin a cake of soap. He sniffed, then placed it under Fiona's nose. She inhaled the rich scent of pine.

"Rosemary," the merchant said before Fiona could inquire.

"'Tis far better than smelling like a bunch of flowers," Gavin said. "I'll take a dozen. And three pounds of beeswax candles."

Purchases made, they moved on, passing a stall with rounds of cheese. The pungent smell was not unpleasant, making Fiona's mouth water.

Next was the cloth merchant's stall. Long pieces of fabric were arranged in neat piles by color and type, stacked one on top of the other, while some were hung over the wooden joists at the top of the stall.

Fiona was impressed. Twisting her head from side to side, she wasn't certain where to look first. There were piles of wool, damask, and linen cloth, of varying texture and quality. Clearly, this merchant knew it was best to offer something for all classes of buyers.

She picked up the end of a piece of yellow wool, amazed at the softness. The tight weave would provide a solid protection against a winter wind, yet it was delicate enough to wear against the skin without chaffing.

"I see the lady has an eye for quality," the cloth merchant said with a broad smile. "That is the finest wool weave you can find, but I have something even better suited to the lady's beauty."

The merchant reached into the wagon behind him and lifted out an armful of silk. Fiona's eyes widened at the vibrant red, blue, green, and gold colors, but it was the feel of the fabric that had her sighing in wonder.

"'Tis light as a feather," Gavin commented as he fingered the silk. "Do ye like it?"

"'Tis beautiful, the finest quality I have ever seen."

Fiona cast a final, longing glance at the beautiful material. "But I'm sure the cost is too dear."

"I can afford to buy ye whatever ye desire," Gavin said.

"Shh, don't let him hear you say that!" Fiona glanced anxiously at the merchant, then lowered her voice for Gavin's ears only. "I thought the Scots appreciated the art of negotiating a good bargain."

"They do," Gavin replied. "But it isn't necessary to beggar a man either."

"He'll make a profit as well you know," she hissed. Turning to the merchant, Fiona assumed an air of indifference. "The silk is pretty, though I'm not certain I like the colors. I find them to be rather ordinary."

The merchant's brow rose. "The lady is English?"

Gavin's hand reached down for his sword handle. "Aye."

The merchant stepped back, holding his hands aloft and waving them dramatically in apology. "Please, milord, no offense was meant. I was merely surprised when I heard the lady speak."

Fiona was silent, her thumb rubbing against the smooth fabric. She had not taken offense at the merchant's inquiry, for she had grown accustomed to such reactions. But it was Gavin's passionate defense of her that made her ache to throw her arms around him and hug him tightly.

"Since the earl insists on buying some of your cloth, I shall ask you for your very best price for a bolt of the blue silk," Fiona said, acting as though she was doing the merchant a great favor by allowing him to sell her his wares. "But before you answer, I should warn you, good sir, an English lady is far more difficult to please than the fair maidens of Scotland."

It took but a few moments for Gavin to realize that Fiona truly was a master at bartering. By the time she was finished, she had acquired bolts of satin, silk, linen, and wool, with thread and ribbons to match and a fine assortment of sewing needles at half the price he would have most likely paid.

From there they moved at a snail's pace, examining and sampling the wares at each cart and booth. As she exclaimed over the variety and quality of the items, Gavin waited with good humor for Fiona to turn to him with pleading eyes when she came across something she desired, but she never once asked. The leather pouch of coins hanging from his belt remained full and heavy.

"Do ye see nothing that ye like?" he finally asked.

She looked surprised. "I don't expect you to buy me anything. 'Tis the looking that I enjoy the most."

Gavin had a difficult time believing her, but for the next hour Fiona stayed true to her word, never once indicating there was something that truly caught her fancy.

A cheer went up and Gavin turned. He saw a crowd clustered at the end of the row of carts and stalls. He captured Fiona's hand and tugged her down to the gathering, annoyed when he saw a wrestling match about to begin. Shaking his head, Gavin pushed forward, but Fiona pulled him back.

"You aren't going to wrestle that giant tree trunk of a man, are you?" she asked.

Gavin wasn't certain if he should feel insulted by the incredulous tone she used or pleased at the underlying worry in her expression. He raised a brow. "Are ye implying that I would lose?"

"Not exactly. Though I will say that I prefer you with all of your limbs in one piece."

"If ye must know, I intend to stop the match from

starting. I don't want any of my men injured. Last year that fellow broke several of Duncan's ribs."

Fiona clucked with disgust. Interpreting that as approval, Gavin pushed himself through the crowd and spoke with his men. When he was finished, he returned to Fiona, took her hand once again and followed his nose to the area where food was being prepared.

He purchased a few meat pies, cheese, and fruit while Fiona waited at a wooden table set beneath a tree. Feeling a need for privacy, Gavin did not join her there, but instead continued walking, motioning for her to follow him.

"Is anything wrong?" Fiona asked in alarm.

"Nay. I'm just trying to steal a few moments alone with ye."

A short while later they were walking down a sloping hill, nearing the lush valley below. The noise of the fair faded, then disappeared completely. They reached a field of yellow and lavender wildflowers and Fiona bent to pick some. When her hands were full, Gavin led her to a shady tree, bidding her to sit beneath it. He nestled beside her, taking in the peaceful view of the distant mountains and the sound of birds trilling in the treetops.

It was strange how this vast space felt so intimate. Perhaps because they were seated side by side? He liked the feel of Fiona's legs brushing against his thighs, reveled in the clean smell of her hair and skin. It was a scent he never grew tired of, because it reminded him of her.

Fiona unpinned and removed her veil, allowing her hair to become loose in the gentle breeze. The curls floated freely around her face, a few of the longer locks cascading down her back. It warmed Gavin's heart to see her looking so peaceful.

"Did ye enjoy the fair?" he asked.

"Well, 'twas very grand, unlike any other I have ever seen. The last time I attended a fair was five, nay six years ago. A band of tinkers was traveling through the village and Henry allowed them to stay overnight. He was not interested in seeing their wares, but I enjoyed the diversion. Spencer and Alice went with me. I remember we returned with our arms laden with goods."

"I feel like a miser," Gavin lamented. "I've bought ye nothing but a few bolts of cloth and some sewing needles and thread."

She waved a dismissive hand. "'Tis what I asked for and I am heartily pleased to have received them."

"I do have a wee token." Gavin reached inside his tunic and pulled out a small bottle made of deep green glass. Placing it in the center of his palm, he held it out to Fiona. "The sparkling color reminded me of yer eyes."

"I've never seen anything so fine," Fiona exclaimed in a hushed voice.

Gavin lifted the vessel higher. Sunlight reflected off the delicate glass, illuminating the tree trunk with a glittering green color. "The bottle is but one part of the gift." He removed the glass stopper and passed it beneath her nose.

Fiona's chest expanded as she took a deep breath. "It smells like heaven," she proclaimed.

"Aye, lass. It smells like ye. Irresistible heaven."

To emphasize his words, he cupped a hand behind Fiona's head and drew her forward. He kissed her temple, then her cheek, and lastly the sweet spot just below her ear.

A giggle bubbled up from her throat. She sounded as carefree as a young maiden. Gavin decided he liked the sound. He wanted to see more smiles, more serenity on her lovely face. He wanted to be the one to relieve the burdens she carried on her shoulders with such grace and dignity, to set to rights the wrongs she had endured.

Being around Fiona made him feel like more of a man, more of a protector, a leader. 'Twas strange, considering the emotions she evoked inside his heart. Many men he knew loudly proclaimed that loving a woman made you weak, foolish. But loving Fiona had the opposite effect on him.

Fiona carefully tucked the bottle of perfume in the pocket of her gown while Gavin arranged their simple meal. He unwrapped the linen cloth of meat pies, cheese, and fruit he had bought, then using the cloth as a blanket, laid out the food upon it.

They dug into the meat pies first, then grabbing his small-bladed eating knife, Gavin cut the pear and passed Fiona a slice. She took it with a smile, the sweet juices running down her fingers. She was dainty, but not delicate when she ate, and Gavin enjoyed the earthy sensuality of watching her savor every bite. The sight of her lips closing around the succulent fruit with such enthusiasm was an almost erotic experience.

Desire raced through his blood like a rampant fever. Her every movement, no matter how mundane, seemed to reach out and beckon to him. He pulled in a heavy breath and looked away. He was a man of experience, not a raw lad lusting after his first wench. Where did she get the power to reduce him to such a randy fool? To fluster him as though he were a blushing maiden?

Gavin stretched out on his side, one hand holding up his head, the other resting on the curve of her hip. He lowered his lids and cast her a bold, suggestive glance, hoping for a similar reaction. Awareness crackled in the air between them.

Yet Fiona pretended not to notice, inspected the palm of her hand with great interest, though she would have to be blind as a bat not to see the evidence of his desire. Gavin tried to hide his disappointment as Fiona busied herself clearing the remains of their repast. His ploy hadn't worked. She had clearly gotten his message, yet preferred to ignore it.

She crumbled the uneaten crust of the meat pie and tossed it on the grass. "For the birds," she explained when Gavin raised his brows.

"Ye're too tenderhearted," he quipped.

"Hardly a fault." Fiona's lips rose into a wavy smile as she leaned down and placed her palms on the sleek muscles of his shoulders. Their eyes met. Gavin felt his body harden, felt the temptation.

"If you are going to ravish me, my lord, you'd best get started while we still have daylight."

Gavin's features contorted into confusion and Fiona's smile widened. She liked that she could surprise him, could catch him off guard. It gave her a feeling of control, a sense that she had an equal part in their relationship.

Fiona pressed herself closer, draping her body across Gavin's. They were face-to-face, chins nearly touching. He leaned back on his elbows to give her greater access, blinking against the glare of sunlight that fell over his eyes from that prone position.

She stared at his mouth and felt desire stir within her, tightening her nipples, heating and dampening her inner thighs. Yet Gavin appeared unaffected. His expression was content, almost lazy, his eyelids lowering as though he were going to sleep.

Does he know how he makes me feel?

Lifting her chin, Fiona kissed him. Gavin's languid pose disappeared instantly and his lips parted eagerly, encouraging the sensual teasing play of her tongue. Lost in the haze of desire, Fiona moved her lips and tongue in a slow, provocative rhythm. Rejoicing in the sensations, she ran her hands over his hard body, drawing infinite pleasure from the touch.

Was this the usual reaction between lovers? Did their hearts race and their blood warm and their breaths catch whenever they drew near? Did they joke and tease and laugh together? Did they share their thoughts and hopes with the same commitment as their bodies? Did they hold and keep each other as fiercely as they claimed one another?

Fiona shifted her position again. Gavin inhaled sharply, then let out a soft groan. The evidence of his arousal was hard and unmistakable, poking insistently into her soft belly. She felt her body responding to his as a matter of course and wondered at the intensity of the mysterious bond they shared.

She looked at him another minute and then allowed the dam inside her to break. The feelings of hope and passion and excitement rushed forth, filling Fiona with purpose.

It took little effort to rapidly divest Gavin of his clothes. His muscles rippled as he stretched his arms over his head, switching to a more comfortable position. Fiona had always admired his fit body, yet seeing it unclothed in the bright light of day was an almost humbling experience.

In her eyes, he was beautiful. Some might object to

the puckered scar across his left shoulder or find the thick, dark swirls of hair that cover his upper chest and lower abdomen unattractive. But not her. Scars and all, imperfect as God made him, her attention was fully captivated by this noble man.

Emboldened, she flattened her palm on the tight muscles of his flat belly. He squirmed as the tips of her fingers sensually traced the heated flesh from side to side. With each movement, her hand deliberately went lower and lower, causing his whole body to clench.

Fiona stilled and put her hand over his heart. The sound of Gavin's breaths coming in short, sharp pants made her feel wicked. And free. She wanted more of it. Glorying in the freedom, she continued with her explorations, this time using her lips. His muscled flesh was warm in most places, yet hot in others.

She began kissing his stomach as she ran her fingers lightly along his inner thighs. Gavin's hips jerked forward. Eagerly, Fiona grasped them and pulled him closer, blowing a warm breath on his turgid penis.

"Is it all right if I . . . ?" Fiona inquired in a throaty tone, her voice trailing off deliberately.

"Ye're a witch to tease and torture me," he rasped, moving his hands down her back until he cupped her bottom.

Fiona raised her head and assumed an air of innocence. "Do you wish me to stop?"

"Minx. Ye know very well my heart will shatter from disappointment if ye turn away from me now."

"That sounds dreadfully serious, my lord." Fiona swirled her tongue teasingly through the springy hair at the base of his manhood. "I simply cannot allow it."

"Jesus, lass," he said raggedly.

She took his straining penis into her mouth, first

stroking his length with her tongue, then surrounding the sensitive tip with her lips. She heard his gasp of shock, quickly followed by a series of deep moans of pleasure.

From this angle it was impossible to see his jaw clench and strain, but Fiona could easily imagine it. She continued her ministrations, her tongue stroking slickly against his hardness, increasing the pressure and rhythm, mimicking the act of love.

She licked and suckled and teased every inch of him, caressing his length with her tongue, massaging his inner thighs and heavy sack with her fingertips. Inexperienced with the act, Fiona let Gavin's reactions guide her moves, his writhing hips letting her know she was getting it right.

Suddenly, he grasped her shoulders firmly and groaned loud and long. He tried to pull away from her, but she held fast, overwhelmed by the trusting intimacy of the act.

"My God, Fiona."

His hips jerked and she felt the searing heat of his seed on her tongue. It was the most intimate, erotic thing she had ever experienced and she sighed deeply with pleasure, savoring every moment, continuing to gently absorb his pulsing quivers as they slowed and then finally ceased.

"Did I please you?" she whispered, when she was at last able to catch her breath.

Like a lazy, contented cat, Gavin stretched his back and shoulders and raised himself on his elbows. His head was tilted against the tree trunk and he watched her through heavy-lidded eyes. "Nay, ye dinnae please me, Fiona. Ye astounded and delighted me. I've never felt anything like it."

"I knew you'd like it," she confessed, running her hands across his damp chest.

His arms tightened around her and he kissed the top of her head. Copying his feline movements, Fiona snuggled against him, stretching and pressing, caressing him with her entire body. It felt wantonly sinful to rub his taut, naked flesh while she remained fully clothed. Gavin apparently felt the same, judging by his low-throated groans.

"Gavin," she murmured, looking down at his large, callused hands. Masculine and strong, yet they held her with such tenderness. It was part of the enigma Fiona found so irresistible. "Will you make love to me now?"

They worked together to push her gown up and out of the way. He grasped her hand and pressed a tender kiss in her palm, so delicately, reverently, as though she were as fragile and precious as the blown glass perfume bottle he had bought for her.

When Gavin spread her thighs with his knees and moved between her legs, Fiona reached up joyfully to embrace him, longing for the moment when they would once again be joined as one. He entered her slick warmth forcefully, filling the emptiness inside with one strong thrust. She moaned and arched, pulling him deeper. Passion rising, she clung to him, kissing his neck, his shoulder, his cheek. She could feel his heart beating against her breast in a synchronized rhythm. Together. As one.

"Fiona, my love," he groaned, sinking deeper.

My love? His gentle words brought tears to her eyes. He doesn't mean it, she reprimanded herself sternly.

He is merely caught in the pleasure of it all, lost in a moment of passion.

Still, the words surrounded her heart as strongly as his body surrounded her flesh. The empty yearning inside her eased, the protective shell she tried so hard to maintain began to splinter and crack. Here and now, in this moment of sheer honesty, she let herself embrace her deepest feelings without restraint, allowed herself to experience what she had never believed possible.

He kissed her hard, pushing himself deeper inside. She flexed her inner muscles, pulling him closer, holding him tighter. Every inch of her throbbed at the feel of him. The tenderness in his eyes seared her heart, scorched her soul.

She parted her thighs to try and bring him deeper, lifting her hips to follow his rhythm. The gesture drove him wild. Gavin moved faster and faster, pounding his flesh against hers, willing her sensitive flesh to crest, to explode. Claiming her mouth once again, he slipped his fingers between their bodies, caressing the delicate flesh where they were joined.

Fiona felt herself responding immediately, her body shattering, crashing. She let out a thin, high cry of exhilaration as the pleasure broke and oblivion claimed her.

The final pulses of pleasure were still rippling through her body when she felt Gavin's urgent, violent shudders begin. It rippled through her body and she felt herself responding, losing herself in the wonder of knowing in this moment he was utterly and completely hers.

It slowed, then stopped, yet Fiona continued to hold Gavin tightly. She could feel his forehead resting against hers. Finally, she managed to open her eyes and found Gavin staring into them, the intensity of his emotions nearly overwhelming. For a long moment she became lost in his gaze, linked to him beyond the physical, beyond the emotional.

Time stilled.

The passionate fire was still evident in the depths of his blue eyes, but it was overshadowed by tenderness. Fiona pressed her face into the solid wall of his shoulder, inhaling the familiar musky scent. The ancients might have developed a method to create perfume, but this was a fragrance that she would pay any price to have within her reach.

Burrowing closer, she basked in the sweet afterglow of pleasure, savoring the protective, loving feeling pouring through her, shutting her mind to any thoughts of the future.

This is, she decided, *a most perfect moment*. And she was determined to catch and hold it tight for as long as possible. Secure and comforted, Fiona dozed, the smile on her lips still evident when she awoke.

Yet as she watched Gavin dress, it was impossible not to reflect on what had just happened between them. What she shared with Gavin was stronger than anything she had ever known. The way he made her feel, the kindness she saw hiding behind his rough command, the tenderness beneath his tough exterior. Fiona closed her eyes, overcome with emotions that gripped her from deep inside.

In that bittersweet moment Fiona admitted what she had long suspected. Despite her best efforts to remain immune, to hold fast to her defenses, it had happened.

I love him.

The revelation made her feel light-headed and she nearly stumbled and lost her footing.

"Careful, Fiona."

His deep voice rang out at the same time his strong arms reached out. To hold her. To steady her. To prevent her from coming to harm.

But for how long? Fiona shivered as the cold, cruel hand of reality closed around her heart.

Chapter 14

The smell of roasting meat drew Ewan's attention to the crackling fire. He had trapped two hares early this morning and the skinned pair were now being slowly turned on a spit over the flames. It would provide a fine afternoon meal for him and his companion, once William returned from the village.

Information was critical for the survival of Ewan and his men and William was his best informant. Not many paid attention to the skinny youth who slid unobtrusively throughout the village, his ears attuned to any and all gossip. With summer coming to a close, it was essential that they learn when the various crops were being harvested and where the yield was going to be stored.

Like any good provider, Ewan was very aware that he needed to start laying in stores for the winter for himself, his mother, the men who followed him, and their families. Since they had no large fields to grow any food for themselves, it was necessary to *acquire* whatever they needed. And just like honest men who toiled in the fields, it was necessary to start planning and storing these goods away as soon as they were able.

A strong wind shifted through the leafy trees, but both the fire and Ewan were well protected. He heard the swallows chirping, but his mind was occupied with more important matters than the singing birds.

A rustling in the brush had Ewan reaching for his sword. William emerged from the woods, a smug expression on his face.

"It smells grand." Licking his lips, the young man sat down on a low boulder across from Ewan. "Is it ready?"

Ewan smiled, remembering well his own ravenous hunger when he was William's age. "Have a care not to burn yer fingers or yer tongue," he warned as he hacked off a quarter of the hare and passed it over.

William bit into the charred meat with relish, wiping the meat juices that trickled down his chin with his shirtsleeve.

"I did as ye bid and stayed away from the shops, but it grew harder when my belly started to growl." William wiped the last bit of meat juice off his chin, then gazed hopefully at Ewan.

Damn, the lad could eat the legs off a table. Silently, Ewan sliced off another large portion of the rabbit and placed it in William's eagerly outstretched hands.

"Did ye hear anything of interest?" Ewan asked.

"Aye. They'll be sending a cart full of grain to the abbey on Friday next," William answered before taking another bite. "'Twill have an escort, but there shouldn't be too many soldiers."

"We can handle them. A full grain cart is too ripe an opportunity to let pass." Ewan poked at the flame with the long end of a stick. "What other news?"

"Well, ye already know about the fair they held last week."

"Aye." Ewan sighed. A fair was no small matter, something that brought excitement and pleasure. Several of his men had wanted to attend, but Ewan had forbidden it, fearing they might be recognized and captured. There was grumbling and annoyance, but as far as Ewan knew, he had been obeyed.

"There was still a lot of talk about the day the McKennas rode through, led by their laird," William reported. "They only stayed fer a few hours, but the earl provided a feast fer them. The cooks were complaining about the food they had to prepare at the last minute since all the McKenna guardsmen were invited into the great hall to partake."

Och, now that must have cost the earl dearly. Hospitality was one thing, a large feast another. The earl obviously wanted to impress the McKennas. Why?

"What else?" Ewan asked.

"The earl's got himself a leman." William tossed the rabbit bones, now picked clean, onto a small pile and rubbed his stomach. "Her name is Lady Fiona."

"Is she blond?" Ewan asked, wanting to confirm the identity of the woman he had seen at the loch a few weeks ago.

"I dinnae see her. The men say she is a golden beauty, but the women, fie, the women said 'tis disgraceful. She's an English noblewoman. A widow with a son."

"English? Are ye certain ye heard that right?"

"I did indeed." William slapped at the bug that had settled on his arm. "Heard it from nearly everyone who mentioned her."

Ewan stroked his chin thoughtfully. Now that was an

interesting tidbit. It had to be a passing fancy, keeping an Englishwoman inside the castle, not a situation that would continue for very long. And when the earl was finished with her . . .

Ewan rubbed his neck. The power of a woman scorned could never be underestimated. All he need do was look to his own mother to see the effects. The hatred she carried was twisted deep inside her soul.

Would this Lady Fiona feel the same way once she and the earl parted?

If so, she could become an ally. Who knew what secrets she had uncovered while living inside the castle, sleeping in the earl's bed? The information that she could provide would be invaluable, making Ewan's goal to cause trouble for his half brother easier and much more effective.

The fire hissed as the dripping rabbit juices fell. William looked toward the spit with longing. Without asking, Ewan pulled off the remaining section of one of the hares and passed it over to the lad. He had more than earned his meal this day.

While William ate, Ewan pondered, his mind again returning to the earl's mistress. He was convinced this mysterious woman was the key to striking at the heart of the earl's holdings. All he need do was figure out how to cross paths with her.

"Have ye made yer decision?" Duncan asked.

Gavin felt a hitch in his chest and the biting pull of invisible chains around his entire body at the question. His duty to his king and his clan could not be ignored or stalled any longer. He needed to make an offer to one of the women Robert had suggested and take a wife.

To that end, he had sent Duncan on a mission to the Sinclair clan three days ago. He had returned with a favorable report of the clan, and Lady Aileen, leaving Gavin with no legitimate excuses or reasons to delay.

He stomped down the corridor and Duncan followed. Gavin was distracted, tired, and ornery and in no mood for this conversation.

"I've taken into account what ye learned on yer visit and have decided to offer fer Sinclair's daughter. Along with his lands and wealth, he's got the best-trained, most disciplined soldiers. That makes marrying her the best choice."

"She's fair to look at, with a lively spirit and a fine figure," Duncan added. "I was surprised to see she has red hair, yet I'm certain 'tis not the mark of the devil."

"She's a girl," Gavin said harshly, the reality of it striking at him with a jolt of clarity.

"She turned eighteen last month," Duncan protested.

"I'm nearly twice her age."

"If yer displeased with the lass, then ye should consider one of the others," Duncan exclaimed, obviously puzzled by Gavin's sour mood.

"I have a duty," Gavin retorted.

"Aye, there's duty and then there's martyrdom."

Gavin glared at Duncan, all the more annoyed because he knew Duncan was right. He was acting like a willful child, ill-tempered because he didn't get his way. His two other marriages had been arranged, and though of short duration, they had been pleasant. There was no reason this third union should not also be successful.

Fiona.

The skin on the back of his neck tightened. The unfairness of it all crept up and seized his heart. Gavin sought refuge in logic and duty, praying that somehow that would make this intolerable situation bearable.

"Aileen Sinclair is a suitable choice." Gavin's mouth pulled into a grim line. "She knows her duty, as do I, and will therefore be a proper, respectful wife to me."

Duncan's hearty agreement was drowned out by the sound of a feminine gasp of outrage. Gavin swung around and spied Fiona standing a short distance away, her face a mask of shock.

"Fiona . . ."

She turned and started running.

Married? He is going to be married? Fiona reared back, feeling as though she'd been slapped. Pain sliced through her like a steel blade, almost suffocating her in its intensity. Blindly, she staggered forward, falling to her knees as a wave of hurt enveloped her, crushing her heart.

Gavin was going to take a wife, pledge himself to another woman. Care for her, protect her, make love to her. She would sit at his side and share his bed and bare his children. It was the thing Fiona had dreaded and feared most, but she had pushed it to the back of her mind, convincing herself that she would be long gone from Gavin's life when it happened.

If it happened. Panic squeezed her chest. Saints preserve her, it was going to happen!

Why? Yet even as the question burst into her mind, Fiona knew the answer. He was an earl, a Scottish earl. He had a duty. To his king. To his country. To his clan. A duty that overshadowed the wants and desires of the widow of an English baron.

No matter how deeply she loved him.

"Fiona!"

Oh, Lord, no! Away, I must get away. Fiona struggled to breathe as panic overtook her. Her chest ached in a way that made her fear there wasn't enough air in the room. She ran as fast as her legs would move, but she was no match for Gavin's agile feet.

He reached her just as she started to climb the stairs, seeking the comfort and solitude of her small chamber. Grabbing her arm, Gavin pulled her to a stop. She could feel his fingers burning through the fabric of her gown into her skin. A touch she had craved, a touch that had brought her such pleasure and joy.

But no longer.

"Ye heard us talking?"

Fiona stiffened and turned away. "Yes, I heard. You have decided to marry again. And you've chosen a young woman named Aileen Sinclair." Fiona kept her gaze fastened on the wall and concentrated on slowing her breath. "I wish you both great happiness."

A sick feeling rushed over her as hot burning tears crowded the back of Fiona's throat. She pressed her closed fists to her eyes, holding them back. All she wanted was to escape to some dark, private corner where she could weep, but that would have to wait. Fiona had no idea how, but she kept her composure and was able to finally turn to him.

He gave her a bleak look. At the sight of it, the tears came, rolling silently down her cheeks. He was everything she could want in a man—kind and funny, strong and loving, intelligent and tolerant. She wanted him to be the man she worked beside each day and slept beside each night. She wanted him forever.

He's going to marry another woman. She looked at him helplessly. Why did it have to be so complicated?

Why did politics and position have to play such a dominant role in their lives?

The trembling of her limbs wouldn't stop. Fiona wrapped her arms around herself, rocking back and forth. Whenever she had encountered adversity, she had always strived to face it head-on, to tackle the problem aggressively and find a solution.

But this, oh this, was unbearable. It felt as though her very soul was shriveling with pain. Bitterly, she wondered why she was surprised. Any emotion that lifted her so soaringly high would logically fall so despairingly low.

"'Tis a political alliance," Gavin declared. "It means nothing."

"Oh, I'm sure your new bride will be delighted to hear that." Despite her own pain, Fiona's heart lurched with pity. "Honestly, Gavin, how can you be so cruel? This poor, unsuspecting girl deserves more from you."

"She cannae have what I cannae give. My marriage will change nothing between us. I care for ye, Fiona. With all my heart and soul."

But that doesn't matter. The unfairness of it all clamped around Fiona's throat like a vise. She was foolish to have ever speculated about a future together, let alone a permanent one. A lasting relationship between them was impossible. It had always been impossible. But she had been too caught up in the beauty and wonder of her love for Gavin to fully consider it. And that mistake was now going to cost her in heartache.

"When I first heard you speak of marrying another, I confess I felt pity for myself." Using the final ounce of her inner strength and resolve, Fiona drew herself up, squaring her shoulders. "But now I shall pity all three of us—you, me, and your bride."

Sounds drifted in from the great hall. Gavin's head turned. Her cheeks heated at the very idea that someone else would appear and witness her mortification. Taking advantage of the distraction, Fiona disappeared without another word.

Sleep was impossible later that night. Fiona remained locked inside her small chamber for the rest of the afternoon and evening, stoically climbing into the cold, unfamiliar bed only when Alice insisted. She had refused Gavin's pleas to speak with him and had rather viciously torn up a note he sent, the sounds of the tearing parchment causing a fleeting moment of satisfaction.

Knowing her restless turning would awaken Alice, who slept on a pallet near the door, Fiona sat huddled beneath the thin coverlet. Tucking her knees close to her chest, she stared out into the dark, miserable night, yearning for what she could never have, could never capture and hold.

She watched the dawn slowly break, bringing the warming sunlight to all it touched. If only it could penetrate her heart and heal the frozen pain, she thought.

But sunshine quickly fled and the rains began, steady and hard. How ironic. Even the weather joined her in sorrow. Fiona bathed her swollen eyes, knowing she had to face the reality of the situation. She wasn't precisely certain what she was going to do next. All she did know was that staying here and watching Gavin marry another woman would crush the already shattered pieces of her heart.

Somehow, she must devise a way to leave.

Father Niall was placing a newly embroidered cloth on the altar when Fiona approached him in the chapel.

She had waited until everyone had broken their fast and left the great hall before slipping away, grateful to have avoided meeting Gavin.

"Have you heard the news about the earl's marriage?" Fiona asked.

"Yes. There is talk of little else." His eyes were kind, sympathetic.

Yet the words brought all the wounded emotions she struggled to control rushing back. "The announcement was not unexpected," she lied. God forgive her, now she was lying to a priest. A man she considered a friend.

A frown gathered across Father Niall's brow. "Still, it must be painful for you."

"'Tis hardly pleasant," Fiona quipped, but her voice fell flat. "I will need to make arrangements to leave. Can you help me?"

"What about Spencer? Will he go with you?" The priest cleared his throat. "I'll admit I had my doubts when you first proposed coming to Scotland, but Spencer has thrived here. Would you take that from him now, my lady?"

"Nay." A grim smile tugged at Fiona's mouth. "Spencer needs the training the earl is providing. Though it adds another layer to my sadness, he must stay."

"You must be strong, Lady Fiona, and trust in God that all will be well."

"I'm trying. Yet 'tis difficult to have faith under these circumstances." She began walking toward the door, then stopped and turned. Fearing the answer, yet needing to know, Fiona whispered, "Am I being punished, Father Niall? For being wicked, immoral, for taking a man to my bed who was not my husband?"

The priest's face crumbled with sympathy. "God understands the weakness of the flesh, for were we not made in his image? He is not a vengeful being, though he expects us to atone for our sins. And I know that you understand it would be an even graver sin to encourage the earl to commit adultery after he has taken a new wife."

"I agree. That is why I need to leave this place as soon as possible."

Father Niall nodded, yet his face looked troubled. "So you've heard?"

"What? There is more?"

The priest's eyes slid over her. "I regret having to tell you, but I heard the cooks talking after morning Mass. Laird Sinclair and his daughter will be arriving tomorrow."

"Maybe this time the earl will find true love," the laundress said. "I've heard that it can happen, even in an arranged marriage."

A group of servants were busy hanging out the laundry, their chattering voices easily overheard. Fiona made a move to turn away, but several highly raised brows let her know that she had been spotted. Curiosity, mixed with a dash of pity along with a hint of satisfaction, lined many of the women's faces.

Fiona's pride rushed forth. There was no help for it. She'd have to test her composure and walk past them.

"I've heard tell that she's young and pretty," one of the women exclaimed as Fiona drew near.

"The looks of an angel, that's what Duncan told me," another chimed in.

Fiona couldn't seem to catch her breath as a large sob lodged itself in her throat. She battled to force it down. She'd rather walk barefoot in the snow all the way back to England than break down and prove that their words were causing her pain.

"If she's as pretty as they say, he willnae be able to resist her, I'm sure." The laundress snickered. "Not that he'd even try."

"Aye, we'll have the heir we've been praying for within the year, mark my words."

Pain stabbed at Fiona's chest. A child. Gavin's child. The sob rose again in her throat, threatening to burst from her at any moment.

Fiona kept her steps slow and measured, but she barely made it beyond them before bursting into tears. Her legs sagged, her steps faltered. Scurrying around, she searched for a quiet, desolate corner of the bailey where she could be alone to vent the misery that was strangling her heart.

Gavin discovered her there nearly an hour later, her back pressed against the wall, her knees drawn to her chest, her eyes staring sightless ahead.

"Dammit, Fiona, I've got half my men out searching fer ye."

She looked at him with anguish in her heart. "Would that not make it much easier, if I simply vanished from the castle?"

"Jesus, lass, there's no need fer such drama." Gavin crouched beside her. "Ye're going to make yerself sick over this situation. I dinnae know how many times I have to tell ye that nothing will change between us."

"What an utterly ridiculous thing to say," Fiona snapped.

As if trying to prove his point that naught was different between them, Gavin leaned forward. His head dipped. Their lips pressed together. At the contact, Fiona felt all the aching love in her soul pour out to him. For a mere instant, her heart pounded with optimism and hope for the impossible, longing to believe what he was saying.

His powerful arms wrapped around her, his ardent heat reaching through the layers of cold surrounding her. Closer. She needed to be closer. Fiona's tongue circled his, urging him on, savoring the moment she knew was fleeting.

The hard, blunt evidence of his desire for her pressed insistently against her thighs. It woke her from the trance of passion. She was in danger of becoming lost, of moving back instead of forward. Fiona yanked her head away, breaking the kiss, struggling to pull back.

But Gavin refused to relinquish his hold. The roughness of his jaw scratched her tender flesh as he trailed hot, moist kisses down her throat. She felt the familiar tingling heat between her legs as her body betrayed her, yet she fought against it.

"Don't! Stop!" Fiona yelled, emphasizing her point by pounding Gavin's shoulders.

It took a moment for her cries of protest to register. When they did, Gavin's head raised. "What?"

"Unhand me," she hissed. "I don't want this, I don't want you."

"Calm down," he replied as if he didn't believe a word she was saying.

She ceased struggling and he looked into her eyes, his expression once more turning dark with desire. At the sight of it, Fiona felt something tilt inside her; the honesty of their passion was now askew. This was wrong. It had to stop. Now! She was no match for him in physical strength. She knew he could take her, no matter how many times she pushed him away. And none would gainsay him—it was his right as lord of the castle and she was his acknowledged mistress.

"Kindly release me, my lord."

This time her icy decree reached him. Looking none too pleased, Gavin dropped his arms. Needing to distance herself further, Fiona stood, then tried taking a step back, but her shoulder blades hit the wall. Her hands tightened into fists, but she hid them in the folds of her gown.

Gavin slowly rose to his feet. "I know the news of my marriage has been a shock to ye, but I need ye to know this is not my choice. I have a duty to my clan and my king that cannae be forsaken." He eyed her with such tenderness her vision started to blur. "I've told ye that nothing need change between us and I meant it. Ye'll have yer own set of rooms in the north tower—"

"What?" Her jaw dropped. "You expect me to stay beneath your roof after you are married? To live here with you and your wife?"

"'Tis the way it's usually done. But if that upsets ye so much, I'll give ye the choice of any of my smaller holdings, so ye may have a home that is all yers. I only ask that it be less than a day's ride from here, so I can easily visit."

Shards of red sprang before her eyes. Fiona had never before felt such fury. Her body shook with it, nearly exploded with it. Reacting to the anger that pumped through her veins, she raised her hand and slapped his jaw with her open palm.

His reaction was swift. Gavin raised his own hand. Fiona braced herself, but an answering blow never came. Instead, she saw a flash of self-loathing, an emotion that he previously kept hidden. The sight of it made her feel worse, and oddly guilty. She had started them down this road with her ridiculous proposal to become his mistress and it appeared they had both gotten far more than they had ever anticipated.

"Oh, Gavin," she whispered.

"What's happened to us, Fiona?"

"The truth has come to light. 'Tis harsh to accept. It makes no compromises, no changes in the hopes of avoiding pain. I now know the truth. I acknowledge the truth." Her voice shook with misery. "I hate the truth."

"Ye must accept what cannae be changed, Fiona."

"I'm trying. 'Tis you who are not being truthful. I must leave—"

"No! I forbid it!" The cold arrogance in his eyes darkened, then slowly started to fade and his harsh expression softened. "Please, Fiona, give me a chance to work this out."

She began shaking her head, tossing it furiously back and forth. Gavin captured it between his large hands, holding it steady, forcing her to look him directly in the eye. She felt the pull of his frustration and her heart broke anew.

He pressed a kiss to her lips. Subtle, sweet, loving. His lips were soft, gentle, his possession of her reverent. 'Twas the most emotional kiss she had ever experienced, perfect in every way. It stole Fiona's breath with tenderness and longing. Yet for all its magic, it could not change the facts nor alter the future.

The earl was going to marry another woman.

God help them all.

Chapter 15

The morning arrival of the earl's betrothed was met with all the fanfare of a royal progress. Crowds lined the streets of the village cheering as the procession rode passed. Fiona stood hidden in the shadows of her small tower chamber, watching it all as a detached numbness settled over her body.

When the last of the Sinclair soldiers, retainers, and clansmen came through the gates and the crowds returned to their work, Fiona took a deep breath to calm herself. There was nothing she could do now. Since running from Gavin yesterday afternoon, she had once again retreated to her chamber, anxiously awaiting news from Father Niall. She knew the possibility of leaving before the earl's intended entered the castle was slim; nevertheless, it had been a fragile hope.

Determined not to wallow in self-pity while she waited, Fiona picked up her needle and thread and began sewing a shirt for Spencer. Concentrating on the tiny, neat stitches provided a slight distraction. The garment took shape as the day wore on; however, when the sun began to set and no word had arrived from the priest, Fiona knew she would have to wait at least another day before departing.

A sudden loud knock on her chamber door gave her a momentary start of optimism, but when Alice answered it, they found Duncan standing in the doorway.

"The earl sent me to fetch Lady Fiona to the evening meal."

Fiona felt her stomach clench into a knot. She heard Alice mumble something, then Duncan raised his voice, repeating his instructions. Fiona could see the strain in Alice's back as Duncan spoke. The twinge of guilt at the sight was not easily ignored. 'Twas Fiona's battle to fight, not her maid's.

"I fear I am indisposed this evening, Duncan. Please send my regrets and inform the earl of my infirmary." Fiona turned away in dismay, mouthing a silent prayer that he would listen.

Duncan's face became impassive. "Ye're to come to the great hall. I'm sure if I go there without ye, someone else will be sent to fetch ye. And I imagine they willnae be as understanding or tolerant as me."

Something inside Fiona went still. She stared determinedly at him, but Duncan never moved a muscle. Visions of being bodily dragged into the great hall fluttered through her mind, bringing on a mild panic.

"I need some time to prepare," she finally answered.

Duncan nodded. "I'll wait, but dinnae take too long or else we'll be making a grand entrance."

With an answering nod, Fiona shut the door, then leaned back against it. Shame washed through her. It was too much. How could she face them? How could she walk into that hall and pretend she was nothing more than a grateful widow to whom Gavin had shown chivalrous consideration?

Yet it needed to be done. The Sinclairs had no doubt heard the rumors about her. It would look suspicious if she were absent from such an important event as their arrival banquet, especially since she had not been seen by any of them the entire day.

"We must hurry. Fetch the new blue silk gown, Alice."

The maid scrambled to do her bidding, shaking out the garment vigorously to ensure there were no wrinkles. Fiona had been daring in her styling of the garment, using the costly blue silk Gavin had purchased as a gift for her at the fair. The tight, square bodice allowed a hint of her breasts to show and the close-fitting skirt hugged the rest of her body like a glove, revealing every inch of her feminine curves.

Having only just finished the embroidery on the neckline and sleeves last week, Fiona had not yet worn the gown. She was planning on surprising Gavin one evening, hoping he would approve of her daring choice. Well, now there would be no intimate revealing of the garment, yet Fiona somehow suspected that Gavin would be *surprised*.

As Alice laced up the back, pulling tightly to ensure the fabric flowed perfectly, Fiona smoothed down the sides. Though it might be considered false, the beautiful dress gave her fledgling courage a boost. She sat quietly as Alice skillfully arranged her hair into an intricate crown of braids and then carefully added the circlet of gold and a white veil.

"You look like a queen, my lady," Alice said passionately.

Well, 'tis better than looking like a whore.

Shaking off that repellent thought, Fiona rose to her feet and opened the door. As promised, Duncan was waiting. His jaw momentarily dropped when she stepped into the light provided by the wall torch. Grateful for another boost to her confidence, Fiona took hold of his arm.

They descended the staircase slowly and stood at the entrance to the great hall. As she had hoped, the celebration was loud and lively, packed with people all eager to catch a glimpse of the earl's intended bride.

Aileen Sinclair was easy to spot. She looked young and fresh sitting beside the earl on the dais, her shimmering red hair unbound, flowing across her shoulders like a river of fire. The sight of the couple made Fiona's stomach twist, yet she managed to force her feet to move forward.

She had thought she and Duncan could get lost in the crowd as they approached, but after traveling a few feet, heads began to turn. The conversation around them died away. Looking neither right nor left, Fiona quickened her step. She kept her mind blank, her chin high, her spine straight.

"Good evening." Fiona stood before the dais and executed a deep, graceful curtsy. She could feel Lady Aileen's gaze on her, but held off looking in her direction for as long as possible.

"Lady Fiona, at last." Gavin gave her an appraising look, his eyes scanning her from head to toe, making her glad she had worn the daring gown. "May I present Laird Sinclair and his daughter Lady Aileen."

"Milady," the laird grumbled, turning his attention back to his meal.

Not precisely a snub, yet close enough. Knowing it was not possible to avoid looking at Aileen any longer, Fiona braced herself, then raised her chin. A lively, intelligent set of eyes met hers, along with a timid smile.

"I am delighted to meet ye, Lady Fiona," the younger woman said. "'Tis a relief to have another lady sitting at our table. The men speak of little else but war and sieges and battles. 'Twill be a pleasure to have a change of topic."

Lacking a reply, and the wits to form one, Fiona merely smiled. An awkward silence grew and her pulse spiked with dread as she waited for someone to shout out the truth, to reveal who and what she really was in this household, but none spoke of it. Not for her sake, of course, but for the earl. To a man, they supported their overlord and would do nothing to disgrace or dishonor him.

"Allow me," Duncan said, taking Fiona's arm and steering her toward the end of the dais.

As she took her seat, Fiona wondered how many hours she would spend on her knees in prayer, asking for forgiveness for this deception. Her only sliver of comfort was knowing that their relationship was firmly in the past, regardless of what Gavin believed.

The sight of Fiona approaching the dais kindled immediate unease in Gavin. A week ago his trust in her to act with dignity and decorum under any circumstances would not have been questioned. But she had been in such emotional turmoil these last few days, he acknowledged that anything was possible.

A part of him—a most cowardly part of him— longed for her temper to flare and her judgment to fail and reveal their relationship in a scene so epic it would turn the hair on Laird Sinclair's head gray and thus force the man to back out of the betrothal contract.

But when she reached the dais, Fiona was all dignity

and graciousness, as befitting her noble rank. She even managed to greet Lady Aileen with a tight smile.

Of course for him there was naught but dagger looks. Still, he felt the connection between them. His chest—along with other parts of his anatomy—swelled when she met his gaze. She looked magnificent!

At the sight of her standing so straight and proud, something wicked stirred to life inside him. Her close proximity was bothering him in ways that could prove embarrassing. Gavin grit his teeth and struggled to rally his control. She had ignored him for days and now she stood before him wearing a gown with such seductive powers his head was spinning.

She'd done it deliberately. He understood why. He'd hurt her and she wanted to show him precisely what he was giving up. He should have anticipated this reaction. At her core, Fiona was a fighter. 'Twas one of the many things he admired about her.

Somehow Gavin managed to keep his eyes from following her like a lovesick pup as she took her seat. It wasn't easy. Startled from his reflections, Gavin forced himself to concentrate on those seated around him—namely his betrothed.

Aileen clearly had no notion of the true circumstances of his relationship with Fiona. The lass was all smiles and innocent good humor, shyly flirting with him and graciously attempting to engage all those seated around her in the conversation, including Fiona.

The occasional scowl on Laird Sinclair's face indicated the man might have more of an inkling of the truth, but he was not about to jeopardize an important alliance because of it.

Gavin lifted his goblet and glanced toward the end of the table. One look at Fiona's white face, enormous eyes, and the set, tight lines around her mouth and the ale in his mouth turned sour. Shame bit at him. He couldn't do it. Could he?

He prided himself on being a man of honor and integrity. Housing his new bride and his mistress underneath the same roof was an act of cruelty, a decision beneath him. It was a selfish solution that only considered his needs and desires while ignoring those of the two women.

No. He would not subject them all to such a wretched fate. Instead, he would ready one of his smaller holdings for Fiona, giving her an independent residence of her own. This would give them the privacy they required and allow all three of them to retain their dignity. Other noblemen might feel at ease housing their wives and mistresses together, but that arrangement would not suit in this circumstance.

He realized Fiona would need time to understand this, and accept it. Yet as long as she resided on his land, she was answerable to him. He would have all the time it required to convince her that this was the best choice, the only choice.

Gavin stared into his empty goblet and smiled with irony. If only it were so simple.

Fiona spent another sleepless night, her chamber door firmly locked, and Alice stretched on a pallet in front of it. The precaution had been a wise one, for in the early morning hours there had been a soft knock, accompanied by her whispered name. Clamping her hands firmly over her ears, Fiona had ignored Gavin's attempts to speak with her, knowing nothing good could come of the encounter.

Bleary-eyed the following morning, Fiona had kept herself sequestered in her chamber through the long day and night, awaiting word from Father Niall. It never came. Disheartened, she again sent her regrets for the evening meal, claiming illness, but this time no one was sent to fetch her and drag her into the great hall. It was better that way, she told herself firmly, for it spared her from the pretense of acting as though all was well and saved her from the pain of seeing Gavin with his intended bride.

However, by the third day Fiona knew she needed to leave her confined space, if only for a few hours, or else she would go mad. She waited until the morning meal ended before sending Alice to verify that Gavin was busy with his guests. Only then did she venture from the safety of her chamber, slipping unobtrusively outside.

The gust of misty wind hit her full in the face, yet it felt invigorating. Hoping the rain would hold off for at least an hour or two, Fiona kept her face down and her feet swiftly moving.

She cautiously approached the kitchen garden, peering left, then right before hurrying toward the gate. Yet the sounds of female voices stopped Fiona cold. There was no time to react; a group of women, Lady Aileen in the center, rounded the corner.

Fiona turned to flee, needing to go somewhere, anywhere to avoid meeting Lady Aileen and her fawning entourage. Alas, she was not fast enough as the younger woman called out her name and sent her a cheerful wave.

"Lady Fiona!"

Inwardly Fiona cringed, but she slowly turned and forced a friendly smile. "Good morning, Lady Aileen."

"Oh, please, ye must call me Aileen." The younger woman approached, her face wreathed with an open, eager expression that reminded Fiona of Laddie when he wanted a treat or a good scratch behind the ears.

"Thank you. I, of course, am Fiona."

Aileen's smile brightened. "Come, let's walk. I've been told ye tend the herb garden near the kitchens. I should like to see it."

Fiona's brows drew together. Why was Aileen being so friendly? Where was her aversion to the English? Her mistrust and loathing of the enemy? The rest of the castle women never had any difficulty showing their distaste for her. Why should Aileen be any different?

But different she appeared to be. Aileen sent the other women on their way and the two of them entered the walled garden alone, the younger woman seemingly unaware of the tension crawling through Fiona.

As the strained silence grated, the need to make conversation for the sake of courtesy—and Fiona's sanity—grew stronger. And still she remained at a loss for words.

Aileen, however, suffered no such ailment. She chattered cheerfully about her journey and the various things she was discovering about the castle and its inhabitants, never seeming to notice, or much care, that Fiona remained silent.

When she finally paused to come up for air, Aileen began meandering down the rows of neatly tended herbs, calling out the names of those she knew. There was a restless quality to her movements that was unnerving. A strange feeling skittered through Fiona's chest. She was just about to make her excuses and leave when Aileen spoke.

"Everyone has been very kind and welcoming, but I was hoping that the earl and I would have a chance to spend more time together."

The flutter in Fiona's chest tightened. "He's a busy man."

"I know. And I applaud his tireless sense of duty. 'Tis but one of the many things I admire about him." Aileen leaned down and plucked the top of a mint plant, crushing the fragrant leaves between her fingers. "Still, I know I can learn some things, if ye help me."

Fiona forced back a wave of panic. "I don't know what I can do."

"Come now, dinnae be coy. Ye have been a guest here fer a few months. Ye must have learned something of his character. Of his likes and dislikes. Though I would prefer to hear them from his own lips, I am a practical woman. If the earl cannae spend time with me, then I must learn about him from others. After all, 'tis my duty as his wife to know how to please him."

Merciful Lord, it hurt! Fiona's chest felt so tight it was difficult to breathe. She could not discuss Gavin's likes and dislikes with his future bride. She could not!

"I am uncertain what you want of me."

"Ye're a widow. As a woman of experience, I was hoping that ye'd have some words of wisdom to impart. Advice that would aid me in becoming a good, proper wife." Aileen brought the crushed mint leaves to her nose and sniffed. "My father says that a husband's word is law, his will is implacable. A mere wife cannae force him to do anything. Do ye believe that to be true?"

"No," Fiona answered honestly.

"Neither do I." Aileen smiled. "I think with a clever approach, a wife can get her husband to do just about anything. I want ye to help me understand the right approach with the earl."

Fiona lifted her head sharply. Was this a trap? A way to get her to acknowledge her relationship—*her past relationship*—with Gavin? But Aileen's expression was open, honest. A facade? Or was she truly that young and naive?

"I fear I have little specific knowledge to impart. I am merely a guest here. The earl does not share his confidences with me, Aileen."

"But he speaks so highly of ye. And with great fondness."

"He was a good friend to my husband, and as such, has shown kindness toward me and my son." Fiona's throat nearly choked as she added, "Nothing more."

Realizing she was frowning, Fiona turned away. Aimlessly, she bent down and plucked a weed from the row of sage. For whatever strange reason, Aileen was drawn to her and Fiona knew it would only be a matter of time before the younger woman learned the truth.

Hopefully, Fiona would be long gone when that occurred. But in the meantime she needed a new topic of conversation—quickly! "Tell me, Aileen, was your journey here an arduous one?"

"Not especially. But we did have a few adventures."

"Really?"

"Oh, indeed."

Fiona lifted her brow in obvious interest. It was the only encouragement Aileen needed to settle down on a stone bench and launch into her tale.

Fiona smiled with relief. In this instance Aileen was very much like any other young woman—she enjoyed talking about herself. With only the occasional prompt necessary, Fiona kept Aileen happily chattering, safely steering the topic away from the earl.

By the time the noon bell rang, Fiona was surprised to discover how quickly the time had passed. Aileen had a natural talent for storytelling and a wry sense of humor that was both refreshing and engaging.

"Will ye be joining us fer the meal?" Aileen asked, as the women moved from the garden.

"Alas, I have felt poorly these past few days and require rest," Fiona replied with feigned regret. "I'll eat some clear broth and bread later, if I feel better."

"Oh. I am sorry to hear it."

Aileen's disappointment seemed genuine, but Fiona had little trouble ignoring it. Attending the midday meal in the great hall meant seeing Gavin, and that she vowed to avoid at any and all cost.

"She was asking for you again," Alice said as she placed a tray of food in front of Fiona.

"Who?"

"Lady Aileen. She saw me with your meal and wanted to know if you were still feeling poorly or making some improvement."

Fiona sighed. Since her encounter with Aileen yesterday morning, the young woman had been solicitous in her concern, inquiring several times through Alice if she could offer any aid or assistance.

"She has a kind heart," Fiona exclaimed, guilt closing her throat so tightly she had difficulty swallowing a small piece of cheese.

"Well, Lady Aileen's not the only one wanting to

know how you are faring. The earl has been hounding me, too."

Fiona washed the dryness from her throat with a long sip of wine, then pushed the food tray away. A longing that was too sharp to endure pierced her chest. It was pointless. Seeing Gavin again would open a wound that was still too raw to heal. She would save herself that anguish at least.

"Tell Lady Aileen that if she wishes, I will join her in the solar with my sewing for an hour this afternoon," Fiona said.

"Are you certain?"

"No. Yet I realize I can't hide in here forever. This seems the best compromise."

Thus, later that afternoon Fiona and Aileen sat together in the airy solar, a respectable distance from the rest of the women, sewing in their laps. Had the situation not been so absurd, Fiona conceded she might have enjoyed herself—a fact that was an even greater puzzlement.

By rights she should dislike this young woman who would become Gavin's wife. Yet on such very short acquaintance Aileen had managed to make Fiona like her, respect her, fear for her future—and yes, be jealous of her.

It was an intolerable situation, a hopeless predicament that would only end once she was gone. Aileen was her usual talkative self and Fiona was relieved to be spared the burden of having to make conversation. The time passed quickly and, having fulfilled her obligatory visit, Fiona began to gather her sewing items.

Laddie chose that moment to enter the solar. His floppy ears perked up the moment he spied her. With a happy yelp, the dog lumbered across the room, his tail wagging furiously.

"Och!" Aileen's screech startled them all. "How did that filthy beast get in here?"

"'Tis not a beast," Fiona said. "'Tis Laddie."

"The earl allows his hounds the run of the castle?" Aileen asked in astonishment.

"Only the special ones." Fiona reached into her pocket. She unwrapped the cloth from the soup bone she had Alice pilfer from the kitchen earlier in the morning. Laddie's eyes brightened. He licked his chops and whimpered, quieting only when Fiona commanded that he sit. As a reward for performing his trick, Fiona tossed the bone at him.

Laddie caught it in midair, then sprawled out at Fiona's feet and began gnawing at it with great gusto. Aileen leaned over cautiously and glared at him, her brow knit in confusion.

"Back home, our dogs are kept outside."

"Yes, that is usually the case."

Aileen drew closer, her expression curious. Laddie growled, pulling his bone closer with his two front paws.

"Laddie! Behave!" Fiona admonished.

"He's very smart," Aileen observed, apparently not insulted by the dog's behavior.

"Laddie was the first friend I made when I came to stay here."

"One does always appreciate a loyal companion," Aileen agreed. "We dinnae allow our dogs inside, yet I can see the idea has merit." Aileen wrinkled her nose. "Though I would have to insist they be clean."

"Well, Laddie is not fond of a bath, but he'll sit for one, if rewarded."

"Hmm. I wonder if that approach would work with

some of the earl's retainers. I confess, Laddie is hardly the most foul-smelling creature in the castle. Thankfully the earl takes pride in a neat and clean appearance, though I'm sorry to say not all of his men follow his example."

Fiona smiled at the truth of that observation. "Perhaps that is something you can establish."

"A weekly bath fer his lordship's men-at-arms?" Aileen's eyes danced with amusement. "Mother Mary, can ye imagine how that demand would be met? They'd most likely toss me in the loch."

"It might be worth it if you could pull a few of them in with you."

"Aye. And toss some flakes of soap in fer good measure."

Fiona giggled at the thought. "I confess, I never understood why some folks fear they will catch their death if they bathe too often."

"'Tis a sad yet true problem."

"For the rest of us."

The two women let loose with a peal of laughter. But Fiona's unexpected amusement vanished as quickly as it had come when Father Niall entered the solar, a purposeful expression on his face.

Hoping for some good news, Fiona bid Aileen a hasty good-bye and hurried toward the priest. He seemed genuinely shocked to see her engaged in such a companionable situation with Aileen. But his mind was on other matters and Fiona was relieved when he came quickly to the point of his visit.

"The arrangements are finally set," he said in a low voice. "You leave tomorrow at dawn."

Fiona had to concentrate on standing very still so as

not to give any hint of her emotions. Father Niall's words were a blessing, a comfort, precisely what she had been waiting to hear. However, Fiona was very surprised to discover that mingled with the great sense of relief was an unexpected twinge of regret.

Chapter 16

Darkness, thick and silent, shrouded the great hall. Sounds of gentle, as well as loud, snoring could be heard as the others slumbered peacefully on their pallets. Holding her breath, Fiona tiptoed across the large chamber. She opened the heavy door slowly and slipped out, offering a silent prayer of thanks that no one had witnessed her departure.

The cool predawn air was bracing against her skin and she shivered. The full moon provided far more light than she expected, altering her to be even more cautious. Lifting the skirt of her gown, she hurried, carefully keeping herself close to the structures, to avoid being seen by the guards.

She paused to get her bearings when she reached the stable, but the distinct crunch of a footstep startled the wits out of her. Barely containing a shriek, Fiona flattened her back against the outer wall and waited.

The footsteps grew progressively louder and Fiona's heart started beating so rapidly she swore the sound must be echoing throughout the courtyard. She restlessly shifted her feet and squinted into the moonlit darkness, trying to decide which way to run should someone appear.

Then, just as suddenly as it began, the sound of footsteps disappeared. Cautiously, Fiona peered around the corner. Nothing. The bailey was deserted, with no sign of any guards or any other shadowy figures.

Run! This was her chance and she needed to seize it. Yet instead Fiona went absolutely still. Oh, no. She had come too far to panic and lose her nerve now. Taking a deep breath, she counted slowly to ten, then nimbly dashed across the empty bailey to the chapel.

She was prepared to hear a shout of alarm, an order to halt, the sound of heavy footsteps in pursuit. Yet none came. Head and heart pounding, Fiona slipped through the church door, wishing there was a bolt so she could lock it behind her. She was flooded with relief, though she knew this was only the start of her journey—she still needed to get past the men guarding the gatehouse.

In anticipation of her arrival, Father Niall had lit two candles. The flickering light illuminated just enough of the darkness to enable Fiona to move about the room without knocking into things, yet was minimal enough to avoid attracting attention.

Fiona stepped gingerly forward. Nerves still unsteady, she felt the perspiration forming on her forehead and upper lip, while a few droplets trickled down her spine. As they had agreed, the priest was waiting for her, dozing peacefully on a wooden bench. She stood over him for a brief moment, marveling at his ability to sleep so contentedly on such a hard, uncomfortable surface.

"Father Niall!"

Her sharp whisper startled the priest. He bolted upright, almost knocking his head on her chin. "Lady Fiona, you are here."

"Yes, at the appointed hour," she replied unnecessarily.

The priest shifted on the bench and looked up, yet Fiona knew all too well his sleepy countenance belied the sharp perception of his stare. As recent as last night, he had tried, unsuccessfully, to dissuade her from taking this action, agreeing to offer her aid only after he realized she would not be deterred.

"I have your belongings," he said, pointing beneath the bench.

She picked up the meager bundle of clothes she had packed and given to the priest to hide and slung it over her shoulder. She was taking only what she had brought with her, leaving behind the blue silk gown she had made from the luxurious fabric Gavin had bought for her at the fair, along with the glass vial of perfume. She had no use for these fine things where she was going and the memory of that happy day was a cruel reminder of what might have been, if the circumstances were different.

"I mustn't tarry. Will you please summon Spencer?" Fiona asked.

Father Niall frowned. "Are you certain? The squires sleep in the great hall. I will endeavor to be careful, but I could be seen, and that puts you at a much greater risk of discovery."

She nodded her head decisively. "I know, but I cannot ride through the gates until I've said good-bye and held my son one final time."

The priest nodded reluctantly. Unable to sit, Fiona paced nervously, waiting with growing anxiety for Father Niall to return. She knew the priest was right. It *was* a calculated risk speaking with Spencer, but Fiona knew she would not be able to leave without saying farewell to him.

Spencer's loyalty to the earl, indeed to all his newfound Scottish friends, was deep. She did not have the earl's permission to leave his castle, yet even knowing this might put Spencer in a moral dilemma did not sway her resolve.

After what felt like an eternity, a yawning Spencer trooped sluggishly into the church, Father Niall's guiding hand resting on the boy's shoulder. He blinked groggily at her through the dim candlelight, surprise on his face. "Mother?"

"Hello, Spencer." Fiona forced a smile. "I'm sorry to have awakened you so terribly early, but I've asked Father Niall to bring you here so that I might bid you a proper good-bye. I'm leaving this morning. Quite soon in fact. And I shall not be returning."

The shock in his eyes brought a rush of unexpected tears to her. Uncertainty clawed at her, along with a strong sense of duty. Had she thoroughly considered how this would affect her child? Would he feel abandoned, deserted by her actions?

"Why are ye leaving?"

A fair question, yet impossible to answer with complete honesty. Squeezing her eyes shut, Fiona pressed her palm to her forehead. "I know this makes little sense to you, yet you must trust that I know what is best."

"If you leave, then I must go with ye."

Fiona's throat tightened. 'Twas not only the loyal sentiment that moved her, but hearing him say *ye*. The Scottish influence she had hoped would be Spencer's salvation was starting to engulf him.

"Oh, dearest. Nothing would make me happier than to have you by my side. But for now, 'tis best if you remain here and continue with your training."

"Where are ye going?"

"Somewhere safe," Fiona answered vaguely, knowing

it was best if her son had no specific information. This way when Gavin pressed the boy for details, as he most assuredly would, Spencer could answer truthfully that he knew nothing.

"I have made the arrangements," Father Niall added. "There's no need to worry. All will be well."

Spencer looked torn, glancing back and forth between them. Fiona's chest tugged. She had to tell him more or else he would never accept her decision. But what could she say?

"I must be practical and go before I wear out my welcome," she explained, her mouth curling in self-mockery. Offering to become the earl's mistress had been the most impractical decision of her life. Yet it was far too late to undue that damage.

"Has the earl asked ye to leave?"

"Oh, no. He is too noble and chivalrous, but his kindness does not give me the right to take advantage of him. Do you understand?"

Fiona could tell by Spencer's furrowed brow that he didn't, but there was precious time left to say much else. Knowing she could no longer prolong the inevitable, Fiona reached for her son. Spencer suffered her tight hug and gentle cheek kiss with manly bravado, yet as she started to pull away, he grasped her tightly. The sweetness of his need melted her heart.

"I shall miss ye, Mother."

In spite of her aching heart, Fiona could not help but smile. Spencer was a fine boy, with a true and loyal disposition. Her pride swelled as she pulled back and gazed at his dearly loved face. Oh, how she would miss him!

Unable to stop herself, Fiona reached for Spencer a second time. His arms also came forward and they hugged each other. For just a moment, Fiona caught a glimpse of the small boy who had always loved and admired her. The child she had raised as her own, who came to her when he was frightened, or hurt, or feeling ill. The child who needed her.

She wiped the tears pooling in her eyes with the back of her wrist and hesitated, her conscience battling with her protective mothering instincts. Was he too young to be left on his own? Should she swallow her pride, sacrifice the halves of a broken heart that would never have a chance to mend if she were near Gavin, and stay?

She clung to her son as long as she dared, until suddenly she felt his hand gently patting her shoulder, a clear offer of comfort. It was a bittersweet gesture, reminding her that he was maturing into a young man who understood and accepted his responsibilities. It also gave her the boost of courage she needed to accept the rightness of her decision.

They broke apart at the same moment. "When the time is right, I will send word through Father Niall," Fiona promised, turning away before her resolve to leave failed.

"Wait here until I come back and tell you 'tis safe to return to the hall," Father Niall instructed Spencer.

Then he turned to Fiona. She busied herself with her bundle of belongings, then looked at the ceiling to prevent any more tears from falling. The priest touched her arm, motioning for her to come. Side by side they walked across the bailey, which was slowly stirring to life.

There were a few people starting their morning chores, but none of them gave her a second glance. Still needing to avoid recognition, Fiona pulled the hood of her cloak high over her head and kept her face deliberately lowered. She stood a respectful distance away as the priest readied her horse, moving forward only after he signaled.

"Go with God," the priest said kindly, as he hoisted her into the saddle.

Fiona nodded, unable to speak. The aching loneliness and longing that hung heavy within her heart was so near the surface she was certain she would burst into sobs if she spoke. She nudged her mount, taking up a position at the rear of the grain cart. The guard circled around the front; none seemed to take any notice of her and she realized Father Niall's plan had been well thought out. She wondered how much he had paid them.

As they rode through the open gates, Fiona's melancholy momentarily abated. Fear took hold. She was certain if any of the guards got a close look at her face, they would recognize her. She would be stopped, questioned. No doubt Gavin would be summoned and then . . . she couldn't even begin to imagine what would happen next.

Fiona tried to take a deep breath, but her lungs felt tight. Bracing herself, she fought for calm. Her horse nickered and tossed his head and Fiona's heart skipped. Visions of being stopped while the alarm was sounded spun before her eyes.

But luck or fate or justice was finally looking kindly upon her. Though it felt like an eternity, the guards never even gave her a glance as she went through the gates along with the cart and its escort. Noisily, they all rumbled down the road that wound through the village.

A thick mist enveloped them as they traveled through the village. When they emerged on the other side, dawn began to break, the distant horizon slowly brightening with an eerie pink glow. Gradually, a portion of the fog began to burn off and the sun began to move up in the sky.

Fiona could now clearly see the breath from her horse's nostrils waft into the air, as well as the road ahead.

She filled her lungs with fresh air and resisted the strong urge to push her mount into a gallop. Nay, though she longed to move with haste to increase the distance between herself and Gavin, Fiona knew it was necessary to keep pace with the slow-moving cart or else the men might start asking questions. Only the armed escort rode with any sense of urgency, keeping a fair distance ahead as they scouted for any signs of trouble.

Though she might wish to ride with them, Fiona was very aware that it was the soldiers leading the escort who posed the greatest risk of uncovering her true identity. It was therefore essential that she shield herself from their notice. Thus, she stayed near the heavily laden cart, doing her best to avoid the dust it stirred as it labored along the road.

It would be hours before she was missed; perhaps days before they thought to search for her along this route. As they dipped into a valley, the swirling mist once again shrouded their tracks. A good omen for the day of her leave-taking, Fiona decided.

If only the pain in her heart agreed.

Despite Father Niall's best efforts and meticulous planning, Fiona's departure did not go entirely unnoticed. Restless and unable to sleep, Aileen gave up trying and rose from her bed. 'Twas no use; no matter what position she twisted her body into, her mind would not remain quiet.

She could no longer deny that the future she had believed to be set was in truth unsettled. She had come to wed the earl with high expectations and an open heart, but these past few days she was filled with a nagging frustration she could not understand.

The earl was polite, yet distant. Kind, but distracted. She knew he was doing his duty in this marriage—as was she—but she had hoped there would be more. A sign that the union brought him at least a degree of contentment, a special look of admiration meant only for her, evidence of a growing affection that someday might blossom into love.

Was that really too much for a lass to ask of her future husband? Was she being foolish? Naive?

Her mind in a whirl, Aileen paced her small bedchamber. She needed air! Fearful of waking her maid, Aileen silently gathered her cloak around her shoulders to ward off the predawn chill and slipped from the room.

There were several startled expressions from the guards as she climbed the circular stone stairs to the curtain wall to watch the sunrise, but none challenged her right to be among them. The view from the tower was a sight to behold. Not only was the inner courtyard revealed, but the village below and the outline of the distant hills were also in plain sight. Seeing the vastness around her brought a calm to her nerves, along with a much needed sense of freedom.

Leaning forward on the parapets, Aileen looked down. The waning moonlight reflected off the water in the moat, its shimmering blackness offering an almost mesmerizing fascination. Turning her gaze to the inner courtyard below, she saw two figures leaving the chapel, walking with purpose toward the stables.

One was a priest, the other was—Lady Fiona? Though the woman's face was hidden in the hood of her cloak, Aileen recognized the garment she wore, for it was a distinctly English style. Her curiosity soon gave way to puzzlement as she saw Fiona hug the priest, mount her horse and then follow placidly behind a large cart drawn by a pair of oxen.

Within minutes, they all disappeared from view. Realizing it was too late to call out and capture their attention, Aileen moved from the battlements. Back in her bedchamber, she dressed quickly and silently, then hurried to the stables.

The young stable boy was slack-jawed when she cast him a flirty smile, never once questioning her orders for her mare to be saddled, nor even noticing that she lacked a proper guard to accompany her.

The next challenge that awaited was the castle gate. Aileen felt her blood surge with anticipation as she drew near. She was a laird's daughter, raised to be respected and obeyed. It would be an interesting test indeed to see if her usual forceful demeanor would succeed in getting the McLendon men to do her bidding.

Alas, she never got the chance to try. The senior guard had left his post to relieve himself and the unfortunate lad who stood sentry with him had been celebrating his brother's marriage until the wee hours of the morning.

Badly hungover and practically asleep on his feet, he paid little heed to those leaving the castle. A disgraceful display, in Aileen's opinion, though to be fair she believed it more important that the guard prevent undesirables from entering the domain rather than scrutinize those who were leaving.

In any case, she was through the gates without incident. Once again feeling an almost giddy sense of freedom, Aileen dug in her heels and urged her mount to increase its speed. She would have to ride hard and fast in order to intercept Fiona and her escort before anyone in the castle realized they were missing.

* * *

With each passing mile, the fear of discovery was slowly easing out of Fiona's mind, lessening the knot in her stomach. Everything was going according to plan. Father Niall had said he told the men she was traveling with that she was a dutiful servant of God in need of the safety of an escort as she began her pilgrimage to the shrine of the Virgin Mother. Clearly they had not questioned the priest's word, for they paid her no mind.

With the heavy cart pulled by the lumbering oxen, they continued the journey at an indolent pace. Fiona's mare swayed, expertly avoiding a low-hanging branch that nearly knocked her from the saddle. She pulled her mount into the center of the road directly behind the cart and was concentrating on avoiding the tree branches when she heard the sound of galloping hooves closing in behind her.

Every muscle inside Fiona tensed. She twisted in her saddle, squinting through the swirling mist, and caught a glimpse of the rider. *Good Lord!* 'Twas not Gavin, nor any of his men, but rather a woman. Fiona squinted again. Aileen?

The sight nearly stopped Fiona in her tracks. Turning forward, she lifted herself in the saddle, peering worriedly at the driver over the sacks of grain piled high in the cart. He never moved his head, letting her know he had not yet heard the approaching horse.

Knowing she had to intercept Aileen before any of the men saw her, Fiona turned her mount and doubled back for a few minutes, seeking a more private area off the open road where they could converse without being overheard. She cantered into an open field, then guided her impatient mount in a tight circle, resisting the strong urge to flee. No, 'twould be best to speak with Aileen and discover why she had followed her. Then hopefully she could extract a promise from the young woman to tell no one what she had seen.

Aileen slowed her horse as she drew closer, stopping at Fiona's side. "Fiona! I knew 'twas ye I saw with the priest in the bailey." Aileen glared at her with accusing eyes. "Where are ye going? And why did ye leave so suddenly, without saying farewell?"

Guilt tore at Fiona's throat. How much of the truth could she reveal before causing Aileen hurt? "I'm sorry. There wasn't time to say good-bye," Fiona replied, deliberately answering only the last question.

Aileen flashed her a look of pure disbelief. "Why are ye leaving?" she asked again.

So many words and emotions besieged her mind, yet Fiona could speak none of them aloud. "'Tis time for me to go, Aileen."

"What? Why? Ye must tell me yer reasons. I swear to ye, I'll not be going anywhere until ye do," Aileen announced, emphasizing her point by getting off her horse.

Fiona tried to contain herself. She had come too far to fail now. Truly. But Aileen's interference was maddening. Did she not realize that this was best for all of them?

Fiona muttered beneath her breath and reluctantly dismounted. In the distance, she could hear the grain cart ambling down the dirt road. No matter. It moved slowly; she would be able to regain her place beside it as soon as she convinced Aileen to return to the castle. And keep her mouth shut.

"I am grateful to the earl for his kindness and support," Fiona began. "His willingness to foster Spencer has relieved me of a tremendous burden, however I can no longer, in good conscience, impose on his generous hospitality. Therefore, I am leaving."

Aileen watched her intently. "Yer explanation sounds so simple and reasonable, but yer actions prove the words false. Why must ye steal away under cover of darkness, like a thief in the night? Does the earl even know that ye are gone? What are ye hiding, Fiona?"

"Nothing," Fiona replied beseechingly.

Aileen pursed her lips and took a deep breath. "On the day of my arrival, there were several women eager to tell me stories about ye. Vile, spiteful, dishonorable things, yet I refused to believe what they said. 'Twas rumors and gossip and I wouldn't be a party to it." Aileen studied Fiona closely, her expression darkening. "Was I wrong to ignore them? Are ye in truth the earl's mistress?"

"Oh, Aileen." Unthinking, Fiona moved forward. Aileen's eyes widened and she moved away. The rejection stung, yet Fiona realized that Aileen's pride must surely be hurting. "I swear to you, anything that existed between the earl and myself ended the moment you stepped inside the walls of his keep."

"And before?"

Fiona lowered her chin, embarrassment heating her cheeks. "The past has no lasting meaning. 'Tis over and done and quickly forgotten."

"Not by everyone," Aileen said flatly. "Certainly not by the earl."

"You are mistaken," Fiona whispered, not daring to let even a sliver of hope enter her heart.

"Nay." Aileen shook her head adamantly. "Something isn't right."

Fiona opened her mouth to dispute those words, but

then a sudden, exhausted weariness overtook her. The days of emotional turmoil, the week of pain and sorrow and loss came crashing down on her. Fie, if she were sitting on her horse, she might very well have toppled off.

"Go back to the castle, Aileen," Fiona said wearily, having neither the strength nor the stamina to argue anymore. "Forget what you have been told, forget what you have seen this morning. Move forward with your life and be happy. Please."

Aileen held herself tightly, refusing to meet Fiona's gaze. Then, as if something snapped inside her, Aileen twisted her lips into a snarl. "Ye think me a child. A silly agreeable lass, timid as a newborn kitten, who believes everything she is told, who blindly follows everyone else's commands without question or complaint. Well, ye're wrong about me. Dead wrong."

"I never thought you were timid, Aileen. Young, yes, and innocent. But I've seen your spark of passion and strength of character. Qualities that will stand you in good stead as you mature."

Aileen shook off Fiona's attempts to placate her. "I will not be shamed by ye, Fiona. I've seen the way the earl looks at ye."

Fiona gasped. "What?"

"He hides it well, but every now and again it emerges. The longing in his eyes, the sadness on his brow. Pray, do not insult me by denying it."

The bitterness in Aileen's voice startled her. Fiona had been so caught up in her own misery she hadn't realized the extent of Aileen's distress and disappointment. Or knowledge.

"Then you understand why I must go."

"Aye. 'Tis best, I know. But I also know if ye run from him, he'll chase after ye."

Fiona's gut tightened. "He won't find me. Especially if you keep my secret and say nothing."

Aileen put her hand on her horse's flank as if to steady herself. "Don't ye see, it will be worse? If he never finds ye, he will never forget ye. How can I live with that truth?"

Fiona looked at Aileen in shock. "You are exaggerating his feelings for me. They are not that strong or that constant. In but a few weeks' time, I will be nothing more than a distant memory for him."

Aileen lifted a wry brow. "'Tis what I pray fer every night." Her breath hitched. "I willnae share my husband. I willnae allow him in my bed while he pines fer another in his mind and heart. He must choose me willingly, freely, or else he'll not have me."

"He already has chosen you," Fiona choked. "You will be his bride, his countess."

Aileen closed her eyes. Fiona could see the rigid set to her shoulders. She was holding herself tightly, striving to remain composed. "The earl made an agreement with my father. I dutifully accepted that decree without knowing the facts."

Fiona couldn't stop the flood of pity that washed over her. Aileen was so young! Yet surely old enough to understand the unfairness of a woman's fate in this harsh world run by men. Women of their station rarely, if ever, had the right to voice an opinion about the men they married. More often than not, they had to suffer their husbands until death dissolved the union.

"You cannot defy your father," Fiona said gently.

Aileen's eyes flew open. "He willnae force me to wed if he believes the earl's offer to be self-serving and insincere. Therefore, I have decided that I will only marry the earl if he freely pledges his honor and fidelity to me. And he must speak that vow while we are standing side by side, so that I may judge for myself its truth and sincerity."

Chapter 17

The words had barely left Aileen's lips when a group of men on horseback burst from the trees on the other side of the clearing, racing toward them at a thunderous speed.

"Well, now that we've been discovered," Aileen said with a pragmatic shake of her head, "we shall continue this conversation once we have returned to the castle."

Her thoughts in a jumble, Fiona squinted at the riders. A sense of relief engulfed her when she realized Gavin was not among them. She was in no mood to face him, especially knowing he was going to be very angry when he discovered what she had done.

The riders continued to bear down on them. Fiona could see clumps of grass and dirt flying into the air as the horses' hooves ate up the distance separating her and Aileen from their rescuers.

Fiona considered trying to mount her horse, but decided it was too difficult and cumbersome without assistance. Aileen also remained on her feet. An uneasy breeze stirred. Fiona could see the tension in the way the men hugged their mounts, the tightness in which they gripped the reins.

What she did not see was a single face she recognized, nor a McLendon or Sinclair plaid.

"Run!" Fiona yelled suddenly.

Aileen stood transfixed, her expression bewildered. "Fiona, there is no need—"

"Quickly," Fiona shouted, shoving Aileen forward. "We have to find a place to hide."

"But—"

"Now, Aileen! These are not the earl's men or your father's. Hurry!"

For a split second everything went still. And then Aileen lifted her skirts and broke into a run. Fiona followed right behind, matching the younger woman step for step. They ran with fear and purpose, yet had no set course. Escape was their only thought.

They made it to the tree line and disappeared into the underbrush. For the first time Fiona was glad they didn't have time to mount their horses, since the large animals would not be able to follow the narrow paths. Branches snapped and swung, whipping their legs and arms, but the women kept running.

"Where can we hide?" Aileen called out breathlessly.

"I don't know," Fiona answered frantically. "Look for a thicket. Or maybe a cave?"

"We could climb a tree," Aileen huffed.

Fiona's eyes scanned the large trunks, looking for low branches. Seeing none, they pressed on, the sounds of pursuit drawing nearer.

"We should separate," Fiona yelled. "When I give the signal, you go right and I'll turn left."

But Fiona never got the chance. A strangled cry escaped her throat as two large hands grasped her shoulders. They pulled her back, then clamped around her waist, squeezing so hard the breath was pushed from her lungs.

At her cry, Aileen turned around. The movement caused the young woman to lose her footing and she tumbled to the hard ground. The moment she fell, another man leapt on top of her, wrenching her arms behind her back and shoving her face into the moss-covered ground.

"Stop! You're hurting her!" Fiona kicked and bucked, struggling to free herself from the iron hold. But her captor's strength was unrelenting, making escape impossible.

"I'll do a lot more than bruise her pretty wrists if ye dinnae shut yer mouth and keep still," the ruffian snarled.

Fiona's heart sank. She immediately went limp. Satisfied that they were being compliant, the men took their time binding first Aileen's and then Fiona's wrists. As they stood facing each other, Fiona caught the younger woman's eyes and pursed her lips tightly, then shook her head sharply.

Aileen nodded. Fiona sighed. Thank the saints the girl understood they needed to keep silent. If they were lucky, these men were minions, under service to another. Their leader might prove more sensible, someone with whom they could negotiate. Someone who would be interested in collecting a substantial ransom for their safe return.

For Aileen, at least. When he discovers that I've run away, Gavin might not be so inclined to part with his coin to rescue me.

Taking her by the arm, Fiona's captor marched her

out of the woods. She and Aileen were brought to the edge of a clearing where the others were waiting.

"Looks like ye've caught a bonnie prize," an arrogant voice proclaimed. "Good work."

Fiona heard Aileen gasp. She turned and looked up. No wonder. The man sitting astride the large white stallion was as handsome as the devil, his eyes sharp and assessing, his countenance foreboding. He was flanked by two armed men on either side of him, both older than he, but there was no doubt who was in command.

Sweat glistened on the neck and flanks of all the men's horses, evidence of their punishing ride. A shove from behind brought Fiona close enough to feel the animal's heated breath on the top of her head. But she dared not shrink away, suspecting that this man would be respectful of a sign of courage.

His hard stare passed coldly over her. Yet try as she might, Fiona could not control her shiver. Beside her, Aileen stood rigidly composed.

"Which one will ye take first?" the man holding her arm asked. "The redhead or the blonde?"

"Now that's a problem I wish I had to confront every day of the week," someone called out.

Several of the men laughed; a few openly leered. Aileen's breath caught in a sharp gasp. Fiona wished she could offer some sort of comfort, but her wrists were bound and she dare not take her eyes off the leader. Their fate rested solely in his hands.

"We have no quarrel with these fine ladies," the leader said, his mouth falling into a grim line. "But the earl will have to meet our demands if he wants to get them back."

"Both of them?" a guttural voice questioned. "Now,

why should he be having two such bonnie lasses while we have none?"

"Aye," the ruffian holding Fiona's arm shook her so hard her teeth rattled. "If ye insist, we'll return one. And keep the other. At least fer a few days."

"That's enough, Magnus," the leader admonished. The words were uttered in an even tone, but the look in his eyes held a hard, uncompromising edge that could not be ignored.

Magnus lost a bit of his bravado. He lowered his head and cursed loudly under his breath, but did not relinquish his hold on Fiona's arm.

Satisfied, the leader turned to the man on his left. "Alec."

The man nodded and moved his horse forward. Catching Aileen under the arms, he lifted her, heaving her up to his horse like a sack of grain. She shrieked in fear as she literally flew in the air.

"Stop wiggling, lass, or I'll drop ye," Alec said, and the men broke into laughter.

Alec swung Aileen forward, placing her rump on the horse, seating her sideways in front of him. Nervously Aileen tried to keep her balance, but her bound hands made it difficult. Even worse, the leader gave a signal and Magnus quickly tied her ankles together. Now she was well and truly secured.

Alec's arms tightened around Aileen and Fiona could see the younger woman lean into the embrace. It seemed odd, but 'twas the only thing she could do—if not, she'd lose her seat and tumble to the ground.

With Aileen settled, the man on the white horse bent low and held his hand out to Fiona. She shook her head and backed away. He nudged his horse forward and she got her first clear look at his features.

There was something very familiar in the depths of those deep blue eyes, and the bold, chiseled angles of his cheeks and jaw. The harsh determination on his features was unmistakable, yet oddly reminiscent of someone else. Someone she knew.

A lump formed in Fiona's throat, nearly choking her with fear when she realized who she faced. For an instant she was stunned into silence, her mind trying to deny what her eyes told her.

"Ye'll ride with me, Lady Fiona," he said, in a voice as smooth as imported silk.

Aileen's breath hitched in surprise, but Fiona had already determined their identities were known to this man.

"As you command, Master Gilroy," she answered.

His eyes widened a fraction at her reply and Fiona knew her suspicion was correct. He was the earl's bastard half brother. His sworn enemy. But Fiona was not so foolish as to challenge him in front of his men. At this point, he was the only thing standing between them and brutal treatment, possibly even rape.

Though the voice in her head was screaming with protest, Fiona stood very still. Gilroy's hands encircled her waist. With a single grunt, he lifted her off the ground as though she weighed no more than a babe and placed her in front of him. Magnus quickly placed the bonds around her ankles, biting into her tender flesh as he tightened them.

"We're off." Gilroy pressed his knees into the horse's flanks and the animal instantly responded.

It was a teeth-rattling ride. Fiona struggled to keep her balance, an almost impossible accomplishment, given her awkward position on the horse and her bound hands and feet. Yet each time she feared she might indeed fall from the horse and be trampled to death,

Gilroy's arm tightened around her waist and pulled her closer to the solid wall of his muscular chest.

Her muscles trembled with the effort to keep her seat. Sweat lined her brow and trickled down her spine. As they rode, Fiona offered a short prayer of salvation, for their safe deliverance. However, her prayers soon gave way to blaspheme and before long she was cursing herself for falling into Gilroy's hands so easily.

She knew he would try to use them in some way to retaliate against Gavin. If they were lucky, he would try to ransom them. What did not bear thinking was the possibility he would harm or even kill them in order to goad the earl.

For all their sakes, she prayed that there was a shred of decency in Ewan Gilroy, a trace of the McLendon honor alive within his heart. It was their only hope.

After what felt like hours, they passed through a very dense section of woods and emerged in a small glade. Fiona had no idea how long they had been riding or even what direction they had traveled. Though he knew his lands far better than she did, Fiona rightfully feared Gavin would have a difficult time finding them.

Gilroy steered his horse slowly around the perimeter of the glen, then gave the signal to dismount. He reined in his snorting mount, waiting for one of his men to hold the bridle until he dismounted. Once on the ground, he reached up and pulled Fiona into his arms and set her on the ground.

Limbs aching, Fiona wobbled, nearly falling over. Aileen seemed to be having similar difficulty, but Alec reached out to steady her. Since Fiona was not afforded a similar courtesy, she was merely grateful she didn't tip over and land on her backside.

With everyone now standing, Fiona got her first good look at the rest of the men who accompanied Gilroy. They were a haggard bunch, almost all older than their leader, except for one of the lads. A few eyed her and Aileen with mild interest, two others openly leered.

Icy talons clutched Fiona's heart at those looks, the fear strong and sharp. She fought to stay calm, knowing she must not allow herself to panic. All was not lost. They had been captured, but thus far were uninjured.

At a nod from Gilroy, Alec moved between her and Aileen. He first grasped Aileen around the waist with his left arm, then did the same with his right to Fiona. Their hands and feet still bound, the women hobbled beside him as he half carried, half dragged them to a shady area beneath the trees.

Alec relinquished his hold and they fell, rather ungracefully, to the ground, each landing on their backs. Amused laughter rumbled from the circle of men who were obviously watching their every move. Fiona was certain they resembled a pair of flapping fish just pulled from the loch. Trying to regain her dignity, she rolled onto her stomach, her chin nearly colliding with the top of Aileen's head.

"We must try to escape," Aileen hissed.

Fiona could not contain a small grin. Aileen's fighting spirit bolstered her own flagging courage, but they could not afford to be foolish. "We will not get very far rolling our way through the woods," Fiona said, lifting her bound hands for emphasis.

Aileen winced. "I meant as soon as our feet and hands are freed from these bonds."

"I'm uncertain if that will occur anytime soon."

"They cannae keep us tied indefinitely," Aileen sputtered.

Fiona merely raised her brow. Aileen glared at her for a long moment before her shoulders sagged. "The earl will rescue us," she declared, yet Fiona could hear the trace of helplessness in the young woman's voice.

Fiona rolled to her side and watched the men, now gathered in a tight bunch, intently. A rather heated discussion was in progress, but most of the words were undistinguishable, making it impossible to follow the conversation. A rustling noise from the other side of the glen drew Fiona's attention—and her hopes—yet they were quickly dashed when the grain wagon she had been riding with appeared.

She gave a short prayer of mercy for the souls of the men who had been riding with her. Perhaps one or two of them had managed to escape?

Clearly, the grain cart had been Gilroy's original target. Capturing her and Aileen was merely a bonus to the outlaw, one he was delighted to exploit. If the situation had not been so dire, Fiona might have laughed at the irony. Father Niall's concern for her safety upon leaving the castle and insistence that she travel with the grain cart had placed her directly in the path of the earl's most despised and feared enemy.

The grain was quickly unloaded from the wagon. The sacks were counted, then lifted and tied on the backs of several horses. Once the bounty was secured, three of the men led the oxen away.

"'Tis a perfectly good cart," one of them muttered. "I dinnae know why we have to chop it fer firewood."

Gilroy shared a long, meaningful look with his men. "I want the job finished by nightfall. Make certain every trace of the damn thing is gone, including the wheels. Then distribute the wood among the houses in our glen."

"Bring the oxen to the butcher in Wrenshire," Alec added. "He'll take a hefty portion fer himself and not ask any questions about how ye got them."

The moment the trio left, another lengthy discussion ensued among the remaining men, complete with a few raised voices. Gilroy abruptly stopped the argument with a slash of his hand and the grumbling men fell silent.

Dirk drawn, Gilroy turned and approached her and Aileen. Fiona scrambled into a sitting position, a difficult maneuver with both her hands and feet tightly bound, yet somehow she managed. Aileen struggled to do the same and the women huddled against each other for support and courage.

"I'll cut ye loose, but I give ye fair warning. As long as ye obey me, no harm will come to ye," Ewan said, crouching down at their feet.

The promise sounded far more like a threat, but Fiona wasn't about to argue. The tight bindings had rendered her hands and feet numb and she was certain Aileen was suffering as well.

"We will do as you say," Fiona agreed, holding out her bound wrists.

With a swift, sharp swing, Ewan sliced through the thick ties and they fluttered to the ground. Blood immediately rushed to Fiona's hands, creating a tinkling, throbbing pain. Wincing, she flexed her fingers, the residual stiffness making it difficult to move them.

He raised the knife a second time and freed her feet. A small trickle of blood ran down her foot where the bond had rubbed the flesh raw. Retrieving the sliced linen from the ground, Fiona searched for a clean section and touched it to the spot to soothe the wound.

"What about me?" Aileen asked in a quiet voice, the small quiver betraying her unease.

Gilroy's eyes narrowed, but his lips curved into a smile. "Ye haven't agreed to my terms, lass," he said, pointing the knife toward Aileen's face. She gave a small cry, hardly more than a whisper.

"Be careful!" Fiona admonished, protectively blocking the knife with her body.

Gilroy pulled back in surprise. "I would have thought ye'd want me to slit her throat."

"What?" Fiona was shocked by the dreadful words he spoke with ominous cheer.

"If she's dead, then the earl cannae make her his wife."

"What a perfectly odious thing to say!" Fiona exclaimed, her eyes widening in horror.

He lifted his chin a bit higher. "Aye, there's horror in truth, milady, make no mistake about it."

He reached out and Aileen gave a soft cry, but that did not deter him. He swiftly cut the ties around her wrists. Then his hand held her ankle and he cut the binding around her feet. Fiona thought his hand lingered too long on Aileen's shapely calf. He glanced up and found her staring at him. He grimaced in distaste, then pulled the hem of Aileen's gown down past her ankles.

But Fiona had seen the gleam in Gilroy's eyes. Frantic, she glanced through the trees, wondering how far they could get on foot.

"Remember yer promise to me," Gilroy warned, as if able to read her thoughts. "Ye'll not get far before I catch ye and ye won't be happy when I do."

"We promised to obey ye," Aileen said with dignity. "We dinnae promise not to escape."

Gilroy leaned back on his haunches. "I can see that Laird Sinclair has raised a bold lass."

Aileen tossed her head. "I am a lady, sir, not a lass."

Gilroy broke into a lazy grin so reminiscent of Gavin that Fiona nearly smiled, too. It tugged at her heart, giving her a thin shard of hope that beneath all the anger and resentment there lay a modicum of decency.

"Be ye lady or lass, ye're still under my control. And ye'll do what I say."

A warm flush of blood pinked Aileen's cheeks. "My father will have yer head on a spike if ye mistreat us."

Gilroy's grin widened. "He needs to catch me first."

"Ewan!"

They all turned. Alec stood grim-faced, his wiry frame attempting to hold back a few of the men. Gilroy's expression became pensive. "Stay within my sight at all times, do ye understand?"

"The earl will pay you handsomely for our safe return," Fiona blurted out.

Gilroy gave her a hard look, his mouth twisting in a thin line. "It's not just coin I'm seeking from the earl. Though I suspect ye already knew that, Lady Fiona."

And with that cryptic comment, Gilroy turned and walked away.

Ewan cursed loudly. Encouraged by a disgruntled Magnus, the men were starting to argue again. Some couldn't decide how much the women were worth in ransom, while others thought it foolish to even let the earl know they were the ones who had taken them. Then there were a few who were in favor of simply getting rid of the *problem*.

The passionate words and heated exchanges let Ewan know it wouldn't take much to spark a fight and have them turn against each other. And him.

The boon that Ewan had believed had come his way the moment he spied Lady Fiona and Lady Aileen riding outside the castle, unattended and with no protection other than the few men riding with the grain cart, was starting to become his misfortune. But only if he let it.

There still had to be a way to turn this to his advantage. Both these women were an important prize, and truth be told, he did not want to waste it on mere coin. Though the raised voices and disgruntled comments suggested he might be forced to compromise and do what the majority of them wanted.

Still, Ewan's mind could not help but run wild with the endless possibilities of requests, most of which involved humiliating his brother in some manner. Having him kneel and pay homage to Ewan in front of the entire clan before proclaiming him a recognized and respected son of the Earl of Kirkland, no longer a bastard with no name and no heritage.

Other thoughts were less grand—forgiveness of any and all of Ewan's past transgressions, a pardon for his men, a promise that they would be allowed to live as free men and not outlaws. Or the grant of a holding of his own on McLendon land, along with the right to keep his own men-at-arms. It didn't have to be a large demesne. A small keep would suffice, but one that was his and his alone, where he would be free to do as he pleased.

It seemed that his requests were only limited by his imagination, yet in reality Ewan knew the earl would refuse to grant even one. Or if he did, he would relent and take his revenge.

"If we hold them fer ransom, the earl will know who each and every one of us are," Magnus insisted.

"Nay," Ewan retorted. "I'll be the one negotiating with the earl. He'll not know any of ye. Ye're safe."

Mollified, a few of the men nodded their heads. But Magnus wasn't satisfied. "The women have seen us. They can describe us, identify us."

Ewan shrugged. "We already live as outlaws. What does it matter if the McLendons know yer names?"

It was the wrong thing to say. Instead of looking at him, several of the men stared at the ground, avoiding his gaze.

"If the earl discovers who we are, we will be hunted men fer the rest of our lives," Alec said. "We'll never be able to return our families to a proper village life."

"Aye, and they might suffer fer our sins," Magnus added.

Ewan knew this was his fault. Magnus was a greedy man. He'd been poised to strike for months, just waiting for the opportune moment to challenge Ewan's leadership. Could he hold him off this time? Or would he finally be forced to fight?

"What exactly are ye proposing, Magnus?" Ewan asked.

Ewan saw the other man's jaw trembling as he fought to contain his excitement. "We cannae risk letting them go. But I say we have our fun with them first."

Ewan didn't bother to hide his revulsion. "Rape, first? Then kill them? Is that what ye mean? Then say it plainly."

Magnus stroked the stubbly beard on his chin. "We cannae risk them betraying our identities to the earl."

Ewan squared off against Magnus. "I dinnae believe Laird Sinclair will let the murder of his daughter go unpunished. Do ye wish to bring the wrath of the Sinclairs as well as the McLendons down upon our heads?"

"Ewan's right. There's no need to look fer more trouble," Alec said, stepping forward. "I say we ransom the Sinclair lass. She's a prize likely worth her weight in gold."

Several angry expressions quickly turned to greed. "What about the Englishwoman?" Ewan asked.

Alec shrugged. "We keep her."

"Keep her?" Ewan's eyes held a steely edge. "As what? Yer pet?"

"I thought it a fair compromise—"

"It's not." Ewan cut Alec off with a withering glare. "I've heard what ye have to say and now I need to think on it. I'll tell ye what we're doing once I've made my decision."

Magnus's eyes narrowed. "And if we dinnae agree with what ye decide?"

Ewan looked at the other men and burst into laughter. Yet he was the only one—none of the others even cracked a smile. Sobering, he gazed at the disgruntled band. "Enough!" he shouted. "I'm still the one in charge. Any man who no longer wishes to follow my lead is free to go."

"We dinnae want to leave." Magnus spit on the dirt

in front of him. "And we dinnae want to take orders anymore from ye."

"Well, if that's what ye want, then so be it." With a determined look, Ewan unsheathed his sword. Magnus and two others did the same.

Damn. This is going to get ugly.

Chapter 18

By the time it was confirmed that both Fiona and Aileen were indeed missing, Gavin's anger was roaring through the castle. Yet as riled and outraged as he was, the earl knew he needed a calm, clear head. Still, it was difficult to keep his temper in check as he waited for Father Niall to be brought to him.

And when the priest revealed Fiona's plans to leave, and his part in her departure, Gavin was nearly spitting with rage.

"I could wring yer neck fer this, priest or no," Gavin said in a low growl.

Father Niall bowed his head. "My regret knows no bounds, my lord. I shall never forgive myself if anything sinister befalls Lady Fiona. Or Lady Aileen."

Gavin could hardly hold still. "Be gone from my sight before my anger overcomes my common sense and I act upon it," he snarled.

Father Niall quickly hurried away. Gavin expelled a deep breath, striving for a clear head. He looked up.

Connor, Duncan, and Aidan stood before him at the ready. Thank goodness.

"At least we know that Lady Fiona left with the grain cart that was heading north," Aidan said. "And Lady Aileen departed soon after, following the cart. It shouldn't be too hard to find them."

"But they left early this morning," Duncan said.

"'Tis a heavy, lumbering cart drawn by a pair of oxen," Aidan replied. "A small contingent of men on horseback will easily catch them before nightfall."

Gavin nodded. Aidan's calm confidence soothed his badly frayed temper. Wasting no time, the men hurried to the stables. The horses were being readied when a shout from the guard tower rained down from above.

Bloody hell, now what?

A bedraggled group of men staggered into the bailey, their faces covered with dust and dirt, their eyes weary with exhaustion.

"We were set upon by thieves, milord," one of the men said in a pitiful voice. "They stole the grain, cart and all."

"'Twas Gilroy and his thieving band of mercenaries," a second fellow declared. "I've no doubt about it."

Gavin's eyes searched frantically among the small group, dismayed to find only a handful of men. "What about the woman who was traveling with ye?"

The man scratched his head. "She only rode with us fer a few hours, then turned to meet another rider. Another female. We think the women rode off together."

"And ye let them?" Gavin shouted.

"Our task was to protect and deliver the grain," the man sputtered.

Connor grabbed Gavin's arm. "Perhaps the women got away?" he asked hopefully.

Gavin took a moment to consider it. "Nay. If they were free, they would have returned. I fear Gilroy has stolen far more than our grain this day."

Gavin leveled a furious stare at no one in particular, then spun himself in a frustrated circle. A litany of grievous harm that might befall Fiona, and Aileen, ran through his mind, causing his heart to slam rapidly against his chest. Seeing his agitation, Aidan stepped forward.

"Do ye think Gilroy knows what a prize he's captured?"

"Aye, he knows."

"Then he'll want to ransom the women," Duncan insisted.

"Some might advise that we wait fer Gilroy to contact us with his demands," Connor suggested.

Gavin ran his hand through his hair. Sit patiently waiting for Gilroy to make his move? Never!

"We'll ride together to the spot where the grain was stolen and then split our most able-bodied men into four groups, each riding in a different direction, north, south, east, and west," Gavin decided. "We four will command the units. We will search our lands and beyond, if necessary. We willnae return until they have been found."

The three brothers nodded. "We will bring them back," Duncan stated emphatically. "Unharmed."

Aidan saw to organizing the men while Gavin gave the order to ready the horses. As he prepared to mount his horse, he laid a hand on his gut, which had been churning from the moment he realized Fiona was gone.

His fears for her safety were making him nauseous and he despised the weakness.

Gavin lifted himself onto his horse, staring impatiently at the rest of the men as they prepared to leave, until a frightened voice caused him to look down.

"What's wrong?"

Spencer stood before him, his eyes darting frantically from one man to the next. Gavin stared down at him for a hazy moment. A grim silence descended upon the bailey as Gavin, Connor, Duncan, and Aidan all exchanged troubled glances.

"Is it my mother?" Spencer sniffled, wiping his nose with the back of his hand. "Tell me. Please."

"Lady Fiona and Lady Aileen have gone missing," Gavin reported. "We are making ready to search fer them."

"But I heard one of the men said the women are in grave danger. Is that true?"

A raw tension stretched through Gavin as he tried to formulate an answer. "There might be trouble," he conceded. "'Tis the reason we are in such a hurry to find them."

The lad looked stricken. "'Tis my fault. I should have told ye."

Gavin felt the hot flames of anger lick at his chest. "What do ye know of this, Spencer?"

"She sent for me earlier today, before dawn. To say good-bye. I asked her not to go, but she insisted it was necessary."

"Did she tell ye where she was going?"

"No. She only said that she would write to me once she was safely settled." Spencer's brow furrowed with distress. "I'm sorry I didn't tell ye."

Disappointment poured through Gavin. Not at the

lad's deception, for he expected him to be loyal to his mother, but at the lack of any additional information that might aid them in finding Fiona.

"Ye need never apologize for being faithful and true, but ye must remember a knight's vow to protect his lady, even if the lady doesn't always wish it."

Looking thoroughly miserable, Spencer gave a slight nod of agreement. Having no time to offer any additional comfort, Gavin drew his horse forward. But he had barely cleared the stable yard when a blur of brown fur darted in front of his horse, nearly unseating him.

Pulling up hard on the reins, he managed to stop his stallion before it collided with the creature. A chorus of curses was heard from the others who had witnessed the encounter, a sentiment Gavin fully echoed. Yet with his efforts so focused on controlling his mount, he was unable to get a close look at what had run across the bailey.

Gavin's initial reaction of annoyance quickly melted, replaced by a renewed arousal of hope when he realized it was Fiona's mangy cur. Almost as if knowing he had barely avoided causing a disaster, the dog sat obediently still, except for his tail, which swished rapidly in the dirt.

"Search Lady Fiona's room and fetch me something, anything she left behind that would have her scent on it," he commanded.

"I'll do it," Spencer cried.

"Hurry, lad," Gavin shouted at the boy's retreating back.

Spencer's awkward gait grew more noticeable as the lad struggled to increase his speed. Yet he returned a few minutes later, carrying a blue silk gown that Gavin immediately recognized.

Burying the pang of dismay at discovering Fiona had deliberately left behind his gift, Gavin knew he could use it to their advantage. "Give it here," he said, motioning impatiently with his fingers. "We'll ride to the place where the grain cart was ambushed, then hope the beast will catch Lady Fiona's scent and lead us to her."

Aidan raised a skeptical brow. "It could work. The dogs are usually successful in tracking deer and rabbits."

"'Tis worth a try," Gavin said, as he hastily rolled the garment into a ball and stuffed it in the leather bag that hung on his saddle.

Spencer took hold of Gavin's reins. "Please, my lord, may I come with ye?"

It was out of the question. They would be riding fast and hard and the lad's presence would slow them down. Yet it was cruel to crush the hope in the child's eyes so brutally.

"I need ye to stay here, in case the women return on their own," Gavin said. "Will ye do that for me?"

Though clearly disappointed, Spencer nodded. Gavin leaned down and patted the lad on the shoulder. "Take heart, Spencer. I willnae rest until she is found."

Fiona and Aileen sat on the edge of the camp, watching the exchange between Gilroy and his men with growing unease.

"If they begin fighting among themselves, we must capitalize on the distraction and seize the chance to escape," Aileen muttered.

Fiona grimaced. "We won't have a chance of getting

away unless we can reach our horses and they're on the other side of the camp."

Both women sighed with frustration at the sight of the two rows of tethered horses, knowing it would be impossible to get near them unseen.

"Maybe we can melt into the forest once they draw their swords?" Aileen suggested, a rising note of desperation in her voice. "They'll be so distracted, they might not notice we are gone fer a few minutes, giving us an advantage."

Fiona glanced at the circle of grumbling men. Though they were intent on airing their grievances, she noted several kept darting speculative looks their way. "There are too many keen eyes trained on us. Let's hope that Gilroy can keep his men under control."

Minutes later, the shrieking sound of swords being unsheathed dashed any hope of that happening. Two of the men stepped forward. Sword drawn, Gilroy stood between them.

"Two against one? Are none of the others going to fight beside him?" Aileen cried in outrage.

"Apparently not," Fiona replied, as a terrible sense of foreboding flooded through her. She set her elbows on her knees and put her head in her hands. *Think!* There had to be a way to use this situation to their advantage.

"Mother Mary!" Aileen hastily crossed herself and moved closer to Fiona.

Fiona looked up. Aileen's face went pale. Fiona shut her eyes at the screeching metal ring of the first strike of sword upon sword, but they flew open when Aileen hissed out a startled breath.

Fiona strained to see between the men assembled around the fight. They fought without shields, making the attacks even more deadly. Gilroy feigned left, struck right, then did the reverse, alternating his strikes with precise efficiency, beating back his opponent. The man stumbled backward into the onlookers, but one of them caught him and shoved him forward again.

But he was forced to wait his turn, as Gilroy was already engaged in combat with the second man. Pushing himself, Gilroy began to roar with each swing of his sword, the battle cry almost as powerful as the weapon. He deflected each blow and beat back his second foe, then tossed his sweat-soaked hair off his brow and waited for the next move as the pair stood side by side.

Gilroy's opponents exchanged a pointed look.

Oh, no. Heart pounding, Fiona watched the two men run forward, charging Gilroy at the same time. Holding his great sword in both hands, Gilroy braced his feet apart and swung the heavy sword high over his head, slashing first to his left and then the right.

Blood spurted instantly from Gilroy's opponents. They fell to the ground, one clutching his stomach, the other his neck and shoulder. Writhing in pain, the mortally wounded men were pulled from the circle by a few of the others, a trail of bright red blood marking their exit route.

Fiona's stomach roiled. So much blood! But even more concerning was the hard, bellowing breaths Gilroy emitted. He was tiring. Which was precisely what that worm Magnus had counted upon. Fiona now realized that allowing the other two men to fight first had been a calculated risk, for it was presumed the one who killed the leader was the next to take the position.

But Magnus was also aware of Gilroy's skill, which was clearly superior, even fighting against two. What better way to increase his odds than to face a tired and breathless Gilroy?

Yet before he stepped forward to challenge Gilroy, Magnus's eyes narrowed on her and Aileen. Fiona felt her throat tighten. Bitter tears filled her eyes and guilt gnawed at her heart.

It was her fault they had been captured and were now in mortal danger. 'Twas true she could not have known that Aileen would follow her, but she still shouldered the blame. Fiona's sins were hers to endure, but Aileen was innocent and did not deserve such a gruesome fate.

And Fiona had no doubt it would be gruesome. She had seen enough soldiers in her time to recognize the signs of desperation in Magnus's eyes, the barely suppressed rage that once unleashed would be uncontrollable.

And directed at her and Aileen. If Gilroy lost this battle, they were doomed.

Glaring venomously, Magnus slashed his sword at Gilroy's head, but Gilroy moved to his left at the last second and the steel whizzed through the air. Magnus snarled at the near miss and charged hastily. Gilroy struck at his kneecap and Magnus went down hard, cursing as he fell.

Gilroy spun around, moving in for the kill, but Magnus rolled to his right and avoided the blow. He came up fighting mad. He attacked with meticulous force, advancing ruthlessly, the harsh grate of metal striking metal rattling Fiona's teeth. Valiantly, Gilroy fended off the blows, but he was clearly on the defensive.

What Magnus lacked in grace and finesse he made up for in brute strength and determination. His arm never seemed to tire as he wielded his heavy sword again and again.

Magnus jabbed at Gilroy's chest. The thrust found its mark and pierced his leather leine croich. Gilroy leapt away. Fiona winced at the certain pain and saw a spurt of blood erupt from Gilroy's shoulder. Thankfully, it soon slowed to a trickle, but the sight spurred Magnus's attack.

He pressed harder, the blows ringing loudly in the clearing. Then Magnus brought his sword up from underneath, striking hard at Gilroy's blade. The hilt of the mighty weapon jolted out of Gilroy's hand and went flying through the air. With a sinister shout of triumph, Magnus pointed the tip of his sword in Gilroy's face.

The other men quieted. Fiona moaned in fear; Aileen covered her eyes with both hands.

Magnus thrust his sword forward, his eyes glazed with excitement. But Gilroy ducked out of harm's way before the blade could find its mark, pulling his dirk out of its sheath as he moved. An off-balance Magnus stumbled forward. Gilroy quickly seized the advantage and ruthlessly struck at the vulnerable hollow of Magnus's throat, burying the blade to the hilt.

Magnus's sightless eyes remained open in shock as he fell to the ground. Fiona stood transfixed, unable to look away from the body.

There was a long drawn-out silence before Alec leaned over Magnus, then looked up at the rest of them and proclaimed, "He's dead."

Still clutching his dirk, Gilroy's shoulders sagged in exhaustion. But he rallied quickly, pointing his blade forcefully in a slow circle toward the rest of his men. His voice was strong and commanding when he questioned, "Is there anyone else in the mood to challenge me on this fine afternoon?"

The fight was over, yet the excitement had just begun. The sound of a barking dog echoed through the glen and then, with no further warning, a contingent of men on horseback rushed into the clearing, Gavin in the lead. He vaulted off his horse and lunged at Gilroy, easily getting past the other men, who were too shocked and surprised to draw their weapons.

"As the Lord is my witness, I shall have yer fool head set on a pike fer this outrage," Gavin shouted, his voice rising to an almost ear-shattering pitch.

Gilroy whirled to face the earl, who agilely ducked beneath the wide swing of Gilroy's dirk. Coming up directly in front of his bastard brother, Gavin grasped a fistful of Gilroy's hair, yanking his head back. He placed the edge of his sword at Gilroy's throat, pressing forward until a trickle of blood ran down the man's neck.

The look in Gavin's eye was easily understood—he meant to slay the bastard without a second thought. But for all his mischief, Fiona did not believe Gilroy deserved such an untimely demise. And she also believed that one day Gavin would come to regret this brutal act.

"No!" Without realizing how it came to happen, Fiona found herself at Gavin's side, clutching the arm that held the sword. "Please, Gavin, don't. Spare him."

"After all that he's done?" Gavin questioned in disbelief.

"Aileen and I are unharmed."

"Aye," Aileen added. "Frightened and a bit bruised, but unhurt."

"Have ye both gone mad? Gilroy kidnapped ye!" Gavin seethed in disgust.

"Not precisely," Fiona countered. "He did not breach the walls and invade the castle to take us. He saw us in the woods and seized the opportunity."

Gavin's stormy blue eyes shifted from Fiona to Aileen and then back to Fiona. He held her gaze for the longest moment, then shook his head. "I fail to see the difference."

In a way, so did Fiona. But she pressed on, knowing she needed to prevent this from happening. "He just killed three of his own men to protect us. I know that does not excuse any of his other crimes, but I beg you to seek justice, not vengeance."

Gavin scoffed. "Those men meant nothing to him. Just as killing means nothing."

"No, you are wrong," Fiona interjected. "I watched his face as he fought. Gilroy did what was necessary, yet he took no joy in the act. He is not merely a brutal ruffian. There is honor in him."

"Then I shall afford him an honorable death," Gavin replied, anger thickening his voice. "At the end of a rope."

"No!" Aileen's voice was adamant. "If ye do this, I shall tell my father to break the alliance with King Robert and withdraw his support."

Gavin cocked his head to one side and stared at Aileen in disbelief. "Don't ye dare to threaten me! The Countess of Kirkland will bend her knee in supplication and reverence to our rightful king," Gavin bellowed.

Aileen pulled herself to her fullest height, tilted

her chin and looked him directly in the eye. "We both know that I shall never be yer countess, Gavin McLendon. So I'm asking ye straight out—do ye want to save the alliance between our clans or toss it on the rubbish heap? The choice is entirely up to ye."

Edict delivered, Aileen turned on her heel and stomped toward her horse.

"'Tis a shame ye'll not have the chance to bed that one," Ewan said with a smirk. "She's a lively lass, assured to offer some excitement between the sheets."

"Shut up." Gavin cuffed the younger man on the back of the head, then shoved him toward two waiting soldiers. "Dinnae forget I can still let ye hang. Best watch yer tongue or I'll toss a rope over a sturdy tree limb and do it right now."

As his men took a still-grinning Gilroy away, Gavin turned his attention toward Fiona.

All expression drained from her face.

The others pulled back. After so much chaos, the glen became oddly silent. Fiona's mouth opened several times, yet she spoke not a word, continuing to stare at him as though she were debating what to say. Gavin folded his arms across his chest impatiently.

She had defied his orders, placed herself in grave danger, scared him half to death, then led him on a harrowing chase. An explanation was the very least he deserved. And it had better be a damn good one.

"I cannae believe it, Fiona," Gavin finally said. "The one time I'm waiting for ye to speak yer mind, ye haven't said a word to me."

She inclined her head. "I am beholden to you for

coming to our aid. I thought traveling with the grain cart as an escort would be safe, but I was wrong."

Fiona fixed her stare over his shoulder, refusing to look at him. Gavin would not allow it. Taking her chin, he angled it toward him, forcing her to look directly at him. "Why did ye run from me, Fiona?"

Her eyes welled with tears. "I did not have the strength to stand docilely by in silence while you married another woman."

"Why?"

Fiona shook her head, pulling away from his hands. "I just couldn't."

"Why?" he repeated.

Fiona moved to walk away from him. Gavin grasped her arm, keeping her beside him, and waited. "Pride," she finally mumbled, her chin sinking down to rest on her chest. "'Twas my pride that compelled me to leave."

"Only yer pride?"

"Yes." Fiona stood without moving, her hands curled at her side. Only the slight trembling of her lips hinted at the extent of her anguish.

It was a feeling he suddenly shared. He had believed she left because she cared for him, even loved him. Hopefully, as much as he loved her. Was he wrong? Had it truly only been pride that prompted such rash action? Uncertainty momentarily plagued him, but Gavin brushed it aside.

He had nearly lost Fiona today. He was not about to let her get away from him a second time. Feeling far less sure of himself, Gavin cleared his throat.

"Lady Aileen just refused my suite. Rather adamantly. And loud enough to be heard in London, I'm sure."

His lips curved, hoping to tempt a small smile from her. But Fiona winced and looked away. "Aileen is upset, and rightly so, after this harrowing ordeal. I'm certain once she speaks with her father, all will be set to rights."

"I willnae marry her."

He threw the words down like a gauntlet, then waited for her to react. Would she be happy that the marriage was not going to take place? Was that enough to entice her to willingly return?

"If not Lady Aileen, then you shall marry some other Scottish noblewoman," Fiona rasped, casting her gaze on the ground. "We both understand that is what your king wants and your duty requires."

"There are other ways to fulfill my duties."

Ah, now that got her attention. Fiona's head jerked toward him and he saw a full range of emotions play across her features. "What do you mean?"

"I mean that I can serve my king just as well with an English wife," Gavin announced.

Fiona let out a squeak. At least Gavin thought it was a squeak, though in truth it might have been a squeal. "You cannot marry me," she said in a whispered rush.

"Why?"

"Why? Why? Saints preserve us, that seems to be your favorite word this afternoon. 'Tis maddening."

She nearly stamped her foot for emphasis. The gesture brought a smile to Gavin's lips. He loved her so much. It didn't matter if her heart was not as engaged as his; he was confident that in time she would come to love him as deeply and completely as he loved her.

"Why are ye getting so upset?" he asked, holding back an even wider grin.

"I don't like being taunted, my lord. 'Tis cruel."

"I beg yer pardon. I never meant to be cruel or brutal, but I know I've treated ye poorly. I only pray that ye can forgive me." He leaned down and placed a gentle kiss on her forehead. And her nose. And each cheek. "Oh, Fiona, 'tis past time I told ye what was in my heart. I love ye, lass. And I always will."

Her expression went blank and Gavin's heart skipped. Wasn't a woman supposed to feel joy at hearing a declaration of love?

"Say it again," she whispered.

Relief poured through him. "Why?" he teased.

"Gavin!"

"I love ye, Fiona. I lay claim to yer heart and live with the hope that one day soon ye will return the feeling."

Fiona blinked at him. "Truly? I know you want me, desire me, but love? Are you certain?"

He crushed her to his chest, almost squeezing the breath from her. "Ye must know the reason I was near out of my mind with worry when I discovered ye were gone was because I cannae bear the thought of losing ye. I love ye that much and now that I've got ye back, I mean to hold and keep ye."

They pulled apart, but he kept his hand wrapped around her waist. The smile that broke out on Fiona's face was brighter than the glistening sunshine rippling on the loch. She leaned forward suddenly and kissed him, her mouth tender, but passionate.

"You've made me very happy, Gavin," she said, nuzzling her nose against his chest.

"I'm glad." Bracing himself to hear the truth, whatever it may be, Gavin once again asked, "Now, tell me truthfully, why did ye run from me, lass?"

Her brow puckered slightly and then she smiled. "Because I love you, you damn fool."

The hope Gavin had been clinging to sprang to life.

He threw back his head and bellowed with laughter, then lifted Fiona in his arms and swung her in a wide circle. He could barely believe his good fortune. He was being given a second chance and by the holy rod, he was not going to waste it.

"So, my sweet English lass, will ye do me the great honor of becoming my wife?"

She paused, staring at him in wonder. "Aye, my Scottish lord. I will marry you."

The joyful emotion in her voice matched the feelings coursing through his veins. "Then come along, Fiona. 'Tis past time to return home. We've a wedding celebration to arrange."

Chapter 19

A strong breeze whipped through the trees, the birds chattered nervously, and dark rain clouds threatened in the distance. But for Fiona, seated in front of Gavin on his horse and snuggled tightly in his arms, it was the perfect ending to a harrowing day.

Her head felt as though it always belonged cradled in the crook of his shoulder. Here at last she felt the wholeness and peace that had been missing from her life. She hadn't moved from this position since they left the glen, not even when they had stopped by a brook to water the horses.

No, she had stayed safe within her love's embrace, observing the craggy hills in the distance with mild interest. Happiness and wonder filled her chest, swamping any other feelings. Worries about the future, concerns about how others—namely King Robert and Laird Sinclair—would react when they heard that Gavin intended to make her his wife, faded.

He loved her. Gavin loved her.

For the first time Fiona had real hope that all would be well. She would become Gavin's wife and live out the rest of her days by his side. It felt giddy to realize that the happiness that had eluded her for so long was finally here.

Joy, it seemed, came in unexpected bursts, buried among the mundane and ordinary, balanced by tragedy and sorrow. She had known all those emotions, experiencing poignant despair and near-crippling fear. Was that what made this moment all the more sweet? All the more valued? Or was it the fact that she had overcome impossible odds and in the end achieved her heart's desire?

Most likely it was a mix of all those things. Love, it appeared, was wont to bloom wherever it willed, with no consideration to politics or propriety. How marvelous!

The landscape rolled past. Fiona shifted in the saddle, trying to ease the stiffness in her legs. Seeing her discomfort, Gavin reached down and began massaging her hip, his strong fingers making short work of the knotted muscles. She sighed and leaned back, smiling when she felt him rubbing his nose lightly against the top of her head.

"Only a few more hours and we shall be home, my love," he promised.

Fiona looked up. She ran her fingers over his forehead, sweeping his hair away from his face. A small smile played around his lips, but his deep blue eyes were alight with happiness.

Suddenly, Fiona's own eyes were stinging, the corners saturated with tears, but she refused to cry. Sobbing meant sorrow and that was the very last thing she was feeling. The joy in her heart knew no bounds, the delight in her soul was limitless.

Riding thusly, they were only able to converse

sparingly. But words were not needed when emotions ran so high. Every now and again, Gavin would lean his head down and rumble some suggestive bit of nonsense in her ear. The provocative statements had Fiona squirming with anticipation. Heedless of decorum, she cooed a few equally graphic suggestions herself, delighted to see the sharp flare of desire heat Gavin's gaze.

It had been far too long since they shared a bed and never as acknowledged lovers. The anticipation of an intimate reunion was foremost in her mind—and judging by the heat and hardness of the arousal pressing insistently against her lower back, Gavin felt the same way.

Would the freedom to open their hearts and express their emotions without restraint make it different somehow? Fiona suspected that it would and she was more than curious to discover if she was right.

As Gavin had predicted, it took them several hours to reach the castle. Fiona hadn't realized they were so far away. She glanced down at Laddie, admiring the dog's stamina. At her insistence, he had been hoisted over Duncan's saddle, sitting mostly in the man's lap, when they first rode out, but had jumped down when they stopped to water the horses and refused to be picked up again.

Instead, the dog ran ahead of the horses, leading the way home. It seemed fitting somehow, since he had led them to Fiona and Aileen. Fiona suspected there would be many soup bones in the dog's future, a fitting reward he had more than earned.

There was a shout of excitement from the men when the castle came into view. The exhaustion that threatened to overtake Fiona melted away as she stared at the impressive gray curtain wall and soaring towers. As they rode into the bailey they were met by a deafening cheer. Bewildered, Fiona stared over at Aileen, but the young woman had already dismounted.

"I thought this lot would have been joyful to see the last of me," Fiona muttered. "Or be wishing that I was eaten by a wild boar."

"There are a few who have taken a liking to ye," Gavin insisted. "'Tis only the witless ones who carry a grudge against yer English heritage."

Fiona smiled timidly at the crowd, determined not to let the many unexpected smiling faces she saw fool her into a false sense of belonging. No doubt the grumbling would start again, loud and long, when it was revealed she was to marry Gavin.

"Father!" Aileen's cry of joy could be heard across the bailey.

Laird Sinclair ran forward, his expression one of shocked relief. He was surrounded by a circle of his clansmen, who trotted alongside him. Within seconds Aileen was enfolded in her father's arms.

"I came the moment my men brought me the news. Tell me true, are ye hurt, daughter?"

"Nay," Aileen replied, her voice trembling. "Though I'm so happy to see ye, I swear I could burst into sobs."

The laird broke into a relieved smile. But his good mood didn't last long.

"I demand to know how this happened," Sinclair shouted, patting his daughter's cheek, his anxious, sweeping glance examining her from head to toe. "I left Aileen in yer care, under yer protection. How dare ye be so careless with such a treasure?"

Gavin stiffened. "Lady Aileen's predicament is entirely of her own doing."

"I dinnae believe it!" Sinclair growled.

Aileen placed a restraining hand on her father's shoulder, yet said nothing to refute the claim. Why was she waiting? Why wasn't she explaining what had happened?

"Lady Aileen?" Gavin's brow raised, and Fiona could feel his shudder as he struggled to rein in his rising temper.

"Milord?"

"Dinnae ye have something to tell yer father?"

Aileen wrinkled her nose. Gavin cast her a threatening glare and Fiona's heart lurched. The coy expression on Aileen's face set Fiona's nerves on edge, but it was Laird Sinclair's expression that worried her most. 'Twas evident to anyone who bothered to look that the man doted on his daughter.

So, if Aileen was upset, then the laird would be angered, perhaps even feel compelled to do something rash. If she so chose, Aileen had the perfect chance to mislead her father. A circumstance that did not bode well for Fiona and Gavin.

"Aye, milord, there is much that my father needs to be told," Aileen declared. Her words were dripping with sweetness, but there was venom in her eyes.

Not wanting the entire courtyard to be privy to the very private conversation that was sure to follow, Gavin led Laird Sinclair and his daughter into the private solar on the third floor of the keep, where their voices wouldn't be heard—no matter how loud the shouting got.

Fiona made a move to pull away, but Gavin held her arm tightly and pulled her up the staircase beside him. He didn't care that Sinclair raised his brow when he glimpsed the gesture, nor did Gavin hesitate to ignore Duncan's sign of warning to tread lightly. They could all sod off. He was not about to be separated from Fiona after having so recently experienced the anguish of losing her, and woe to any man who dared to question his action.

The tension in the chamber was thick as a bowl of porridge on a cold winter's morn. Sinclair had his stern gaze pinned on Gavin's chest, Aileen had her arms crossed and a mulish expression on her face, and Fiona looked as though she'd rather be mucking out the stables instead of standing among them.

He caught her gaze, mouthing silently not to worry. Her answering smile went straight to his heart.

"We are reasonable men," Gavin said calmly, tamping down his own ire. "The truth of the matter is that Aileen has returned unharmed."

"That may be, but I've yet to hear the reason why she was in danger in the first place. Have ye been telling tales about the strength of yer defenses? Did the scoundrel breach yer walls and steal my Aileen from under yer very nose?"

"Nay! The walls of my castle have never been breached, nor has my keep fallen in a siege," Gavin said. "Lady Aileen left the castle of her own accord, without a proper escort and without telling anyone."

Laird Sinclair's face blanched. "Is that true, daughter?"

Aileen gulped. "'Tis."

"Damn ye!" The laird bellowed, slamming his fist on the table. "What did ye do to my daughter that caused her to run from ye?"

"Me? I did nothing," Gavin countered, outraged that Sinclair would assume he was responsible.

The laird blinked, but the fury still burned in his eyes. "Aileen?"

"The earl speaks the truth, Father," Aileen said in a bitter tone. "He did *nothing.*"

The laird peered suspiciously at Gavin, then stole a look at his daughter, clearly trying to make sense of their words. "I need a drink," he finally announced.

Gavin scowled. The dull throb in his temple pounded a tad harder. *Christ, the last thing I want is to have to reason with an angry,* drunken *Sinclair*, he thought, but there was no help for it. He walked across the solar and yanked open the door.

Duncan, Aidan, and Connor practically fell into the room. Obviously the trio had been listening at the door. Gavin scowled with condemnation at his cousins. "Make yerselves useful and tell Hamish to bring us ale, wine, *and* whiskey."

Orders delivered, he forcefully shut the door. The tension in the chamber escalated as they waited. Gavin risked a glance at Fiona. Both Sinclair and Aileen were staring at her. Sinclair looked suspicious while Aileen was visibly distressed.

Fiona's lips were pressed into a thin, tight line and she appeared unnerved by their scrutiny. It was obvious that her careful attempt not to call attention to herself had failed.

Bloody hell, where was that damn whiskey!

In a noisy blur of shuffling feet, Hamish entered with a tray of tankards, goblets, a pitcher of ale, another of wine, and a jug of whiskey. Without being offered by his host, Sinclair helped himself. He downed a tankard of ale, then filled the vessel with whiskey. He took three swallows before slamming it down on the table, then dragged the back of his hand across his mouth.

"Tell me again, daughter, what happened to ye today?"

Aileen showed her teeth in a humorless smile before answering the laird. "I awoke very early this morning and was unable to get back to sleep, so I walked the battlements in anticipation of the sunrise.

"It was from there that I saw Lady Fiona in the bailey riding behind the grain cart. I was curious about this most unusual occurrence, so I followed her. Due to the early hour, there was no time to gather any men to accompany me and no one to tell of my plans. I grant that I acted in haste, but I know of the dangers and never intended to ride very far. I assumed the men guarding the grain cart would also provide me with protection."

Sinclair gave Fiona an appraising look. "What exactly were ye doing traveling with a grain cart, Lady Fiona?"

Fiona's head jerked up. "I was making a pilgrimage to the shrine of the Virgin Mother. The cart, with its escort, was going near, so I rode with them. Father Niall kindly made the arrangements for me."

"Why did the earl refuse to provide ye with a proper escort for such a holy journey?" Sinclair questioned.

"I didn't ask him," Fiona stammered. "He has far more important matters to consider."

"The moment I was alerted that the women were missing, I followed them both," Gavin added.

"I thought ye were a man of honor, milord," Aileen challenged, her eyes narrowed and shrewd. "I'm wondering if ye would have bothered to chase after me, if Lady Fiona was not also missing."

Indignation heated Gavin's face. "Ye were under my protection. I would never leave any female in my care without aid."

Aileen's brow shot up. "Even one ye are being forced to marry?"

"No one forces my hand," Gavin declared.

"Really? Then ye'll be wanting to make me yer wife as soon as possible. Is that what ye're saying?"

Gavin cringed. The lass was too bold for her own good. Or rather his good.

"He's yer betrothed, Aileen," Laird Sinclair insisted. "Of course he's going to marry ye."

She gave her father a patronizing glare. "He might have fooled ye, and even himself in this matter, but I've seen it with my own eyes. He wants Lady Fiona and he'll not give her up, no matter who he marries."

Sinclair gave Gavin a hard look. "Is that true?"

Gavin clenched his jaw. The laird would learn the truth eventually, so there seemed little point in keeping it from him. Yet there had to be a way to explain it that would not offer such great offense. "There is no denying that I love Lady Fiona. With all my heart."

Sinclair's ruddy face grew even redder and he nearly spewed a mouthful of whiskey all over the room. Instead, he swallowed, took a second swig and faced Gavin. "Are ye saying ye won't honor our agreement and marry my Aileen?"

Now how was he supposed to answer that without starting a lifelong feud? Stalling, Gavin rubbed his chin, trying to find the right words. He glanced at Aileen and his spirits immediately lifted. Mayhap he wouldn't have to answer Sinclair. One look at the defiant tilt of Aileen's chin said it all.

"I think 'tis important that we remember the reasons fer this marriage in the first place," Gavin began in a rambling tone. "We need to secure and strengthen King Robert's throne to keep the English—"

"It doesn't matter what he says," Aileen interrupted impatiently. "I willnae marry him, and that's the end of it."

"Aileen Margaret Gertrude Sinclair," the laird bellowed, pounding his fist into his hand. "I'll not be having a lass of yer tender years dictating to me what's to be done. If I say ye're to marry him, then by the holy rod, that's what ye'll do!"

Gavin waited for the storm clouds to break when Aileen's temper ignited and she fought back. But she proved to be a far more clever lass than he realized. Instead of digging in her heels and acting like a shrew, she bowed her head, brought herself directly in front of her father and knelt at his feet.

"I know ye're wise and loving and that ye only want what's best fer me and our clan. But, Father, please, I beg of ye not to press this marriage. I beg that in yer mercy ye'll grant me a reprieve from a loveless marriage that will bring me a lifetime of unhappiness, misery, and regret."

Unhappiness, misery, and regret? That was a bit dramatic. Gavin lifted his brow, uncertain how he felt at being labeled such a poor husband. But then he realized she had the courage to speak the truth; it would not be a happy life for either of them.

They all waited anxiously for the laird to answer. Yet as one minute turned into two, Gavin realized no matter what Sinclair said, he would not marry Aileen. The woman who would share his life, and his bed, for the rest of his days was Fiona.

"I—" Gavin began, but Aileen cut him off.

"Please, milord. Have the decency to allow my father to make this all-important decision without any interference from ye!"

"I shall pray fer guidance," Laird Sinclair finally answered, draining his tankard.

"If ye think it best," Aileen replied meekly. "Though I vow if ye search yer heart, the answer will be revealed."

Damn, she was good! Despite the gravity of the situation, Gavin smiled. Whoever Aileen Sinclair married one day would be a lucky man, though he would surely be led on a merry chase by his clever wife.

"Will ye truly be so miserable as the earl's wife, Aileen?" Sinclair asked, peering down at his daughter, who remained on her knees before him.

"Aye. Today was a horror-filled day, being taken by those brigands. I've never been so frightened in all my life, nor in such grave peril. It made me realize how fleeting life truly is, how quickly it can all end. And when the end comes fer me, I want to have something beautiful and happy to remember." She took a deep breath, her chest rising visibly with the effort. "I was willing to do my duty and I still am, but I cannae bind myself to a man in love with another woman and be happy. I know that fer certain."

The laird gave a sharp hoot. "I suppose if I grant yer wish and dissolve this contract, ye'll be wanting to choose yer own husband?"

"Nay. 'Tis too great a responsibility to be left to a young female such as myself." Aileen's shoulders sagged. "The choice will be yers."

The laird eyed his daughter shrewdly. "Hmm. I'll choose the man, but then ye'll decide if ye'll wed him. Is that what yer saying, lass?"

For a long moment Aileen simply stared at her father. Then she broke into a guilty smile. "That sounds like a fair and just arrangement."

Sinclair threw up his hands, then turned his gaze to Gavin.

"I gather ye have made yer decision?" Gavin asked.

"Aye," the laird grumbled. "I've decided that I'm the biggest fool in all of Christendom fer letting a spoiled child sway my opinion."

"Oh, Father, thank ye." Jumping to her feet, Aileen wrapped her arms around the laird and hugged him tightly. "All I want is the chance fer love. I want to marry a man who will at least try to find a place in his heart fer me. Some might call it foolish nonsense, but I believe that can happen, even in an arranged marriage."

Sinclair's eyes softened. "It can. It does. I met yer sainted mother the morning of our wedding. We lived and loved together for nigh on thirty years until the good Lord called her to sit at his side in heaven. I want the same fer ye, Aileen. Ye deserve it. Even if ye are a bold and impudent wench."

Aileen laughed, her smile brightening the chamber. "I get my strength from ye."

"And yer willful attitude," the laird finished.

Seizing upon Sinclair's even mood, Gavin switched the direction of the conversation. "Though our families willnae be allied through marriage, I hope that King Robert can count on yer support."

Sinclair's eyes narrowed and he stared at Gavin fiercely. "Given how ye've insulted my daughter and broken yer word, I should ride with the MacDougalls against the king just to spite ye," the laird retorted. "But I'm not such a fool as to be driven by pride. Aileen fell to harm while under yer protection, but ye rescued her and kept her safe from any true danger. She has made her feelings about a marriage to ye very clear and they are good reasons. In the end, I'll allow that no real harm's been done."

"Yer support?" Gavin prompted.

"Will rest with the Bruce. Ye have my pledge that my best fighting men will flock to the king's banner when called." Sinclair paused. "And unlike ye, I honor my pledges."

Gavin released a breath he hadn't even realized he'd been holding and met the laird's sharp gaze. "'Tis a wise choice, and one ye'll never regret."

"That remains to be seen," Sinclair scoffed.

"The Bruce's cause is just, as ye have stated on more than one occasion," Aileen said, taking an anxious step forward. Sinclair looked none too pleased at his daughter's revelation, but did not correct her.

Gavin remained silent, grateful that he had been given the chance to redeem himself in Sinclair's eyes and secure the support the king so badly needed.

"There are plenty of good men who have showed an interest in my daughter," Sinclair said. "Men on both sides of this conflict, as well as those who have yet to declare their allegiance."

"'Twould make more sense to choose someone who will stand with ye, rather than against ye," Gavin replied, taking a long sip from a tankard of ale.

Sinclair nodded and held out his empty tankard. Gavin obligingly filled it—with whiskey. "I think Brian McKenna could be such a man."

"Thus far he has fought for neither side," Gavin mused.

"Aye," Sinclair replied, his gaze fixed upon his daughter. "I hear he has a keen appreciation fer a bonnie lass."

Aileen's head tilted. "If ye so desire, Father, I shall be pleased to meet him."

"And?" Sinclair prompted.

"And then I'll decide if it's worth listening to his offer. Agreed?"

Sinclair sighed, then nodded. "'Tis criminal how I cannae deny my Aileen anything. Just wait until ye have daughters of yer own. 'Tis enough to put the gray in yer hair and the worry in yer brow."

Gavin answered with a slight grin, though his heart was momentarily heavy. He would never have any daughters, or sons for that matter. Fiona was barren. Yet as he gazed over at Fiona, a warm, contented feeling began to surge through his blood. He could never let her leave him. He knew now it would feel as though a part of him were being torn away.

The lack of children to enrich their lives was a sorrow they would face together. It would not weaken their love, nay, 'twould make it stronger for it was a shared sorrow.

That knowledge alone was enough to bring Gavin a feeling of acceptance. In life it was necessary to recognize that no one escaped heartache. It therefore made it even more essential to hold tight and savor every drop of happiness that came your way.

"I'm glad we have weathered this storm together and come through it as allies," Gavin said, offering his hand in friendship to the laird.

Sinclair looked down for a long moment before grasping it firmly. "I'll see ye when the king next calls us to arms." Then turning to his daughter, he added, "Come, daughter. We are fer home."

Before leaving, Aileen allowed Gavin to send her a courtly bow, though she did not return the gesture with a curtsy. As for Fiona, Aileen never once glanced in her direction, silently voicing her resentment.

"Well now, that was thoroughly unpleasant," Gavin announced the moment they were alone.

"For all of us, I fear," Fiona concurred. "Except perhaps Laird Sinclair, but I think that's only because he drank so much of your fine whiskey."

It took but three long strides to get close enough to gather Fiona in his embrace. Taking her chin, Gavin angled it so she had to look directly at him. She smiled and he felt a pang deep in his heart. There was no feeling on earth that could compare to having her in his arms. Though he vowed never to lose her again, it had not been an easy feat, and knowing he had achieved that goal made him feel almost invincible.

Gavin pressed a soft kiss on her lips. He felt her hands clutching his shoulders to hold him near. The heat rose quickly between them, the restless hunger yearning to be satisfied that increased to a shimmering ache.

Gavin knew he could take her now, right here on the table, rough, hard, and urgent. She would not deny him. Hell, she'd probably be the one to suggest it. But she deserved more—and so did he. A warm bath, a soft mattress, and all the time they needed to explore each other's bodies, to relearn what gave them gentle pleasure and what drove them wild.

Reluctantly, Gavin pulled back, trailing a soft line of kisses up Fiona's neck to her cheek. "Were ye really going to journey to the shrine of the Virgin Mother?" he asked.

"Yes, and from there I planned to continue to the convent at St. Ives."

"To join their ranks?"

Fiona laughed. "To seek asylum. Though I cannot fathom why you are looking so shocked. Do you not think I would make a good bride of Christ, my lord?"

"I know you would make a terrible nun, milady," Gavin declared, kissing her hard and fast. "And for that, I am truly thankful."

Chapter 20

Gavin faced the church doors and listened closely as Father Niall recited the vows he was to repeat. Fiona, dressed in her elegant wedding finery, stood beside him, her expression solemn but for her eyes, which glowed with joy. Gavin could not stop looking at her.

"My lord?" Father Niall cleared his throat. "Do you need me to recite the words again?"

"Nay." Gavin drew a ragged breath. He knew what to say. This was, after all, his third marriage. But it felt completely different this time. There was an aura of hope radiating from deep inside him, mingled with amazement at his good fortune. He was binding himself to the woman he loved beyond measure, was willingly, nay *eagerly*, pledging his body and soul to her as long as they both drew breath.

The emotions coursing through his blood gave greater meaning to his vows. This was a fresh start, a new hope, the beginning of a life that offered endless possibilities.

Gavin's voice was strong, powerful, as he spoke, ringing throughout the courtyard. He wanted each and every one of his clansmen to know how committed he was to this union, how determined he was to cleave to his new bride.

When it was Fiona's turn to speak, she first lifted her hand and placed it on his chest, directly over his beating heart. Her voice trembled with emotion, but she never faltered.

Gavin tilted his head, fascinated at seeing the glow of his happiness reflected in her sparkling eyes. He longed to bend down and taste the sweetness of her lips, to kiss her senseless, but that would have to wait.

As was the custom, the first part of the ceremony had taken place outside, in front of the chapel doors. When the vows were done, all that remained was for the bride and groom to enter the chapel and kneel at the altar for the final blessing.

They did not, however, have the chance to enter the church, as there was a sudden commotion at the castle gates. They could hear men shouting and swearing, followed by the distinct sound of approaching horses.

"Make way for the king!" someone yelled.

Gavin met Fiona's gaze and he watched the color drain from her face. He pulled her in a tight embrace.

"What will he do?" Fiona whispered fearfully, as the king rode into the bailey.

"Hush now, all will be well," Gavin insisted, sweeping a stray piece of hair from her face with the back of his hand and tucking it under her veil.

Fiona gave him a look of such confidence and trust his chest tightened. The crowd parted seamlessly, and Robert rode boldly through the mob until he was positioned directly in front of Gavin and Fiona.

Gavin's arms fell from around Fiona's waist and he stepped away. Duncan, Aidan, and Connor instantly moved in, surrounding him. Though dressed more formally in honor of the occasion, each still wore a sword. Gavin noted all three men already had their hands on the hilts of their weapons.

Gavin stepped forward. Without breaking formation, the trio moved with him—one man on either side with the third guarding his back.

"Nay," Gavin ordered. "Stay here and protect my lady wife."

The king's great warhorse pranced nervously, agitated at being in close quarters with such a large crowd. Looking every inch a royal presence, Robert controlled his mount with graceful skill, a true warrior king.

"Lord Kirkland, I am most displeased to discover that my invitation to this important event has been waylaid."

Gavin looked up at the man seated so regally on horseback and met the angry gaze of his king. Resisting the answering anger that flared inside his own chest, Gavin instead assumed a casual, confident demeanor. King or no, this was the happiest day of his life and he wasn't about to let anyone ruin it.

"I sincerely beg yer pardon, sire. We decided but two days ago to wed, leaving no chance to invite any guests, save for my clansmen."

"That was rather convenient. For ye."

Gavin nodded, but remained silent. The white lines around Robert's mouth indicated his growing fury. 'Twould be foolish indeed, to poke at an already snarling bear.

"Is the ceremony completed, good priest?" Robert asked, his angry voice cutting through the tension like a sword slicing flesh.

Father Niall's face froze in horror as he hastily went

down on one knee in supplication. "'Tis done. Save fer the final blessing," he croaked.

A muscle twitched under the king's eye. "So, I have missed the part when one can voice an objection if they know of any reason or just cause why this couple should not marry?"

"Aye." The priest blanched, then nodded nervously. "They are indeed wed in the eyes of God."

"But not their king!"

There was a collective gasp from the crowd. Father Niall pulled a linen cloth from his sleeve and wiped his sweating brow, looking as though a few years had been taken off his life.

Gavin's eyes immediately sought Fiona's. She appeared to be holding up well—her back was straight, her head held high. But no matter how hard she tried to hide it, he could see the small tremor of her hands, clasped together so tightly the knuckles were white.

"Perhaps 'tis best if we speak of this in private," Gavin suggested.

There was a long pause. Robert favored him with a mulish expression, looking far less like a king and far more like a petulant little boy. Finally, he leapt from his horse. Without waiting to see if Gavin followed, the king took several long strides and entered the chapel. The moment Gavin stepped inside, Robert slammed the door behind him.

"I've always known that ye are far too stubborn fer yer own good, but I never thought ye'd go this far." Robert's mouth fell into a grim line. "When did ye plan on telling me that instead of marrying the Sinclair lass, ye've taken it into yer fool head to wed an English widow?"

Gavin hesitated. It was important that he show remorse or else Robert would never be appeased. Yet he could not let the king believe there was any room for negotiation—Fiona was his wife and would remain so as long as they each lived.

"I sincerely beg yer pardon fer being so impulsive, but once the decision was made there seemed no point in waiting."

"Ye willfully defy me without a qualm, giving no thought to the consequences," Robert shouted, his gaze boring into Gavin. "And then ye have the gall to stand before me, unrepentant, righteous, and arrogant."

"What's done is done, sire."

The king made an exasperated sound. "For ye, perhaps. But for a king, what's done can be undone, if he so commands."

They squared off, each determined to maintain their position. Gavin knew that Robert was at his core a fighter and could be impossibly stubborn. But he was fair, and most importantly, he rarely held a grudge.

Still, Gavin acknowledged the incident was his own fault. He could have waited until Robert sanctioned the marriage. The consequences of ignoring a dictate from his sovereign was one of the risks he had taken into account when insisting that Fiona become his wife.

Yet in his heart, Gavin knew there was no other choice. He could not, nor would he, live without Fiona. It was a fact that Robert would have to accept, in spite of his justified anger.

"Do ye want me to pay ye a bride price?" Gavin offered, knowing that years of warfare had left little time for Robert to collect the rents owed to the crown, usually leaving his coffers dry.

"I should demand twice the normal payment." Robert made a frustrated sound. "I probably will."

"I'll willingly pay whatever ye require."

Robert let out a huff. "A Scotsman willingly parting with his gold? Bloody hell, she's turned yer head with her passion."

"Aye, but 'tis more, so much more. She's captured my heart. I would gladly give my life fer her."

"Love? Well, then, that's another matter entirely." Something approaching understanding flashed in Robert's eyes. "Love is a rare occurrence, an emotion that most men believe is an illusion. In my experience 'tis also an impression that many women seek to change, fer they value love far above the more practical aspects of marriage."

"'Tis no illusion," Gavin answered readily. "True love is difficult to describe, but fer me it has brought a completeness to my life that I never believed possible."

Jaw locked, the king rocked back on his heels. "And how did Laird Sinclair take the news of yer decision to forsake yer promise to his daughter and wed the English widow?"

"Better than I had hoped." Gavin grinned. "Lady Aileen also rebelled at honoring the betrothal, making it harder fer Sinclair to insist. But in my quest fer my own happiness, I did not neglect my duty. Sinclair has agreed to support yer claim to the throne and swear allegiance to ye."

The king paused. "What will become of his daughter?"

Gavin slowly let out his breath, relieved that Robert's anger was visibly cooling. "Sinclair said he was considering a match with Brian McKenna."

The king stroked his chin thoughtfully. "Now that Sinclair rides with me, the marriage would create a strong alliance fer my cause. The McKennas are fierce warriors and there are few who equal Brian's fighting prowess. I much prefer him to be fighting at my side than to face him across a field of battle."

"If ye so desire, I shall undertake the duty to broker the match, at my own expense," Gavin volunteered.

There was a short pause. "And achieve the same outcome as the last time I asked ye to arrange a marriage? Do ye think me daft?" the king said sarcastically.

"Please, sire, ye must allow me the opportunity to redeem myself," Gavin asked humbly.

Robert's mouth twitched. "I suppose I must. I need yer loyalty and yer sword too much to push ye toward my enemies."

"Ye have both, as well as my unwavering devotion," Gavin replied, wishing there was a way to further prove this in deed as well as words.

As if reading his mind, the king gazed at him expectantly. Gavin was just about to offer Robert more gold when a thought struck. A brilliant thought! A way to placate the king and relieve himself of the nagging complication that sat languishing in his dungeon—Ewan Gilroy.

Gavin had lost more than a few hours of sleep trying to decide the fate of his bastard brother. He wanted him executed, but Fiona had begged and pleaded that the rogue's life be spared. Though determined not to let anyone, even his beloved wife, dictate his actions, Gavin found he could not gainsay her in this request.

"In fact, not only do ye have my sword, but I'll pledge ye the loyalty of my bastard brother, Ewan Gilroy," Gavin offered.

"Ewan Gilroy? I've never heard any mention of him. Has he always been a part of yer army?"

"No, Gilroy's always fought against me. He's a legendary outlaw in these parts, who's led a band of mercenaries intent on causing mischief. He's never killed any of my people, which is the main reason he hasn't been put to death. To be honest, he's been a royal pain in my arse fer far longer than I care to recall—no disrespect to yer royal personage intended."

Robert waved his hand. "None taken. Tell me more about this Gilroy."

"Well, I'm ashamed to admit he's run me in circles on my own lands fer years. He's cunning, ruthless, and a natural leader. He's got a fair hand with a sword and dirk and he's a fearless rider. I was thinking ye could use a man with his talents."

"I could. But can I trust him? The last thing I need is to be guarding my back in my own camp."

Gavin nodded. "I spared his life when I captured him a few days ago. He knows he'll only gain his freedom by repaying his debt to me. Though he was raised to hate our clan, he oddly carries the McLendon honor within him. If he agrees to serve, he'll do it with his whole heart. I wouldn't have suggested it otherwise."

Robert's eyes were alight with interest. "This man intrigues me. I wish to be present when ye pose this proposition to Gilroy, so I can look into his eyes and judge his character."

"Fair enough. Shall I have him brought to ye now?"

Robert's face creased into lines of puzzlement. "In the middle of yer wedding?"

Gavin groaned. *Bloody hell, how could he have forgotten the rest of the ceremony?* "The blessing willnae take long," he said sheepishly.

"What of the celebration that follows? No—Gilroy can be brought to me after it ends."

"Ye'll stay?"

Robert quirked his brow. "If I am welcome? After all, I was not invited."

Gavin laughed, his amusement genuine. "We would be honored to have our good king as our guest on this most sacred and special day."

Robert's mouth turned up with obvious delight. "Excellent. I have made it a practice to never miss an opportunity to kiss a lovely, happy bride."

It was a wedding celebration for the ages, one that would be talked of for years and years to come. Attended by the king, who offered the first toast with the earl's private stock of whiskey, followed by music and dancing and more specially prepared food than most had seen in their lifetime.

Tables laden with food and kegs of ale had been sent to the villagers, so that they, along with the hundreds of guests filling the great hall, could share in the earl's happiness, too.

Yet it was not only the bounty of food and drink, but the obvious love and affection shared by the bride and groom that made this event so markedly different from any other. Gavin's solicitous care and affection for his bride was swooned over by all the women, while Fiona's obvious devotion to her groom was the envy of many of the men.

The celebration continued into the wee hours of the morning, but the king departed before nightfall. Bellies full of good food and drink, the people lined the road trying to catch a glimpse of their sovereign. A riotous cheer went up from the crowd when Ewan Gilroy, leading a contingent of his men, rode out with the king. There seemed little doubt among the common folk that

Gilroy would acquit himself well in his service to the crown and thus bring honor to the clan.

Naturally, the wedding night followed the wedding celebration, yet another event that led to discussion and speculation, for the earl took his new bride to his bedchamber and did not emerge again for four days.

Two months after her wedding, exhausted from too little sleep, Fiona sprawled in the center of Gavin's enormous bed—nay, *their* enormous bed—and regarded her husband. Naked, Gavin lay on his side facing her, bathed in the streaks of morning sunshine that streamed through the chamber window.

The sight of him sent her stomach spinning and her heart skipping. The love she felt for him was so complete, so intense, so overwhelming at times she couldn't think straight. So, too, was the need to be near him. Feeding that need, Fiona reached out, caressing the curve of his jutting hip with her fingertips.

His eyes remained shut, but a grin tugged at the corner of his mouth. "Have ye need of me again so soon, dear lady wife?"

"Gavin," she admonished in a tone that usually had Spencer bracing for a lecture, "we cannot spend every waking moment making love."

"Why not?"

"'Tis indecent," she said primly. "And sets a lazy example for our people."

Gavin released a rumbling shout of laughter and pulled Fiona into his embrace. "My former mistress is now lecturing me on proper behavior? What has happened to the world?"

"Enough," Fiona shrieked as they tussled on the bed.

His flesh was hard and hot. As always, the feel of him entranced her, but Fiona refused to be distracted. "I am no longer your mistress, but your wife. And I say there is more to marriage than bed sport."

Suddenly, his mouth came over hers, silencing any protests. Sprawled on his back, Gavin drew her down on top of him, showering her face and neck with kisses. Fiona felt her body start to respond, her resistance slowly melt. She slid her fingers into his hair and stretched, twining herself around him.

"Feel what ye do to me, love," he groaned.

"The same that you do to me," she whispered, lifting one leg to climb astride his hips.

Heat enveloped Fiona as her body joined with his. She breathed in his familiar scent, savoring each sensation, every delicate caress as though it were the first time they were together. Following his erotically voiced instructions with an almost languid reverence, Fiona moved her hips with daring sensuality, beckoning her lover to share her passion.

Gavin ran his hands up her legs, over her hips, and along her back. She leaned forward and his eyes darkened. She adored how every emotion he felt showed so clearly on his face, in his eyes. It made the connection between them more forceful and intense.

She could feel urgency inside her building and she answered the need with a faster rhythm. Gavin approved, lifting his lower body off the mattress, thrusting upward. Clinging to him tightly, Fiona moaned as the sensations surrounded her. The strain was climbing higher and higher until it felt as though her very soul was clamoring for completion.

"Now, my love, now," she panted, begging him to take her to that place where nothing else existed except the two of them and their intense love and need for each other.

He obliged, reaching down between their bodies, caressing her most delicate, sensitive spot. Fiona screamed as she lost all control. She felt the sparks skitter over her heated flesh. Quivering and shuddering, she let the pleasure wash over her, almost melting her body.

The muscles in Gavin's body seized as he climaxed, too, his cock pressed to the very edge of her womb, pulsing and spurting deep inside her tight warmth. Unable to keep herself upright any longer, Fiona collapsed against him. Resting her cheek against his chest, she could hear his pounding heartbeat gradually begin to slow.

Afterward, when she finally came back to herself, Fiona stirred in his arms and perched her chin on Gavin's broad chest to look up at him. Could a person die of pleasure and happiness? She almost asked, then decided she would relish the delight of the moment instead and worry about dying another day.

"'Tis two months since our wedding and you have yet to tell me everything that King Robert said to you when he pulled you inside the chapel. You were with him a long time. Was he truly that angry over our marriage?"

"He wasn't pleased," Gavin admitted.

"Yet the king sat beside you on the dais at our wedding celebration. He smiled at me throughout the day, kissing me heartily and wishing me well. He even offered a toast to our good health and happiness, so somehow you managed to make amends."

"I did." Gavin cast her a teasing grin. "It will cost me dearly, but 'twas worth every piece of coin."

Despite his joking manner, Fiona shuddered, pulling

her fingers away from the springy hair on Gavin's chest. *Pay? He had to pay the king for forgiveness so that they could marry?* "Oh, Gavin."

"'Tis a hardship, I know, make no mistake about it," he said with an exaggerated sigh. He placed his hand on the top of Fiona's head and gently stroked her hair. She pressed into his touch, stretching like a kitten. "I've thought it over and have decided that ye'll have to start working off yer debt to me as soon as possible. Since I, my good lady wife, intend to take yer bride price out in trade."

Fiona felt the vibration of his chest when he laughed. She turned her head and he flashed a wicked grin. Fie, he was handsome when he smiled. She moved closer, rubbing her nose against his, then pulled back.

"I'll have to start making payments another day, husband. We mustn't stay abed so late," she said forcefully, tossing back the bed linen. "The servants will gossip and then the entire castle knows our private business. Heavens, my face already turns ten different shades of red every time I go near the barracks. Why, just the other day I heard two of your soldiers wagering on how soon after our wedding day I will bear the fruit of your prowess and quicken with child."

Gavin sat up suddenly, nearly knocking her off the bed. "Tell me who dared to speak so disrespectfully and I'll have them severely disciplined."

Fiona placed her hand on Gavin's shoulder. "There's no need for punishment. If you disciplined every man who makes a bawdy jest, there would be none left to guard the castle walls."

"Their words were hurtful," Gavin said, his eyes blazing with concern. "I'll not have any man cause ye pain, especially one that is pledged to serve ye."

Feeling a sudden chill, Fiona pulled the bed linen around her, surprised at the vehemence in his tone. "I've endured far worse snipes from the women in this castle and lived to tell the tale. Besides, the men have a right to speculate about the heir to the earldom and the clan."

"They already know the heir. Since I have no brothers"—Fiona frowned and Gavin hastily corrected himself—"no *legitimate* brothers, Duncan, as the eldest, will inherit my lands and title when I am gone."

"What of your own child?"

Gavin knelt on the edge of the bed and grasped Fiona's hand. "I know ye love Spencer as though he was yer own, and I too have come to think of him the same way. But he can never inherit my properties. Duncan is my cousin, the son of my father's only brother. If fer any reason he cannae follow me as earl, it would be Aidan next and then Connor. The Earl of Kirkland must be a man of McLendon blood."

"I didn't know they were your cousins. Why did you never tell me?" Gavin shrugged and Fiona snuggled into the warmth of his chest. "I know that there are some members of the clan who will never fully accept me as your wife, but I was hoping they would feel differently about our child."

Gavin stiffened. "They might have, but there's no use wishing fer what can never be. We know a child of our own is an impossibility."

"Why?"

"Oh, Fiona. Yer barren state was what persuaded me to accept yer scandalous offer to be my mistress in the first place. I'll not lie and say it doesn't pain me now, but it brought us together and therefore I cannae be angry."

"Ah, yes, my inability to bear a child." Fiona cleared her throat. It didn't feel like the opportune moment to correct that very erroneous impression; then again, would there ever be a good time? "If memory serves, Gavin, I never specifically told you that I was barren. 'Twas an assumption you made because it suited your needs."

Gavin squeezed her hand, his expression filled with uncertainty. "The evidence was telling. Ye were married ten years and never conceived."

Fiona tried not to blush at such frankness. "I never carried a child because I very seldom slept with my husband."

"I thought ye had a loving marriage?"

"We did. But it was a very different kind of love from the one we share." Fiona dipped her chin self-consciously. It somehow seemed wrong to discuss her former husband with her current one, yet she wanted no misunderstandings between herself and Gavin. "Henry thought of me more as a daughter than a wife. He showered me with affection, but never passion."

He swallowed hard. "Are ye telling me that ye might yet have our child?"

Fiona stared at the wonder and hope in his eyes and nearly burst into tears. Guilt gnawed at her heart, for she had kept the news from her beloved that would bring him great joy. Would he be angry? Or worse, feel betrayed by her silence? She pressed a hand against her still-flat belly as a shudder of uncertainty rolled through her.

"We will become parents sooner than you think, the good Lord be praised."

Breath held, Fiona waited for Gavin's reaction. He

looked shocked for a moment and then he blurted out, "We've only been married a few months."

"Aye. And we've spent most of that time in bed."

"Bloody hell!" Gavin ran a visibly shaking hand through his hair. "Are ye telling me that ye're with child?"

Fiona nodded vigorously. "All the signs are present. I thought my overset emotions were the reasons for my strange symptoms, but they have persisted. And I've missed my courses for the second month, and the smell of freshly baked bread in the morning makes my stomach ache and . . . Gavin, put me down!"

Ignoring her plea, Gavin lifted Fiona in his arms and spun her around in a wide circle. The look on his face was indescribable—shock, awe, and wonder.

"'Tis a miracle," he yelled.

"Hardly," Fiona replied as she struggled to control her queasy stomach. "You know, I've heard that some men coddle their wives when they learn they are expecting a child instead of tossing them about the room like a rag doll."

Her words stopped him cold. He set her gently back on her feet, then ran his hand down her side, placing his palm against her belly. "Is something amiss? Tell me."

"I'm fine and so is the babe. And we shall remain so as long as you promise never to spin me like that again."

"I promise, my love."

He lifted her hand to his lips and kissed it respectfully, solemnly. They drew closer, and then at the exact same moment broke into luminous grins. Words were unnecessary; their expressions said it all.

Fiona could feel the ache of emotions creeping into the back of her throat. Her sight went hazy for an instant, but was then suddenly brought sharply into focus.

Gavin. Her beloved. This man who held her heart from the moment she witnessed his strength and kindness was the one she wanted, now and forever. A vision shimmered in her mind of a peaceful sun-drenched morning and life filled with endless possibilities.

Their life.

Epilogue

Seven years later

"Are we getting very close, Mother?" the child asked, punctuating his question with an exaggerated sigh.

"We are but ten minutes nearer to our destination than the last time ye asked that very question, Angus," the earl answered in a stern voice. "And I can assure ye, the answer will be exactly the same when ye pose it to yer mother again, ten minutes hence."

Fiona tamped down her weariness and smiled patiently at her six-year-old son. They had been traveling for nearly two weeks and the initial excitement of going on a grand adventure had long since faded for Angus, and his four-year-old sister, Colleen. Only baby Andrew endured the long days without fuss; then again, he rode—well, mostly slept—in the comfort of a cushioned cart, his nurse by his side.

"Once we ride to the top of that hill, Arundel will be within our sights," Fiona said, smiling as she adjusted her reins.

Bored with being confined in the cart with his

youngest sibling, Angus was now riding with Connor, while Colleen was held in the protective circle of her father's arms. Fiona had hoped this change would make the journey more tolerable for her children. Alas, the novelty of this arrangement had worn off within the hour and the pair were alternatingly asking the same question with exhausting regularity: *Are we there yet?*

"Are we truly that close to our journey's end?" Gavin whispered, pulling his mount beside Fiona. "Or are ye just saying that to buy us a few moments of peace?"

"Both," she answered with a wider smile. "The trees are taller and fuller than I remember, but I'd recognize these landmarks in my sleep."

"England." Gavin shook his head. "I still cannae believe I've brought my entire family across the border."

"When we agreed to undertake this journey to visit Spencer, you were the one who bellyached the loudest about being separated from the children for so long. Besides, Spencer would be terribly hurt if they did not come with us," Fiona replied.

"I insisted they be included because I knew we wouldn't make it out of Scotland without them. I even bet Duncan that we'd get no farther than three miles before ye'd have me turning back to collect them," Gavin countered with a wry grin.

Fiona laughed. Her husband knew her all too well. Yet the miracle of having whole and healthy children was something that neither of them took for granted. To be blessed with three was a joy beyond their hopes, and while he'd never admit it, Gavin doted and spoiled them even more than Fiona.

"We've reached the top of the hill, Mother!" Angus shouted. "The castle is up ahead."

"I want to see," Colleen exclaimed. "Lift me up high, Papa."

Gavin obliged his squirming daughter. Fiona also lifted herself, straining her neck and then finally catching a glimpse of her former home. Memories flooded into her mind, along with a pleasant, tender feeling. She had been happy living here, first as a girl and later as a young bride.

"I cannot believe we are about to be reunited with Spencer," Fiona said, her eyes welling with tears for the child she had not seen in over a year.

"I, too, am anxious to see him, but I'll be happiest at finally having a private moment with ye," Gavin declared, settling a protesting Colleen back in the saddle. "I find our sleeping arrangements less than ideal and our tent far too crowded at night."

The smoldering look he cast at her caused Fiona's heart to flutter and her skin to tingle. Aye, privacy would be welcome, though by morning there was often at least one child sleeping in their bed.

"We've been spotted," Connor announced, circling back to ride beside Gavin.

The sound of squealing metal chains was clearly heard as the drawbridge slowly lowered. The people toiling in the fields ceased their work and started running to the castle gates.

"Is all as ye remember?" Gavin asked.

"Yes. No. Everything looks smaller, especially compared to our holdings." Fiona lifted her arm and shaded the sun from her eyes. "I worried that a drought would harm the yield, but the crops are growing tall and straight," she observed. "My son has done well."

"I never doubted Spencer's ability," Gavin confessed. "To first take the castle and then to hold it."

Fiona had shared Gavin's confidence, but a mother's worry had kept her on her knees in prayer when Spencer had gone to retake his birthright, leading a small army of retainers. The siege and subsequent battle had been accomplished with minimal losses, and the people had welcomed him back with surprising loyalty.

Word of their arrival spread rapidly through the village and it seemed as though everyone had stopped what they were doing to watch them. Mouths dropped, tools were put aside, tasks abandoned. Suddenly, one of the women cried out.

"Lady Fiona? Is it really you?"

"Bertha!" Fiona answered, pleased to discover a familiar face among the crowd. "I'm so happy to be back."

"Why is the lady crying, Mama?" Colleen asked. "Did she hurt her finger?"

The little girl held up her own bandaged thumb. Ever since she had somehow wedged it between two rocks a few days ago, Colleen associated any sign of tears with a bruised finger.

"No, dearest, the lady is fine," Fiona replied, near tears herself. "She's crying because she is surprised to see me."

Gavin swooped down and kissed his daughter's bandaged finger and she giggled. The distraction worked like a charm and thankfully there were enough new and exciting things going on around her to successfully garner the little girl's attention.

While she loved her daughter more than words could say, Fiona was the first to admit that once Colleen set her mind to asking questions, she was relentless. A trait of tenacity she shared with her father.

"Oh, my lady, we never thought we'd see you again," Bertha said, placing her gnarled hands reverently on

344 Adrienne Basso

Fiona's stirrup. "First Lord Spencer came and now you have returned to us. 'Tis truly a day to give thanks."

The crowd surrounding them all murmured in agreement. Fiona glanced down at the beaming faces, recognizing many. Some were too thin and the clothes they wore were threadbare, but most looked healthy. More importantly, they were smiling.

Fiona smiled back. In all these years, she had never forgotten the people who had been left behind. She had prayed for their safety and comfort and was rewarded to see her prayers had been answered.

"They do realize that ye're only here for a visit," Gavin muttered.

"Worried, my lord?" Fiona asked with a saucy grin, but her attention was soon diverted by the sight of a man hurrying across the lowered drawbridge. He was tall and broad-shouldered, his dark hair hanging past his shoulders, his gait revealing a limp—

"Spencer!" Fiona practically vaulted from her horse, landing on her feet in an awkward and undignified manner. Arms outstretched, she began running, not caring one wit that she was a countess, a matron, a woman of propriety.

They met in the middle of the drawbridge, their bodies nearly colliding. "We weren't expecting ye until next week," Spencer exclaimed.

"The weather has been better than we hoped, so we rode each day until nightfall," Fiona said, hugging him tighter, absorbing the love and joy this moment brought. "Now, let me have a good look at you."

Obligingly, Spencer pulled back and Fiona drank in the sight of him like someone denied water for a fortnight. She framed his face between her hands and leaned closer. His cheeks were thinner, his beard fuller.

There was a scar over his left eyebrow and a small chip out of his front tooth. He looked so mature and manly that she nearly started crying, but was saved that embarrassment by the arrival of Gavin and the children.

Still, Fiona started sniffling as Spencer embraced the earl before turning his attention to the children. Angus hurled himself at Spencer and was rewarded with a toss up in the air. Colleen was momentarily shy, hiding behind Fiona's skirts until she saw her brother being lifted and twirled in the air. Then she was at Spencer's side as quick as a flash, clamoring for attention.

She wrapped her arms around his neck and her legs around his waist. Not about to be outdone by his pesky younger sister, Angus hoisted himself up Spencer's back. With both youngsters dangling off him, the newly appointed Baron of Arundel walked slowly into the courtyard.

Fiona's eyes darted in ten different directions as she took in her surroundings. She noticed the kitchen garden had not been planted and the stables needed to be whitewashed.

Gavin leaned down and whispered in her ear. "This is Spencer's home, not yers. Cease making notations in yer mind about things ye want to change."

Fiona shrugged and batted her eyes innocently, but Gavin wasn't fooled. She already had several improvements in mind that she wanted to speak to Spencer about, but apparently that would have to wait until she was alone with her son.

"Sir George awaits you in the hall," Spencer said. "He would have come to the courtyard, but he suffered an injury to his leg on the hunt this morning and needs to rest it."

"Is he badly hurt?" Fiona asked with concern.

"'Twas a deep gash, but I made certain it was properly stitched and dressed. I daresay the sight of ye will hasten Sir George's healing, Mother."

Fiona nodded. Seeing that loyal knight was the final piece to a perfect homecoming. Yet before she stepped inside the keep, Fiona gathered her family around her to savor this perfect moment of happiness.

Gavin stood on one side, Spencer, Angus, and Colleen on the other, and her youngest, Andrew, lay contentedly in her arms. The most precious beings in her life all together in one place, even if only for a brief time. It was enough, nay, more than enough.

Never in her wildest imaginings would Fiona have believed her desperate journey into Scotland seeking justice those many years ago would have yielded such bounty, would have resulted in such fulfillment and delight.

For if she had known, she just might have left sooner.